The
False Messiah

By Leonard Wolf

Voices from the Love Generation
The Passion of Israel
A Dream of Dracula
The Annotated Dracula
The Annotated Frankenstein
Wolf's Complete Book of Terror (editor)
Bluebeard: The Life and Crimes
of Gilles de Rais
The False Messiah

The
False Messiah

Leonard Wolf

Boston

HOUGHTON MIFFLIN COMPANY

1982

Library of Congress Cataloging in Publication Data

Wolf, Leonard.
  The false messiah.

  1. Shabbethai Tzevi, 1626–1676—Fiction. I. Title.
PS3573.O488F3 1982   813'.54   82—6243
ISBN 0—395—32528—5   AACR2

Printed in the United States of America

10 9 8 7 6 5 4 3 2 1

This book is for Harry Sions
in memoriam

Author's Note

This book is a historical novel, a fiction based on history. Although I have been attentive to the known facts about Shabbatai's life, I have not hesitated to manipulate people, places, and dates for the sake of my fiction.

Book I

1

Smyrna
July, 1633

The women were quarreling at his bedside. His grandmother, who had the face of a fat-tailed sheep, spat against
the evil eye and said, "Yes, I slapped him; the boy is too
young to have nightmares. Now he has something real
to be afraid of."

"He's only a child," his mother whispered, complaining
as much as she dared against her more powerful enemy.

"A sniveling brat," the grandmother replied, provoking
from Shabbatai a renewed whimper, and from his mother
somewhat frenzied caresses. The grandmother had oily,
fat, beringed fingers, and when she slapped, she put heart
into the blow. His mother's fingers were warm, their touch
light — and guilty. He sobbed again and was rewarded:
his mother clasped him against her breast and rocked him
in her arms. When his sobs quieted, she slipped a sesame-
seed cake into his hand, pulled the covers over him, and
whispered, "Sleep, lambkin. Sleep," and left him in the
alcove where he had his bed above the chicken coops.

As the voices of the bickering women receded, Shabbatai
tried, as best he could, to sleep. Sometimes on fearful
nights, if he put his mind to the clucking of the poultry,
he almost caught sleepy meaning in their phrases, which

3

helped him to drowse off. He listened, trying to distinguish words, but tonight he could neither decode their language nor invoke the angel sleep. For a long time, he stayed awake, stroking his cheek where his grandmother's fat hand had struck it, where his mother's fingers had soothed it; then, without warning, he was back inside the nightmare from which his screams had awakened him.

It was still the same — a country in which darkness was the weather and pain the landscape. Whatever he saw, whatever he touched, hurt. A tree winced when he went by; a pond shrank away when he kneeled to drink. Haystacks wept and orchards mourned; the earth on which he walked was like a skin, more sensitive than his own lips. When he paused, he heard the pattering of hooves, the lowing of cattle sinking in distant quicksand, and the wild, lost cry of jackals on fire. Close by, there were disembodied voices snuffling or bubbling; in the underbrush, there was a barking of rodents whose names he did not know. The boy, who was too young to have nightmares, moved, nevertheless, through this one across streams that ached and over rocks that, like Shabbatai, dreamed of God, hoping He would wake them with the sun.

And yet, it was still Smyrna, the same houses and gardens, the same walls, domes, minarets; but the city was as if printed shadow upon shadow, and the shadows rustled. When Shabbatai moved through them, they stank. Frightened, Shabbatai turned toward the east and tried to dream the sun.

Instead, he saw an enormous rooster standing on cruel, blue-plated legs, its pearl-gray claws planted in the membrane of the sky. It was an auburn-feathered rooster, with gleaming, iridescent throat, pale brown eyes, a jet-black beak, and a lurid red comb, that stood, overwhelming the sky with quick, audacious movements of its head.

Shabbatai stayed hopeful. In a moment, the rooster would crow, and the sun, waiting below the horizon for a signal, would rise, and the nightmare would be over.

4

For a while, it looked as if the rooster meant to do what Shabbatai expected. It lifted itself on tiptoe, stretched its neck, searched to the north, to the south, to the west, and then to the east. Pointing its head toward the stagnant sea, it drew a long breath; then, straining and flapping its wings, it uttered, instead of a rooster's crow, a serpent, which struggled and flowed from its parted beak to make a malevolent, thrashing curve of darkness in the sky. The lower half of its body still in the rooster's throat, the serpent looked about with its yellow eyes, then twisted and squirmed. The rooster gagged, gasped, and opened its bill. Again, it expanded its chest, flapped its wings, and tried to crow. This time, it extruded the last of the snake, which convulsed slowly, unwound and wound itself in the free space of the sky, and looked about for a victim. Fascinated, Shabbatai watched as the snake, endlessly convoluted, flowed toward *him*, in its eyes a cold yellow look of recognition.

It was too much for the boy. With a stifled cry, he woke, his bed wet, his throat aching. Inside his head a message lingered: "Go, Shabbatai. Go save the sun." The spit in his mouth tasted of tin, but, obedient to the portent, he got out of bed, threw his cloak over his stained nightdress, groped for the sesame cake that was his mother's gift, and went softly through the sleeping household and out to the cool forecourt of his father's house, into a crisp night glittering with midsummer stars.

There, for a while, he stood, shivering. The words in his head were clear: *Go, Shabbatai. Go save the sun.* And the reason was equally clear. A serpent had stolen the rooster's voice; and without it, the rooster could not crow, the sun could not rise, and the world risked staying a place of stinking shadows forever. A tear trickled into his mouth and he licked it away. What was he to do?

The *chenar* tree beside the courtyard gate was a stately presence, a judge signaling decisions with many arms. Shabbatai went to it, wrapped his arms around its old trunk, pressed his face against the spotted bark, and whispered questions to it; but the only answer he got was a burst of chiding song from the nightingales in its lower branches, who did not care that he was worried and wet and ashamed and charged at too early an age with the fate of the sun. Shabbatai accepted their scolding and clung to the chenar with a sweet objectless yearning that was nearly its own consolation. Then a memory of his dream returned, and he saw again the gelatinous sea, the quivering mountain, the slow thrashing of the serpent emerging from the rooster's mouth. Reluctantly, he took up his duty to the world, let go his hold on the chenar tree, opened his father's gate, and slipped into the street. When the latch clicked behind him, he looked back and saw the single blasted branch, high near the chenar's crown, where Azrael, the vulture, came to brood each day during the noontime heat.

At Ibrahim Square, there were hushed noises at the water ditch, where a twelve-year-old girl was letting a pair of goats drink before driving them the three hundred yards they still had to go before they reached the shop where the Moslem butcher in his stained apron was opening his shutters, readying himself for the market. On other days, Shabbatai's gouty and asthmatic father would be doing the same thing, but today was Saturday, the Sabbath of the Jews, and the hens could cluck one morning more without alarm. Afraid of imperiling his mission by too much friendliness, Shabbatai edged around the girl, who knelt, one arm companionably around the shoulder of the younger goat as she whispered endearments to the other.

"Greetings," Shabbatai said, hoping she would not hear.

To his relief, she replied indifferently, "Greetings." He was almost past her when, out of an alley, there stumbled a tall figure in a ragged caftan, his arms flailing. It was Barot'ali, the water-carrier's idiot son, who grasped at the rent in the goat girl's smock. Not particularly surprised, the girl twisted away and sent the idiot sprawling with a kick. "Low-born wretch," she said, laughing. "Own brother

6

to a camel's turd. Were you not witless and foul, I would snatch your things out and give them to my sparrow to hatch." Holding closed the rent in her smock, she whistled to her goats and moved arrogantly away. Barot'ali, having neither ventured nor gained very much, grinned and scratched at the lice in his pubic hair, reasonably contented with himself. But Shabbatai, not understanding what the scene meant, took to his heels, only to be pursued by the howling Barot'ali.

The idiot meant no harm. He and the boy knew each other and, in daylight, were friends; but now Shabbatai's flight seemed a disloyalty that needed to be punished. Shabbatai, running on his short legs, was easily caught but not so easily subdued. Goaded by the image of the silenced rooster, its mouth agape as it struggled to rid itself of the serpent, Shabbatai wrenched and kicked, crying, "Let me go, Sir Idiot! Let me go. I have to save the sun."

Barot'ali held him with one hand and caressed Shabbatai's shoulders and thighs with the other. The girl — whose haunches, seen through the rent of her garment, had gleamed like starlight — was gone. Now, here was Shabbatai, soft and warm and pleasantly squirming.

"The sun," said the boy, gasping. "Sir Idiot, please. Please let me go. I have to save the sun." Barot'ali pulled him closer and let his coarse hand explore the boy's inner thighs. At his touch, Shabbatai burst into tears. Barot'ali, immediately ashamed, held him more gently and patted his thick brown hair. "Hush, Shabbatai. Hush."

"The rooster," Shabbatai whispered. "The sun . . . I have to hurry . . ."

"Where?" the idiot inquired. "What?" The boy's locks were soft as silk in his fingers.

Shabbatai did not know, but needing to give an answer, he replied, "Kadifekale." Still sobbing, but clever beyond his years, he commanded, "Take me there."

To Barot'ali, it seemed a sensible thing to do if it stopped

7

the boy's tears. He rose, took Shabbatai's small hand in his huge one, and started off toward Kadifekale.

They made a singular couple. Barot'ali, who had never hurried in his life, tried to obey the white-faced boy's urgings, but his limbs, hinged rather than articulated, shuffled aimlessly, so Shabbatai had frequently to pull the idiot back on the road. The one swaying, the other tugging, they reached the high road out of Smyrna, whose dust, in the predawn starlight, was beginning to be stirred by the first movements of the market traffic: the lame beggars with their palm-leaf turbans who would congregate at Suleiman's mosque to accost the morning worshippers with their cry "O thou, the open-handed!"; the gardeners from the outlying villages who set their feet down in time with that of their donkeys burdened with panniers of beans and cucumbers, baskets of tulips and lilacs, hampers of melons or tightly filled skins of curdled *mast*. Shabbatai, oblivious of others, poked and prodded at Barot'ali and cast fearful glances at the sky, but the night looked the same as it had when he left his father's house. His heart sank when he considered that he might already be too late, that the darkness would last forever.

Barot'ali panted and wheezed. Then he turned up the footpath for which he had been watching. It was the winding way that would take them to the low summit of Kadifekale, the mountain that overlooked Smyrna. "Slowly." Barot'ali groaned. "My bones ache!"

"Hurry," Shabbatai begged. "I must save the sun."

"But why?"

Shabbatai tugged at the idiot's caftan, and Barot'ali cranked his shuffle to a more energetic pace as Shabbatai, sensing an advantage, told his dream, punctuating the tale with pokes and shoves while they made their way up the hill. Barot'ali did not mind. The boy's voice was so sweet, its accents so thrilling as he recounted his dream of a serpent and a rooster and a sky that was in pain, and a mountain that trembled, and a serpent that had stolen a rooster's voice and now the rooster could not crow and the sun would not rise, and the world would stay plunged in darkness. It was a sweet, sad tale.

A sad tale, and sadder still were the problems it posed for the idiot, who struggled to think what Shabbatai could do to avert the evil.

Barot'ali often tried to think — as when he ambled along beside his father, the water-carrier, who told him to keep his mind on the horses, but the fascination of their tails plaited in green and red ribbons switching back and forth occupied him for only a little while; then their movement blurred the colors, and he found himself, like a sleepwalker, drifting through the bazaar or on the Street of the Perfumers, where, before a sunlit shop, he ended dozing cross-legged, breathing an atmosphere of frankincense, attar of roses, and sandalwood.

Shabbatai, tugging at his sleeve, gave off an odor of sesame cake, urine, and body warmth. Barot'ali closed his eyes and gave up trying to solve problems and surrendered himself to an ecstasy as intense as it was incoherent. When Shabbatai pulled at him, the idiot moaned and balked and pawed blindly at the boy.

"Come on," Shabbatai urged, fending off the caresses. "Come *on*. We have to go." His dream was like the sting of acid behind his eyes. "Help me, please, Barot'ali. Help me. How shall I save the sun?"

The music of the boy's voice, and his fear, reached the swaying idiot. He opened his eyes and for Shabbatai's sake tried again to think, but in the mists that served him for a brain, he could find no notion that would do any good. Of one thing he was certain. Remembering the smell of sesame cake, he whimpered, "I'm hungry."

Shabbatai glanced first at the sky, still starlit, still unchanged, then at the idiot, and made a desolate decision. Plunging his hand into the waistband of his sleeping garment, he retrieved his mother's seed cake and put it into Barot'ali's already outstretched hand.

9

Barot'ali chewed, and felt contentment flowing from his mouth to his brain, while Shabbatai clenched his own jaw muscles to keep from crying. The boy studied the idiot's face for helpful signs, but all he saw was the motion of Barot'ali's mouth making sesame-cake crumbs and sweet spit out of his seed cake. Overhead, the night was still the night. Shabbatai's heart sank.

It was then that Barot'ali, swallowing the last mouthful of the sesame cake, had his illumination. His face wreathed in the smile of an incandescent saint, he said, "Crow, Shabbatai. You must crow."

Shabbatai looked toward the harbor, where the riding lights of half a dozen ships swayed with the motion of the incoming tide. Except for the torches of the night watch, the streets of Smyrna were dark. Turning to Barot'ali, he asked, "How? How shall I . . . ?"

Barot'ali, no longer puzzled, replied serenely, "Flap your wings. Flap your wings and crow."

He was right, and the boy knew it. The idea was so simple, so powerful. It was exactly what was needed, and yet, like every prophet who ever quarreled with the angel of the Lord, he hung back. "I don't know how to crow."

"Open your mouth," the idiot said. "Open your mouth, stand on your toes, flap your wings, and crow."

Shabbatai, the poulterer's son, understood and did as he was told. Facing the bay toward the east, he spread his arms. When the breeze fluttered his cloak, making a gentle tug at his throat, he lifted his head and crowed. Hesitantly at first: *co co ri co.* It was the thin, clear, but still uncertain call of a cockerel testing his voice. Then, with a more vigorous flapping of his wings, there came a richer, fuller cry: *co co ri co, co co ri co, co co ri co, ri co ri co ri co ri co* — a rooster's triumphant welcome to the sun, which rose now, like a golden tangent to the sea, and turned to an expanding glow that became a circle of fire as it mounted the sky to pour its light on the bay, the rooftops, and the streets that Shabbatai had saved.

The rooster hushed; his arms dropped.

From a minaret in the town there came the muezzin's cry:

Allah, o Akbar,
Allah, o Akbar.

Ashadu an la ilah illa 'llah,
Ashadu an la ilah illa 'llah.

Ashadu anna Muhammad rasul 'llah,
Ashadu anna Muhammad rasul 'llah.

God is great,
God is great.

I assert that there is no god but Allah,
I assert that there is no god but Allah.

I assert that Mohammed is His messenger,
I assert that Mohammed is His messenger.

The boy, weak with joy at the miracle he had made, rested awhile against the idiot's muscular thigh and heard the muezzin out; then, remembering he was a Jew, he stood away from Barot'ali, the Moslem. His palms together, head bowed, he replied to the infidel prayer:

Kadosh, kadosh, kadosh
Adonai ts'vaot.
M'lo kol ha arets
K'vodo.

Holy, holy, holy
Is the Lord of Hosts.
The whole earth is full
Of His glory.

And yet, the glory was in him, in Shabbatai. He was a light-filled boy who had seen the worst of the dark and conquered it. The light was in *him,* and it flowed from him outward. Then why, as he descended the low mountain, followed by an admiring idiot, did he feel the light pressing against his bowels, like a serpent coiling itself for a long, long stay?

11

2

Smyrna
March, 1641

Though the provincial rabbis of Smyrna had conferred
on the fifteen-year-old Shabbatai Zevi the title of *khakham,*
or wise man, Rabbi Joseph Escapa, Shabbatai's teacher,
was not pleased. The boy, it was true, had an amazing
memory and a dazzling capacity for textual exegesis, but
— there was something missing. Shabbatai might be a
prodigy, but in Escapa's view, he was in danger of damnation, and the old man, bitter with his own lot, did not
intend to brood silently about him any longer. He had
come to a conclusion about his pupil and had sent for
the boy's parents to tell them what he thought. Since the
parents, like everyone else in Smyrna, were used to hearing
what a genius Shabbatai was, Escapa expected the interview
to be painful, and looked forward to it.

Outside the rabbi's house, Shabbatai, slim and tall for
his age, dressed in the white caftan he affected as the Wise
Youth of Smyrna, stood in the sunlight of a hot spring
morning, his hands piously inside his sleeves, as he cast
secret, sullen glances at his parents, who hesitated to open
Rabbi Escapa's gate. Inside the house the envious rabbi
waited with who knew what poisonous proposal against

his freedom. One day, Shabbatai would declare himself and would no longer acquiesce to the restraints of *olam hazeh,* this world. A petty place, sadly in need of change.

Suddenly, in the crowded road, there was a shriek as a wrinkled Turkish woman chased the donkey she had tied by a foreleg to a stone at the gates of the bazaar, higher up the road. The donkey, nibbling at a wisp of hay, had been stirred into action when a boy, leading a jenny in heat, passed by. The donkey, overwhelmed by its opportunity, set up a braying and plunged after the jenny, lugging the stone to which it was hobbled. The old woman, seeing the beast disappear, followed, her toothless mouth agape, howling at the outrage, while the boy slowed his pace to allow the fun to happen. It was the old woman's shriek as her donkey mounted that had startled Shabbatai.

It was not an edifying sight. The donkey, in the grip of its lust, fought the pull of the stone tied to its foreleg even as it clambered over the panniers of hot flat bread with which the jenny was loaded. The old woman, enraged at the imminent loss of a stud fee, beat at the donkey's rump; the jenny cast hopeful glances behind her; and the water-carriers and market porters roared encouragement to the donkey, which sought, with its distended member, to find its way.

From the walkway, Shabbatai and his parents watched with distaste. Then there was the sound of a military drum roll as half a dozen red-capped Janissaries, their sticks of office in their left hands, their whips uncoiled in their right, came riding at a trot down the hill. Instantly, there was a new commotion in the street — the porters fled, the hangers-on remembered other duties. Only the beasts, unaware that the Kaimakam Pasha's dignity was at stake, pursued their enchanted searching as before, and were rewarded with success just as the Janissaries, their whips swinging, bore down on the innocent tableau.

It was then that Mordekhai Zevi, Shabbatai's father, drew

himself up and, to the accompaniment of the squealing but ecstatic donkeys, led his son, Shabbatai, and his wife, Clara, into Rabbi Joseph Escapa's house.

Barot'ali, Shabbatai's idiot friend, watched the family enter the rabbi's gates. Of all the panicked onlookers, he alone had nothing to fear from the horsemen, because, an idiot, he was regarded by the Turks as kissed by God and therefore already assured of his place in paradise. So it was that, while the Janissaries wielded their whips impartially on the backs of the old woman, the donkeys, and the bystanders, Barot'ali, with whom the soldiers were familiar, was spared their attention and was free to do as he liked.

What he liked best was to keep an eye on Shabbatai, who enjoyed the idiot's devotion, which had grown over the years since he had helped him to crow up the sun. Barot'ali, at twenty-three, was an enormous, uncoordinated lout with a body as muscular and hard as a gladiator's and a mind as dim as it had always been. He was still feckless, still filthy, still groping toward whatever flesh, male or female, came his way; but the light of adoration that a glimpse from Shabbatai kindled in his eyes burned as brightly as ever. As for the Jew, he never drove the idiot away; rather, he welcomed Barot'ali's nearness. Over the years they had maintained a largely silent and, for Shabbatai, sometimes embarrassing friendship. As if the idiot's sheer brutality needed to rest near the clear light of Shabbatai's intelligence — and the other way around.

While Barot'ali watched Shabbatai and his parents disappear into the rabbi's house, he was rewarded with a smile and the familiar wave of the left hand with which the Jewish youth acknowledged the presence of his friend.

In the darkened entry hall of Rabbi Escapa's house, Mordekhai Zevi shifted his weight from one foot to the other. He wheezed and coughed and in other clumsy ways tried to achieve the dignity of a father getting ready to speak with the most powerful rabbi in Smyrna. The dignity of a competent businessman who did not need his wife's advice, though he had brought her with him, because, as he told the rabbi, she fretted so about the boy — and one knew how women were. How his Clara was. His Clara, who stood calmly, five paces from him, tall and pale, enveloped in the silks *her* father, Isaac ibn Leon, had paid for over a score of years ago, when, in a fit of poor character-guessing, he had given his fifteen-year-old Clara to be Mordekhai's wife.

Mordekhai's mother, Zipporah, had warned against the match because, though both families had the true Spanish-Jewish blood in their veins, the ibn Leons still spoke pure Castilian in their home, but the Zevis, adrift for generations in the Morea, in southern Greece, had lost contact with those Spanish graces and had declined into a family of wandering petty merchants and guildsmen that had come to rest, finally, in Smyrna. Zipporah, the hardheaded widow of a not entirely successful poultry dealer, foresaw the trap into which her slow-thinking Mordekhai was being drawn, but her son would not listen to advice. He was, then, already thirty years old, a *bakhur*, a bachelor, in a country where, because the hot sun ripened the flesh quickly, early marriages were commonplace. He was tired of his lonely nights and of being the butt of jokes about unmarried men. When ibn Leon's marriage broker proposed the match — but more, when he had caught a glimpse of the elegant, fifteen-year-old bride — he would hear nothing his mother said about the social distance between the two families, and signed the marriage contract in such haste that he spilled the inkwell. The marriage broker, a shrewd, pot-bellied toper, said it was a good omen.

It was a joyous wedding feast. The plump groom ate so well that his face steamed, as if he himself were the cook who had made the dainties in the kitchen at the back of the house. He drank so much, the tears streamed from his eyes. His bride, sitting at his left, kept her hands folded in her lap and her eyes lowered, as if she were studying the sugared dates in the silver dish before her. When Mordekhai offered her his cup, she touched it with her lips, not to shame her husband. Her father, sensitive to her moods, was quick to see the mistake he had made, but though he felt a twinge of remorse, old ibn Leon was too good a businessman not to know when to cut his losses. She was, after all, only a woman, and he would comfort her with presents later.

Meanwhile, the guests ate and drank and sweated. Toward midnight, the bride and groom, accompanied by flutes and tambourines and a score of jubilant well-wishers, were taken to a freshly spiced room at the top of ibn Leon's house, where, with a final burst of music and laughter, the pale bride was shut in with the trembling groom.

Below, in the banquet room, Zipporah, Mordekhai's mother, sat over a pile of broken sweetmeats, gorging. She remembered her father's advice to her brothers: "To avoid a lifetime of regret, you must descend a step in choosing a wife." It was too late for her son, Mordekhai. He had married upward and believed his fortune was made. The stuffed and sugared dates were good, and the *halvah* better. Zipporah, as realistic in her own way as ibn Leon, did what she could to sweeten her life.

God, no doubt, arranges marriages, but what He wants from them is not always clear. Mordekhai and his bride, Clara, started out well enough. The groom, sobered by his new responsibilities and emboldened by the ten thousand *rials* that were the bride's marriage portion, showed signs of financial ambition. He was seen in the coffee houses, having long, important talks with Smyrna speculators, whom, later, he followed along the docks. He learned to kick at bales of silk, to peer into the baskets of pears and sacks of spices, but having breathed for a little while the heady air of speculation, Mordekhai panicked and invested his ten thousand rials in poultry, the only business with which he was comfortable. It was his father's calling, and Mordekhai liked the familiar sounds of the cackling and clucking birds. No doubt people like ibn Leon got rich on more grandiose ventures, but such schemes were not for him. He preferred the heat and the noise and the smells of his dirty little shop, and he settled down to live out his life in its comfortable confusion.

He might have been happy but for one thing. His wife despised the shop and the stink, and it was not long before she despised her plump, asthmatic husband. Despised him silently, it is true, since she had been trained to be an obedient wife. Silently, then, she picked the bits of down from his beard in the evening, and silently fed him the steaming mounds of saffron-flavored lamb and rice that he adored.

On Friday nights, which devout Jews set aside for love-making, Clara lay beneath him, clean and perfumed, elegant and cool as a naked statue with movable limbs, which, unsuccessfully, he sought to stir into motion with his fat fumbling. Whatever he did, she permitted without a word or gesture. At the very peak of the frenzy to which her silence drove him, she remained as calm as alabaster, and as beautiful, enduring everything until he subsided, when she asked politely, "Are you done?" If he nodded, she reached for the vinegar-soaked napkin she kept beside the bed and wiped her loins as if they were not her own.

For five years, Mordekhai's lonely Friday night wrestlings bore no fruit, then in quick succession, there came the three sons: Elijah, who did as he was told; Shabbatai, the prodigy; and Joseph, the greedy one.

Now, Shabbatai, sitting on a low stool in Rabbi Escapa's study, listened as his teacher spoke about him. "Your son," the rabbi said hoarsely; "you have reason . . . to be proud of him . . ."

Mordekhai, sitting at his end of a bench, leaned forward to agree. "Proud of him. Of course. Yes. And thanks to you, Rabbi Escapa. He is what you have made him."

Escapa winced. Shabbatai put a hand to his mouth to hide a smile. Though Escapa was the finest Talmudist

17

among the rabbis of Smyrna, he and his pupil both knew that Shabbatai had surpassed the old man's learning long ago. Escapa was sixty years old and a passionate voyeur of God's light. He had spent a lifetime mastering the necessary texts without coming one step closer to illumination. Enviously, he had seen Shabbatai, unmindful of his teacher's frustrated longing, toy with the Shekhina, the Indwelling Presence of God, as if it were a token in a child's game that had been hidden for his amusement on the other bank of a swift stream. Escapa was miserably certain that the boy, with clever hopping from stone to stone, would find the glory hidden on the other side. "He is what he is," Escapa finally said. "He is quick and has an excellent memory. But lately — you understand, I say these things for your own good — lately, he has become impudent . . . arrogant. He will not bend to the rod . . ."

Clara took a deep breath and said, "We have never beaten him."

"Nor have I," replied the rabbi. "Nor will I. What is happening to him is . . . perfectly usual."

"He is a good boy," Clara insisted.

Escapa's voice was strangled. *"No.* He is no longer a boy. Understand, Clara. I am his teacher; I know. He is in danger of losing what I have taught him." Escapa closed his eyes, hoping to snatch some strands of piety out of the tangle of envy he felt for the boy. Silently, he prayed, Let me teach him, O Lord, for he has within his grasp Thy word, Thy Torah, the fruit of which may be eaten in *olam hazeh* and in *olam haboh,* in this world and the world to come. O Lord, let me teach him so that where I am yet thirsty, he may continue to drink, for the sake of Thy people, Israel. Amen.

Clara sat very straight, her lips parted. "Rabbi, he is still a boy. I am his mother. I know."

"Between a boy and a man, Clara, there is another place, a place of danger. He is young" — Escapa tried to soften

18

his words — "he is young. His blood runs strong. It is not his fault."

For Clara, there was something grim in the air, something she chose not to understand, but which she felt was strangely like the aura in her room on those Friday nights when she endured Mordekhai's pawings. She gazed at her son. He did not return her look, but stared insolently at the rabbi. "Reb Escapa!" she cried. "What is not his fault? What are you hinting at?"

Fatigued by his effort at kindness, the rabbi snapped, "The boy must marry."

Mordekhai chuckled and rubbed his hands. "Good news, Rabbi. Good news. We will find a bride, at once."

"No," said Shabbatai.

"Insolence!" Escapa hissed. "Be still. Would you fall into sin? Would you succumb to temptation?"

The blood rushed to Shabbatai's cheeks as he remembered what the rabbi had in mind. It was in the synagogue on a Sabbath morning, just before the blessing of the New Moon was to be given. Shabbatai had been honored with the task of holding the Torah before it was to be put back into the ark. The cantor's wavering voice called, "Blessed art Thou, O Lord our God, King of the universe, who, in giving us a Torah of truth, hast planted everlasting life within us . . ." Shabbatai's eyes glazed over as he felt the stirring of that life in his loins, and he drifted into a musing. It was hot in the synagogue, hot as a communal bath, where the air smelled not unpleasantly of steaming bodies. Shabbatai pressed the Torah to his breast, and his fingers caressed the nap of the velvet cover. He sighed and watched the pattern of pulsations the blood made across his closed eyelids, like bursts of red starlight. Far, far away, the cantor was saying, "Magnified and sanctified be the name of God throughout the world . . ." and Shabbatai's slender fingers moved around the curving sides of the Torah. His fingertips glowed; there was a sudden warmth in his forehead and heat surged and throbbed in his loins. A voice, dry as a cricket's, was saying, ". . . before the sacred scrolls of Thy Law, we here renew the ancient covenant with our fathers . . ." Shabbatai panted as, from the Torah cover, there rose the same perfume that had floated long ago through the trees in Eden. He felt his tongue grow thick as his fingers pressed the velvet, and the naked youth Shabbatai-Adam, in a slow swoon, opened his arms toward the naked woman drifting from the tree-tops overhead. She was not Eve, that pliant flesh of his flesh, bone of his bone, who was made to be supine, to keep her eyes lowered, obedient to the commands of men. No. This was not Eve who drifted from the treetops, whose branches she gilded by her passing. This was the splendid Other — Lilith, willful and hot as fire. Lilith, the tigress whose skin had the velvet smoothness of the Torah cover over which his fingers played, tracing the outline of her firm thighs, over the gold embroidery of the fringes; then his hand, probing under the skirts of the Torah, plunged upward to the darkness between the scrolls while, from the incandescent treetops, Lilith drifted toward the fifteen-year-old Shabbatai-Adam, who was neither asleep nor awake, but waiting, ready, swollen, enkindled, but not for Eve. Never for Eve, that pallid, yielding thing. This was Lilith, woman enraged, lusting, her eyes glittering like coals, her breath acrid as the breeze over a lake of fire, her lips insatiable. Lilith, the dark devourer, with breasts like desert sand dunes. Lilith, who would not lie beneath a man, who throbbed with life, who confounded angels, and who smelled of the swamp and roses, of sesame cake and lilacs, of orange peels and urine. It was Lilith in the Garden who fell toward Shabbatai while the mice raced in the undergrowth, warning the creatures to make way for her fall; and Shabbatai fell with her slowly, slowly, as his right hand stroked her shoulder and his left clawed at secret places in the Torah that had no name.

They fell on the moss, the youth and the flame, squirming while macaws and apes screamed in the treetops and the cascade of fragrant serpents that was her hair scalded his eyes. He gasped and tore at the velvet thighs of the Torah as the cantor begged, "May Thy Word ever be a lamp unto our feet and a light unto our path, showing us the way to true and righteous life . . ." Then Rabbi Escapa was pinching Shabbatai's shoulder so that he started up with a real cry, which he managed, bewildered as he was, to join with the congregation's *"Sh'ma Yisrael, Adonai Elohenu, Adonai Ekhod.* Hear O Israel, the Lord our God, the Lord is One." How he managed to get the Torah back into the opened ark, he did not know; but when it was closed and the curtain drawn, he turned to stumble from the dais, shamefully emptied and afraid of what terrible stains his white caftan might betray.

It was clear, then, that Escapa had seen and understood, though not nearly as much as Shabbatai supposed. For the old man, it was enough that Shabbatai, too, was enmeshed in the senses. It explained the insolence with which the boy put forth ingenious but wicked interpretations of biblical texts. It explained, too, the stories that had come to the rabbi of Shabbatai's nighttime wanderings, his secret fasts and frequent ocean-bathing. Escapa, remembering his own youthful writhings, thought he was being merciful when he repeated, "The boy must marry. And soon."

Mordekhai bobbed to his feet. "He will marry. If the rabbi says he must, then he must."

There sounded a hollow "No" from Shabbatai.

"No!" his mother cried.

Shabbatai stood, his face drawn, his eyes luminous. *This* was olam hazeh, the present world. Petty tyranny, envy, spite. "No," he said.

"It is written," Escapa replied, "that if both parents are thirsty, then the son will bring water to the father first . . ."

"It is not written for me," said Shabbatai.

"It is written further," Escapa went on, "that it is the

21

father's duty to care for his son's instruction in the Torah."

"It is not written for *me.*"

"Well, what says the father to his dutiful son?" Escapa demanded.

Mordekhai sent a timid glance toward his wife; then, swallowing his words as rapidly as he spoke them, he said, "Married. He will be married. At once."

Because Mordekhai was too plump to feel confident in his sternness, the rabbi quoted approvingly, "It is written, 'While your hand is on your son's neck, see that he marries.' "

Shabbatai felt himself towering over the room. It seemed to him that he had only to reach his hand out and he could make all of Smyrna crumble. If he only desired it, he could heave the city into the sea, turning his tormentors into the prey of dolphins. If he chose, he could . . . he could . . .

Outside, across the nearly deserted street, Barot'ali, the idiot, who had been dozing in the heat, rose and, like a ruined version of Achilles, lurched across the roadway into the rabbi's courtyard. Inside Escapa's study, Shabbatai, with an authority that made the rabbi tremble, said, "It is not written for me."

"Blasphemer . . . fool . . . Shabbatai . . ." The words came from the rabbi, from Mordekhai, and from Clara. Mordekhai, determined to deserve the rabbi's respect, raised his hand to slap his son, but was arrested in the act by a wild sound that filled the room.

It was Barot'ali, who stood in the courtyard below, his cheek pressed against the whitewashed wall as he howled a full-throated warning.

3

Peter Harleigh, in Tunis,
to Nicholas Tyrell, in London
April, 1649

. . . to be brief with you is neither in my nature nor in
the terms of our friendship; therefore, be of good heart.
These letters will be as long as you desire, since I propose
to tell you of my voyage into Turkey-land neither more
nor less than — everything!

But, since your orderly mind will have it so, let me begin
at the beginning.

See me, then, wrapped in my cloak, already afraid of
seasickness, sitting beside my father as we are rowed by
a rascally crew of dicers and drunkards out of Gravesend
harbour — scurvy knaves, who would defer neither to my
father's black-garbed mercantile dignity nor — more blame
to them — to my pale young presence. No. The scum
growled amongst themselves the whole wretched time they
rowed their leaky boat that we were Presbyterians who
would fee them with a farthing and a prayer when they
had taken us to my ship, the *Demeter*, which bobbed at
anchor half a mile off shore.

My father, always the fearful merchant, would not acknowledge his sentiments for the King, lest the rowers
should prove to be secret Roundheads testing him. As

always, he thought it was a time for caution: King Charles was in the hands of the Parliament; London was in turmoil; there was not a day went by but the cry of "Treason" was raised against old friends. So he kept silent and paid the rowers well, and blessed his stars that I was soon to be aboard the ship that was to take me to Turkey, where, whatever the fate of the King may be, the Harleigh fortunes, at least, might be secured.

Moments later we bumped the sides of the *Demeter*, where the water men, dazzled by the sight of my father's gold, and promising themselves more from his hands, turned nimble as apes and had my bedding and chests aboard the ship so quickly that I found myself alone at the rail, my hand at my lips already bidding adieu to my father, who looked fearfully shaky standing in the stern of the receding boat, waving his sober hat at me as the sun went down.

He is a difficult man, and, since my mother's death last year, more irritable than ever. And yet, shall I confess? I felt a tremor at the heart to see him bobbing like a bottle in the sea — so middle-aged, so unsteady — as the space between us widened like a stain. Who knows whether I shall ever see him more?

But let me turn from such reflexions.

Two days later, the *Demeter* was wallowing in tempests in the Sleeve,* while our captain, too much taken in drink to know whether to sail upon a wind or to tack on the occasion, left the charge of the helm to a dark-eyed third mate, a muscled Yorkshireman who stood, stripped to the waist, fronting the storm, eyes glistening, mouth opened with delight. The rain came down in slanted sheets that turned to silver in the play of lightning. The waves crashed against the ship's bow, sending foam scudding along the quarterdeck. Four several times the sea drenched the helmsman, but the half-naked Yorkshireman only shook himself like a mastiff, bared his teeth, and laughed, his

---

* The English Channel

24

great hands turning the wheel, keeping the ship headed to the wind. He exulted, and I exulted with him, all thoughts of seasickness forgot. From the entryway where I was being buffeted nearly senseless, I yearned towards him, already in the grip of love.

For more than ten days, we had a brisk wind at our backs, which sent us scudding first into the open Atlantic, then south along the coast of France. At Cap Blanc Nez, we were joined by seven sail from Plymouth, also Turkey-bound, with whom we formed a convoy. We had smooth sailing, even into the Straits, which we reached twelve days out of Gravesend. All those fine days, you may be sure, I stalked my Yorkshireman. By the time our ship was pointed eastwards, he had grown accustomed to the warmth of my daily greeting and to the admiration in my eyes. Insensibly, he spent ever-longer moments in my presence, drawn by what strange magnet he could not know.

He was to learn soon enough. We dropped anchor in the harbour of Algiers. There, once we debarked, my York-shireman and I found ourselves amidst a very fine bustle and stink, what with camels and jackasses and goats under-foot and throngs of turbaned men jostling about, shouting, *"Ballock, ballock,"* which is to say, in their language, "Way, give way." There were lousy squint-eyed confectioners' boys with trays of sweets swarming with flies, and poulter-ers shouting their wares — for all sorts of fowl, wild and tame, are to be had in great plenty and very cheap: par-tridges and quail, hens and chickens.

You will acknowledge, Tyrell, that I am not without re-sourcefulness. You will not then be surprised that, without knowing a word of the Berber speech, I yet found a nimble-witted lad who understood the language of my eyes and tongue so well that he led me and my blushing Yorkshire-man to a sort of *bagnio*, where, in a hushed twilight, half a dozen fat-bellied, moustachioed men in flannel undergar-ments sat cross-legged on cushions puffing at water-pipes, while behind them an old man plucked lingering sounds from an instrument like a swollen guitar.

"Kif, kif," our boy guide said, shoving cushions under us. *"Kif, kif."* I understood nothing, but the smell of the smoke and the attitude of the smokers (at once dazed and contented) let me know we were in a *hashish* shop. As my eyes grew accustomed to the dark, I saw alcoves in the shadows from which endearing sighs and other sounds could be heard. From time to time, like the swift passage of moths, white-clad youths appeared and disappeared as they tended to the water-pipes or assisted some fat smoker to his feet and went with him to yet another alcove.

Though my Yorkshireman's eyes burnt with eagerness for the coming mystery, he scratched an ear and made a Christian face at where we were, and would have left; but I, pretending innocence, urged the pipe upon him, which he, with much laughing and mock reluctance, had so soon mastered that he lay across his cushion, glassy-eyed and unbuttoned. For myself, I breathed only lightly of the fumes, having other tastes in mind.

With the help of the white-clad youths, who looked upon the venture with great sympathy, we got my young giant into the farthest alcove, where, on a well-worn Turkey rug, I laid him down. The young attendants helped me to undress him and marvelled with me at his broad shoulders, his muscled arms and splendid chest; at his neck, "like the tower of David, builded for an armoury." When he was altogether naked, and the lads had seen what else there was to see, they let me known by signs how they envied me my good fortune. Two of the more forward of the youths made as they would stay to share it with me, but a box on the ear and a piece of gold each sent them laughing softly away.

He had wrestled the wind and the rain and been caressed by the sun. Now it was my turn. The sweet, strong smell of his warm body turned me dizzy. "Until the day break, and the shadows flee away, my beloved," I whispered, "be

26

thou like a roe or a young hart upon the mountains . . .
All night long, he was supple flesh in my arms to the sound
of distant music and endearing sighs. When the boy guide
came for us in the morning, he found us nestled like a
couple of spoons, and fast asleep.

At Algiers, we took on water, fruit, and two score of passengers, their cargo and baggage, and a dozen black slaves,
young and strong, male and female. There was also a rich
Jew of Algiers, a surgeon, Haim Nakhman Yerushalmi,
who, having ransomed six Polish Hebrews from the slave-
tents of a desert *sheikh,* is escorting them to Smyrna, where
he hopes to settle them amongst their kin. They are, despite his kindness, a miserable-looking lot, who survived
last year's massacre at Chernigov in Poland when that wild
Cossack, Bogdan Chmielnicki, ran amok amongst the Jews.
These Polish Hebrews are alive because they were captured
by Tartars, allies to the Cossack, who care more for money
than for Jewish blood; and yet, what dreary survivors they
are: an old man, three young men, two women, and a
child of three. Even the child has their age-old look of
woe, and sits, like his elders, for hours on end, staring
sadly into the bottomless depths of his soul.

On board, there is also a Spanish Arab merchant, with
blackened teeth and drooping moustaches, who tells me
that to do business in the East, one must be ever ready
with gifts. For instance, the slaves in his charge are being
sent as gifts to the Kaimakam Pasha, the provincial governor of Smyrna, by the Bey of Algiers, who wishes to keep
the Emperor in Constantinople from interfering with his
profitable piracies. The Kaimakam Pasha of Smyrna is not
an important man; yet the gift is sent to him because of
this twisted reasoning: First, none but an emperor can
send the Padishah a gift worthy of him; second, the Kaimakam Pasha of Smyrna, though merely the governor of a
province, is, nevertheless, the brother-in-law of the Sultana

Torchan, mother of the Padishah, Mehmet the Fourth. The gift of slaves is the feather whereby the Kaimakam Pasha's nose is tickled in order to make the Emperor sneeze. Because the Emperor is young, and his mother is sly; and because she dotes on her younger sister, who is the Kaimakam Pasha's favourite wife. Out of this tangle of favours given and received, acts of state will emerge. The Emperor, you may be sure, will sneeze.

I have almost forgot, in this babble about Turkish statecraft, to tell you of a beast that was put on board the ship in Algiers — a camelopard, the first that ever I saw: a creature spotted like a leopard, with a body resembling a horse, but with a neck as long as a leaning pillar and a head at once silly and graceful. The thing had been brought hundreds of weary miles up from the African plains below the Sahara and was confined to a sort of pen on the afterdeck, where it made a forlorn figure, its legs spraddled, its inordinately long tongue reaching towards a bunch of dried mimosa my Yorkshireman had tied for it in the rigging a dozen feet above the deck.

It was a misfortunate animal, uncomfortable enough while we were still in port; but once at sea, as the weather grew warmer and the motion of the ship increased, its real torment began. Whether it was the fatigue of its overland journey, or the diet of mimosa branches, or whether because it had eaten whatever scraps of human food the passengers and sailors threw to it, the creature began to heave and sway, growing sicker and sicker, until, towards evening, it began sensibly to bloat before our eyes. The Jew surgeon offered to cut a vent in its sides to permit the noxious gases to escape, but the creature's keeper, a tiny black man, slave to Rustum Pasha himself, turned ashen at the suggestion, protesting that his own life was forfeit should the thing die.

He might have done better to let the surgeon work. As night came on, a crowd of us gathered on deck to watch the beast's final agony. With the slave chattering beside it, imploring it to live, the camelopard, its long tongue lolling, heaved and retched, until it was seized by such violent dry vomitings as were dreadful to behold. It was then that, kneeling on its forelegs, it seemed to make a last obeisance, stretched its spotted neck towards the sea, opened its mouth, made a nearly voiceless bleat, rolled over on its side, and was still.

My Yorkshireman could not conceal his tears and would have had me lament with him, but as the long-necked creature's body was being shoved over the rail, I had so strong a revulsion against the brawny mate as made me gag. I turned away and went to my cabin, where I lay in my hammock, studying the knot-holes in the timbers over my head, listening to the slap of water against the ship's sides. A couple of fathoms below in the dark, cold sea, the fish were poking their blunt noses against the camelopard's hide.

My spirits are disordered, Tyrell. The sea is calm, the winds steady. We shall make Tunis tomorrow.

On deck, the black slave huddles, his turbaned head on his arms as he rests them on his knees and waits for Constantinople, where he will die. Nearby, the rescued Jews wait as impassively for life. Why will they not rejoice, when a hundred thousand of their numbers died and they were saved? Why do they sit, looking towards heaven as if *it* harboured crime?

We are ten days out of Smyrna.

How fares King Charles? Does my father speak of me?

4

Kalisz, Poland
1648

"You see, Jew," the young Cossack said as he pounded
the wooden tent peg through the loop he had tied on
the woman's wrist. "You are a hateful people. You hate
God, you hate Cossacks, and you hate the Polish poor.
For your hatred of God, you will answer to God; your
hatred of Cossacks, the Cossacks ignore; but for your con-
nivance with the Polish *panyi* to steal our freedom and
oppress the Polish poor, you must die." He grunted and
leaned across the woman's swollen belly to catch at her
other wrist, which he pegged down into the hard-packed
turf so that she lay spread-eagled. "You understand, Jew
. . . it is for your crimes and not your sins that you pay."

The words were not addressed to the woman, who, for
all he knew, might be already dead. A pretty, fluttering
thing who had collapsed the moment he touched her,
though he had meant only a little harm. The Cossack was
talking to her husband, a thickset middle-aged man whom
he had tied a couple of yards away to the hitching post
in the courtyard of the inn. The husband licked at the
dried blood at the corners of his mouth, but his tongue,
too, was dry and gave him no relief. The cavalryman
waited, then asked again, "You understand, Jew?" Still

there was no reply. The young man scratched his head and got to his feet, embarrassed. The speech had sounded fine when Hetman Chmielnicki spoke it to an entire battalion of his Cossacks at dawn, sending them out against the Jewish bloodsucker villages to achieve justice, but in this place, this sad cluster of houses leaning like gravestones in a vast field of stubble, the words, with no one to hear them but the victims, seemed to lose their power.

Still, the Jews had to die, or there would be nothing to show for the day's hard riding except his fatigue and the lame excuses he would have to make for having lost first his companions, and then his way to Lvov, where his troop was gathered. The Cossack had considered lying about his vengeance against the Jews, but he was a proud youth. He knew how he detested empty bragging, and would not be guilty of it to his comrades. The Jews had to die, because they served the Polish landlords. But they were worse than chickens to kill. They died without a squawk.

The man at the hitching post leaned into his bonds. The Cossack grinned, confident that his prisoner was well tied. That husband, a man with muscles like a wrestler, might have been a problem. Fortunately, he had been asleep when the Cossack, walking softly, entered the tiny inn and asked for water for his horse. The wife, not more than eighteen or nineteen, unwilling to wake her husband, had hurried out to the well. The rest was easy.

There was a whinny, and the Cossack turned toward his horse, where it stood beside the well nibbling at a tuft of grass. The foam on its neck, he saw, was drying to a crust. The cavalryman hesitated between the Jew squirming at the hitching post, the unconscious or dead woman he had pinned to the sod, and the weary horse. Then, moved by the silhouette of faithfulness his horse made standing there, head down, tail drooping, he threw aside the rock with which he had pounded the tent pegs and went to the well, from which he drew a bucket of

31

water. Then he went to the woman. Tearing a hem from one of her long skirts, he dipped it into the bucket, wrung out the excess water, and sponged the horse's neck and sides, murmuring, "Good girl. Good Katya. Katya, *dushenka,* Katya, darling."

The sob he heard must be the woman's, he thought. When he turned, it was the uprooted hitching post that crushed his skull.

✻✻

The man wielding the post was Nehemiah Ha-Kohen, and the calamities at Kalisz made the second of three times in his life when Nehemiah, who passionately believed in Him, hated his God.

Nehemiah was born in a Jewish settlement in Slovenia, far to the west of Kalisz, and he had had green forests and snow-clad mountains sealed as images in his eyes from the time when, as a child, he had trailed after his father's logging sledge through the snow on the wooded hillsides bordering the Tisa River.

Behind them, in the settlement, there were aprons of snow before the brown huts from whose chimneys smoke rose into the thin blue air. The boy, leaning against the wind, watched his own breath puff out of his mouth and remembered the throaty gurgling of pigeons in the attic of the house he and his father had left behind that morning. A warm house with clay ovens in the middle of the *stieb,* the large family room whose windows, beginning in October, frosted into illustrations for stories no one ever told. At night, those traceries were illuminated by yellow moonlight. When he put his ear to the windows, Nehemiah could hear the frost crisping and crackling, and, in the white wastes of the windowpanes, the howling of wolves etched into the glass. They were imagined wolves, like those which pursued the bride and bridegroom in the fairy tales; but there were also real ones, who, in bad winters when their prey high up the mountain failed them, appeared like so

32

many beggars, twelve dark forms, snuffling and shambling before the settlement, their tongues out, puffing the air, howling their sad story, yet never striking any chord of pity. Twelve gaunt wolves, their tails sweeping the snow; sad — so sad and *Jewish,* Nehemiah thought — prowling darkly, hungrily, finally helplessly before the muskets brought to bear against them, till they lay down, one wolf at a time, and turned stiff corpses in the snow. After that, the vultures came to perch on the bodies and gorge themselves, despite the ice in the muscles and the eyeballs crystallized with cold. The vultures were patient, and picked the bones clean while the wind swept around them, rearranging the snow.

Green forests and shifting winds and snow lying like endless sheets down the slopes of the hills to the river, or snow falling. Falling silently all night long and, in the morning, so beautiful, the heart ached lest something disturb its purity. Once, there was the fox running, the hen in its mouth still complaining, though each outraged cry was already gurgling with the blood that splattered the snow. Nehemiah saw it all as a design of shapes and colors: the trotting auburn fox, its curving trail of black pawprints, the droplets of blood on the snow, and the new sunlight enclosing the scene in a silver glow. A complex design whose meaning he would one day understand.

Nehemiah had the family look. They were all born lumpy, and they all grew into great squares of men who, like himself, could heave a door off its hinges by the determined shrug of a shoulder. They had been that way for generations, the Ha-Kohen males and the Ha-Kohen females. A family of Jewish loggers and loggers' wives, swarthy, muscular, with low foreheads, broad shoulders, and tremendous strength.

The men were *ba'alei m'lokha,* as the Jews call their unlettered men — masters of labor, which, in terms of prestige, meant that they were not masters at all. They were, here in this mountain settlement, literally hewers of wood,

33

whose sons seemed to leap to the axes beside their cradles and out to the forests, where they cut down the pines, the oaks, and the birches that, all winter, they stacked along the river, until the spring floods made the Tisa navigable for the rafts of timber they floated to the Danube.

On Sabbaths and holy days, the Ha-Kohens sat in the back of the synagogue, holding their prayer books in callused fingers. They could read, but just barely, and followed the order of the service with hesitation, watching the congregation carefully so as not to make a response too soon or too loudly. Always they worried lest the rabbi call them to the altar to read the prayer over the week's portion of the Law. It was an honor that sometimes happened, and they were forced, before the whole assembly, to utter God's words in their uncouth accents.

They were an honest, forthright family, and, if they had small *yikhus* or prestige, they were respected as hard-working and devout Jews; but for generations, they had shared a fixed idea that one day one of their sons would break out of the mold of ba'al m'lokhim and show himself a scholar. Because, after all, they were, as their name indicated, *kohanim,* which is to say, they belonged to the priesthood established by Moses himself. As kohanim, they were entitled to bless Israel on holy days, to make the mystic sign with their spread palms over the heads of the congregation.

Clumsily lettered though they were, they knew how, in the time of the Temple at Jerusalem, the elders separated the high priest a week before the fast of the tenth day and cleansed and purified him so that he might be sanctified when he made the blood offering within the Ark of the Covenant. "If the [priest] was a man of erudition, he lectured on both the written and oral law; if not, those who attended him read unto him till midnight to keep him awake." The kohanim were the inheritors of that mystery. Once *they* had been taught how to receive the burnt offering of the morning; how to pour out the drink

34

offering; how to wear the golden garments brought from Egypt, of the value of eighteen *minim*. It was a *kohen* who slew the spotless bull and dipped his finger in the blood and performed the expiation by sprinkling it according to the Law, counting "one, one and one; one and two; one and three; one and four; one and five; one and six; one and seven."

It was an expiation for men, a service to the Lord performed by kohanim. And the Ha-Kohens wanted one of their number to be a man of erudition who could lecture on the written and the oral law. With the birth of Nehemiah, it happened. Thick and square and strong as the rest of his clan, he also had the gift of learning. To his parents, and to the Jews in the community, it was further proof that God attended to His covenant, even on the snow-swept banks of the Tisa River.

Learning came easily to him. Harder to endure was love.

He was eighteen when it surprised him. Until then, the woodsman's axe, the Torah, and its handmaiden, the Talmud, were what he knew best. In the forest, he cut a clean stroke; in the House of Study, his mind moved with agility through the maze of reasons the Gemarah gives for why a man may not stand in a private domain and make water in a public one, or why, standing in a public domain, he may not make water in a private one. He saw no contradiction between the rough simplicity required in the forest and the tortuous reasoning needed for his studies. The oak had to fall because the timber was immediately needed; for that, his axe must be sharp and his stroke clean. But the study of Talmud was a testing and a braiding of the strands of the Law. There, subtlety and intricacy were required. In Talmudic scholarship, there were no petty scruples. The most minuscule questions, since they were a form of doubt, deserved to be answered.

It was an equable view for the young scholar, and it

kept him cheerful until, without warning, he fell in love and stayed impassioned long enough to learn a grief that neither logging skill nor Talmudic subtlety assuaged.

Her name was Hannah *die Lome,* Lame Hannah, though she was not truly lame. As a child, she had had an illness that affected her bones in a way that made her body seem asymmetrical. It was not a dreadful disfigurement. It was only that, in repose, sitting in a chair, her left shoulder appeared to be a trifle higher than her right, and when she walked, though she did not limp, there was a certain unsteadiness in her gait.

Hannah was an orphan of fifteen when Nehemiah, his head down, as befitted a Talmud khakham walking in a public path, passed by her, carrying a volume of Torah under his arm. It was a summer morning, with bluebells and forget-me-nots nodding their heads along the river. Nehemiah was not thinking of flowers or Torah. He was simply walking in an intensely concentrated mood in which he was considering an extraordinary humming, a music made of the noises of the forest where he had spent the morning and the intricate chiming of his own bloodstream in his ear. It was a sweet, puzzling meditation in which he was engrossed, only to be snatched from it by the wild beating of wings, a cry of *"hiss, hiss, hiss,"* and the raucous gabbling and honking of Hannah's flock of geese, into which he had stumbled.

"Hiss, hiss, hiss," she cried, and the geese went after her, gabbling and beating their wings, bobbing their heads in a hurry to snatch at the grubs and snails buried in the spring-warmed sedge beside the pools left by the recently flooding river. Nehemiah, still lingering in the echo of his inner music, was not wholly aware of where he was, until Hannah's laughter made him turn. At the sight of her, he emerged slowly from his daze and smiled.

He came by again the next day, in the middle of the afternoon, when the House of Study was hushed with scholars dozing over their texts. This time, Hannah, sitting on a rock under a willow, was engrossed in pulling the stems from her apronful of gooseberries, the geese prattling around her in the grass or wading in the river shallows. When he stopped to look at her, she affected not to notice, then said, "You're too tall to be a Talmud khakham. To be a scholar, you have to be short and pale with pasty cheeks and egg-white eyes." Because Nehemiah said nothing and avoided looking directly at her, she thought she had hurt his feelings and said, "Here, have some gooseberries."

Properly, he should not have talked with her. Woman, he well knew, was temptation, a stumbling block to the Torah. And according to the Kabbalah, whose secrets he was already exploring, the female mystery in the flesh gives rise to the demonic. Furthermore, it was a woman who lured Adam to walk in the Garden, there to transgress God's Law, for which sin, though God punished Adam with heavy labor and with loss of the Garden, He punished Eve with *nine* curses, as well as death. But Hannah's gooseberries made a tempting heap in her apron; if he continued to avert his gaze from her face, he might eat one without danger.

He sat on a stone, sharing her gooseberries and two or three bits of coarse brown bread. She laughed at his height and the size of the book he carried; then she told him that she could not read. "Will you teach me?" she demanded. "Will you teach me?"

He considered the matter. It was not forbidden for a woman to read. There had been instances where a father had taught a daughter, even Talmud. But it was unusual, and it might prove dangerous. On the other hand, there were secular books . . .

The next day, he brought with him a *mayse bukh* — a Yiddish book of children's tales — and while the geese plunged their bills into the mud, she sat beside him and let him read to her the tale of the Talmud khakham who went out into the world with a thousand of his father's

37

dinars to make his fortune, and spent the money to purchase a funeral for a great rabbi in a wicked Turkish land . . . and returned home empty-handed. Next year, his father gave him ten thousand dinars with which, this time, the young scholar bought a Spanish galleon captured by the Turkish navy. But the youth was cheated, because the galleon turned out to be empty. Once again, the investment would have been a loss, except that a secret panel in a cabin wall opened to reveal a beautiful girl, who was the King of Spain's daughter. No sooner did she see the youth than she fell in love with him and showed him a hidden fortune of jewels and precious stones.

When Hannah finished weeping a tear or two for the young lovers, Nehemiah offered to teach her the Hebrew alphabet. She brushed the crumbs from her apron and moved even closer to him on the log.

"Would you?" she asked. "Would you?"

"Yes," he said, grumpily, afraid he might be doing something wicked.

"Then . . . teach me. To read words. Words."

Nehemiah cleared his throat. He tried to imagine what she might feel as she looked at the lines of print, which for her had no more meaning than any jumble of twigs and grass and mud along the riverbank. "Look here," he said, pointing. "This is the letter *aleph*."

She stared, then put her finger out as if to touch the letter, then bent her head to study it once more. Then, as if she had been stung by a bee, she cried, *"Aieee,"* leaped to her feet, snatched the book out of his hand, and ran away, only to turn and face him, squeezing the book to her breast as joyfully as she sometimes hugged a gosling. Her face beamed. Watching her, he thought of the Kabbalistic mystery of the letter aleph, which held that when the throat readies itself to say the first letter of the alphabet, it takes on the same attitude of expectation that the Primal Nothing assumed just before God condescended to utter the universe. As the letter aleph is about to be spoken, the silence gathered over the vocal cords is like the gathering of intention that rippled over chaos, after which there was the Word. The beginning. The Creation.

Now Hannah danced, holding the book to her breast, singing, "Aleph. I know aleph." It was Hannah's dance, as the world must have danced in the whirlpool of Creation. She danced, twirling, whirling among her geese, scattering them with her cry of "Aleph! I know aleph!" Danced breathlessly, lurching a little.

Nehemiah, watching, was not sure whether he should laugh at or pity her, but she calmed down and came back to him to sit at his feet, the book still pressed to her bosom, and whispered, "Oh, blessed be the Lord, and blessed be His Name forever and ever. I know aleph."

"But you can't stop with knowing aleph, you monkey. There are twenty-two letters in the alphabet. The next one is . . ."

"No, no, no, no, no."

"The next one, you little goose, is . . ."

She put her fingers to her ears and would not listen and closed her eyes to retain the light that still burned in them, and pressed her lips together to keep the power of aleph trapped in her throat.

It was then that he stroked her hair and felt love overwhelming him. He touched the poignant twist of her shoulders and said, "Hannah, Hannah . . . what about the rest of the alphabet?"

To the tenderness in his voice, she replied, "No. You mustn't. Please. Aleph is enough. It is the beginning, and therefore better than all the rest. If I have the beginning, can't you see, I don't need the rest. If I had them, then I would no longer want them. Aleph is better. It brings all the rest to me, still dark and beautiful. Still mysterious. All the words, still waiting to be known. Prayers, still waiting to be prayed. No. No, Nehemiah. Don't teach me. Don't teach me. I'll have so much less to long for."

Suddenly, desiring her, he understood — and did not

39

understand. She, for her part, sensing the strain her words had made, tried to ease it by saying, matter-of-factly, "Besides, you shouldn't teach me. I'm a woman. It would only spoil me for the geese."

He heard himself saying, whether with the crudeness of the axeman or the subtlety of the scholar he was not sure, "It will not spoil you for a bride."

"Hush," she begged, her head pressed against his knees. "Hush . . . please. Please, please, please . . . hush."

❧ ❧

He asked for her hand in due form, and as she was an orphan, a ward of the community, there was no trouble about arranging the marriage.

When he came to tell her that the date was fixed, she took his hand and made him come with her, alone, without the geese, higher up the mountain and tried to dissuade him. "I'm not beautiful, Nehemiah. I'm crooked. How can you know what sorts of children we will have. I'm not a fit wife for a logger *or* a scholar. Let me go . . ."

He took her hand and said doggedly that the date was set. She would be his wife. And added, though the words were strange to him, "I love you." She leaned against him and they watched a water ouzel dart under a fall, where it strutted among the splashed stones, pecking and snatching at water grubs that sparkled like emeralds.

He made her sit and told her of all the loves he knew: of the devoted love of Jacob for Rachel, the loyal love of Abraham for Sarah. And of the sad love of Potiphar's wife for Joseph, and the criminal love of Tamar for Judah, and the destructive love of David for Bathsheba. But he ended, as he knew he would, with the timid love of Ruth for Boaz, her near kinsman, on the threshing floor in Bethlehem.

She listened, she sighed, and asked him to take her home. There was a strange light in her eyes, and her gait was more than usually awkward. By the time they reached the hut in which she lived, she could hardly drag herself along.

40

Nehemiah had to put her to bed himself, though he was afraid of touching her garments, and ran all the way home to get his mother.

His mother recognized the cholera at once. She and Nehemiah stayed beside Hannah's bed for three days. They wrapped her body in cold wet towels, and they offered her tea. Finally, the rabbi came and prayed. By then, Nehemiah knew that Hannah would never get past the letter aleph in this world. He sat, holding her hand, watching her turn a brown clay color. Once she opened her eyes and seemed to see him; then they closed for good.

Nehemiah, a powerful woodsman and a subtle scholar, dug Hannah's grave himself, wielding the pick in the rocky soil with the same cold anger with which, thirty years later, in Poland, he swung the uprooted hitching post against the Cossack's skull. In Poland, burying his murdered wife, he hated God once more.

5

Zamosc, Poland
1657

The wind swept through the last of the leaves in the line of poplar trees on the east side of the Jewish cemetery, making a new drift of yellow and brown and gold to rustle against the old headstones. All morning, it had been cold. So cold that Ephraim, the gravedigger, paused frequently in his work to take off his heavy mittens so that he could warm his fingers over the scalding tea his granddaughter had brought him from his hut near the cemetery gate. "The ground is tired of the dead," he grumbled, "so it makes me tired."

Khavah looked up at her tall grandfather laboring over the grave; like herself, he was swathed to the eyes in wool. She wished he would hurry with his tea. The dead were nothing to her. What she wanted was to get back inside the hut, where the stove roared and her grandmother was rolling the dough for the noodles that, with sugar and cinnamon and eggs, would be turned into a steaming *kugel* for the evening's supper. Khavah was twelve years old, an orphan, a fat lonely child who ate to keep herself company. She shifted from foot to foot, letting her grandfather know he was keeping her from the warmth of the hut.

Ephraim drank more quickly, wiped his mouth with the sleeve of his coat, and handed the cup back to his granddaughter, who waddled off to be with the noodles and the cinnamon and the fire. Ephraim turned to his work.

The grave was for another young man dead in a winter that had been bad for Jews and Christians alike. Ephraim knew from the frequent tolling of the iron bells in the Convent of the Holy Sisters of the Poor that eleven nuns had been laid to rest since early November. In the Jewish village in the valley, there had been fourteen deaths, men and women. Ephraim buried the Jews. Who, he wondered, made the graves for the nuns?

Looking up toward the walled buildings of the convent on the slope of the hill behind the cemetery, he marveled at Christian customs. There were said to be forty-two women behind those walls, women whose sole work in life was to pray to Jesus and to knit woolen garments for the poor. The nuns themselves chose to be poor, and spent their lives collecting holiness. Strangest of all, they had nothing to do with men. Still, they were a courageous band of women. Ten years ago, when Chmielnicki's Cossacks raged through the valley of the Zamosc, cutting down Jews at a gallop, the nuns opened their postern gate and dragged in wounded Jews, whom they nursed back to health. Later, when Chmielnicki returned, the nuns denied that there were Jews within the walls. For a wonder, the Cossack believed them — or said he did — and rode away.

Ephraim, noting the wisp of smoke curling from the smallest of the convent's chimneys, thought the nuns this winter must be poor to their hearts' content.

All morning, he hacked at the clay. The dead were courteous to a gravedigger only in the spring, when the ground was moist. Spring was a fine time for the living, when the juices flowed through the flesh, but it was a particularly congenial time for the dead, who had easy graves in which to lie and a swift moldering. Grave-making in November

43

was a curse, but there was no help for it. Death was an unexpected guest about whose coming no grave-maker should complain.

By noon, just as the first snowflakes of the day drifted to his eyelashes, the grave was ready. If the mourners did not get here soon, and the snowfall should turn heavy, there could be trouble settling the body in the grave. Snow looked fine coming down or spreading across the fields, but it could be treacherous in an open grave, where it could interfere with setting the body in its place. And relatives read the slightest misadventure at a funeral as an evil portent. Already the cemetery paths were pale with snow, and the headstones were acquiring white cloaks. Ephraim climbed his short ladder and drew it up after him. Setting it aside, he took up his spade and stood against the slowly whitening mound of yellow soil he had taken from the earth and wished again that the body and its mourners would get here.

Then he said a prayer in contrition, because one who hastens a burial unduly is to be despised; but as the snow fell more thickly, he could not forbear stamping his feet. To delay an interment was also a sin. Then he heard the creaking of the burial society's cart and the voice of the rabbi urging cart and mourners on. Ephraim glanced into the grave and breathed more easily.

The cart with the shroud-wrapped body was first into the cemetery. On either side of it walked the half-dozen members of the burial society. Behind them followed Yankel Fuchs, the dead youth's father, walking with the rabbi and such of the male members of the Fuchs family and their friends as had been able to come. After them came the female relatives, with Miriam Fuchs, the dead Benjamin's mother, in their midst. Miriam's weak "no, no, no" was all that was left of her first hysteria at her son's deathbed. Now, she let herself be led in a nearly introspective silence by her two grown daughters. As the procession made its way toward the grave, the cart stopped, moved,

44

then stopped again — seven times, at intervals of six feet each, as a reminder of the seven gates of Gehenna and the seven judgments that are passed on the dead.

The mourners, their shapes and voices muted by the snow, formed a semicircle around the grave. The tiny rabbi, his pointed hat drawn low over his ears, gave a sign to the mourners, and those who had not been to the cemetery within the past month repeated the required prayer: "Blessed be the Lord our God, King of the universe, Who created you in judgment, Who nourished and sustained you in judgment . . . Who is like unto Thee, Lord of great acts?" Their muted voices were like a disturbed silence colliding with a deeper stillness. The rabbi hurried the prayers on with discreet signals, and the mourners whispered more quickly, "Who resembles you, O King, Who orders death and restores life and causes salvation to spring forth?"

The prayers could be hurried, but not the eulogy, since Benjamin had been a favorite in the village. The snow fell on while the young man's piety and kindness and filial devotion were extolled. Finally, the rabbi was done. The women continued to sob respectfully, but it was too cold to cry at length. Besides, there was the week of mourning still to come. There would be plenty of time for more tears.

The members of the burial society stepped forward. The mourners bowed their heads a final time and said, *"Al m'komo yevo besholom.* May he come to his place in peace," and the shrouded body was lowered into the grave. Ephraim listened to the sound it made and gave a satisfied grunt. The body had settled well. Then, knowing how the relatives hated to be the first to throw dirt into a grave, he seized his shovel and threw in the first clods himself. Then he set it down, stepped back, and waited. Yankel, Benjamin's father, looking yellow and shrunken, pressed his teeth together and reached for the shovel. When he was done, the male relatives and friends, one after the

45

other, threw their clods into the grave. When they had all had their turn, Ephraim went to work neatly, professionally, to cover the body. The mourners turned away and followed the empty cart out of the cemetery. Near the gate, some of them paused to dig in the snow, searching for bits of grass to pluck so that they could recite a last prayer that expressed their hope that the people of the towns would flourish like the grass of the earth.

At the cemetery gate, Miriam Fuchs looked back at Ephraim, who was working diligently over her son's grave. She opened her mouth to say something, then changed her mind and allowed herself to be led away.

Not many minutes later, the last clod of earth was in place, and Ephraim stopped to look about. The snow was a thinner veil now, and through it he could see the curl of smoke from the convent chimney, as well as the smooth curves of the snow-filled meadows sloping toward the village. The sky was getting lighter. Soon, if the rising wind kept up its fraying at the clouds, the sun would shine through.

Out of the corner of his eye, Ephraim caught a glimpse of movement on one of the larger tombstones near the line of elms. It was an angular, white motion — neither bird nor rabbit — where nothing should have stirred. Ephraim seized his shovel and moved forward to defend his graveyard.

He knew the tombstone well. It was Jacob Stern's, and it represented his daughter Rachel's extravagant affection for her father, as well as her haughty sense of herself as the richest widow in the village. But that had been more than ten years ago, before Chmielnicki's Cossacks overran the district. Rachel escaped that terror with her life, but with very little else. Her father's imposing tombstone was all that was left of her wealth, and now she spent her days in a hut that was darker and many times poorer even than Ephraim's.

Again, the movement on the stone, as if a shroud of

46

snow had twitched. Then there was a moan. Ephraim stopped, more puzzled than afraid. His neighbors could afford fancies about graveyards and ghosts and demons, but years among the graves had made a skeptic of Ephraim. In his cemetery, he had never seen anything but the living or the dead. Whatever it was that twitched on Jacob Stern's tombstone belonged to this world and would bear looking at.

Ten paces from the grave Ephraim was brought up short by a sneeze that sent up a powdery cloud from the tombstone. There was a second sneeze, and a bare arm poked out of the mound of snow. The wind died down as the sun found a rift in a cloud and it became, suddenly, a bright clear day.

The figure on the tombstone shook itself and turned into a woman, who sat, her legs drawn up, her head pressed close against her knees, trying to make a ball of her body in an unsuccessful effort to keep warm inside the shawl wound round the ragged smock she wore. Ephraim stepped forward. At the sound of his boots, the woman peered out at him from under her elbow and sighed. The gravedigger, who was not afraid of spirits or demons, started. Slowly, the woman unwound herself from her spiral crouch and faced him.

"*Riboyno shel oylom,* Lord of the universe," Ephraim said, gripping his shovel. She looked so grim and pale, so cold and ill. Turning her luminous, dark eyes on him, she said, "You are not my father?" Her effort at speech weakened her, and she leaned her head upon her knee.

She seemed young enough to be a child, but the smock that imperfectly covered her revealed the body of a woman. A woman suffering, indeed, but a woman so extravagantly beautiful that old Ephraim had to close his eyes to deal with a rush of dizziness that would have made him stumble had he not leaned against his spade. The child — the woman — had the oval face, the densely curved brows, and full lips of a Bathsheba. When she stretched toward

47

him an arm bare to the shoulders, the movement revealed her full breast, so that Ephraim could hardly bring himself to answer when she said again, "You are not my father?"

"No," he said. "No."

She gazed at him, a look of baffled longing in her face and echoed, "No, no." Then she tottered to her feet.

She was tall, nearly as tall as Ephraim, and when she moved toward him, the old man thought that his fearful neighbors might after all be right — there were demons and goblins in the world. Succubi who could appear in a graveyard after a snowstorm to enfold an innocent grave-digger in hot caresses to destroy him. Then Ephraim, who had raised five children, two of them daughters, responded to the tears in the woman's eyes, and she became once more an ill-clad waif on a freezing day who needed to be warmed and fed. Throwing his shovel aside, he un-wound the fastening of his coat.

"You are not my father?" came the question again, as she put her arms out toward him, whether to ward him off or to implore or to embrace him he could not say, because at her third step she fell and lay trembling at his feet.

"Rivkah," Ephraim called toward the hut as he knelt beside the woman. "Rivkah. Come." When his wife ap-peared in the doorway, he turned his attention to the woman. His first thought was that she was an epileptic; then that she was in a seizure brought on by the cold. When he wrapped her in his coat and took her up in his arms, her tremors subsided. She put her head against his chest and murmured sleepily, "No, you are not my father. My father hates me, though he is dead." She burrowed her head closer against him. Through all the layers of wool, he could feel the pressure of her breast like a zone of warmth and memory. Almost, he regretted having called his wife. The absurd thought sent him marching resolutely toward the approaching Rivkah.

Rivkah wiped her flour-covered hands on her apron and

48

stared at her husband and his strange burden. Behind her, her plump granddaughter stared too, blinking her eyes in the sunlight. When Rivkah saw that it was a human form Ephraim carried, she clasped her hands and cried, *"Gott zol unts hiten.* May God protect us," and ran toward her husband. She was alternately rubbing snow against the woman's forehead and chafing her stiff fingers when there was a shriek from her granddaughter.

Her fat face twisted with fear, Khavah pointed at the woman in Ephraim's arms and cried, *"Zeyde, Zeyde. Kuk, kuk! Zeyde, der tseylem.* Grandpa, Grandpa, look! Look! The cross." Ephraim and Rivkah stood, petrified. In the excitement of the woman's need and her nearness, Ephraim had noticed only her beauty and that she was freezing. Rivkah, whose natural talent was to comfort victims, had noticed nothing at all except that the woman needed help. Now they saw what Khavah had seen: the silver crucifix dangling across the woman's bare shoulder.

Ephraim looked uphill toward the convent, from which there continued to rise the wisp of smoke he had seen earlier in the day. The woman's fingers moved against his neck, though her eyes remained closed. Despite the sunlight, Ephraim felt a grayness like a fog descending on them all.

There were always stories about convents. Women living unnaturally behind stone walls. There were always stories. Dark stories of hungering women throwing themselves at gardeners, peddlers, Gypsies. Or women who crept out at night to meet shepherds or priests. And then there were the runaways: noblewomen, hidden in convents to keep them from unsuitable marriages, who climbed down rope ladders and rode off with their lovers to distant lands. But that was in folk tales. Slowly the implications of their situation reached him. She was a runaway nun. And they were Jews in Zamosc.

Rivkah said the words first. "You can't bring her in here. Take her back where you found her."

"In the snow?"

"Oh my God, what am I saying? No, no. The poor thing. She'll freeze to death. But you can't bring her inside. A . . . a half-naked nun in a Jew's house. They'll flay us alive."

The woman in Ephraim's arms groaned, *"Matko boska, Matko boska,* Holy Mother." Then she lapsed again into what seemed to be a deep sleep.

Ephraim stood, waiting for Rivkah to help him out of his dilemma, but Rivkah's mind was too full of the remembered screams of dying Jews when Chmielnicki's troops had swept the district to be able to think what to do for a fugitive nun, however young and cold she was. It was Khavah who broke the long silence. "Take her to the church," she said. "To Father Gyorgy."

"Matko boska," the sleeping woman whispered, and Ephraim turned toward the entrance to the cemetery. Father Gyorgy in the Christian village was a kindly priest. A decent enough man to the Jews; but nowadays how could one be sure? Ephraim could already hear the questions he would ask: "Why isn't she wearing a habit? Where did you find her? How long has she been with you? How did her clothing get torn?"

Rivkah urged Ephraim on. "Go. Go. If you go now . . . it's beginning to snow again . . . maybe no one will see you. Hurry. Open the little door of the church . . . the little one. And leave her there."

The whole scheme was unreasonable. It was half a mile to the Christian village, and despite the snow, it was unlikely that he could get there unseen, and, with his burden, once seen, he would be stopped. What could he say then? Who would believe a story he could hardly credit himself? What the Jews believed need not matter, but a Gentile . . . A half-naked nun in the arms of a Jew! It was too horrible. But Rivkah still urged him on. "Hurry. Quickly, quickly. Go. With God's help it will . . ."

It was then that the woman in his arms grew rigid. Her

50

arms thrust out before her as if she were pushing away a weight. Her face was suffused with blood, and her teeth ground against each other. From her throat there came a harsh gasp. Her head was thrown back, the muscles in her neck tensed. Whatever had been beautiful about her fled, and Ephraim stood holding a rigid female *thing* out of whose mouth there issued a series of Polish reprimands:

"Have I not forbidden you the ways of the Gentile?

"Have I not forbidden you the flesh of the swine?

"How long will you play the harlot among women?

"How long will you worship a forbidden god?"

At the end of each question, there was a pause into which there seeped a faint cry as of a child being pinched, after which the accusing refrain was resumed. When the litany was done, there was a long cry. The woman's body went limp and she sobbed, *in Yiddish, "Gotenyu, Tatenyu. Vos tust Du mir? Vos vilst Du fun mir? Ikh bet Dikh, Tatenyu, Tatenyu . . . Ikh bet Dikh . . . Ikh bin azoy shlefrig . . . loz mikh shoyn a bissele zu ru.* O God, dear Father, what are you doing to me? What do you want of me? I beg you, dear Father, dear Father. I beg you . . . I'm so sleepy . . . let me rest for a little while."

The snow fell heavily. Ephraim and Rivkah and Khavah stood, their heads bowed, each of them aware how everything had changed. It was Rivkah who said what they all understood: *"S'iz a Yiddish kind.* It's a Jewish child. *Gebentsht zol zayn der Oybershter.* Blessed is the Almighty. A lost Jewish child, newly found with God's help."

The gravedigger, his wife, and his granddaughter knew how much more fearsome their situation was now than it had been before. The woman in Ephraim's arms was Jewish — perhaps a forced convert escaped from the convent on the hill. For Jews to help her, for Jews to hide her, was to court worse than death. Ephraim and his wife and the lonely fat Khavah knew all that, but now at least they were no longer unclear about what to do. It was Khavah who led her grandparents through the snow and opened the door of the hut. A tired Ephraim, with Rivkah helping him, brought the unconscious woman inside.

❧ ❧

Her name was Sarah. That was the one clear thing she told them before she became a thrashing prisoner of the illness that overwhelmed her from the moment they put her into Khavah's bed above the clay oven. For a week she raved in Yiddish and Polish while she was tossed between fever and chills with such violence that Rivkah, who was a patient nurse, was tempted to believe the devil was in her.

Rivkah spat three times and blamed herself for being jealous of the woman's beauty, which, despite the ravages of the illness, was a constant presence in the hut. She could not help being lovely, Rivkah told herself, and yet what, if not the devil, was it that made her patient, tossing in her fever, seem to be moving in a sensual dance? At such times Rivkah, exasperated by her own feelings, turned her old husband around and made him go stand at the window to look out at the gravestones in the moonlight.

When, on the other hand, Sarah was overcome by chills and sighed and moaned and rolled herself deeper and deeper in the eiderdown as if she meant to bury herself in it, the effect was equally startling, though her body was entirely covered. She lay, her long gleaming hair making a black pool on the pillow, her eyes closed, her face drained of all color, looking so abused and worn, so helpless and lonely, but still so desirable and female that Rivkah, looking down at her, felt stirring in her bowels something of a man's ambiguous compassion. The mystery of Sarah's beauty, in such moments, seemed to be in the tremors that passed over her eyelids, in the faintly cruel aquiline curve of her nose, and in the contradictory innocence of her sweetly parted, full lips.

"She is a Jewish child," Rivkah said sternly, "and she

52

is sick." With that, she sponged Sarah during her fever or wrapped her closer in the eiderdown during her chills; but in the early morning hours, when Sarah's delirium was most intense and only Rivkah was there to hear it, there was plenty of reason to think the devil was mixed up in the matter. Rivkah, listening, tried not to understand, and when the ravings became too explicit, she shut her ears. Sooner or later, Rivkah knew too much, and, though she never stopped ministering to Sarah, she vowed that as soon as she was well, she must be gotten out of Zamosc with the utmost speed.

The scandalous ravings were in Polish.

※ ※

"Rapture." The nun's voice was dry, patient. "What I will teach you is rapture. No. No. Do not blow out the torch. What I will teach you is condemned by men and proscribed by God. Heaven forbid that you should achieve damnation in the dark."

The twelve-year-old girl spoke without fear, but with a questioning note. "Rapture? I understand rapture. I feel it in adoration of the Virgin, or in praying before Christ."

"For which the Virgin and her Son will bless you. But that is the rapture of the spirit. The joyful soul beating its wings to fly like a dove toward heaven."

"Yes. Yes. Yes." The girl's voice was soft, hurried, silken. "It is a flight. You will teach me such a flight of the soul?"

"Of the senses, darling. A flight of the senses, here, below."

"Not toward a supernal light, as Sister Olga says?" The listening nun restrained herself. The girl could not be teasing her. With even kindness, Sister Irene said, "No. Toward overwhelming darkness. That is why the torch must be allowed to burn."

"To help me see my way to darkness?" There was no blame in the question, only perplexity.

53

"To help us see *our* way. For we shall be together."

"Will you hurt me?" the girl asked unaccountably, but calmly and curiously.

"Sometimes," Sister Irene answered. "But not more than you can bear, and never less than you will learn to desire."

"I will learn to desire pain?"

"For the sake of rapture. Yes."

"Then," said the girl, "teach me slowly, please. I would not like to be afraid."

Sister Irene was overwhelmed. "You marvelous child," she said and kissed Sarah's forehead.

Sarah smiled. "Surely, Sister, I will not be damned for such a kiss as that. I have felt more rapture kneeling in the chapel."

"No doubt you have," Sister Irene replied, her voice rich with anticipation. "If we are to study rapture, we must begin with our clothes."

"As Adam did with Eve?"

"No." The nun's hand was at Sarah's cheek. "Adam and Eve learned to cover their nakedness after they fell."

"And we . . ." Sarah's voice was charged with heat and hurry.

"Will uncover ours."

Slowly, slowly, button by button. Each piece of clothing carefully folded; the torch flickering, giving off a heavy resin smell.

"Naked, we are very beautiful," Sister Irene said. "See how unlike we are, Sarah, and how alike. I am fully a woman, and you are no longer a child. Come. Lie close and let us touch. There. Yes, put your hand there, on my breast. Now. Close your eyes. Move your hand while I touch . . . your breast. There. See how alike, how unlike, we are. I, a woman. You, no longer a child."

Sarah lay in the nun's embrace, grateful to be held. It was fine to be warm, fine to be held close. Better than to remember the clinking of harness gear, the creaking

54

of saddle leather, and the endless trot-trot-trot-trot-trot-trot of horses' hooves and the smell of horses and the cries, plucked like bloody rags, from distant throats.

She remembered the horses more than the men who rode them, or the shouts and the shooting. Horses. From where she lay, she could see the movement of their legs, the flash of steel shoes. And hear their startled neighings, their coughs, their whickerings. A river of horses trotting round and around the village. Sometimes a horse was shot, or a brand fell across a mane and the horse screamed and reared and sometimes died.

"This is also forbidden, Sarah," Sister Irene was saying. "And this. And this. And this."

The horses stank and shrieked, but there were other voices, too. Hissing words. Sharp commands that made the horses jostle and wheel around the village square. There were voices that gave commands, as if someone understood why the sabers should flash in the light shed by burning huts, and why a ten-year-old girl in a long dress should be snatched up to be crammed inside a shed beside a couple of startled sows. Why a hand should press against her mouth, keeping words jammed in her throat along with the nausea that kept rising in it. A hand that should have been familiar, but that now was fierce and would not let a sound out of her mouth, though the sows complained and grunted, and the horses went round and round, and the flames roared, and the horses squealed and trotted, round and round.

It was better to be held by the soft, strong arm that held her now. Better to lie in the flickering tent of light the torch made. Better to touch with her tongue, as Sister Irene bade, the good sister's earlobes, the hollows of her neck. Better to bite the soft flesh of the nun's shoulder.

The sows grunted and shat and quarreled. They poked at her long dress with their hard, hungry, wet noses. They trod on her with their mean little hooves and belched against her face; but the hand at her mouth held every

55

protest in so that she could not cry nor curse nor retch, while out where the horses went round and round there were women screaming, as well as horses, and children shrieking, until the sounds abruptly stopped.

"Do it. Do it. Do it," Sister Irene implored. "Ah, do it. There. Rub, my darling. Kiss. Tongue. Yes. Yes. Slowly. Feel, ah feel. See, where I swell, there you curve. There. That's right. Slowly — there!" From the nun's body, there came an odor of dry cleanliness, not the rank odor of sweating horses, the smell of farting sows, and the dribble of their turds against her hair while the hand (whose it was she *ought* to have known, and didn't) pressed against her mouth until, at some moment when the fires were at their highest and the screaming in the square had stopped, the hand went limp.

The pigs understood what happened sooner than she did and tore at the dead fingers, then at the arm, so Sarah never found out whose it was, but sat cowering in a corner of the shed, being sick and weeping softly, until at last it rained.

Now Sister Irene moved. Her fingertips were at Sarah's nipples, then her mouth. Then the girl and the woman were entwined. Opening her eyes, Sarah watched with something like affection as the nun's face grimaced into a mask of sensual attention as her body mounted toward achieved desire and then delayed it. "Wait. Wait." Sister Irene gasped. "Not yet. Sweetly, Sarah," she panted, "let's not make a hasty abomination. There, *mo koteczku,* there, my kitten. Use your tongue . . . . . . your tongue . . . . . . your teeth. *Your teeth!*"

It had rained all night. She heard it pattering against the shed and felt it drenching her, but when she opened her eyes, she was somewhere else, in a spacious stone room, naked, her hair, matted and stinking, over her shoulder while two nuns led her to an oak tub half-filled with hot water. She did not mind the coarse yellow soap with which they washed her hair, but all the while they worked

56

at her, scrubbing and washing and drying and clothing her, she peered into the shadows of the large chamber, from which she expected would emerge at any moment the first of several million horses to throng the streets of the village, their harness metal jingling over the sound of creaking saddles and the terrible clatter of their hooves.

"Deep, darling. Deeper. Deeper," Sister Irene begged. "Higher. Gently." Sarah's fingers moved. "Twirl them," the entranced nun whispered. "Pull them. Pluck them. Harder. Harder. Not so hard." Sarah smiled. Sister Irene's eyes were tightly closed, her mouth twisted, her teeth clenched. As her body reached in quicker smaller motions toward something beyond her grasp, Sarah's fingers moved more quickly, more lightly still.

The nun's mouth opened wide. Still watching her mentor's face affectionately, the girl bent her head and let her tongue dart around a nipple while her right hand repeated the motion down below. When the low scream came from Sister Irene's throat and the nun's body thrashed in her arms, Sarah wept for gratitude and joy.

Perhaps, as Sister Irene believed, what they had achieved was iniquity, but after her friend's throbbing cry subsided, there descended so sweet a hush upon their bed that for a long, long while Sarah could not hear the sound of hoofbeats or screams or the crackling roar of overwhelming fires.

6

Peter Harleigh to Nicholas Tyrell
May, 1650

Within a month, it is your birthday and you will be thirty, listening, as I did last night, to the crack of doom which woke me from an indifferent dream to the realization that, not two days past, *I* was thirty.

Thirty! And I have been gone more than a year. And Cromwell has loosed the wrath of his unsmiling God on Scotland. And the theatres are dark, and you have taught yourself to wear a sober face no matter what lovely legs go twinkling by. Ah, Tyrell, can it really be true that our England has turned into a tradesman's parlour in which only the chastest kisses may be kissed? And is wit really dead? And does it have piety for a headstone?

My news is not so grey — yet how to write it? How shall I, the skeptic of love whom you know, confess to you that love's rude arrows have pierced my heart? Like any witless Romeo or haughty Troilus, I have been humbled by Aphrodite's blind bastard.

To put the matter soberly, I am well and truly in the toils of love. The Ganymede whom I adore is a youth named Shabbatai, a Jew, whose name signifies that he was born on a Saturday, the Sabbath of his people.

If Shabbatai were an ordinary London lad, making his

58

way in the world, and capable of gratitude, he should long ago have been mine, because, since my coming to Smyrna, I have enriched the tribe of Zevi, to which he belongs, by employing his father Mordekhai, a groaning, fat, gout-and-asthma-ridden man, as my factor in the town. Mordekhai is not particularly prudent or wise or yet intelligent. Nevertheless, amongst so many greedy Turks and Jews, he has two qualities that make him worth his considerable weight in gold: First, he lacks ambition, so that, finding his comforts to flow from me, he serves me faithfully; and second, he suffers from the most un-Jewish curse of honesty, which makes him render up his accounts to me with the same scrupulosity with which he makes up the jot and tittle of his sins to God. These traits serve us both. Mordekhai has grown rich in my employment and goes home each evening much cleaner than once he did from the poulterer's shop in which I found him. I, his patron, grow richer still, and prove a trusty steward of my father's goods.

But for his son Shabbatai — my ill luck is that he is one of those light-struck young men who is indifferent to wealth, since he is intent on climbing a shimmering ladder to God.

You smile, Tyrell, to see me brought to bay by sanctity. And yet, his beauty baffles me. There is about him an aura of odours: warm skin in secret places mingled with the smell of the sea — and those smells are mixed in some way with the odour of — there is no other word — holiness.

Shabbatai seems to glide through the streets of Smyrna. Dressed always in a clean *caftan* — sometimes white as the snow, sometimes a brooding blue — he is followed in his morning wanderings by a crowd of learned Jews, who, grown impatient with the dusty wisdom of their old rabbis, yearn after Shabbatai, thirsting to hear the new truths that fall from his lips.

In addition to the wisdom-seekers, there is always a scattering of the Jewish humble and the Jewish poor, who, looking up from their lives, are enchanted by Shabbatai's serenity (and perhaps by his cleanliness) and trail after him.

He walks among them like a promise, and those who follow him seem clothed in expectation, but what it is that is to come, no one yet seems to know.

In the mean while, he lifts their hearts.

As yesterday, when I mingled with the crowd to walk after Shabbatai down the Lane of the Basket Weavers on the way to the stairs that lead to the lower port. At the head of the stairs, by common consent, the crowd stopped to let Shabbatai precede it down the stairs. At the first landing, he was stopped by a shrieking Jewess, who staggered towards him, a huge child in her arms.

"Help me!" the woman cried. "Help him."

Shabbatai hesitated, as if he feared the woman's touch. Then he studied the child's face, then its mother's. His calm outraged the mother, who shouted, "You goddamned holy man — help him. Help . . ." Flecks of spittle came from her mouth and dribbled down her chin. "See." She seemed to cough. "See, he does not move." Enraged again, she cried, "Take him, you goddamned holy man! Take him," and thrust the boy at Shabbatai.

He sighed and looked up at the crowd behind him on the stairs. To the woman he said, "Why are you angry?" His voice was like the clear hush that comes over the mind when one is about to fall into a restful sleep. "Why are you angry?"

She hitched the boy higher against her and said, "Because he is sick. Because I am poor. Because you are beautiful."

Shabbatai approached her. "You are afraid," he said. "You are lonely."

She averted her face and nodded. Shabbatai reached out his arms for the boy, and the mother relinquished him. "Yes," he said. "Afraid and lonely. Lonely and afraid. You are angry, and he sleeps. He sleeps, and you are angry. Together, sleeping and angry, you make a frightened de-

60

nial of God. Hush. Hush. When you are not afraid, you will not be lonely." He rocked the boy in his arms, as if what he had spoken was a melody whose echo still hung in the air. The woman, relieved of her burden, swayed before Shabbatai, and the crowd on the stairway also swayed.

Shabbatai held the boy as if he were weightless. Softly, he reproached the mother for her fear; then he reproached us all for insufficient faith in God. Whatever he said (and often I was far from knowing what he meant), what floated over the harbour was a gleaming strand of encouragement. God alone knows what ailed the sleeping boy, or what it was the mother expected from Shabbatai, but all at once, what had been unheard music changed into a veritable song as Shabbatai tilted his head and sang.

Where the young Smyrna Jew found the Spanish ballad, or why he sang it, I do not know; yet the people on the stairs, the merchants in the *bazaar* below, even the gulls circling over-head, seemed to be caught in the same crystal-line silence as Shabbatai uttered his "Song of Meliselda":

> *As I rode down a winding way,*
> *Down through a valley winding,*
> *I chanced on Meliselda there,*
> *Her dark long hair unbinding.*
>
> *The daughter of the King of Spain*
> *Was Meliselda bathing.*
> *She washed her raven tresses and*
> *She took me for her darling.*
>
> *I combed her hair, I kissed her lips,*
> *I whispered love and wonder,*
> *But when I bent to kiss her breasts,*
> *The sky grew dark with thunder.*
>
> *And when I kissed her secret hair,*
> *And drank her secret fountain,*
> *She swore that I would always be*
> *Her love upon her mountain.*

> *And Meliselda sweetly swore*
> *We would be parted never;*
> *But then the sky grew dark — oh dark,*
> *And she was gone for ever.*

That was the song, and that was the whole cure. Or almost all of it, for when Shabbatai had done singing, he handed the boy back to his mother, after which he reached out and stroked the sleeping face. Lo and behold, the great lump of a boy opened his eyes and looked about him in surprise. His mother, as amazed as he, set him on his feet, where he stood tottering; then he leant against his mother whilst Shabbatai reached into the bosom of his own *caftan*, from which he extracted a boiled sweet which he popped into the sleepy-head's mouth.

"Miracle! Miracle!" shouted the crowd, but Shabbatai had already resumed his solemn walk towards the lower port. His band of scholars, disputing the mystical meaning of the song, followed after. I, too, was in that multitude.

Ah, Tyrell. At thirty, I am learning how it is that a man may stand in the midst of three fires at once: the flames of rapture, the radiance of heaven, and the coals of hell.

I ask myself a delicious question: *Est-ce qu'on peut faire l'amour à un vrai saint? À un saint aux jolies fesses?*

7

Smyrna
1650

After the wedding ceremony under the canopy, after the wine and the feasting and the vulgarities, Shabbatai brought Leah, his sixteen-year-old bride, to the room at the top of his father's house. Leah was a slight young woman, full of self-importance because of her marriage to Shabbatai, the famous *khakham*, the Wise Youth of Smyrna; but as Shabbatai led her from landing to landing up the stairs, her hand in his sweated, as if she would melt away in her excitement. She laughed a forced little laugh that allowed him to smell the odor of the cinnamon stick her mother had taught her to chew after drinking wine. As they came closer and closer to the bedroom, he noticed too the changes in her body's smells, from acrid to pungent to very bittersweet.

Inside the bedroom, with the door finally closed, they stood looking at each other, neither of them ready to make a first move toward the bed. Finally, Shabbatai dropped her hand and went past the bed to the open window, where he stood looking out toward the stars, which glistened peaceably enough. Sometimes, because it was midsummer, a star or two fell, streaking briefly across the sky. Leah, who had not moved, called, "Shabbatai? My husband?"

Abruptly, Shabbatai left the window and began to pace before the bed, his hands folded behind his back, as though he were intent on a particularly knotty Talmudic problem.

Leah was not to be so easily intimidated. Like the gawky child she had been not long ago, like the wily woman she meant to become, she planted herself before him and smiled coquettishly. It was not a successful maneuver. What Shabbatai saw was a suddenly moistened, gleaming lower lip and a mouthful of strong white teeth. He whirled away and resumed his silent pacing, but in a smaller circle. He could feel, seeping into the room, the invisible mist of female desire.

Again, she placed herself before him, but now she had undone the thrice-folded crimson and gold scarf that had been wound around her hair to make a cone-shaped peak. From the garden, there came the biting smell of nasturtiums. Leah's fingers worked at the scores of tiny knots in her velvet bodice. Shabbatai thought she moved with uncanny speed, and yet she was clumsy and breathless. Half-unwillingly, Shabbatai reached out to help her unwind the soft linen cloth that had been wound eight times around her neck. He moved it slowly, fascinated with the mystery the cloth concealed. She was small and trim, yet Shabbatai wondered about her neck. What if it was square or thick or stringy? What if the skin was blotched or coarse? Into Leah's eyes there poured a dark languor that stilled for a while the shapeless warnings drifting toward him along with the mist of her desire.

Her neckcloth fell away, and Shabbatai stood, enchanted. Her bodice was gone, her shift, her robe — all gone. She stood, her head proudly raised in the full consciousness of her beauty. Stepping carefully on her high, silver-embroidered blue shoes, she went closer to him, her small hands out, palms up, and whispered, "Shabbatai, my husband."

Shabbatai averted his head, as if the gesture could avert the sight of her nakedness. He felt the weight of his blue

64

linen robe and the irritating stiffness against his skin of his woolen *arba kanfot,* the ritual four-cornered fringed undergarment. This moment, he thought, was not of his making. Almost to the last, he had fought against marriage, knowing that it "was not written" for him. He, Shabbatai, had been born for something else, but what that was had not yet been revealed. Certainly, it was some boundless destiny, brimming with power and light. Because he was Shabbatai.

"Shabbatai. Shabbatai." It was Leah leading him to the bed. Following her, he wondered at what a trivial thing a marriage night really was. Not more than an occasion for a display of female flesh and darkness, of the rising mist that is the yearning of the female for the male.

At the bedside, Leah poured wine from a copper ewer into two silver cups and handed one to Shabbatai. He took it, closed his eyes, and drank. Then Leah's fingers were among his clothes, and he was lying heavily beside her on the bed, doing what he could to remember that a wife was needed to complete a man. That it was not good for man to dwell alone. That the Shekhina, the Indwelling Presence of God, was also female. That when the infinite En Sof and the Shekhina embraced each other face to face, then the Creator and His creation too became as one.

But that was not in a perfumed bed in which his Leah squealed like one of those faces in his dreams of the night demon Na'amah. Leah seemed to be everywhere — over, around, and under him. Her body was entirely made of small hot breasts and finely curling hair through which he was made to swim like a blind fish, his eyes shut, as light shattered inside his head in angry bursts. Then he was above her, and she hissed out of her serpent's throat, "Shabbatai! Now. Quickly. Do it *now.*" Her tiny hands pulled against his hips. He felt the weight of his great member and let out a roar of wild intention as he plunged.

Nothing.

Nothing.

A dry, small emptiness between his legs. Something wilted. A wrinkled mushroom. Leah still wriggled, unwilling to accept so much defeat. If movement and heat could make it happen, then she would move and burn. She was the bride of Shabbatai, the Wise Youth of Smyrna. She would not be shamed. She moved. She kissed his throat, his shoulder, his breast.

He growled and pinioned her arms against her sides, then bent to suck some power from her nipples. Again, his member was a stallion's or a bull's. Huge. Huge. More dangerous than when he stroked the Torah or fell upon Lilith in the steaming Garden. His hand touched some nerve in Leah, and she cried, "Hurry!" He reared and plunged.

To nothing. The same shriveled emptiness between his legs. The same female hunger thrusting up at him.

Leah rolled away and lay silent, her head pressed against her pillow. She sat up. "You loathe me," she said.

He tried to think whether that was true. "No," he replied. "You are beautiful." When she moved toward him as if to try again, he said hurriedly, "No. No, Leah . . ." and waited for an easy flow of speech to come to his help, but his nakedness and hers made him feel lumpish, incompetent for speech. Muttering "No, no," he left the bed, put on his clothes. Dressed, he felt the power of speech returning; in another moment he would feel competent again to invent reasons.

But when he turned to Leah, he gave a halting performance. It was not her fault, he explained. She must never think it. But her misfortune was that she had married a holy man. It was his own holiness, he said, that he had been testing. He had always known that marriage was not for him, but Rabbi Escapa and his parents had insisted. He would not have succumbed to their urgings had it not been for the glowing reports of Leah's virtues and her beauty. And she was all that had been said of her. Tonight, in her arms, he had prayed that he might after all be only

66

a man like other men; but God, as she had seen, had sent him a sign that he had another destiny.

Leah, in the bed, was cold. What, she wondered, was she to say to her father when he came next morning to see the proofs of her virginity? How was she to face her mother and friends, who, this very moment, were thinking she was the most enviable young woman in Smyrna? Licking her lips, she writhed before him, trying to remember the very small store of lasciviousness her mother had taught her, but Shabbatai, at the window, said sternly, "Leah, daughter of Israel, count yourself blessed. You have lived to be a witness to the secret motion of the hand of God. For the rest of your days you will have reason to bend the knees of your heart before Him in thankfulness that He has taught you, in time, to mark the difference between the holy and the profane."

A moment later, walking with a light step, he left the room, leaving a furious Leah to tear at the silken coverlets with her fingernails.

✻ ✻

Less than an hour later Shabbatai was running on the white beach below the cliff a mile west of Smyrna. In daylight, the cliff towered over the beach, a huge half-devoured promontory of carelessly piled stone. At night, in the light of the quarter moon, it seemed to have shrunk to a gnome-like black hump, its sinister outline reflected in the water as in a rippling mirror. Shabbatai, no longer encumbered by his wedding clothes, was wearing wide Turkish trousers. He ran as hard as he could, his white blouse open to the breeze, his hair streaming behind him. Though he was tall and well proportioned, he was anything but an athlete, and found himself gasping at his unaccustomed pace along the shore.

But that was the idea. To be in pain. To hurt. Whether in the soft sand near the cliff's base where his feet sank in and he twisted his ankles, or on the packed sand along

67

the water where stranded jellyfish shone whose stings might make him so dizzy that he would fall and lie paralyzed until the advancing tide should come and roll him gently out to sea. Harder and harder he ran, his hair falling in wet, lank wisps into his eyes. Between intervals of pain, he bit his tongue until the blood flowed into his mouth, covering with its salt stickiness the taste of Leah's cinnamon-flavored kisses.

Two hundred yards behind Shabbatai, there lurched a tall figure. Someone else running, but without haste. Overhead, the stars shone.

Shabbatai wove across the beach, sometimes splashing his scraped feet in the salt water, sometimes bruising them among the more and more frequent rocks at the base of the cliff. Then his feet were in running water, and he turned to follow the little stream to the cave below the cliff from which it flowed. There, in the all but total darkness, he found the long flat rock for which he was searching, and collapsed on it, all in a heap, his right arm under his head, his left trailing in the icy water.

He lay listening to the chirp and flutter of the bats and tried to keep himself calm in the darkness, which he detested. When the numbness in his left hand became an ache, he withdrew it from the water and sat up. He could see better now. There was a weak trace of moonlight in the cave that marked the winding of the tiny stream as it moved toward the sea. The cave breathed the dankness of old seaweed.

Something blocked the bit of moonlight. Shabbatai held his breath. There came a wet sound. "Shhhh . . . Shabbatai." It was Barot'ali.

"Oh! It's you." Shabbatai would have preferred to be alone, but with Barot'ali it was not possible to give reasons or excuses. The idiot stumbled through the stream and into the cave, followed by streaks of moonlight. Shabbatai pressed himself against the edge of his rock, making room

68

for Barot'ali, who lighted a candle and set it on a ledge. "I have food," the idiot said.

"Good."

"Eat," Barot'ali commanded, and, as scrupulously as his huge fingers could manage it, he divided the bread. Shabbatai smiled and said, "A feast." Together, the idiot and the khakham, after Shabbatai had made the appropriate blessing, settled back to eat by the candle's light.

The bread had the musty salt taste of Barot'ali's body, but as Shabbatai chewed, he felt how hungry he had been. It was cold in the cave, but the candle made a yellow-orange flickering light that kept away the shadows and the chill — and the bats. Shabbatai savored the bread and held it a long while in his mouth, passing it with his tongue from cheek to cheek until it was dissolved. Then he swallowed the sweet paste. Beside him, Barot'ali stopped tearing at his bread long enough to demand, through a crammed mouth, "Tell . . . Shabbatai . . . Tell me a . . . sssstory."

Shabbatai laughed aloud. The idiot's request, so misplaced, so unrelated to Shabbatai's adventures on this long wedding night, was ludicrously dignified. Shabbatai often told him stories. What did it matter that Shabbatai had left his bride in a fruitless bed in search of punishing nightmares in a cold cave? Shabbatai told stories to his friend, and he should do so now. "Tell," Barot'ali urged. "Tell . . . tell . . . tell."

And Shabbatai, taking the idiot's huge hand in his, put it into his lap and told.

"Once upon a time," he began, "before there was a time, and long before there was our light, there was a light beyond space and beyond description that crouched in the timeless egg of itself. A light without need or attributes floating in eons of stillness."

Barot'ali, deeply versed in the formulas of tale-telling, echoed the teller. "It floated," he said, "once upon a time."

"Yes," Shabbatai agreed. "Once upon a time, though there *was* no time, this light floated, until one day it gave a tremor of intention. A tremor of self-conscious light. That tremor was the sign that the light intended an event."

"What happened?" the idiot, in a soft voice, asked.

"The light contracted. It pulled away from the edges of itself (though it had no edges — but how else am I to tell the story?). It pulled away. It shrank.

"That was a wonderful moment: the light fleeing from itself at the same time as it flowed toward itself . . . Flight without diminution; contraction without loss."

"Without loss," Barot'ali repeated.

Shabbatai resumed. "Then, because perfect consciousness cannot leave a space without leaving an aspect of itself behind, the place where the light contracted was soon flooded with the residual light that lurked therein."

"Lurked therein," Barot'ali echoed.

"Now comes the wonderful part," Shabbatai said, gripping Barot'ali's hand. "The light that shrank and the light in the space abandoned by it yearned for each other. So great was their yearning that, finally, the contracted light sent an arrow of its essence into the abandoned space, which, striking the residual light, created Man."

"Me." Barot'ali sighed, ecstatic.

"Not you, you idiot. *Man.* And not ordinary mankind either, but Adam Kadmon. A creature of light. A fountain, an erupting volcano, sparkling, gleaming, burning. Light, restless and turbulent, surging and spouting. Adam Kadmon's fingers blazed, and his toes, his nostrils, and his eyes. His hair, his lips, his all-consuming organ. Everything alive with light. A fire so intense, it could not be contained within the splendor of that Man; so that there was an overflow of light that jetted from him, spewing and splattering, gushing. Light colliding with light until En Sof, He Who Has No End, determined to contain the gushing and sent . . ."

"Sent help!" Barot'ali cried. "A servant."

"Of sorts. But not a scullery maid. Instead, He formed vessels, also made of light, that would contain the light spewing from the body of Adam Kadmon. And the light poured into the vessels, age upon age; poured in an endless flood, filling up the vessels, which, though they were also made of light, took on a brighter glow, until . . ." Shabbatai's voice dropped.

"Until . . . until . . . until . . ." clamored the idiot.

"Until they broke."

"Alas!"

"And from that spilled light, no longer wholly perfect, no longer absolutely pure, descend the worlds we know; and the light of Adam Kadmon lies, to this day, obscured by the broken shards of those first vessels."

"Can they be mended?" the idiot inquired.

"Yes, Barot'ali. When the Messiah comes, he will gather up the scattered light and mend the vessels, too."

From inside the cave, Shabbatai became aware that dawn had touched the Aegean. Barot'ali, still chewing on his bread, said impatiently, "You mend them, Shabbatai. You mend them."

"Come on," Shabbatai said brusquely. "Let's go home."

8

Zamosc
1652

The apple trees were heavy with fruit, and the birds, noisy in the branches, were overwhelmed by so much opportunity for food. Summer flies, their bodies gleaming like burnished bullets, hung in the air as if asleep. In the high grass under the trees, occasional flag irises waved their purple ruffs. Sarah and Sister Irene, on their hands and knees, were waiting for a turtle to emerge again from his shell. They had been watching him for half an hour as he crossed the space between the pea vines and the apple trees, pushing the grass aside like a swimmer breasting waves. It was because Sarah had picked him up that he had withdrawn his head and feet while she studied his blue-gray-plated upper shell and the butter-yellow armor of his belly. "His eyes are so lonely," the fourteen-year-old Sarah said. "So patient and lonely. As if he had everything . . . and regretted it." She touched her upper lip with her tongue. "But I, Irene, when *I* have seen everything and touched everything . . ."

"Yes?" Sister Irene asked, caught up, as she frequently was, in Sarah's loveliness. "Yes? What will you do?" The child was passionate and unpredictable, with an eager intelligence that could turn suddenly labyrinthine and — as Sister Irene privately named it — Jewish.

Sarah's body, like her mind, was mercurial. She could be, in certain moods, no more than the bumptious four-teen-year-old she seemed, making their lovers' bed delight-ful with her innocence; at other times, she became an ageless sensualist, sleepy and languorous; at other times, she was overwhelmed by strange heats, gushes of intense necessity that no embrace and no caress could still. After such a seizure, Sarah lay quietly, the glittering hunger still unextinguished in her eyes, and looked past the bed, past the wall, out into the night beyond the convent, beyond the world itself to a chosen point of meaning hovering between the stars. After such a time, when Sarah was finally asleep, Sister Irene had taken her in her arms, wanting to breathe more closely Sarah's young fragrance. Sarah had stirred and opened her eyes and said, "Irene? Irene. Ah, it's you. Oh, Irene. I want to bear your child." Then her eyes had closed, and she had slept the sleep of the sinless young.

Now, musing over Irene's question, Sarah said, "I? When I have seen everything and touched everything . . . I will pray to remember everything — except . . ." She gritted her teeth and seemed to be shrinking away from painful words.

Just then, the turtle, satisfied that he was no longer in any danger, put out his small beaked head and resumed his slow swimming through the grass. Sarah, instantly cheerful and alert, crouched with Irene beside her and followed his majestic progress until he came to rest on a bare little sun-drenched mound, where he waited. The sun beat down, steeping him and the grass and the women in its midsummer warmth. The turtle's head was far out of its shell, poised like a beady armor-plated ball on the sinewy stalk of its neck.

"Shhhh," Sarah whispered. Sister Irene saw what her

73

friend had seen: a stag beetle was climbing the mound, its black body gleaming, its curved antlers held out before it like questing lances. The turtle made no movement. The beetle advanced quickly up the slope of the mound. Sarah touched the back of Sister Irene's hand; both women held their breath. There was a click and a blink. The turtle stood as still as before, but now, from either side of its poised old head, there feebly waved a beetle's antler and a delicate, barbed black leg.

"Lovable, your friend," Sister Irene said, getting to her feet.

"He is a turtle," Sarah replied, also standing. "He only followed his destiny."

"And the beetle?"

"He followed his as well. But you see, the beetle was in the greater hurry. If there is any blame, it is his."

"Ah, Sarah!" the nun cried. "So wise, so young." She shivered and embraced her friend compulsively. "Oh, Sarah, Sarah. How dangerous, how deadly is God's world."

"Not only dangerous." Sarah laughed, disengaging herself from Irene's embrace. She ran up the walk away from the orchard, calling back, "Come, I'll race you to the bins." Sister Irene, as decorously as she could, ran after Sarah, past the apple trees, past the pea vines, to the convent granary. Behind them, the turtle withdrew into his shell until the sound of their footsteps no longer vibrated in his earth; then he eased himself out again and waited. This was a favorite walkway for the beetles. Sooner or later, another one would pass.

❧❧

The bins were in a high, tile-roofed loft of the granary. The sunlight coming through the chinks in the red tiles and the knotholes of the rough board walls was diffused by the wheat and barley dust, which turned the loft's dimness into a cozy glow. Each of the long, wide bins, now that the summer harvest was in, was filled with wheat or

74

barley. Sarah, busily undoing her clothes, was eagerly sniffing the dry smell of the grain, the odor of the old pine boards, the more distant smell of mouse-droppings in the rafters.

A moment later, a naked Sarah sat in a scooped-out space in the barley, like a naiad on a golden basin. Sister Irene, more meticulous than Sarah, still folded her clothes and laid them across the upper board of the bin. Then she too climbed into the pool of grain.

Sarah caught up a handful of barley and put some of the grains into her mouth. She chewed reflectively. A beam of dusty sunlight fell slanting across her breasts. The barley was dry and hard and sweet. She closed her eyes and tried to remember the grains when they were green. They had been tender in the spiky stalks that waved in the wind. "You know," she mumbled, her mouth crammed with barley, "if I could, I would chew sunlight."

"If *you* could, my darling, you would chew darkness or any other thing that you could get between your teeth."

Sarah hesitated for an instant. "You're right!" she cried, and flung herself on Sister Irene. "Anything I could get my teeth . . . or fingers on . . ."

The grain under their bodies flowed against and bit into their skin. With each turn of their embraces, new valleys formed in the barley, and new hills. The women moved slowly, and the grains poured around them slowly. As their hands passed over each other and the pace of their desire quickened, the barley rose and fell more quickly. There was barley in their ears, in their navels. When their fingers and mouths touched or strayed to their body openings, the barley followed every gesture, and they met grain mixed with sweetness and with salt. They moved and turned and groaned as they sank ever deeper into the barley, whose dry smell mingled with sunlight and the moist odor of sweat and love. There was a final tumult of barley, flesh, and sunlight, and the women fell into the last tunnel of amazement with a single cry. As they subsided, they

75

were followed into the redeeming dark by a cascade of grain that all but covered them.

Much later, they lay beside each other and held hands. "You make me very happy," Sister Irene said.

"You" — Sarah considered the matter — "you make me . . . almost happy."

"Almost? What is it, darling? What is it I don't do?"

"I feel abused," Sarah said. "I feel just like those silly girls men seduce and run away from in the tales that old Sonya tells."

"But . . . I don't abandon you. Look at us. Here we are!"

"Yes . . ." Sarah's tongue searched the crevices in her teeth for a recalcitrant barley grain. She found it, chewed it, and swallowed it. "Yes," she said finally. "Here we are. But" — she smiled more than half seriously — "you never talk of marrying me." Abruptly, she turned over on her stomach and faced the older woman. "Listen to me. Are you listening?" Sister Irene nodded. "Good," Sarah went on. "I don't care about the damnation and the abomination and all of that . . . I love you. And you love me. And . . . and . . . I want to be wholly yours and I want you to be wholly mine."

"But I am. We are."

"No! Just because I'm young doesn't mean I don't know what it is that all true lovers desire. They want to be *one*. Body and soul, forever, in the sight of God and man. If you loved me . . . if you truly loved me . . ."

"Yes?"

"You would marry me."

The nun gazed at Sarah and saw that there was real grief in her face. Sarah was serious. "Sarah," Sister Irene began. "Sarah, darling. You know that can't be."

"Why? Why? Why?" Sarah beat against Irene's shoulder with her fists. "Why? Because you don't love me? That's it, isn't it? That's it."

Sister Irene stroked Sarah's hair. Looking around at all

76

the golden grain, she felt how it had lost its former luster. She closed her eyes and tried to think what she could say that would feel truer to Sarah than the physical truth her lover had chosen to ignore. "No, sweetheart. I *do* love you, with all my heart and soul. There. There. You know why I can't marry you, Sarah darling. It's because . . ." She held out her hand to show Sarah the gold ring on her finger. "It's because . . . I am already the bride of Christ."

Sarah buried her head in Sister Irene's shoulder and would not stop her sobbing. "What shall I do, Irene?" she moaned. "What shall I do? Oh Irene, if you love me, tell me, whatever shall I do?"

9

✿

Smyrna
1650

Esther, Shabbatai Zevi's second bride, was a plump, phlegmatic seventeen-year-old, who, having no secrets of her own, assumed that everyone around her was as uncomplicated as herself. Being married to Shabbatai, she had supposed, would be like living in her scholar-father's house. She would be loved and dandled and fed and kissed. Everything would be as she had known it, with one difference: her father was poor, and Shabbatai was rich. But in the wedding bedroom, nothing happened as it should.

Instead, there was a long, gloomy silence while she sat on the bed looking toward Shabbatai, who, a bunch of black grapes in his hand, stood at the trellised window that looked out over Smyrna harbor. Sometimes Shabbatai plucked a grape and ate it. Eventually, it occurred to Esther that this was the wrong behavior for a wedding night. Tentatively, she reached a hand toward him and said, "Shabbatai . . . husband . . ."

He shook his head. "No, Esther. I am not your husband."

"In heaven's name!" she cried. "What are you, then?"

The question seemed to soften him. He stepped away from the window and moved toward her as if he meant to impart a secret. And, indeed, that was Shabbatai's temp-

78

tation just then. He would tell her . . . confide in her
. . . She looked so sad, so bewildered and ignorant there,
swathed in her silks, her lips parted, her eyes wide. What
a relief it would be to tell her . . .

Tell her what? What would this plump young woman
with the liquid eyes say if he told her of his vision of the
three Patriarchs dressed in robes of light who had stood
at the foot of his bed and called to him, "Shabbatai, Shabbatai, Shabbatai"? First, Abraham, as having the most authority; then Isaac, as the one who had experienced the
greatest pain when he was brought, a sacrifice, to the altar;
then Jacob, bowed by tragic paternity. Each addressed him,
their voices like the various winds that blew from God:
"Shabbatai. Shabbatai Zevi. You are the beloved of the
Lord. Take up your burden. Yours is the task."

And Shabbatai: "What is my task?"

The Patriarchs held their arms out in blessing. "Shabbatai Zevi, O lord of light, perform thy destiny . . . thou
savior of Israel!"

Then they were gone, and he was left, light streaming
from his eyes and fingertips.

How say all this to Esther, squirming in her innocent
lust? Outside in the garden, cats yowled. He remembered
Leah, his first bride, her thin hands on his hips, and her
obscene cry, "Quickly, quickly, Shabbatai."

He set the grapes down on the window ledge and said,
"I am not . . . what you need." Turning, he walked from
the room, leaving Esther to writhe in a drama that, to a
lord of light, was less than trivial.

❧❧

He thought of himself as a solitary figure, but in the year
of his marriages, young men began increasingly to collect
around Shabbatai. Particularly in the late afternoon, the
scholars at the House of Study would prevail on him to
lead them to the beach at the southern outskirts of the
city, where, as the shadows of the day lengthened, they

79

discussed the texts they had been reading. When Shabbatai tired of text explication, he taught the young men the discipline of whirling.

Among the most eager of the youths who gathered for instruction from Shabbatai there was a fifteen-year-old named Itzhak ben Shimon, whose father, a prosperous dealer in hides, was after the boy to avoid Shabbatai's company. Shabbatai was the object of considerable rumor these days in Smyrna. There were the two marriages, contracted for, solemnized, and dissolved for mysterious reasons within a few months of each other, not to mention other *ma'asim zarim,* strange acts.

One thing in particular had made the leather dealer nervous. It was said of Shabbatai that his body gave off a peculiarly sweet odor. The elder ben Shimon, who himself carried about with him the strong smell of the leather he sold, found himself especially affronted by the idea that Shabbatai gave off the odor of sanctity. "There's witchcraft in it," he complained to the rabbi of his small synagogue. "Witchcraft or the devil." The idea weighed so heavily on his mind that he began to plague the rabbi, demanding that the shy old man investigate what might be a source of corruption to the young Jews of the town.

The rabbi was in an agony, pressed on the one hand by his rich but unlettered congregant to investigate the source of Shabbatai's smell, and worried on the other by what the even richer Mordekhai Zevi, Shabbatai's father, might say to such an investigation. Fortunately for the rabbi, Shabbatai himself treated the matter with good humor. Putting his arm around the old man's shoulder, he said, "Come, Rabbi Gamaliel. Let us both go to the *mikveh,* the ritual bath. There you may see and smell to your heart's content."

And that was how it had been. Shabbatai, with no diffidence whatever, had removed his clothes and, standing naked beside the somewhat murky water of the mikveh, had said, "See, Rabbi. This is the entire mystery. A clean body. I love to bathe."

Pressed by his duty, and by a curiosity he did not entirely understand, the rabbi moved closer, sniffing the air around Shabbatai. There *was* an odor, but it was not, as had been rumored, so sweet that anyone who smelled it would fall into a swoon; nor did it, as another story went, send swarms of evil thoughts into one's head. Though, the old man acknowledged, it did touch him in some manner. As if he had caught the fragrance of something infinitely beautiful that had once had a greater presence in the world. Or as if nostalgia had an odor and it came from Shabbatai. A nostalgia for what? The rabbi, keeping his eyes closed and trying to dream toward the vanishing presence, still could not find it. though he had a sense of sea-washed distances or of something green that was flecked with sunlight, or sprinkled, that very moment, by a pleasant rain. Tears came to the rabbi's eyes and he murmured, "Forgive me, Shabbatai. It must be that you are truly blessed."

"As you may be, Rabbi Gamaliel," Shabbatai replied.

The hide dealer, Itzhak ben Shimon's father, heard Rabbi Gamaliel's report and muttered that Shabbatai had bewitched him, but when Rabbi Gamaliel repeated before an assembly of synagogue notables his conviction that Shabbatai smelled of nothing more than youth and cleanliness, the leather merchant was silenced, and his son, Itzhak, was free to join the youths who trailed after Shabbatai.

It was Itzhak, whose voice, though he was fifteen, had not yet found the timbre of manhood, who wanted Shabbatai to explain the Talmud story of the celestial lion.

The story goes that the Emperor of Rome and the great Rabbi Yehoshua were arguing. "Your God," said the Emperor, "may be a lion of whom it can be said that when he roars, all who hear him are immediately fearful. But this comparison does little honor to Him. What is there

81

astonishing in it? The roar of a lion is frightening, and yet my horsemen can kill a lion."

"Indeed, indeed," Rabbi Yehoshua said, "your horsemen can kill *their* lion, but my God in no way resembles such a beast. Ah, no, *my* God, may His name be blessed forever, my God resembles the celestial lion."

"The celestial lion?" the Emperor wondered.

"The celestial lion," the rabbi replied, rocking on the balls of his feet.

"You say that he is fiercer than the lion my horsemen can kill?"

The rabbi nodded.

"Show him to me," commanded the Emperor.

"Ah, my lord. That may not be. The celestial lion cannot be seen by mortal eyes."

"Show him to me," the Emperor insisted, "or you die."

"Bethink you, my lord," Yehoshua said, "the celestial lion . . ."

"Show him to me!" cried the Emperor. "At once!"

The rabbi closed his eyes and prayed to the Holy of Holies while the Emperor and his courtiers smirked. Then the celestial lion emerged from his secret place. When he was four hundred miles away from Rome, he roared lightly, and every pregnant woman lost her child, and every city wall collapsed. When the celestial lion was three hundred miles from Rome, he roared a second time, and men and women lost their teeth at the sound, and the Emperor fell from his throne.

The Emperor cried to the rabbi, "I beg you, Jew! I beg you, make a prayer to send the beast away. I beg you."

And so it was. The rabbi prayed, and the celestial lion returned to his secret place.

"Ahhh," the young men said, when Shabbatai had finished telling the story. By now, they were at the beach, where young Itzhak, in a burst of pleasure, stood on his head, which made Shabbatai smile. Ezra, a dark, oily-skinned youth, was instantly jealous. Turning querulously

82

to Shabbatai, he said, "You tell the story well enough to satisfy Itzhak's simple question. But what *I* want to know is how we are meant to understand it. Are we to assume that God is the celestial lion, as one reading of the text permits us to suppose; or, since the rabbi prays to have the lion sent back to his secret place, are we meant to believe that God stays in heaven and sends the celestial lion to be His messenger?"

"Well, Itzhak, what do you think?" Shabbatai said, thereby darkening Ezra's mood. "How do you interpret the story?"

Itzhak, his heart in his mouth, watched as the afternoon breeze plucked at Shabbatai's robe. He knew what he should say. What, in fact, he wished to say. But the word *you* struggled in his throat, yearning to be uttered. With all his heart, he longed to say, "You! You, Shabbatai, are the celestial lion." Instead, he heard himself croak, "The celestial lion . . . represents the power of the Messiah," then waited to die of chagrin. But Shabbatai smiled sweetly at him, and Itzhak felt forgiven.

"Come," Shabbatai said to the others, who did not notice that anything untoward had happened. "Come, let us whirl. It may help to clear our sight."

And so they whirled beside the sea. It was one more effort at *hitpashtut ha-gashmiyut*, divestiture of the flesh, to send flesh and blood into a spin so intense that at its center one could achieve the holy moment of No Consciousness.

They started slowly, following Shabbatai's lead. Slowly, slowly. Six young men, each at his own place in the sand, turning. Turning more quickly, and more quickly still, as they pursued vertigo. Round and round they went, throwing off consciousness, throwing off memories and dreams. Faster and faster, throwing off the capacity to reason; round and round, no longer able to imagine or to hope. Faster and faster, whirling in an indiscernible waste; spinning at the center of endless miles of emptiness in which

83

light disappeared, as well as longing. Only the notion of a circle persisted, aching like a whirling membrane. The notion of a circle and a sense of speed forming a careering darkness. Round and round, until even vertigo was no longer a memory, and there was only the sensation of being at a summit, a pinnacle on which all was calm and dark and still, while far below whatever Was flowed away in a great spiral.

Round and round and round, until the silent pinnacle was invaded by an attenuated heartsickness, a roaring in the ear, and one by one they collapsed at the end of a long steep slide toward death.

From which, slowly, slowly, sprawled on the cool sand, one by one they returned to the light of the late afternoon.

Shabbatai lay where he had fallen at the water's edge, the waves caressing his lips. Itzhak was beside him, nearly immersed in the sea. The weary youth looked into Shabbatai's eyes; the tears ran down his cheeks. "Shabbatai," he begged. "Oh, Shabbatai. You know. You . . . you are the celestial lion. No one but you."

For answer, Itzhak received what he had dared to hope for only in his dreams. Shabbatai crawled through the sand and the foam. Kneeling beside Itzhak, he took his face in his hands and kissed him full on the mouth.

10

Kalisz
1647–1648

When Lame Hannah died of cholera, Nehemiah Ha-Kohen
was eighteen years old. With a youth's impetuosity, he
vowed never to be in love again, and cursed God. That
done, he sank back into his Talmudic studies as into a
safe parchment cavern, where every shadow was known,
each terror tamed and codified. But in the midst of a thoroughly abstract debate over whether a weasel could be
properly classified as a wild animal, or in a quarrel over
the number of degrees of uncleanliness the touch of human
semen could convey, Nehemiah would find himself gasping
for air and movement, and the House of Study, the rabbi,
the twelve swaying scholars around the table, and the old
books on their shelves, all turned into a single ball of dust
on his tongue, which needed to be spat out. When that
happened, Nehemiah packed his belongings and walked
eastward or westward to any center of Jewish learning that
required months of slow traveling to reach. It was the motion he wanted. Mile upon mile: Lvov, Nemirov, Kiev, Vi-
tebsk, Kovno. Cities or villages, wherever there were Jews,
he moved, his clothes in a bundle, his axe swinging from
a belt against his side. Wherever he went, he was sober,
silent, and useful. Where there were forests, he worked

as a logger; where there was none, he earned his keep by teaching children their *aleph-bet*.

It was many years after Hannah's death, in the course of one of his longer journeys, that he came to the Polish village of Kalisz. He was forty-seven years old, strong and vigorous as ever, but firmly settled into the pattern of his wandering life as a morose and lonely bachelor. From the time in the early morning when he put on his phylacteries to the midnight hour when he closed whichever book he was studying, he did not think of woman except as she might be mentioned in the text.

Kalisz, in 1647, had eleven Jewish families living on the outskirts of a village of three hundred Poles. Nehemiah, on his way eastward, stopped to rest and repair the sole of one of his boots at the village inn, which was kept by a bald and wispy Jew Named Yudel Abramowitz. The inn, like the village itself, was set on the edge of a plain of wheat. Everything — inn, village, wheat — was owned by the Pan Ulanowitz, a permanently absent landord who lived sometimes in Paris, sometimes in Bayreuth, while his holdings were looked after by a hierarchy of Jewish factors, overseers, tax collectors, and licensees. Yudel Abramowitz was licensed to sell vodka to the peasants who worked Pan Ulanowitz's wheat.

Abramowitz was a bad innkeeper, unable to be firm with his two Polish barmaids. He was also clumsy with his accounts. To the Jews of the village, he seemed arrogant and withdrawn; to the Poles who clustered around his rickety tables, his obsequious behavior was entirely insincere. Yudel had two things more to worry about: he was dying of tuberculosis, and he did not know what would become of his seventeen-year-old daughter when he was gone.

The daughter's name was Feigele — little bird — and indeed she was shyer than a wren. She brought Nehemiah water in a birch cup, which she set down before him so quickly that, as she made her escape, the water spilled over the shoe sole he was about to mend. Annoyed, but trained to patience, Nehemiah laid the shoe aside and looked after her. Why is she so frightened? he wondered. She retreated, wiping her hands on her apron as she walked backward. "I'm sorry, sir," she whispered. "I'm sorry."

Like a bird, she came running back, snatched up the cup, and was off again, only to return with it a moment later, full to overflowing. This time, though the water trembled at the brim, she set the cup down without spilling a drop. Nehemiah smiled and asked for a bowl of soup, a handful of nails, and a hammer.

She brought the soup, the nails, the hammer, and, on her own account, a small loaf of black bread. Then she stood beside the table and watched him eat. When he pushed the empty bowl aside, she darted off into the kitchen and was immediately back beside him, as if afraid that she may have missed some precious movement of his hands.

Nehemiah worked at the shoe and tried to ignore her. Her attention was so eager, so intense. He could feel her eyes studying the contours of his face, the shape of the shoe, and the veins on the back of his hands. "What's the matter?" he finally asked. "Have you never seen a man mending a shoe?" When she did not reply, he worked on. "Well," he asked, "is it that you've never seen a man before?"

She sprang away from him, then forced herself to stop. "Not like you," she blurted. He looked at her, amazed to see her panting. Whatever could be the matter with her? Then a thought occurred to him that made him blush. Then it annoyed him. The whole thing was absurd. She could not possibly be flirting with him. She was much too innocent, and he was much too old. He wriggled against the texture of his wool shirt and remembered that it had not been washed in many weeks. "Not like you," she repeated, and Nehemiah felt a rush of pleasure. But it was all absurd. Altogether absurd.

They watched each other, while Nehemiah drove the

87

nails into the shoe with precise taps of the hammer. She was thin-boned, with a slender body and an oval face. Not at all beautiful. She was dark, with the cheekbones of a Tartar; but her lips were full, and her eyes wide and wondering. Still, she was no beauty. Moreover, she was no more than a child, and he was forty-seven years old. An aging Talmudic scholar, a logger, an occasional *melamed* teaching the aleph-bet.

Feigele stood and watched him with what could not possibly be a look of adoration. Behind them, there was a step. It was Yudel, the innkeeper, come to join his guest. "There is no salt, Feigele," he grumbled. "No pepper at the table. Is that a way to treat a Jew?" Feigele hurried off, and Yudel, sighing, settled himself on the bench facing Nehemiah, to whom he promptly poured out his heart.

With the candor of a dying man, he explained that he would be dead soon, that Feigele was seventeen, that there were no marriageable men in Kalisz, that the nearest large community of Jews was in Lvov, from which, from time to time, a marriage broker did appear. "But you see where we are?" Yudel said, waving his arm at the landscape. "And what I am. The marriage brokers are interested in bigger things. It's something, isn't it — something for a father to worry about. And every day it gets a little worse." As if to explain his meaning, he was seized with a fit of coughing just as Feigele brought back the entirely unnecessary salt and pepper shakers and put them on the table; then she returned to the kitchen. Nehemiah, looking past her father, watched her shadow moving there and heard the clatter of the pots and pans.

Nehemiah pulled on the repaired boot and reached for his axe, which he had leaned against the table. Deliberately, he attached it to the belt at his side and stood up. The innkeeper, a look of panic in his eyes, also stood. Nehemiah put his right hand out to bid Reb Abramowitz good-bye, but what he said, as if it were the most natural thing in the world was, "Reb Yudel, if Feigele will do me the honor to accept my hand, she will make me the happiest of men in Israel." Reb Yudel burst into a prolonged coughing fit. From the kitchen, a furiously blushing Feigele came running to see what she could do to help.

⁂

Yudel Abramowitz died a month after the wedding, having had time enough to teach his burly son-in-law those rudiments of his trade which he himself had mastered so poorly. Nehemiah, for Feigele's sake, put aside his axe and acquired the patience needed to serve vodka to Pan Ulanowitz's peasants. When, six months after their marriage, Feigele told Nehemiah that she was pregnant, the inn was more prosperous than in all the years it had been in her father's hands. The coming of the baby was a golden omen, nearly as lovely as their wedding day.

Feigele was in her eighth month when disturbing news of trouble among the Jews east of the Dnieper reached them. The stories dealt with what seemed to be sporadic Cossack brawls, and Feigele, in the happy daze of her pregnancy, looked out at the miles and miles of wheatfields surrounding Kalisz and could not bring herself to worry about distant horrors. There were immediate things to think of: Would the peddler from Lvov remember to bring the ribbons and the flannel cloth she had ordered? Nehemiah, too, had the baby and its needs in mind. There was the cradle to make, and the *moel*, the circumciser, to keep track of, in case the baby turned out to be a boy. Beyond all that, the new prosperity of the inn kept him too busy to spare much thought for events beyond the Dnieper.

It was because of the late hours he kept to maintain their new prosperity that Nehemiah had taken to napping each afternoon for an hour or two on a bench just inside the door of the inn. He was sleeping there when the young Cossack rode into the courtyard and asked Feigele for water for himself and his horse. He was still sleeping, minutes

89

later, when the Cossack's pistol butt crashed down upon his head. Later, tied to the hitching post, he was horribly awake, unable not to see each detail of the Cossack's playfulness with Feigele, whose neck snapped at the moment of the Cossack's ecstasy, leaving him the master of a corpse.

Feigele, the little bird, lay, her head twisted on her shoulder in a most awkward sleep, while the Cossack, outraged that she no longer resisted his manhood, manipulated her limbs in one imitation of desire after another. Finally, even the pressure of her swollen belly no longer excited him. He got up and looked around and thought what else there was that he could do.

It was after that that he staked Feigele to the ground, stubbornly refusing to believe that she was dead. Then his horse called. The Cossack tore strips from the silent girl's petticoat, dipped them in water, and went to wipe the dried foam from his horse's neck. "Good Katya," the Cossack said. "Good girl. Katya, *dushenka*, Katya, darling."

Nehemiah, at the hitching post, strained against his bonds. Inside his head, below the sharp ache where the pistol butt had struck, he could feel an icy wind blowing. There was a red haze, then a gray one across his eyes, and he heard the howling of wolves filing down a mountain through the snow. He heard them snuffling and shambling, wailing to be understood, as one by one they were brought down by musket fire to become stiff dark shapes in the cold, waiting for the vultures to pluck their crystallized eyes.

"Good Katya," the horseman murmured as Nehemiah, with a final tug, parted the rope at his wrists and moved. The sound of the hitching post against the Cossack's skull was like a melon squashing, or a sob.

※※

After that, Nehemiah entered another long period of darkness and wandering, during which he asked God, both in his prayers and in his dreams, to show him what plan,

90

if any, He had for the universe. Sullenly, he insisted that there had to be a design. "I demand to know!" he shouted. "It's *Your* world. Your creation. Surely, You are no bungler. Teach me; teach me, Lord, to know Your intent." In reply, there came only a long silence. Silence by day, silence by night.

"Tell me," Nehemiah begged. "Tell me." But the days followed each other. Sometimes there was cold, or a strong wind from the north. Nehemiah felled trees in the forests or taught little children their aleph-bet. Sometimes he waved his axe at God and vowed not to budge from the spot until He should send him an answer. But Nehemiah was not the great Rabbi Honé Hammeagal, who stood fast in a hole until God sent the children of Israel the rain they needed. "Reasonable rain," the master specified, "falling with Your blessing and free will," and not some trivial spurt of water that might be sufficient as an answer to a prayer, but not enough to nourish fields of corn. And reasonable rain had fallen. For the great Rabbi Honé Hammeagal. Nehemiah, waving his axe against the sky, stirred nothing from the heavens. In the forests, the resin oozed from the pine trees in the spring. On the river, clouds of gnats hovered over the water.

Then Nehemiah discovered drink. If there was no coherence in God's world, He at least had had the good sense to put alcohol into it. For months, Nehemiah had served vodka to the Poles without ever having the slightest temptation to drink it. But after Feigele and the Cossack had been buried, Nehemiah found himself staring at the empty inn. There were barrels of vodka there, behind the counter. A clear, white, burning liquid that nightly glazed the eyes of unhappy Poles. He would see what it could do for him.

It was dreadful stuff, with a taste he could hardly stand, but if he drank it steadily, bracing himself against its fire, he found that it could, not so much wipe out his memories, as at least congeal them. Perhaps this was God's voice speaking from the whirlwind to men who were not on the level of saintliness with Job. A steady flow of clear white liquid in which God's mystery (or His bungling) was concealed. Chaos moved more slowly; pain lost its edge; and the voices of anguish lost their capacity to echo.

Nehemiah resumed his wanderings, wrapped, now, in a gauze of vodka-muted grief, only to discover that he was still a prisoner of longing. Direct, physical, brutal longing. Day and night, despite vodka and hard labor in the forests, despite fasts and frequent cold baths, an unyielding erection stood between his legs.

It was not an erection *for* someone. It was merely there, unrelated to any fantasy, any memory or hope. Merely a stern rod of flesh, uncomfortably waiting, interfering with his work.

11

Smyrna
1650

Late in July, a dour Rabbi Joseph Escapa finally signed
the decree that declared invalid Shabbatai's marriage to
Esther, his second wife. Rabbi Escapa had listened to the
woman's sobbing complaint and to her father's indigna-
tion. He made note of Shabbatai's assertion, offered without apology or constraint, that as far as he was concerned,
Esther was still a virgin. Though Shabbatai's father, Mordekhai, blustered and would have asked for more time
to reconcile the couple, Clara cut him off with a shake
of her head, and Escapa signed the annulment. The dreary
business, gone through once before with the first bride,
Leah, had to be done all over again: the dowry was repaid,
the wedding gifts returned, and the costs of the wedding,
since the fault lay with the groom, were assumed by Mordekhai. The bride, Esther, declared passionately that Shabbatai was a saint, the hem of whose garment she was not
worthy to touch, and the two families parted, sharing (all
but Shabbatai) a common bewilderment. Rabbi Escapa was
left with a renewed respect for the groom, who, he supposed, had, by an amazing discipline of the flesh, found
a way of punishing him, Escapa, for his part in arranging
the two marriages. When the families were gone, the rabbi

sat in his darkened room and thought what an ingenious opponent he had raised up in his former pupil, and could not be sure whether he feared or envied him.

Now, in August, Shabbatai woke in the small room on the ground floor of his father's house to the sunlight streaming in across the roughly woven rug on which he slept. His eyes opened from a dreamless sleep to a sense of himself as a point of joy in a perfect day. Properly, he ought to have felt grief, because it was Tisha b'Ab, the ninth day of Ab, the day on which Jews recalled the Roman destruction of the Temple of Solomon. The week in which the Ninth of Ab comes is a time of mourning. But the Ninth of Ab was also Shabbatai's birthday, and this year it fell on a Sabbath, which made the morning feel even more propitious.

For Shabbatai, who had been born on the Sabbath, the Saturday hours always had a golden glow. Today, on his birthday, Shabbatai could actually feel the taste of the morning's perfection on his tongue. On such a day, Rabbi Shimon, son of Gamaliel, said, "one must change one's life." Off in a window corner, a brown spider was swinging tirelessly from a silver thread, making effort after effort to reach a projecting ledge of the window frame where it was building its web. The spider launched itself and failed, then poured more thread from its body to make a longer arc for its swing. It swung and failed and tried again.

It was a summer morning. For an entire night, his body had lost contact with his soul, and the separation had left them both refreshed. Already, he could feel himself expanding outward, touching trees and rooftops, meadows and streams, with his happiness.

He lay still and tried to listen, as Solomon had, to the sounds of the day. And heard them as a mixture of exultation and woe. His ear caught the *brrrrrr*ing flutter of the swallows as they moved in rolling flocks from the orchard to the garden, from the garden to the eaves of the house, and from there to the olive trees bordering the meadow.

Not far away, in the courtyard of the Englishman Harleigh's house, a servant girl, waiting her turn at the well, sang of two highborn cousins who, from the tower in which they were imprisoned, saw a yellow-haired princess in the garden below them. The princess was gathering roses and singing a song of love. No sooner did the imprisoned cousins see her than they were enamored with her. The servant girl's voice trembled as she sang of the griefs that followed.

It was a gilded morning. From the street there came a carter's cry and the continually surprised bleating of kids, being driven to the bazaar, who paused in their progress to leap toward the eaves of the house, where orange-colored poppies waved in the crevices between the tiles. Off in the barley fields, corncrakes and larks made their songs and were interrupted by the braggart quarreling of the crows. From the sesame-grinder's mill there came the slow creaking of the stone wheel that the blind camel dragged round and round the circle he had paced for a dozen years.

Shabbatai, lending himself to every sensation, felt himself to be a network of sweetly pulsing veins into which the entire creation was indulgently pouring itself. On such a day as this, nothing ought to be disappointed. The spider should make its web, the blind camel should find rest, the leaping kids their poppies, the carter a rich patron, and the singing girl should become the happy princess of her song.

Because it was *his* wish. Shabbatai's.

He smiled, remembering who he was. A twenty-four-year-old naked scholar under a woolen coverlet. What did it matter what he wished? "It matters," he replied firmly to the universe. Then, because the Zohar teaches that nothing naked can be manifest, he leaped out of bed and reached for his clothes, still repeating, "It matters. It matters."

He studied himself in the mirror as he buttoned the many buttons of his red caftan. White was the appropriate color, but it was his birthday. He would wear red because it is the color of the Creation and because it was a day on which to change his life. When Shabbatai looked at himself in the mirror, he saw a youth around whose head there glowed a nimbus of healing light. He smiled as he felt power surging to his fingertips.

❧❦

The Zevi family was on its way to the synagogue.

Shabbatai walked first, and his father, severely crippled by his gout, clung to his right arm. Elijah, Shabbatai's older brother, walked at his left, keeping a shy pace away from the prodigy. Behind him, Joseph, the youngest son, who did as he was told, escorted Clara and Zipporah, his mother and grandmother. The family was on its way to the Portuguese Synagogue.

The morning was still cool. Shabbatai, in his red caftan and blue-canvas hemp-soled slippers, walked with the dignity of a sage, though to maintain the manner, he had to ignore his grandmother's frequent angry interjections. She was past eighty and had grown both strong-willed and unfocused, though she continued faithful to her lifelong aversion to Shabbatai. "Who is he?" she demanded. "What is he? Making me hurry. Rushing me to my grave. My egg uneaten — on the Sabbath. My tea not drunk. And the household collapsing around me because he, the lord and master, wants to be early at his prayers.

"Piety? Don't tell *me* it's piety. You and another fool may believe it if you like. Piety! Say, rather, he wants to be seen. Young Shabbatai. The First among the Pure. And my egg uneaten and my face not properly washed. God has sharper eyes than you may think, my pretty boy. The First among the Seen. That's who you are.

"Ha, ha! Sea-bathing and midnight prayers. Fasts and lamentations. For whose sake — if you'll be good enough to tell me? Silent, are you, Clara? Well, I'll tell you. And my tea not drunk. I'll tell you. He's all prayer, is he? All

96

alms and blessings? Watch his eyes, my girl. Peering out of the corners of his eyes to catch who may be watching him. Seen. Seen. Seen. Seen. Well, I see him and I know what I know. Sea-bathing and penitence don't put his kind of fat on a body. Don't I know?" The tears sprang to her eyes as she considered her own bulk. She dashed them away with a pudgy hand.

Clara, trained by years of patience, said quietly, "Enough, Mother," and bided her time. Clara had only to look from the splendor of Shabbatai to the ruin the grandmother had become to know whose side God was on.

Clara sighed, because it was not easy to be the mother of a saint. Though her heart swelled with pride at his radiance and the awe he inspired, she knew, in the most practical way, that sanctity could be a difficult domestic guest. It was Clara who knew (because Shabbatai would not trust such matters to a servant) what Shabbatai required in the way of clean towels, spotless undergarments, and endless pairs of slippers and freshly ironed robes.

As the family turned the corner into Nasser al Din Street, they were caught up in a crowd of Turks who were pushing their way through the open gates of the tax gatherer's house, moving toward an already dense throng around a scaffold built beneath a handsome laurel tree. Mordekhai, jostled by the hurrying Turks, wanted to turn back, to find another way to the synagogue, but the usually biddable Joseph cried "Stripes" in a high, excited voice. Trembling with eagerness, he pushed his mother and grandmother into the crowd flowing into the courtyard. Shabbatai and Elijah, unless they were to abandon the women to the Turks, were constrained to follow, dragging a protesting Mordekhai with them. They could hear Joseph, already some distance from them, crying, "Stripes! Stripes!"

A Turkish tax offender was about to be flogged.

Sitting in a capacious chair beside the scaffold, Moham-

97

med Reza Hadj, the wrinkled district tax gatherer, was reading over once again the document he would sign in a moment; it declared that judgment had been carried out on a tax offender in the Smyrna district on this date. The judgment: one hundred blows on bare flesh administered with rods wielded by a rod-master.

The tax offender, Sammi al Garmizani, was twenty-eight or twenty-nine. He stood beside a table set near Mohammed Reza Hadj, patiently folding his tunic. When he was done, he handed the clean garment to his fifteen-year-old brother to hold. Sammi's wife, a woman of twenty, stood nearby, holding a pot of unguent. When the flogging was finished, it would be her turn to be useful.

Mohammed Reza Hadj rolled up the document he had been reading and slipped it into his green sash. The sash signified that he had made his pilgrimage to Mecca. The Hadj was sixty years old. He had a wrinkled narrow face and shrewd, melancholy dark eyes. He hated this aspect of his work so much that when the sums the state was owed were small enough, he sometimes paid them out of his own pocket. But young Sammi, who had a flourishing sandal factory, had bragged over a period of many months that he had been outwitting the tax gatherer. After today, though he might cheat, it was certain that he would never brag again. Proportion, the Hadj thought; if only men would keep a sense of proportion. The old man hated blood. The sight of a fellow Moslem naked below the waist, his buttocks and calves exposed to the rod, was a continually renewed grief. His tongue found a stray pomegranate seed and dislodged it from his teeth. The Hadj prayed, *"Bism Allah al-Rahman al-Rahim,* In the Name of God, the Compassionate, the Merciful," after which he signed to the rod-master to begin the work of chastisement across Sammi al Garmizani's thin buttocks.

"Piety, piety," chirped Zipporah. "See, Shabbatai, how the Turk is pious." And as the rod-master raised his rod, she cried, "Beat him. Crush him, pious rod-man. Let him bleed. Piously, piously." Shabbatai and his brothers turned toward her, alarmed. As long as she babbled in her native Judeo-Spanish, the Jewish family was in no danger, but if she should lapse into street Turkish, the anger of the Turks might easily come down around their heads.

Mohammed Reza Hadj ignored Zipporah's outburst. He was counting with great deliberation, ". . . eleven, twelve . . ." When the rod-master, keeping time with the Hadj, struck the sixteenth blow, he saw the first signs of blood on his rod. It was the signal that he must, for a while, strike lower down, at Sammi's calves. At the next stroke, however, the rod broke. Swiftly, the rod-master's alert apprentice was at his side, ready with a fresh stick, and the rhythm of the beating was hardly interrupted.

Shabbatai, watching, was afraid. He grimaced with every blow and was certain that if he were ever struck this way, he would die before the third stroke fell. And yet, like his brothers, he could not tear himself away from the place. It was the formality of the torment that held him; its deliberation and its slowness. The courtesy that everyone involved in the expiation showed.

Behind Shabbatai, his mother wept silently. Mordekhai, short of breath, his joints aching, tried to gather his women together, but Zipporah refused to go. "Flog on. Flog on," she piped. "Higher, lower. There. There." When Shabbatai put a hand to her arm to restrain her, she tore from his grasp and spat, "Don't *touch* me, you honeyed saint. It was you who hurried us. But for you, I should have had my tea instead of blood for breakfast."

At the count of twenty, the Hadj raised his hand. The rod-master's apprentice stepped forward to trim the wounds with the keen knives of his profession. Sammi al Garmizani raised his head and prayed in the direction of the Hadj, his swollen tongue giving his voice a furry, distant sound: "Blessings . . . Blessings, O Hadj. I thank thee for my stripes."

The Hadj, as a kindness to the sufferer, nodded to the

rod-master, who, with his apprentice's help, deftly laid Garmizani face down on an inclined plank so that the soles of his feet could be beaten, giving his buttocks and calves some rest. The crowd murmured its appreciation of the dignity with which Garmizani received his stripes and the consideration with which the Hadj supervised them. They praised, too, the rod-master's skill as he carried out the decree. In a sense, Zipporah's sarcastic "Piety, piety," was an accurate description of what was going on. For the Moslems, the beating was more than an administration of justice. The beating also had a religious function. The rod was an object of veneration, since the Turks believed that the first rod had descended to earth directly from heaven. Chastisement, therefore, blessed all who participated in it: the judge, the rod-master, and the sufferer, who, while he paid for his misdeeds in this world, comforted himself with the knowledge that the parts of his body abused by the rod would be freed from pain in purgatory.

At the thirtieth blow, when Sammi al Garmizani's feet were bleeding, Clara pleaded, "In the name of God, will it ever stop?" At the thirty-second blow, she groaned and fell in a dead faint against Shabbatai, shaking him out of his somnolent fascination with the scene. With Elijah's help, Shabbatai half led and half carried Clara from the courtyard while Zipporah and Mordekhai, the one very old and doddering, the other old and lame, followed. Minutes later, a reluctant Joseph caught up with his father. The Turks, intent on the penitential ritual, hardly noticed the passing of a family of Jews.

※※ ※※

In the synagogue, the heat was heavy, without yet being uncomfortable. The cantor for the morning was a visitor from the Holy Land, a *sheleakh,* or messenger, sent by the Jews of Jerusalem to gather funds for that chronically indigent community. The sheleakh, a thin, wiry man, given to nervous blinking, was overwhelmed by the prosperity of the Smyrna Jews and nearly paralyzed with gratitude at the inexpensive kindnesses they had shown him. He had been invited to many fine dinners; he had been seated in a place of honor in the House of Study; and now, at the bidding of Rabbi Escapa, he was leading the congregation through the morning service. He sang the prayers in a high voice and, by way of gratitude to his hosts, decorated the melodies with swirls and twists and runs.

Shabbatai, wrapped in his prayer shawl, leaned his forehead against the rail of the dais and murmured his prayers well ahead of the sheleakh. His mother was somewhere among the women behind the latticed alcove reserved for them. His father and brothers sat in the rich men's pews.

The congregation was mostly traders and artisans, money-lenders, jewelers, textile merchants, and commission agents. In the synagogue there hung a cloud of Sabbath aromas of soap, pomade, and snuff, of coffee and leather-bound prayer books, of cedar boxes in which the woolen prayer shawls were kept.

"We give thanks unto Thee Who art the Lord our God, the God of our fathers, the God of all flesh . . ." droned the congregation. From the women's alcove there flowed, like an underwater current, a mixture of female odors. The smells of aging women, sour with regrets. The brash, clean smell of virgins fragrant and scrubbed under their modest Sabbath gowns. The redolent odor of married women, their flesh still glowing with the Friday night sexual mysteries, or the astringent odor of repeated disappointment. Shabbatai, immersed in his prayers, felt the presence of Woman in the air. The cleft instead of the rod. The female principle, the Shekhina, the Indwelling Presence of God. The lowest of the ten *sephirot* without which the male principle, Tipheret, was incomplete.

There was a dizziness of male and female; a giddiness of the Ninth of Ab, when the Temple of Solomon was destroyed; a mingling of the senses with a haze rising from

Jewish history, touched also by the memory of his birthday and the exultation of his early morning. Hoping to contain the tumbling giddiness, Shabbatai prayed, "O my God! Guard my tongue from evil, and my lips from speaking falsely. Open my heart to Thy Torah. Let the words of my mouth and the meditation of my heart be acceptable before Thee."

Shabbatai opened his eyes. Inside the warm hollow he had made for himself within his prayer shawl, there glistened Sammi al Garmizani's open wounds, above them the patient pale face of his young wife waiting for the beating to stop so that she could be useful. The wife's face was like a blanched almond, her eyes secret and narrowed.

The open wounds pulsed. The rod-master's apprentice stepped forward, his bright little knives flashing. He was so courteous. Mohammed Reza Hadj was so kind. Sammi al Garmizani was so grateful. Only his wounds, like voiceless mouths, complained. Only Clara cried aloud, "In the name of God, will it ever stop?"

The wiry sheleakh, who had, all week long, eaten more and better food than in many months in the holy city, flung his voice out in an extraordinary spiral of cantillation as he read, "We will sanctify Thy Name in the world, even as they sanctify it in the highest heavens." Shabbatai looked about him, but everything was as usual. Rabbi Escapa was in his seat on the dais. The congregation was in its place. Overhead, the calcined dome of the synagogue arched in an imitation of the sky.

And yet, on Shabbatai's birthday, on the Ninth of Ab, Rabbi Shimon, the son of Gamaliel, had decreed that "one must change one's life." It was time.

Shabbatai folded his prayer shawl. He had promised the morning that nothing should be disappointed: the spider would make its web; the blind camel would find rest; the leaping kids their poppies; the carter a rich patron; and the singing girl the happiness of which she sang.

And what of his mother's question? "In the name of God, will it ever stop?" Which of the names of God would make the suffering stop and the bright morning of his birthday glow forever? Adoshem? Adonai? These were the daily euphemisms used in prayer to avoid taking the Great Name in vain. Or the Great Name itself, the Shem ha m'foresh, the Name of Names. A name so secret and so powerful that it had formerly been used only by the priests in the Temple when they gave the sacerdotal blessing, and by the High Priest on the Day of Atonement. The Shem ha m'foresh is the Name of Awe, the Tetragrammaton, forbidden to ordinary Jews except as the last cry at the moment of their martyrdom. So dreadful is the Name that even the way to pronounce it is hidden, to be revealed only to uniquely blessed men, who guard the secret with their lives, though its knowledge makes them holy all their days.

The Tetragrammaton. The Shem ha m'foresh. The gates of paradise are closed to the man who pronounces it lightly.

The Name of Awe. Had not He Himself said, ". . . My people shall know My Name; therefore they shall know in that day that I am He that doth speak: behold, it is I." It was time.

Shabbatai left his place beside the dais and walked around the rail and up the three stairs that led to the pulpit. The sheleakh was readying the Torah scroll in its carved box so that the weekly portion of Scripture could be read from it. He had already removed the blue cover and was untying the simply braided inner girdle that bound the scrolls together when Shabbatai brushed him aside with the sweep of an arm. At the shove, the Jerusalemite, who had been reciting a prayer of thanks for the Torah, squeaked, "What?" and looked for help, first from the congregation, which, for the moment was as paralyzed as he, and then, inanely, to Shabbatai himself. Rabbi Escapa took a step toward Shabbatai, only to be arrested by an imperious gesture from his former pupil.

Shabbatai stood before the Torah, a tall young man

garbed in red, feeling himself to be the radiant youth who had looked out at him from his mirror, and led the congregation in its prayers. His lips were bloodless; the pupils of his eyes dilated. According to the liturgy, the next interval was devoted to a meditation from the Zohar, which begins, "Blessed be the name of the Sovereign of the universe . . ." Shabbatai, his head unbowed, waited for the congregation to murmur their supplication and thanks. When they were done, every eye in the synagogue was on him, on Shabbatai.

There then began a powerful surging, a long and in some ways sweet tug between their expectations and his will. As their attention nourished him, Shabbatai felt himself growing lightheaded at the same time as there flowed into him a stream of power. He was Shabbatai Zevi, clothed in red. Shabbatai Zevi, to whom the Patriarchs had spoken. From his toes to his eyes there flowed the incandescent power of Adam Kadmon. He had only to put out his hand and he could bring joy to all of Smyrna or plunge it into the sea.

Then, subtly, the light of Adam Kadmon in him changed. The blazing sparks cooled, and a darkness, deeper and blacker than any he had ever feared, poured through his veins where the light had been. He could feel his eyes growing wider and wider, but there was only more darkness to see. Then the darkness became a sound, low at first, then mounting, mounting, its pitch high and thin, until it became his mother's cry, "In the name of God, will it ever stop?"

Shabbatai inhaled the close air of the synagogue and felt it searing his throat. Then he read the prayer that belonged to the moment, but as it issued from his lips the Name of God was stripped of all euphemism. Shabbatai pronounced it letter by letter:

"*YHVH, YHVH, LORD, LORD.*" And again, "*YHVH, YHVH, el rakhum v'khanun erekh* . . . Lord, Lord, God is merciful and gracious." The whole prayer is repeated three times on festivals, and Shabbatai sounded the forbidden Name each of the six times that it occurs:

"*YHVH, YHVH, el rakhum v'khanun erekh* . . .
"*YHVH, YHVH, el rakhum v'khanun erekh* . . .
"*YHVH, YHVH, el rakhum v'khanun erekh* . . .*"

The consternation in the synagogue gathered slowly, as if the presence of the Forbidden Name had stupefied outrage during the time that Shabbatai's magnificent voice uttered and repeated it. Even the children, locked in their parents' horror, were silent.

Then Shabbatai surpassed the farthest bounds. Lifting the Torah in his arms, he raised it toward the heavens and cried:

"*Shema Yisrael, YHVH Elohenu, YHVH Ekhod.*

"Hear O Israel, the L O R D our God, the L O R D is One."

Old Rabbi Escapa was the first to strike — a blow so violent across Shabbatai's shoulders that he almost fell. There was a screech as the Jerusalem sheleakh leaped, clawing at Shabbatai's face with both hands. Shabbatai clung to the Torah, despite the pain that erupted like simultaneous flames in his cheeks and neck. There was a tumultuous roar and a babble of motion. Then kicks, screams, blows, and a buffeting darkness, from which, as Shabbatai gratefully descended, he let the Torah go.

12

Zamosc
1658

Nothing he drank ever diminished the relentless clarity of Nehemiah Ha-Kohen's mind or blurred the efficacy of his axeman's eye. In the forests, the trees he cut fell where he directed them. In Talmudic disputation, his seamless logic, bolstered by a memory that recalled the most distant commentary or the subtlest ambiguity of a minor text, had given him a reputation for formidable learning. Nor did Nehemiah's drinking interfere with his performance of the many daily acts and prayers that are incumbent on the Jew. Nehemiah blessed God in his prayers with precise devotion, never slurring or losing a word in the catalogues of praise. God, no doubt, heard the irony that also trembled in Nehemiah's voice, but the axeman's fellow Jews, who had before them his piety, his poverty, his silence, and his Talmudic wisdom, whispered that he was a *lamedvovnik,* one of those thirty-six saints, masters of the Holy Name, who live secretly among us, preparing the world for the coming of the Messiah.

Nehemiah smiled at such notions and thought affectionately that his Jews were a credulous people. If a man showed up in their midst and wielded an axe to their profit and did not ask for wages; if he sat with their children

and taught them the aleph-bet and did not ask for wages
. . . such a man, they were willing to believe, might be a
saint.

For the most part, his reputation for sanctity was a harm-
less by-product of his wandering life, but once, in Polish
Zamosc, it involved him in a startling confrontation.

On his way to Lvov, he had stopped in Zamosc because
it was late Friday afternoon in January, and the Sabbath
was coming on. The local rabbi, Aryeh Nissan, a man in
his early forties, treated Nehemiah with the respect due
the axeman *tsaddik*, but in the midst of nervous courtesies,
he broke into sighs and babblings. "You are here, Reb
Nehemiah, by the will of God. I . . . we . . . rabbis of
Zamosc . . . Has there ever been such a curse? Blessed
is the name of the Lord Who sent you . . . What in the
world are we to do? This is a matter beyond us. A Jewish
child . . . or a nun . . . a *makhsheyfah*, a witch . . . or an
orphan? You must help us, Reb Nehemiah. You will . . .
I know you will."

On Sunday, Nehemiah, at the behest of the three rabbis
of Zamosc, Rabbi Aryeh, Rabbi Nakhman Asher, and Rabbi
Reuben Halperin, presided over the interrogation of
Sarah, the woman found in the cemetery. The meeting
was convened in Rabbi Aryeh's study. In addition to the
four rabbis, the two women of probity who, all week, had
guarded Sarah in the seclusion of Rabbi Aryeh's house
were present. The men, constituting themselves a Rabbinical Court, intended to probe the truth of Sarah's story.
Was she truly a nun, or had she been schooled by the
Christians to ensnare the Jewish community? Was she a
Jewish miracle — a forced convert who had stumbled back
into Judaism? Or, given the accounts that had reached
them of her ravings, was she possessed by a *dybbuk*?" Or,
worse, was Satan involved in the case?

She was pale, Nehemiah noted, and, as Rabbi Asher's

questions revealed, she had been ill. When she came in, her hair was covered by a seemly black shawl, but when Rabbi Aryeh, the youngest of the rabbis, asked for her family name, Sarah, with a sweep of her hand, removed the shawl and loosened her hair, letting it fall in a shimmering wave of black down her shoulders.

"Why do you display your hair?" Rabbi Aryeh demanded.

Sarah turned to him, her lower lip, for a moment, between her teeth. "Display? No. It is my hair. It feels better loose . . . I have been pent up."

"Pass on, pass on," Rabbi Nakhman Asher interposed. "How did you come to be in the cemetery, where Reb Ephraim found you?"

"He is a kind man, Ephraim . . ." Her eyes narrowed, as if she were trying to distinguish something among the faces of her interrogators. "I do not wish to talk . . ." she said. Then, "No. I do not wish to talk. It is enough that I am here."

"You must talk," Rabbi Reuben grumbled. "Tell me. Can you say a Hail Mary?"

"Of course I can."

"Yet you say that you are Jewish!"

She smiled — sadly, Nehemiah thought. "We are speaking Yiddish, aren't we?"

"The devil," Rabbi Reuben said angrily, "can speak Holy Writ if he wishes."

Sarah walked to the oak table, where she addressed the plump rabbi directly. "If it comes to that, the devil, when he likes, can inhabit the form of Rabbi Reuben of Zamosc."

"See, see," Reuben squealed. "A dybbuk. There speaks the dybbuk in her." Sarah, as if he had wearied her, walked away from the oak table to stand at the window that looked out into the courtyard, where, now, snow was falling.

Nehemiah rose and followed her. At the window, they stood facing each other, like people meeting on a narrow path.

108

"Sarah," Nehemiah inquired, "where have you been?"

"Ah," she said, "you are the rabbi with the secret."

The Zamosc rabbis looked at each other. Had she guessed that Rabbi Nehemiah might be a lamed-vovnik? Nehemiah, for his part, wondered what woman's wisdom it was that had told her of his perpetual erection. Nehemiah made fists of his logger's hands and contained himself. It was forbidden to be angry at the truth. "Where," he persisted, "where have you been?"

"In a place," she said, her shoulders drooping, "in a place of horses . . . the cracking of whips . . . men shouting . . . the smell of fire . . . of pigs . . ." She shook herself, then said, "Your eyes have seen . . . what mine have."

Nehemiah felt his throat constrict as he remembered the sunlight on the Tisa. The moist riverbank. The geese. The volume of women's tales in his lap from which he had taught a not quite lame Hannah the first letter of the alphabet. "Aleph," he said. She leaped to her feet and snatched the book out of his hand and ran away, dancing, holding the book to her breast, singing, "Aleph. I know aleph." Dancing and singing as the world must have danced in the whirlpool of creation. Hannah. Crooked Hannah who would never learn more than aleph in this world. Death had confirmed her instinct not to spoil illumination with detail. Hannah, whose eyes were first dimmed by cholera and then extinguished by it.

"Where I have been . . ." There was a mist across his eyes. "There was . . . a horse . . ." The horse was named Katya; after God had sent him Feigele, the little bird. An extravagant gift to send a man well advanced into middle-aged loneliness. A fragile, thin-boned creature, who offered him water from a cup, as if she were a princess offering her prince a drink from an enchanted well.

"Horses . . ." He peered into Sarah's dark eyes. "I did not see them." Because they were somewhere else. Files upon files of Cossacks; perhaps here, in Zamosc; Chmielnicki's men. Not even near Lvov. While Nehemiah served vodka to the Polish peasants and Feigele sat, her arms folded across her swollen belly, seeming to say "See what I can do."

The axeman tsaddik and the woman seemed to share the same trance. Rabbi Reuben spat three times to ward off the evil eye; Rabbi Nakhman Asher repeated a verse against Lilith. Rabbi Aryeh, reposing his trust in Nehemiah's holiness, tapped his wedding ring against the top of the table, hoping to get Nehemiah's attention. The veins stood out on the axeman's tightly clasped hands.

"Why," he asked hoarsely, "why have you forgotten?"

"Why," she replied, "do you remember?"

Blood roared in Nehemiah's ears as he remembered himself remembering. Every day he begged his memories to rewrite themselves, hoping to make them once achieve a happy ending. Instead of being asleep on the afternoon when the Cossack rode into the courtyard, Nehemiah was awake. The Cossack, seeing a burly Jew wielding his axe on the log beside the inn, found it prudent to drink his vodka quickly and ride on. Or, in another version of the scene, the Cossack started toward the inn door, where Nehemiah stood. The Cossack swung his sword, Nehemiah his axe, and a dead Cossack lay on the ground. Or the Cossack arrived, young, fatigued, and hungry. Touched by Feigele's youth and sweet demeanor, the Cossack warned the Jews of the danger they were in from his troop riding hard from Lvov. The Cossack helped them to hide in the cellar, and when his comrades came, sent them off on a false scent.

None of the variations that he begged for happened. Hannah, in his memories, always died; the Cossack always destroyed Feigele and the baby in her womb; and Nehemiah, always, smashed the cavalryman's head with the uprooted hitching post.

"I remember blood," he said. "It is the real world."

"When the Messiah comes, he will wash it clean," she replied.

"The Messiah . . . Did she say Messiah?" called Rabbi Aryeh.

"Whose bride I am destined to be," she serenely replied.

As the women led her away, Nehemiah turned to the waiting rabbis. "There is . . . some force in her."

"Is there evil in her?" Reb Aryeh hurriedly asked.

Nehemiah closed his eyes and tried to pray without irony. When a sufficient time had elapsed and there was still no interior reply, he said, "What is in her, God's will . . . will manifest."

For a man who might be a lamed-vovnik, the Zamosc rabbis thought, that was a puny judgment.

13

Peter Harleigh, in Smyrna,
to Nicholas Tyrell, in London
1655

Banished.

Banished.

Shabbatai is banished, Tyrell. Sent from Smyrna. Driven away by a pack of whining, scurvy rabbis whom he has offended.

Banished . . . just as there was growing between me and my *saint aux jolies fesses* a most delicious tenderness. After so many years of paying me no more than the scantest of courtesies, two months ago he looked into my face.

Until that moment, and despite my wiles, I was less than a shadow to him, and for no better reason than that I am no Jew. Whether it is because the Jew is as stiff-necked as we have been taught, or that he has been so long accustomed to expect only the worst from the people in whose midst he lives, the fact is that, except in matters of essential business, the Jew regards unbelievers with an unseeing eye. And for Shabbatai, busy with his pieties and visions, I have been less than a distant presence.

But in late February, all that changed.

It was on an otherwise indifferent morning when I was vexed with a letter from a thieving Spanish shipmaster who claimed an act of God to excuse the loss of seventy-two bales of linen bound for Marseille. The scoundrel captain claimed that his boat, going around on the Candy coast, he was forced to lighten it by the amount that *my* bales weighed. And all the while, I had by me a letter from an English merchant in Salonika offering to sell me seventy-two bales of (*my*) linen, lately acquired from a Spanish captain, whose they were in default of payment from a Greek merchant of that city. My bales of linen. Mine!

I was growling and swallowing oaths enough when Shabbatai came into the counting-house on an errand to his father. He stopped at my table as if he wished to be attentive to my swearing. I had disposed of Christ's bones and His blood, His mouth, His teeth, and His tongue; and I was tearing at His nether bones when Shabbatai asked courteously whether it was the custom amongst Christians to pluck at God's body so fiercely or was it a trait reserved only to Englishmen?

My counting-house, Tyrell, at any ordinary moment has in it the smell of four infrequently washed Greek scriveners, two bilious Jewish clerks, and the fat and wheezing Mordekhai; but when Shabbatai asked his question, the place turned redolent with spring. There was the smell of mimosa amongst the ledgers, and the very Greeks breathed the scent of almond blossom. Dizzied by my good fortune, I got to my feet. I commanded coffee to be brought. I smiled. I sent for sweet cakes. I danced attendance.

I hesitate to tell you what we spoke of in that time. Do not snicker, Tyrell, but Shabbatai and I, as soberly as any bishops, talked of Jesus Christ. It was a strange conversation, during which I, an all-but-unbeliever, told the story of Christ's life to the scholar Jew, who surely knew it. But he was avid to hear it from the lips of a Christian, as if it had more authority that way. My father, I think, would have been moved by my rendition of the tale.

I honoured the pathetic moments in the story: the star shining in the East, the birth in the stable among dumb beasts; the prophecies of John; Jesus' sojourn in the desert, where the devil tempted Him. I described the scourging of the scribes and Pharisees. When I had told of the Last Supper, the betrayal by Judas, and the crucifixion, Shabbatai put down the sweet cake on which he had been munching. "No, Peter Harleigh," he said, "it is a dreadful story for which the world is owed a better ending. Your Jesus came at the wrong time." This was said in a level voice that had in it a poignant portentousness. And into his eyes there came a considering look, but whether he was gazing back into the past or was being attentive to some vision of the future, I could not say.

That, then, was the beginning of our friendship, and little by little we were progressing towards an ever-greater tenderness. It pleased Shabbatai to have in his train a Christian who, so he chose to imagine me, would have been Jesus' friend.

Then came the new series of blasphemies, and the Smyrna rabbis banished him.

Mordekhai, Shabbatai's old father, tells me that banishment is the lesser of the two punishments with which the rabbis threatened his son. "Blasphemy is no small crime, Lord Harleigh. To utter the forbidden Name once was bad enough; but to persist in it, against all warning! O God . . . O God . . . The boy is a scholar. He knows well that the crime merits death by stoning . . . in the stoning field. Think of him . . . my Shabbatai! His head crushed, his limbs bleeding . . ."

"Come, Mordekhai," I protested. "Surely in this Turkish realm, where cruelty is a pastime reserved to the Turk, not even the sleepiest Kaimakam Pasha will delegate to the Jews a punishment as severe as stoning."

"Lord Harleigh," Mordekhai said bitterly, "you have truly said that the Turk, who has a talent for cruelty, reserves chastisement in the empire to himself. But the Infidel has not ruled these many years without learning *not* to interfere in the lesser affairs of the subject peoples in the empire. We live here, a jumble of faiths and creeds: Turks, Arabs, Kurds, Armenians, Greeks, Nestorians, Copts. The Padishah, for the sake of the prosperity of the realm, wisely enough prevents the sects from cutting each other's throats. But should the Copts or the Armenians or the Jews wish to punish one of their own, then that is a very great convenience to the state. Oh, Lord Harleigh, Jews will be found to punish Jewish blasphemy. For the moment, Shabbatai has escaped the last decree, but if he means to provoke the Salonika rabbis as well, who knows how long their patience will endure?"

Old Mordekhai wept — and no wonder. I learned later from my clerk, Benjamin, a furry-voiced, pale-fingered toad-eater of a Jew who would have given me his mother, trussed and roasted on a platter, had I had a taste for so unlikely a morsel, just what the punishment of stoning entails. It is not a pretty method of execution, though it *is* prescribed by Holy Writ.

The blasphemer is taken out into a wide field by a judge and twenty-three witnesses, the chief of whom will be the one to cast the first stone. The person to be punished lies on his side, naked but for a cloth covering him in front. He is then thrust forward upon his loins, and it is then that the chief witness lets fall, from a very great height, a heavy stone. If the victim is lucky and dies with that first stone, the thing is finished. Otherwise, the second witness takes up his stone and casts it at the heart. In this fashion, all those who are assembled take up their stones, flinging them one by one, until the blasphemer is dead.

When Benjamin, the humble slug, was gone, I was as woeful as Mordekhai had been. All that day, I could see nothing but a cruel rain bruising and crushing Shabbatai's fine skin and tender bones. It was some while before I remembered that Mordekhai and I were grieving over a sentence that had *not* been passed; that Shabbatai had been exiled. It was then that I resolved to go to Salonika, where, not only will I get to see my exiled Shabbatai, but I shall have the further pleasure of taking my deceitful Spanish captain by the throat. In Salonika, I shall make him squeal.

I spoke too soon, Tyrell. I had forgot we are in the Orient. It will be a week or more before I can make the journey to Salonika. In the meanwhile, the time hanging heavy before me, I have taken to sitting in a *chai-khane*, a teahouse on the public square, where, with a cup of tea in my left hand and the mouthpiece of a bubbling *narghile* at my lips, I watch the sale of Christian slaves who have been lately brought to Smyrna in great numbers from southern Russia. Usually, the men and strong youths are kept here in Turkey, and the women and children are sold good cheap to Egyptian traders, who disperse their wares throughout the Mediterranean.

The prisoners are a sorry spectacle. The Turks, the better to sell them at a higher price, garb them in finery that is both ill-fitting and awkwardly worn. The men and youths stand for sale at one side of the square, the women and children at the other. The boys have their heads shaved, with the exception of a single lock, which is permitted to show from beneath their caps — as a sign that they are still Christians.

Though the Moslem faith prohibits the immodest display of female slaves, yet so strong is the chapman's instinct that many a Turkish slave-dealer will make secret arrangements with a would-be buyer to let him view the females' faces and to touch their breasts. Nay, it is well known that there are unscrupulous merchants who permit wealthy customers to test the virginity of the reputed maidens amongst their wares.

Yesterday, my melancholy musing on the spectacle was interrupted by the sight of a youth who was thrust forward for sale. Except that he was blond and a Circassian and not yet fully grown, he was the very image of my Shabbatai: the same arched eyebrows and carved full lips; the same *jolies fesses* under the out-sized silk tunic that he wore. To put the matter briefly, I bought young Pyotr for a sum not exceeding forty English pounds. He is hardly fifteen years old and as nervous as a newborn colt. Between thanking God that he has been bought by a Christian, and wondering about the meaning of my as-yet-tentative caresses, he sleeps badly by night and jumps when I call him by day.

So you see, Tyrell, what the Orient is. Even consolation may be purchased in the marketplace. I look forward to taming my *quasi*-Shabbatai.

Peter Harleigh, in Salonika,
to Nicholas Tyrell, in London
1655

These days, I am as touchy as a menstruating woman. No sooner do I lie down, but I must leap to my feet, or go to the window, where I look out and think of seven unnecessary errands on which to send Charlie (formerly Pyotr). I give him instructions; I reverse them. I beat him for having done what I commanded. When he cries, I kiss him and get a hateful pleasure from the taste of his tears.

Salonika is hot and moist. All my routines are disrupted. There is no one here, Greek or Turk or Jew, who can make a decent cup of tea. The wine is atrocious; the *ouzo* of the Greeks a foul and poisonous liquid that makes one headachy, feverish, and erotic all at once.

The Apostle Paul walked in these streets, but was he here in a time of such killing heat or amidst a rout of such scabby folk? Salonika is the very navel of squalor. I can feel the dirt through my shoes. There are only two moods in this city: deceit and unrighteousness. It is a place where humankind is rank, and the touch of a hand feels like vermin crawling against the skin.

Shabbatai is missing, Tyrell. It is known that he is in Salonika, but he is nowhere to be seen. I feel a Byzantine politics at work. Or worse.

Where is he?

It is hard for me to stay calm amongst these frenzied Jews. They have no Attic coolness. It is as if they were born panting, or at the edge of rage. What scurriers they are! Busy. Busy. Unlike the bees, whose lives are spent buzzing under the orderly sign of the hexagon, these Jews move only by fits and starts and rages. The only stillness they know is the paralysed ecstasy of prayer, or the final stillness of death. If there *is* a reasonable map of their commotion, it is safely hidden by their God behind His stars.

As the days go by, I fret and worry like a very Jew. At night, when I am a little calmer, I have taken to wondering what it is in Shabbatai that makes him such a public wonder. I am not always blinded by a lover's partiality. I can see the man behind the monument. But the Shabbatai I see is somehow opaque, as if he were a *silhouette* by the sea whose outline was known, but not his human features. And yet, he stirs the cities where he walks. Why?

It may be that his very vagueness moves us. His beauty is instantly manifest; but behind those sweet features, there glows not his, but *our* yearning. In the imprecise grandeur of his phrases, in the unlined benevolence of his face, we get the sense of something close by that we need. In him, what in others would be lack of focus, seems to be immanent power, as if behind his eyes are hidden the possible answers to our impossible prayers.

And so we dream of him. Or follow him. Or bathe in the glory that shines from him, because the Shabbatais of this world seem to cancel the past and refresh the future. We need them, and we find them, just when the rhythms of history are faltering, when the world is threatened, not even with darkness, but with the victory of the most usual shades of grey. In a time when our highest mountains mimic hills, when what was passion declines to habit, when even dreams, which made us tremble or which swirled with hope, turn unremarkable — in such a time of torpor, *ennui*, or unheroic shame, suddenly there is a Shabbatai, and we wake to the possibility of our lives. We feel the resin flowing in the pines; we touch water, earth, fire, and air as if we, and they, had just this moment, and together, entered into the world.

14

Amsterdam
1661

"I won't." Sarah, at the blue and white tiled stove, shook her head. "I won't. I won't marry Mijnheer Leibtche or Mijnheer Mendele, or Mijnheer Lazar, or Mijnheer Schmendrick, the richest Jew in Amsterdam. Why, because I am your sister, must I bow my head and curtsy and say *'Dank je weel'* to every creature with a beard?"

"Sarah." Her brother Shmuel groaned. "Sarah, the things that are said about you. Have you no pride?"

Sarah paced the kitchen. "Ah Schmielekhel, my poor little Shmuel. It's not my pride or *my* reputation that troubles you, but yours. Tell the truth. Mijnheer van der Veen left without buying cigars, isn't that true?"

Shmuel nodded disconsolately. "He's my best customer. If it gets out that you've upset him . . . Oh, my God. Sarah, Sarah, the whole town is talking about you. You come and go where you please. You drink with this man. You walk with that one. It's not . . . it's not womanly, Sarah."

"And it's bad for the cigar business, too. Isn't it?"

"Don't sneer, Sarah. Every mouthful we eat is paid for by my cigars. I make good cigars," he said, thinking of the years it had taken him to find the blend of pale American leaf and dark Turkish tobacco that went into the cigars that he sold under the name of the White Raven. The cigars had made a prosperous man of him, and now Sarah, with her amazing ways, was threatening to ruin him. "Sarah," he pleaded, "Sarah, think again. Where is the harm in marrying? There are still half a dozen men willing to . . ." He caught himself up.

"Yes?" Sarah asked.

"To make a respectable wife of you," Shmuel finished.

"A wife in Amsterdam! May God preserve me from Amsterdam, or else He will need to preserve me in it. I would die here, Shmuel. I would die in Amsterdam. It is a city of bricks and greatcoats, and unimpassioned water. A city of low clouds, long rains. A city of cheese and chocolate, where the men keep their hands in their pockets by day and slip them into the plackets of whores on the Heerengracht by night. A city . . ."

"Enough," Shmuel begged. "Enough. It is a civilized city, decent and good to the Jews."

"But will it be good to me, Schmielekhel? Or do you want to see me drowning in my fat year after year? Do you want to see me live with no greater excitement in my life than the cycle of my menses, or the coming of some mijnheer's infants out of my belly, one by one?"

"If you marry," Shmuel said doggedly, "it will make a respectable woman of you. Don't you care what they say of you — in coffee houses, in homes, in the synagogue?"

"I know what they say. That I am a *kurveh*, a *zonah*, a *hoor* — because I lie with men of my own choosing."

Shmuel covered his ears. "Don't say any more. I don't want to hear it. Please."

"Because I lie with men, Shmuel. I lie with them for my pleasure *and* for theirs. Because my body pleases me, and I am pleased by bodies. But, dear Shmuel, your sister is maligned. I am no whore. I have never taken money for giving or receiving joy."

"Stop, Sarah. I don't want you to talk to me this way.

It's not decent. Don't say another word." Shmuel closed his eyes, as if that would block out the words his fingers at his ears could not prevent his hearing.

"But I must. I will say more. Listen, Shmuel. Do you know what will happen to me if I stay another month in Amsterdam? If I do what you want me to and marry one of your respectable mijnheers? I will become a duck. A fine, fat duck, fit for roasting and serving to a decent Dutch family: a father, a mother, five sons, three daughters, and a maiden aunt who helps out in the kitchen. Twenty-two apple cheeks will glow when I am brought in on a platter; twenty-two eyes light up at the sight of me gleaming in the gravy. They will admire my glossy sides, they will lick their hungry lips. Then the *va-aaader* will poke me with his silver fork, and the *moe-oe-der* will pronounce me ready to carve, and the *kinderleeeek* will hang out their tongues for joy as they get ready to devour Sarah, the Polish *katchkele,* the Polish duckling. Ah Shmuel, dear Shmuel. My darling brother, is this what you want for me?"

Shmuel smiled uncertainly but would not be placated. "What's wrong with marrying some good Jew in the town, Sarah? You're young and" — he looked away shyly — "and beautiful. Marriage is a good Jewish woman's destiny."

Her voice was like ice. "I have told you what my destiny is."

She had. It was enough to drive a man mad. "Come, Sarah. Be reasonable. How can I announce to all of Amsterdam that you mean to marry the Messiah? People will think we've both gone out of our minds." He went to the high, leaded window and looked out on the canal. The sight of passersby drawing their thick collars up around their ears against the icy February wind made him shiver. There had been a sudden thaw the week before, which had melted the ice on the Scheveningen Canal. Now it was frozen again, with heavy blocks of the old ice trapped in the new, making the canal look at once lumpy and gray — and bright. "Besides," he added sadly, "there is no messiah. It's still an ordinary, dreary, human world."

"The Messiah is not ordinary. And neither am I."

That was certainly true.

The first week of her return had been luminous with joy. His little sister Sarah. His lost, his dead, sister, whom he had held in his lap when she was a tiny child. He had fed her her porridge, blowing it cool lest it should scald her tiny lips. He had held her close and touched each of her ten rosy fingers twice as he sang to her the Yiddish counting song she loved:

> *Ela bela boo, ela bela boo*
> *Ela bela bela bela*
> *Ela bela boo.*
>
> *Ver se ken kayn tsvontsig tseylen*
> *Tsvontsig zenen du.*

At the last touch, laughter had always burst from her as from a pent-up fountain.

Then she was dead, thrown into one of the mass graves the Jews had dug for Chmielnicki's victims. Dead, along with his father and his mother. His mother had died of a lance driven through her breast, and Shmuel had seen his father running with Sarah, then ten years old; running with her straight through the Cossacks trotting through the village toward a Gentile's hovel where he could hide the child. Shmuel had seen the glittering sword that cut his father down. Three days later, when he and the two other Jews with him had dug themselves out of the potato cellar in which they had taken refuge, the Jewish dead were already buried. His father, his mother, and Sarah, presumably, among them.

Then, impossibly, a tall young woman showed up at his door. In her face — after he had read the letters of proof that she brought with her from Polish rabbis of repute — he recognized the outlines of his sister Sarah's features. She was his sister, returned from the dead.

But the letters had not said what sort of woman she was and had only hinted at the messiah-madness that she flaunted, and that was driving customers from his shop and prospective husbands for Sarah from his door.

She had turned out to be a strange, impetuous, intelligent, scalding woman by day who, late at night, could become a creature of great tenderness. Then, she could look as vulnerable as the little girl he remembered. At night, she did not sneer at Amsterdam or poke fun at him or his friends or his bachelor habits. Instead, she sat quietly and talked about the childhood she could not remember, a childhood that had become, as she put it, a clean black ribbon in her memory. She listened as Shmuel talked, eager for the minutest details about the house in which they had lived, the clothes they had worn, what her father and mother had looked like, how they moved and talked. But when Shmuel, speaking always in Yiddish, had done telling her, she seemed to sink deeper and deeper into her own dark eyes, and she whispered, "I see nothing. I can see none of it at all." After which she got up and made him his evening cup of chocolate, just the way he liked it, and brought him a hot brick for his feet before he went to bed, and told him he was the best brother any woman ever had and that she loved him. At such moments, Shmuel believed again that God had been miraculously good to him.

But when her messiah-madness was on her, she was impossible.

Now, realizing for the thousandth time that her scorn had wounded him, she said gently, "I *will* marry, Shmuel. But I cannot marry any man." Then, as he had feared she would, she went on, "The world is no longer as ordinary and dreary as you think, Shmuel. The Messiah is coming, and then, I promise you, when the time comes, I will do my woman's part. I will marry him. It is my destiny."

"Your destiny," Shmuel echoed, almost under his breath. "I wonder what that means."

15

Salonika
1655

Joseph Florentin, a physician of Salonika and a devotee
of Shabbatai's, employed market spies to find his missing
house guest. It took two weeks. Then, in the home of a
cobbler who lived in one of the mean streets near the
port, the bedraggled Shabbatai was found.

He had gone there, he whispered to the worried physician, to make a penitential pilgrimage into the Abyss. For
two weeks, he had subsisted on a few crusts of bread,
moistened in a cupful of water. Occasionally, he had
scourged himself with a carter's rope. And there, in the
cobbler's filthy room, he had received an instructive vision.

Joseph Florentin took Shabbatai home with him, but
by the time they reached the physician's house, the square
before it was already thronged with Shabbatai's followers.
The physician tried to lead Shabbatai indoors, but the hag-
gard penitent pushed his host away and turned to face
the crowd.

"Friends," he called, his voice cracked and strained.
"Friends, I have been on a great journey. Among the *kelipott*,
among the powers of evil. Wonders . . . wonders . . ."
His voice gave way. He staggered, and Joseph Florentin
propped him up by the elbow. "Later," Shabbatai begged,

straining his head toward them, toward the sunlight, toward the harbor. "Come back later . . . I will tell . . . I will tell . . ." He swayed, then mastered himself. "Come back — at four. At four! I will reveal . . ."

At the stroke of four, Florentin's brass-studded door opened, and Shabbatai emerged, newly bathed, dressed in white, and looking as if Jehovah Himself had just that minute finished making him. The huge crowd which, until then, had been chattering, hushed.

Shabbatai stood at the top of the long staircase and raised his arms. "I have been," he called, "into the Great Abyss. I have been in darkness. I have been . . . in that most great darkness to which all that is most evil inevitably sinks.

"And there . . . there I found . . . Amidst serpents, amid beasts and human bestiality, in the very roaring ground of Satan, I have received a *simon gadol,* a great sign."

The crowd was so still that only the water spurting in the circular fountain in the middle of the square could be heard.

"That sign, received from the power above, and received from the power below, I give now . . . to YOU." Shabbatai turned and nodded to Florentin's door, from which there came four young men, walking two by two, shoulder to shoulder. Each youth carried in his right hand the silver pole of a folded marriage canopy. When they reached the street, they stepped apart and faced each other, making, with that gesture, the tented space beneath which Jewish weddings are performed. It was a handsome canopy they spread, made of white silk, thickly embroidered with leaves and flowers. The tassels at its edges were fringed with gold. The young men took their places, stiff as statues, almost afraid to breathe.

Shabbatai walked down the steps and waited a couple of paces from the canopy. Again he nodded. This time, Joseph Florentin, wearing a prayer shawl, and appropriately garbed as the father of the groom, emerged from the house and made his stately way down the steps to stand just behind Shabbatai.

Shabbatai nodded a third time. Again the door opened, and two old men, carrying a carved box containing a Torah scroll, walked solemnly down the steps and took their places under the canopy, facing Florentin and Shabbatai. The white-bearded men leaned toward each other like sticks as they held the sacred scroll between them.

There followed now a long silence as Shabbatai waited for the crowd to understand the meaning of the scene.

It was the shabby cobbler who first gasped and cried, "The Torah! The Torah is the bride, and Shabbatai . . ." He stopped, not daring to say what was by now clear. The crowd stirred. There was a frightened babbling. Heads craned; women whispered.

Another nod of Shabbatai's head, and now a gaunt rabbi, dressed in a silk caftan that was only a shade less white than his beard, emerged from the house. The rabbi's eyes were sunk in his head; his transparent skin was deeply flushed. He walked quickly down the steps and took his place under the canopy. He would be, as everyone understood, the officiating rabbi at the wedding.

The gaunt rabbi touched Shabbatai's arm; he touched the Torah. In a cracked and reedy voice he sang, "May the Almighty, the Supreme Ruler of the world, deserving of praise, bless this bridegroom. Let Him bless this bride."

A cooper, horrified by what he saw, opened his mouth and almost said the word *blasphemy!*, but choked it down when someone held a fist like a mallet before his eyes. But the crowd swayed as it was moved by fear or by belief.

Under the wedding canopy, the gaunt rabbi led the "bride" seven times in a circle around the groom. Then bride and groom stood before him while he filled a silver goblet with wine. The rabbi prayed, "Blessed art Thou, O Lord our God, King of the universe, Who hast made us holy by Thy commandments . . . Who hast ordained the wedding canopy, and made holy the covenant of wedlock." The wine trembled. Shabbatai drank; then the rabbi presented the cup to the Torah-bride and spilled two drops of wine on its silk garment. Joseph Florentin shuddered as the wine stained the silk. The rabbi called out, "The ring. Where is the ring?"

Shabbatai produced a large ring and, without the slightest hesitation, dropped the gold band over a protruding handle of the Torah scroll. "Behold," he said, his voice rich and steady, "by this ring, I make thee holy unto me by the law of Moses and Israel."

From the crowd came fitful bursts of applause. Someone cried, "The glass. Where is the glass?" and Joseph Florentin kneeled to set a wineglass beside Shabbatai's shoe. Shabbatai smashed it with a stamp of his foot, and the crowd finally went mad with joy. *"Mazal tov, mazal tov,"* came the good luck cry. Despite the late afternoon heat, the happy Jews put their arms around each other and danced. When Shabbatai, too, took his bride up in his arms and danced, it was as if a tide of love had washed the square. Someone appeared with a drum; someone else had a fife. Old men danced with boys; young men with old women. Merchants cavorted with water men; sages with market-idlers. There was whirling and singing, kissing and caressing. Round and round went the revel, until over the street Shabbatai's voice floated, singing his mysterious song:

> *As I rode down a winding way,*
> *Down through a valley winding,*
> *I chanced on Meliselda there,*
> *Her long dark hair unbinding.*

> *The daughter of the King of Spain*
> *Was Meliselda bathing.*
> *She washed her raven tresses and*
> *She took me for her darling.*

He danced before the fountain; he danced in the midst of the crowd; and as he danced, he pressed his lips against his bride, his fingers stroking the blue-lacquered sides of the box in which she lay.

Far up the street, a squad of mounted Janissaries watched the scene of Jews gone mad, and trotted off. At the corner of an alley, the cooper, now at the center of a weeping group of Jews, whispered with them, *"Yitgadal, v'yitkadash, sh'may rabba . . ."* It was the prayer for the dead.

16

The current was swifter now; soon they would be at the rapids, where Nehemiah, the sweepsman, would need to be quick to find passage for the raft. The wind, blowing up at him from the south, was cold. He narrowed his eyes against it and leaned against the sweep. Along the shore, willows and birches, their roots exposed by the force of the stream, leaned perilously over the water. Sometimes, one toppled and drifted slowly away from the shore, until, caught by the current, it was hurried into midstream, where it could endanger the raft.

Old Velvel, Nehemiah's companion, poured coffee for himself from the clay pot in the ashes of the little hearth built in the middle of the raft. As he drank, he kept one eye on the changes in the surface of the river, another on Nehemiah at the sweep.

The old man, Velvel, could not understand Nehemiah's pleasureless drinking. Velvel enjoyed his vodka — its taste, and the fiery trail it made from his mouth to his stomach, where it created a fine sunset glow that found its way back to his head to cheer the day. He liked the giddiness, the bright false memories it could create, and the occasional stunned oblivion it gave him. But Nehemiah's drinking was a grim and painful thing. "You don't even like it," he would protest. "You take it like medicine. No, worse. Like the wrong medicine. Or the only medicine on the shelf . . ."

"Shut up," Nehemiah always said, without anger. "Shut up and pass the bottle." And Velvel passed it. Vodka was cheap, and Nehemiah was a valuable man on a timber raft, no matter how much he drank. He stood long hours, like a statue made of beaten leather, leaning into the wind, his eyes concentrated, not on the river ahead (whose turns and dangers he managed with instinctive skill), but on some image of perplexity that seemed to dangle only inches before his eyes. The vodka kept him steady at the sweep. When it was Velvel's turn to guide the raft, vodka kept Nehemiah silent and sleepless, lying on his pallet amidships, watching sometimes the ashes fading or glowing in the hearth, sometimes the night-long brightness of the stars.

The wind blew more strongly and rippled the surface of the water. On either side of the raft appeared the first rocks that signaled the nearby rapids. Islands of grass and other rubble that had been floating on either side of the raft swept past it quickly now. Soon, they would be in white water. Velvel rose to his feet, thinking to take the sweep before they reached the channel through the rapids, but Nehemiah waved him away. Velvel shrugged. He bent and took the long pole that lay between the logs and made his way forward, where he stood, ready to push off any threatening debris that might come floating their way. The wind tugged at the old man's white beard, and the first drops of rain struck his cheek. He looked back at Nehemiah, who had the sweep tucked under his left arm while with his right he tilted the vodka bottle toward the sky. Velvel, not for the first time, prayed that at least God might know what He was doing. It would be pleasant to survive the rapids, because not many leagues away was Zlitin, a little river village, where he looked forward to a day or two of rest.

The raft swayed and rolled and bucked. The water rushed by, boiling and hissing. From a massed cloud ahead, there came the first lightning bolt, then thunder, then a driving rain. An enormous tree, its roots high out of the water, bore down on the raft. In the sudden illumination of a lightning flash, Nehemiah saw a doe cowering in a tangle of roots and soil as it swept closer. He leaned against the sweep, and the raft veered away until the current caught it and flung it between two rocks, where it hung wedged. The doe opened its mouth and bleated; then the tree plunged by.

There was a long creaking sound as the raft raised itself on its left side, like a bludgeoned man trying to rise. At the sweep, Nehemiah stood at a crazy angle, showing no surprise. The wind pulled at his beard, at his woolen coat and trousers. Velvel, clinging to the pole he had thrust between the logs to keep himself from being swept overboard, had time to think how good it was to be so old that he could think of death as nothing more or less than the next event; another something, like the thunder and the lightning and the rain. Then, as a wave drenched him and threatened to tear him loose from the pole, he found himself regretting the good meal of crumbled cornbread and yoghurt, and the glass of strong, strong tea that he would miss in Zlitin if he died.

There was a shriek of wood being tortured by stone. The raft trembled like a creature shaking itself. There was a lurch, a bump, a splash, and the raft was free, racing downriver toward the deep-water bend that would carry it around the rapids. Nehemiah, as silent as ever, stood at the sweep, holding the vodka bottle in his left hand. As the raft swept close in toward the bank, a wet branch slapped the bottle from his hand and sent it crashing against a rock. Nehemiah shook his head, took a firmer grip at the sweep. They were through the rapids. From here on to Zlitin, the raft would have unobstructed passage all the way.

Overhead, the heavens put on a final display of bravado: thunder and lightning and a howling wind. But it was all rhetoric. Half an hour later, the storm blew itself out. Within an hour, the sky was clear, the river calm. When Velvel tied the raft to the overhanging beech tree in Zlitin, Nehemiah stepped ashore carefully, drunkenly. Soon, there would be another bottle. There always was.

❧ ❧

Velvel was seventy-five years old, Nehemiah was sixty; but Velvel talked with the vehemence and the embarrassment of an older adolescent giving his younger brother advice. "You have to go," he said. "Ask for the younger one. I've seen her. She's . . ." Velvel spluttered.

He was having trouble giving sexual advice in the broad light of day, and he had a mouthful of cornbread and yoghurt. "You *need* a woman." He growled. "You can't keep on like this. It isn't natural. Your flesh will rot."

Nehemiah listened, unoffended. He spun a hardboiled egg idly on the table top and waited for the tavernkeeper's wife to bring the bottle he had asked for. He breathed deeply. One needed to breathe deeply to deal with contradictions.

In his pocket there were two letters. He shifted, then thrust his hand under his woolen shirt and found the folded papers in his money band.

The question, always, was how to take the present world. Young women named Sarah who could look past their memories and, without a hint of madness, claim to be the destined bride of salvation. The bride of the Messiah!

And now, further riddles. The world was one great rubble of blood, crushed bone, and anguish . . . a place where the Turks slaughtered Persians and Tartars. Where Tartars killed Jews and Russians murdered Poles. Where the

133

French and the Dutch slit the throats of Spaniards; Spaniards murdered the Portuguese; men waded in blood in Transylvania, in Sweden, in Denmark; the English immolated the Dutch, themselves, and the Irish. The cry for blood was so vehement in this century that one might well believe it came from the infant Satan wailing to be nourished.

Further riddles. In the age of blood, another perplexity.

He opened out the first letter. It was one of dozens like it that had been sent by Joseph Florentin, a rich and pious Jew of Salonika, in Turkey, to Jewish Houses of Study in Europe. Proof, Nehemiah grumbled, that wealth was no safeguard against madness.

The letter read:

> To the Children of Israel, peace!
>
> Praise, praise unto the Lord.
>
> Know that the great day of healing and the redemption of Israel is upon us . . . The fulfillment of God's words pronounced by the Prophets.
>
> Shabbatai Zevi, the Holy Youth of Smyrna, now walks the stones of Salonika. In his face is the morning light; in his smile, Salvation.
>
> Fear no more. The time of the Messiah is at hand. Rejoice. Rejoice.
>
> Let those that have ears to hear, let them hear and believe.
>
> *Joseph Florentin*
> Salonika

Beside this ecstatic letter, Nehemiah put the angry one from the Chief Rabbi of Vilna:

> To the Jews of Europe, peace!
>
> Though it has been well said that "silence is a fence to the Torah," yet frivolous letters that have lately appeared in Vienna, Vilna, Frankfurt, and Livorno prompt us to take pen in hand to warn of deceitful claims made

by the followers of a certain Shabbatai Zevi, known also as the Wise Youth of Smyrna.

We have been told to "fear no more, for the prophesied time when the celestial lion will descend from the heavens for the Messiah to mount is at hand."

Brethren in the Dispersion, beware of dazzling light shining in the East; for is it not written, "And I will bring forth a seed out of Jacob, and out of Judah an inheritor of my mountains . . ."? Then how shall a glowworm out of Smyrna light up the sky with salvation?

Our enemies compass us around. May the God of our Fathers bless you and keep you. May the misleaders of Israel perish; may their names be blotted from the Book of Life.

Avram Karschenboim
Chief Rabbi,
Vilna

"You need a woman," old Velvel insisted. Nehemiah folded up the letters and put them back in his money band. Need. That he understood. "Let them hear and believe." That was not so easy. He believed what he saw. The tavern in which he sat and the wrinkled features of Velvel, his friend. And Zlitin, where the raft was to be broken up, where they would be paid for their timber. Where, if the bottle did not come soon, the world would come back into that knife-edged focus he could not bear. The brandy would help put distance between himself and the thick presence of the erection in his loins. More than a woman, what Nehemiah wanted was to be enclosed in the glaze of the inertia brandy created. Once the bottle got there, his erection might go on with its perpetual throbbing, and he would feel it only as a distant presence, not much more urgent than his pulse.

"I'm old enough to be your father," Velvel said apologetically. "If you were my own son, I'd send you to the *kurveh*, to the whore. For your health's sake. You're a strong man, in the prime of life. You know, because you are a learned man, that . . . that in some cases . . . it is not forbidden." Velvel's tongue licked at the two black teeth in his upper jaw, then at the three in his lower, and found bits of cornbread to swallow. "What am I?" he said deprecatingly. "Nothing but a *proster Yid,* a simple Jew. But *I* know it's not forbidden. Read the *Shulkhan Arukh,* where it is practically *prescribed* for a learned man so that his sleep will not be tormented with longing that will make him too weary the next day for study of the Torah.

"You think I don't know, Nehemiah. Well, I know. Old men sleep very little, and I hear you groaning. I watch you hump the deck at night; I'm afraid you'll break the damned thing off in a knothole in the middle of one of your dreams. You ought to hear yourself. The sounds you make — as if your heart were being nibbled by mice.

"So go, for heaven's sake. Her name is Gina. She knows enough Polish for her work. If you haven't got the money, I'll pay for it. You can't go on grieving for a dead wife forever. It's been twelve years since you buried your Feigele. I tell you, it's a positive *mitzvah,* an act of grace, for a learned man to go. You need to be only a little bit discreet, not to bring scandal to the Torah. It is written — you know better than I — that you should travel twenty miles from where you're known."

" 'Dressed,' " said Nehemiah, with something like a grin, " 'in sober clothing, and his hat drawn low.' "

"You see!" Velvel cried. "Rabbi Karo understood young men." Then Velvel, overwhelmed at how much that was unseemly he had allowed himself to say, addressed himself fiercely to the crumbled cornbread in the bowl of yoghurt, but into his eye there crept an old man's tear.

Nehemiah stopped his heavy swaying and considered the tear. Slowly, as if it had to part the invisible layers of vodka surrounding Nehemiah's heart, it reached him. "Yes," he said. "Yes." And tilted himself forward in his chair so he could reach the axe lying on the floor. With its haft in his hand, he pushed the chair back and stood, just as the tavernkeeper's wife brought the bottle of brandy he had ordered. With the gross courtliness of the very drunk, he took it from her; then, indicating Velvel, he said, "Give . . . give my friend . . . give him . . . give him anything he wants." He put a handful of silver on the table.

When Nehemiah reached the mud street, he turned to the left, not even wondering how it was that he knew the way.

❧❧ ❧❧

The only brothel in Zlitin was in a tidy thatch-roofed house surrounded by a neat kitchen garden. It was open to the general public on Mondays, Wednesdays, and Fridays, the market days, when the outlying farmers and cattle drovers crowded into the small house from early morning until late at night. On Sundays, of course, the brothel, like any other Christian business, was closed. And it was more or less closed on Tuesdays, Thursdays, and Saturdays, when the two women — Amalia, the older, and Gina — took care of themselves and the house. The women washed clothes, bathed, oiled their hair, and slept at delicious intervals. They fed their two pigs and their twelve hens and counted their money.

It was a Tuesday morning when Nehemiah pushed open the heavy door, came in, and found Amalia sitting on a couch before the fireless hearth. She was shelling peas into a copper basin in her lap and nodding her head at a story that Abdul Hamid, the one-legged former Janissary, was telling her. Both of them stared at the thickset Jew who stood in the doorway, an axe in one hand and a bottle of brandy in the other. Abdul Hamid took a sip from his own brandy glass and smoothed a hand over his drooping mustache. Amalia caught the hint of a stagger in Nehemiah's step and noticed the look of puzzled emptiness in his eyes. It was Tuesday. If the Jew wanted anything more

137

than a quiet place to nurse his misery, he would have to pay well for the privilege.

Abdul Hamid looked with interest at Nehemiah — another of those northern Jews who came floating down the Tisa to the Danube. This one looked as if he were a walking statue, planting his feet into stone when he walked. He was a broad, storm-swept man, so different from the Jewish merchants, sleek and silken, whom Abdul Hamid had seen in their countinghouses in Constantinople.

He sighed. That had been long ago, before the fortunes of war had cast him up here, in Zlitin. Abdul Hamid had been with Sultan Murad the Fourth at the siege of Erevan, and again at Baghdad when that city was retaken from the Persians. He had stood not ten yards away from Murad when the Sultan split a giant's skull with his battle-axe after the giant had challenged Murad to single fight. Under Murad's drunken and baleful eye, Abdul Hamid had participated in the great blood bath that followed the battle for Baghdad. Thirty thousand defenders of the garrison, disarmed and helpless, had stood waiting their turn to have their throats cut by Murad's troops. It had been a long, reeking slaughter. Horrid and — satisfying. There had been screams and entreaties, useless spasms of resistance, blood spattering, curses, prayers. When it was over, Abdul Hamid had slept for days and days.

After that, his fortunes changed for the worse, though at first it had seemed quite otherwise. Promoted after Baghdad, he was put in command of a troop of Janissaries sent to guard a galleass packed with Persian women and children destined for the slave markets of Tunis. Off the Candia coast, the galleass was overtaken by a Venetian galley. Half an hour after the sea fight that followed, the Turkish captain of the galleass struck his colors, though Abdul Hamid, his right leg blown away by chain shot, protested weakly from the pool of blood in which he lay. An hour later, the galleass was in the Venetian's tow, and a nearly dead Abdul Hamid was flung below deck to join his disarmed troop, now prisoners along with the Persians. For three weeks, fever and gangrene tore at his body, but he was still a young man, descended from hardy Albanian stock, and he recovered.

For his Venetian captors, however, he was a useless prize. As a one-legged Turk, he was too damaged to be sold into slavery or to be put to a galley oar; and his soldier's rank was too low for them to offer him up for ransom to the Sublime Porte. Finally, he was turned loose to starve in the streets of Venice, where a Turkish dyer, a convert to Christianity, who was passing through Venice on his way to Austrian Zlitin, gathered him up and carted him home. The dyer, in that one gesture, managed to exercise Christian charity, a lingering loyalty to his Moslem past, and a mercantile shrewdness that recognized the hard lean toughness in Abdul Hamid, which, despite the absence of a leg, would make a profitable servant of him.

In Zlitin, Abdul Hamid thought of stealing back to Turkish Belgrade, some eighty river miles away. At first, he was delayed by a sense of gratitude to his master, the dyer; then he found a wife, who promptly gave him children. What with one thing and another, it became easier and easier to stay in Zlitin, where, after some years, except for his baggy Turkish trousers and the turban, which, as a conscientious Moslem, he always wore, he became simply another of Zlitin's unassuming citizens.

The Jew, swaying in the brothel doorway, had the look of a disoriented exile, so it was with some fellow feeling that Abdul Hamid called, "Put your axe against the wall, Jew, and bring your bottle here."

Nehemiah shook his head. "No. The axe stays . . . with me." He stumbled into the room and sat heavily beside Amalia; then he leaned forward and peered into Abdul Hamid's eyes. He sighed, laid the axe across his lap, pulled the cork from the bottle with his teeth, tilted it, and drank, after which he passed it to Abdul Hamid. "F'give me," he said. "I couldn't wait." Abdul Hamid accepted the bot-

139

tle, poured generously from it into his glass, and passed it back to the Jew. Both men drank; then Nehemiah offered the bottle to Amalia, who shook her head and went on shelling peas. "It's too early in the day for me," she said.

Abdul Hamid drank. Nehemiah drank. The Jew filled the Turk's glass. The Turk found a glass and filled it for the Jew. Plump Amalia watched them with a professional eye. One or the other of the men would want her soon. Abdul Hamid would be no surprise to her. He came regularly on Tuesday, when the brothel was quiet and his wife made her weekly visit to her mother in a village eleven miles away. On the other hand, this broad, muscular Jew with the axe in his lap might prove interesting. The Jews she had met had the look of frightened rabbits when they came to her. In her arms they were white and trembling, easy to soothe, easy to send away. This fellow was like a butcher's block. His veined fist around the brandy glass looked as if it had been carved out of oak.

An hour later, the men were still drinking, but more companionably. Abdul Hamid's crutch was propped against the table, beside Nehemiah's axe, and when they drank, they leaned toward each other, as if to hear each other better.

Amalia had long since left them to join Gina, the younger whore, at the stove, where they tasted and stirred the strawberry preserves boiling in the iron kettle. The room was filled with the fine smell of strawberries and brandy. Except for the all but whispered conversation of the men or the gentle noises of the women at the kettle, the house was quiet. An enormous fly hummed at the sunlit window that looked into the garden. There, hens clucked, and behind the house, the sows grunted at their swill. It was a slow afternoon, restful to the women, who waited with easy confidence for the masculine affability around the bottle to change to lust. Meanwhile, they stirred the strawberries and, with a wooden spoon, lifted off the rosy white scum that formed on the syrup.

"No. No, friend Jew," Abdul Hamid was saying as he pounded on the floor with his crutch. "Not souls. Souls are . . . Allah's business. Here . . . nnnnnow . . . a mmman is mmmeat. Meat on a hook. Meat mmmmmoving. M—— meat," he concluded firmly.

"Yes . . . No . . . Yes." Nehemiah tried it both ways, striking the floor in his turn with his axe. Then he remembered what he meant to say. "No! No design. No pattern. I have seen it. There . . . there is none. No." Then it occurred to him to tell the dear Turk everything: Lame Hannah; broken Feigele; the dead Cossack. The years of wandering. The dear, dear Turk had also suffered. "I have heard," he said, as if it were an illumination, "I have heard it said that . . . God . . . hides inside a mirror. Which is why . . . which is. That's the reason we stare into . . . the glass. Thinking to see . . . Hoping to see . . . Him . . . Him . . ." Nehemiah nodded thoughtfully, then added, "Is it?"

"Meat." Abdul Hamid breathed hard. "Meat. Thirty thousand . . . throats. Like calves . . . like lambs . . . like . . . like . . ."

"Bullocks," Nehemiah helped his friend.

"Bullocks. Ballocks." The joke was too funny. Abdul Hamid twittered; Nehemiah chuckled; little by little they worked their bit of amusement into a fit of hysterical laughter, which left them holding on to each other's shoulders, their faces touching, cheek to cheek.

"Meat." Abdul Hamid returned to his conviction. "If there had been souls there, there would have . . . there would have been a wind."

"Meat," Nehemiah compromised. "Meat looking in the mirror. Daring God to come out. 'Come out, come out,'" Nehemiah mimicked a child playing.

"He never does," Abdul Hamid said sadly. "Because we're meat. On this earth, stinking meat. Rotten meat. But there" — he pointed toward heaven — "there, Allah be praised, He prepares . . . He . . . He . . ."

141

"He gets ready," Nehemiah encouraged.

"He gets ready the Garden, Jew. He gets it ready."

"No. No design. Not . . . for me."

Abdul Hamid thought Nehemiah was grieving for the Moslem Bower and hurried to reassure him. "Yes. Yes. You too. Because we are . . . cousins. Ver—— verily. Allah has chosen . . . Adam . . . and Noah . . . and the family . . . of Abraham. Ishmael . . ."

"And Isaac," Nehemiah rocked back and forth, agreeing.

"Cousins. You and me."

"But meat," Nehemiah said, obligingly taking up the Turk's refrain.

"Looking . . . into . . . mirrors," Abdul Hamid replied, trying to repay the compliment. For a while there was silence as Nehemiah refilled their glasses.

"Where," Nehemiah asked, "where do we come from?"

"Where?" the Turk inquired.

Nehemiah closed his eyes and crooned the argument in the melody of Talmudic disputation. "Akabia, son of Mahallalel, said, 'Ponder on three things.'"

"One, two, three," Abdul Hamid intoned.

"'Ponder . . . consider. Whence thou comest . . .'"

"Erevan . . . Baghdad . . . Venice . . . Zlitin."

Nehemiah ignored the Turk. "'Whither thou goest?'"

"Amalia. Gina. Gina. Amalia." Abdul Hamid gloated.

"'And in whose presence you will stand to give an account of yourself at the Judgment Day.'"

"In whose *what*?" the Turk asked suspiciously.

Nehemiah ignored him. "To the question 'Whence thou comest?' we make answer: 'From a stinking drop.' To the question 'Whither thou goest?' we reply, 'To a place of dust, to be the food for worms.'"

"Meat. Meat. Meat," Abdul Hamid chanted. "Meat, pounding at the mirror to be God."

"To the question 'In whose presence will you stand at the Judgment Day?' we say, 'Before the King of Kings, the Lord of Lords.' Amen! Amen! Amen!" Nehemiah burst into tears, only to be lovingly enfolded in Abdul Hamid's arms. The Turk, hiccupping, held the Jew close and whispered in his ear, "Amen! Amen! Amen!" like a father soothing a frightened child. Nehemiah, overwhelmed by gratitude, but vaguely responsible to his sense of manhood, struggled away from the embrace. In the affectionate wrestling that followed, Nehemiah lost his peaked Jewish hat, which went rolling away toward the newly swept hearth. The fate of his hat redoubled Nehemiah's grief, and he sobbed.

"Don't cry, little Jewish cousin," Abdul Hamid said soothingly. "It's only a hat. Here, take mine." In the next moment, the greasy turban was on Nehemiah's head, and he heard Abdul Hamid's voice in his ear: "There, now. There. See. It is the will of Allah. We are no longer cousins. Now we are brothers, brother dear. Brothers in Allah. Having put on the turban of Allah, you are a Moslem, like me. A sinful Moslem, with a bottle, but a Moslem just the same."

Nehemiah felt Abdul Hamid's hand on his shoulder in a grip as firm as steel. Between his legs, there was the undiminished erection. In God's planless universe, why should these bits of chaos seem out of place? Meat could hang on a butcher's hook, dreaming of a soul. A Cossack could manipulate Feigele's limbs to make them imitate the postures of lewdness. And a turban on a Jew's head could turn him into a Moslem. If he looked in a mirror now, what would he see? Meat staring in the mirror to find God? Or the motion of a whirlwind angry once again that meat should darken counsel with mere words?

Abdul Hamid, who was not perplexed at all, was on his one leg, drinking to the miraculous conversion of the Jew. *"Allah Akbar,"* he roared. *"Allah Akbar."* Nehemiah found himself dancing in the Turk's embrace. Drunk as they both were, each of them felt strangely solemn as they considered the power of Abdul Hamid's turban on Nehemiah's head. Had they been sober, and in a Moslem coun-

143

try, the turban on the Jew's head would indeed have been the irrevocable sign that Nehemiah had embraced the Moslem faith. Two huge tears appeared in Abdul Hamid's eyes. "Welcome, welcome, my Jewish brother. My Moslem brother, welcome."

Abdul Hamid's tears reminded Nehemiah that Velvel, too, had wept for him that morning. These were great gifts, compassionate tears, able to open the gates of paradise for one who sheds them.

Abdul Hamid was roaring in his ear, "Choose. Choose, O former Jew and now my brother. Be thou the first to choose." And there were the two women, plump thirtyish Amalia and the slim seventeen-year-old Gina. Velvel had advised Nehemiah to choose Gina, a dry, forward creature with darting, black eyes and oiled, coarse hair that reached to her waist. Nehemiah, still in Abdul Hamid's grasp, thought of the raft, the wind blowing, the roaring rush of the waters at the rapids. He hitched his belt around his axe — and chose.

❧ ❧

Amalia.

Amalia, naked, lay on her back, her head turned to watch the logger Jew removing his woolen shirt, his thick woolen trousers. His chest was thick as a wine barrel, his arms as heavily muscled and hairy as an ape's. When he removed the fringed woolen religious garment that he wore against his skin, he turned to face her, still drunk, but no longer unsteady. Except for his already towering member, which he held in one hand as if it were the handle of his axe, his body was built of square planes. When he approached the bed, still holding his erection, she had a moment of apprehension that he might have violent, strange hungers. He made no startling moves, however, but stood beside the bed, looking down at her ample breasts, her wide hips, her thick, cushiony thighs. From the next room, they could hear Abdul Hamid, already grunting.

The Jew took his hand from his erection, closed his eyes, and seemed to be trying to remember something. Then spreading his arms out over her, he murmured a Hebrew prayer. What he said, she did not understand, but the words did not sound hostile. Quietly, she waited.

Nehemiah opened his eyes and looked down into Amalia's plump wide face and her chestnut hair spread over the blue-embroidered pillow. Between his legs stood the shaft of his erection, pointed toward heaven. If the mirror was necessary for the meat, who had the right to say the meat was not just as necessary for the mirror? That was the notion which, when he considered it, allowed him, finally, to fall upon Amalia like a tower.

⚜ ⚜

The soft whore stroked the strange Jew's forehead. She passed her fingers through his gray earlocks and his beard, which, she knew, tasted of willow bark. He lay as still as if he had been clubbed, as if he meant to sleep for years.

A strange Jew. Stranger than any man she had ever known. Who had held her in his arms, plunging endlessly, his teeth grinding, holding her as if he had caught and meant to impregnate the wind. How tender she felt toward him. And how amazed. He had been a dark body laboring over her, but the very force of his indifferent hunger touched her. His climax, when it overtook him, had in it such a shuddering of unrealized hope that the gathering tenderness with which she endured him was suddenly transformed to ecstasy, and Amalia, the village whore, and Nehemiah, the exiled rabbi, shook together in the common cry of flesh.

Now he was asleep. Amalia put her hand to her bush. Men were so absurd: " 'Whence comest thou?' To which we answer, 'From a stinking drop.' "

Well. Well. It was not always such a stinking drop. Amalia pressed herself against the sleeping Jew and dozed.

145

Book II

17

Jerusalem
1656

The boy Nathan believed that there were miracles and messages in every stone and bit of straw that he encountered in Jerusalem. God, as Nathan understood, had spoken the universe, and Torah was its written record, written with white fire on black. Every phrase, every word, every punctuation mark, had a meaning on the page and its visible counterpart in the world. One had only to be attentive to the text on the one hand, and to life on the other, and one could learn to feel the two flowing into each other. He knew all this, and he believed it; but, being ten years old and cooped up in the *yeshivah,* where his father, who was often absent, left him, he much preferred to slip away from his study of the texts, when he could, and prowl the streets and alleys of Jerusalem, where the phrases, words, and punctuation marks could be touched and seen, tasted and felt and heard. One never knew around which corner one might bump into a miracle.

What bumped him, in fact, was Barot'ali, the rich Smyrna rabbi's lumbering idiot servant. The huge creature, genial as always, was pursuing a crippled sparrow that fluttered under the feet of carters, peddlers, and mules. Time after time, Barot'ali lunged in his thick way toward the bird, which waited until the penultimate moment before it flapped its uncrippled wing and managed to stagger another dozen yards through the air. Barot'ali huffed after it, laughing, his arms out, the spittle of delight sliding down his chin. "My bird," he called after the sparrow. "My bird." The sparrow fluttered away and found a precarious footing in a potted lemon tree that stood before a money-lender's shop, and Barot'ali ploughed after it, jostling Jews and Arabs out of his way. This time, the weary bird missed its timing, and the idiot's huge hand knocked it in midflight to the stone pavement. Barot'ali, squealing with triumph, flung himself upon it.

Barot'ali cupped the dying bird; kissed the beak, which opened and closed in agony. "My bird," the idiot said tenderly; "my bird." But the light was already fading from the creature's yellow eye. The idiot stared at the bundle of crushed feathers in his palms and scolded it in some idiot-Turkish language of his own. When the bird refused to open its eyes or flutter its wings again, Barot'ali sat cross-legged on the pavement, put the tiny body down, and began a bitter howling.

"Hush," said a voice. "Hush, Barot'ali." It was Shabbatai Zevi, the rich Smyrna rabbi, in his clean gray caftan, who knelt beside the idiot and stroked his greasy hair. Nathan watched the couple, who had been the talk of Jewish Jerusalem for months. The idiot was well known for his expansive friendliness and his enormous strength. Nathan had seen the simpleton holding up a cartful of sand for half an hour while its owner went off to hunt for a wheelwright, and he had heard it said that Barot'ali could bend iron bars with his hands.

His master, Shabbatai, was another sort of wonder. For one thing (rare for a Jew in Jerusalem), he was rich. Then, he was handsome, tall, well fleshed, and stately. Nathan, watching him kneel beside the idiot, was impressed by the clarity of his large brown eyes and the golden glow of his complexion. Shabbatai's voice, almost in Barot'ali's ear, was low and thrilling. The idiot was older than the thirty-year-old Shabbatai, but Shabbatai, talking to him, sounded like a gentle father telling a sobbing child a story while he bathed a wounded knee.

It was not a scene like the one Nathan watched that disturbed the rabbis of Jerusalem. The Smyrna Jew could be as kind as he liked to his idiot servant. It was the man's public behavior that disturbed them. In the synagogue, when morning prayers were done, Shabbatai Zevi had lately been found sitting in his seat, so deeply entranced by an inner vision that the beadle had to shake him to rouse him. And those who prayed near him swore that they had heard him say the Shem ha m'foresh under his breath — something for which he had been in trouble in Smyrna.

There were scandals outside the synagogue, too. Reb Menakhem, Nathan's teacher in the yeshivah, complained, "He will get us thrown to the dogs. As if he had never heard of Moussa Pasha, ready to pounce on us for the slightest cause. And there he is, Shabbatai, the rich Jew, riding around the city on a white horse, wearing a yellow robe like Suleiman the Magnificent! A Jew! A Jew, riding on a horse before the sealed Golden Gates of the city! Sealed until the Messiah comes, and not fixed till then. Sitting on a white horse and being rich won't open those gates.

"Nor will they open just because Shabbatai Zevi takes it into his head to have a fit before them, yelling, 'My God, my God, why hast Thou forsaken me? Why art Thou so far from helping me, and from the words of my roaring?' Oh, it was unbelievable. A Jew, a rabbi, prancing about on a horse in the midst of a crowd of camel drivers and shepherds and Moussa Pasha's spies! Foaming at the mouth, crying, 'I am poured out like water, and all my bones are out of joint. My heart is like wax; it is melted in the midst of my bowels.' Wax is what the Turks will melt in *our* bowels, unless that madman is stopped.

151

"It's what comes of being rich," Reb Menakhem said sadly. "If *I* stood before the Golden Gates and made such a scandal, the Rabbinical Court would get after me soon enough. Stripes, my boys. Stripes. And well deserved, too."

Now, here he was, the strange rabbi from Smyrna, comforting his snuffling servant. Shabbatai put some coins into the idiot's hand, turned him around, and pushed him in the direction of the fowler's market, where singing birds in cages could be bought. Barot'ali grinned and trotted off, first flinging the dead sparrow into a pile of rotten grapes.

It was then that Nathan decided to stalk Shabbatai. The strange rabbi would be the prey whom he, Nathan the secret hunter, must follow. Shabbatai, all unaware that he was being followed, made his way into a nearby grocer's shop. Nathan crept to its barred window and peered in, curious to see what the Jew from Smyrna would buy. Among the other stories about Shabbatai were those that told of his week-long fasts. He began the penitential exercise, it was said, on *motseh Shabbat,* Saturday night, and fasted until *erev Shabbat,* the following Friday night, subsisting on no more than a mouthful of water. The wonder was that the holy man looked so strong and well nourished.

Nathan pressed his nose against the rusted bars of the grocer's window, but he could see nothing through the bottle glass except a vague green haze in which white bubbles were suspended. At a sound from the grocer's shop, Nathan darted away and hid behind a market porter's wicker basket. Then, there was Shabbatai carrying his purchases in a paper cornucopia. When he turned into a thronging David Street, Nathan was on his trail.

Nathan followed Shabbatai through the din of the Coppersmiths' Arcade, where boys Nathan's age dipped rags into molten tin, with which they wiped the insides of the bowls they were plating. It was a brave arcade, with charcoal glowing in braziers, the sound of hundreds of hammers shaping bowls, trays, and ewers. Old men sat cross-

legged, incising on the sides of pots and pans delicate
leaves, horses' manes and tails, scenes of meadowland and
forest, romantic moments between kings and maidens,
polo games, and, in a dreamlike calligraphy, prayers from
the Koran.

At the entrance to the Jews' Quarter, where Yehuda
Ha-Levi and Solomon ibn Gabirol streets crossed, there
stood a tower, an inner citadel in an earlier epoch of the
city's history, but used now, in its upper stories, as a store-
house for building stones. The lower story was leased to
Shabbatai, who now went down a set of cobbled stairs
and disappeared from Nathan's view. The boy stood in
the shadow of a water jar and waited until he could hear
Shabbatai's door creak and close. Then, in the sauntering
way of a boy showing the world that he is doing nothing
sinister, he followed the Smyrna holy man down the
stairs.

Nathan was brought up short at Shabbatai's door, which,
except for the usual small peephole, had no window. To
Nathan, it began to seem that his adventure was over.
There was nothing to be seen. Walking a little way back
up the stairs, Nathan studied the tower. Fifteen feet above
ground level, a window, looking toward the Kidron Valley,
had been cut into the tower. Shabbatai's window, but ap-
parently inaccessible to sleuths and hunters. Nathan looked
again and saw a line of iron brackets set into the masonry
of the tower from ground level to the upper stories where
the stones were stored. The brackets, meant to guide the
ropes of a pulley that once had been used to hoist stones
into the tower, formed neat handholds, one above the
other, leading right to and beyond Shabbatai's window.
Nathan smiled.

Minutes later, he was peering into Shabbatai's steep,
round room, at the bottom of which Shabbatai stood, looking distant and distorted. Nathan, clinging to the brackets,
admired the room. It was exactly the sort of place a ten-
year-old would be happy to live in: round and high, and

153

not like anyone's house, with ordinary doors and hallways. Instead, there was one round space, like the bottom of a clean, dry well.

The furnishings were simple, too. There were two wine-colored rugs, laid end to end, on which there was a scattered tumble of bedclothes. Near the door, there was a brass charcoal brazier, in whose ashes a clay coffee pot leaned. A little distance from the brazier there were two chests inlaid with mother-of-pearl, one large and the other not much bigger than a jewel box. At various places on the floor there was also a copper bowl holding fresh plums, a clay water jar, and a basket with four golden pears. The watching boy's eyes widened.

Shabbatai stood irresolutely holding the paper cornucopia; then he started toward the bowl of plums, but there was a peremptory knock at his door. He turned and asked, "Who is it?"

"Rabbinical officers. Open up!"

The boy saw Shabbatai stiffen; one arm went across the cornucopia as if to defend it; then he went to the door and opened it. Before Nathan could shout, "Don't, Reb Shabbatai! Don't let them in," the three dark men, who went about chastising offenders against Jewish law, were standing in the white cylinder of Shabbatai's room.

The oldest of the officers, Eliezer Kherev, had the eyes and the acquisitive nose of a ferret. He introduced himself as the chief officer, and his colleagues, Yom Tov Gedaliah on his right, and Mosheh Sopher on his left. Gedaliah was a portly man with thick, fleshy lips, and eyes he had trained to deny that he had any lusts; Sopher looked about greedily, assessing the cost of everything he saw.

"Be easy, Reb Shabbatai," the stout Gedaliah said, speaking hardly above a whisper. "It is already late in the afternoon. We will be quick."

Shabbatai, clutching his paper parcel, asked, "Quick about what?"

"The rabbinical judgment," Sopher replied. "Surely, you haven't forgotten?"

"Surely, surely," Shabbatai mumbled, and swayed before them like a man reciting silent prayers. Then he asked, "What judgment?"

"Ah, ah," said the unctuous Gedaliah. "The *dayanim, da-ya-nim,*" he said, pronouncing the word carefully so that his sly insult at Shabbatai's bookish Hebrew should not go unnoticed. "The rabbinical judges," he said, licking his lips, "have condemned you."

"Condemned me," Shabbatai agreed vaguely. He turned from his visitors and walked about the room, making an aimless figure eight; then he returned to stand near Kherev, the chief officer. He looked up at his window but failed to see the alert Nathan, who had withdrawn his head. From somewhere in the Kidron Valley there came the sound of a braying donkey. Shabbatai, who had been in a daze of meditation most of the day, tried, as a gesture of politeness, to understand why the men were in his room. They did not seem angry, and yet they spoke of condemnation.

"Yes," said Gedaliah, the man with the moist lips. "You have been condemned to stripes." Gedaliah had been wondering whether there would be a bribe in this case. There was no harm in a bit of brusque language. It would put the fear of God into this rich man.

Eliezer Kherev said more kindly, "Yes, Reb Zevi. This morning, at a meeting of the Rabbinical Court, you were condemned to stripes. You were there; you heard the judgment and you acknowledged your guilt."

Shabbatai looked about vaguely. It was all possible. He was pale and hungry. Barot'ali was off, buying himself a bird. This morning, in the synagogue, there had been such a stupefying amount of talk. He had heard it, like the whine of the knife-sharpener's wheel, through the throbbing of a week-old headache. The Jerusalem sunlight was intense; wherever one walked there was something sacred or dreadful. Graves of prophets. Mount Moriah, where Isaac had been bound to the altar waiting in the voracious sunlight for his throat to be cut. And now, these men were here, talking about stripes. "Stripes?" Shabbatai echoed.

Sopher, who had decided that the mother-of-pearl chests were immensely valuable, said crisply, "Come, come. You could hardly expect to go on unchecked. The white horse was bad enough. Making the prayer for the new moon in the middle of the month was worse; but haranguing the Turks before the Golden Gates was both blasphemy and provocation to the Pasha. You acknowledged your acts. We are here to administer the punishment." Here, Sopher reached into his sash and brought out the subtly braided cat-o'-nine-tails of his office.

Nathan, at the window, winced. He had seen what the thongs could do.

Shabbatai closed his eyes. "No," he said softly. "I can't bear stripes." He was not Sammi al Garmizani. He was no Turkish tax evader whose skin could be shredded by the quick strokes of a rod-master. Shabbatai recalled Mohammed Reza Hadj's tired face and the ancient fever in his eyes. He heard again his mother's "In the name of God, will it ever stop?"

"Stripes," Sopher said hoarsely, shaking out the thongs. "They are for the good of your soul."

"Come now, Reb Zevi," Kherev said. "Thirty-nine stripes are quickly endured. Here . . ." He took Shabbatai's elbow and led him to the wall. "Put your hands out before you. Against the wall. So. Palms up. So. And now . . ." He nodded at Sopher, who nodded to Yom Tov Gedaliah. The plump man moved with lightning speed. Shabbatai's gray caftan was pulled back from his shoulders, and he found himself helpless, his arms restrained. "And now," Kherev said contentedly, "we are ready."

What followed next was decidedly strange. Nathan, watching from the window, was suddenly unable to hear any more of what was being said below. Though he could

156

see clearly enough, it was as if all human speech had been in some way erased and he was watching a pantomime.

Sopher, holding the cat-o'-nine-tails loosely in his right hand, stood beside Shabbatai's for a long time. Words were spoken back and forth. Shabbatai's head went up and down. Kherev shook his head in negation. Gedaliah seemed to speak; then Sopher shook the cat-o'-nine-tails and smiled grimly. Shabbatai's lips moved faster and Kherev shrugged his shoulders. There was a pause, after which the punishment began.

It, too, went on in silence. Sopher's arm went up and down. The cat-o'-nine-tails came down on Shabbatai's bared back, but Shabbatai never flinched. It seemed to Nathan that Kherev was counting, but he had a look of indifference on his face, and so did Sopher, the whipper. And so did Yom Tov Gedaliah. No one in the room showed signs of heat or pain. Nobody sweated; nobody moaned. And Shabbatai, who had cried out against the mere word *stripes,* stood patiently, enduring the whip.

Then it came to Nathan that he was watching a miracle. Shabbatai, the Smyrna rabbi, had prevailed against the Rabbinical Court in precisely the way that Daniel had triumphed over the lions, who, though they had raved and gnashed their teeth, had had their mouths stopped by an angel of the Lord.

". . . thirty-six, thirty-seven, thirty-eight, thirty-nine." And it was over. The rabbinical officers stepped back. Shabbatai straightened and reached inside the waistband of his caftan. Then, one by one, he shook the hands of his tormentors. It was as the men walked to the door that Nathan could suddenly hear voices again from below. Kherev was saying, "You have borne your punishment well, Reb Shabbatai, and the Rabbinical Court will be so informed."

Yom Tov Gedaliah licked his lips and added, "I hope you understand, dear sir, that we are merely the instruments of the court. We have acted in the performance of a difficult duty."

"I quite understand," a smiling Shabbatai said.

And Sopher, with a final, no longer evaluative, glance around the room, said, "It was a pleasure to know you, Reb Shabbatai."

Then they were gone. For a while, Nathan clung to his perch. Having seen one miracle, he thought that if he waited, he might see another; but Shabbatai had his forehead pressed against the wall and gave no indication that he planned to move. Finally, when Nathan felt the afternoon sunlight moving down his back, he turned and made his careful way down the wall.

Inside the tower, Shabbatai roused himself. He now knew that in addition to being endless talkers, Jerusalem Jews were also men who were inexpensive to bribe. He sighed and remembered that he was hungry. He found the still unwrapped cornucopia of goodies where he had left it beside the mother-of-pearl chests. Sitting cross-legged, he unwound the paper and laid his purchases out on the larger chest.

With the deliberation of a disciplined gourmand who knows in what order he means to please his palate, he arranged his six orange-colored, honey-steeped barley cakes, the three slices of sesame cake, the four rose-flavored pieces of sweet *loqum,* and the three sugared nut-filled dates. When everything was as it should be, he poured himself a cup of the thick, strong coffee from the pot, which he had had the foresight to leave in the smoldering ashes of his brazier.

Outside in the street, the boy Nathan, who had been cheated of his wish to know what sorts of food a holy rabbi from Smyrna ate, had to content himself with having seen a miracle.

18

Cairo
1664

It was Shabbatai's third wedding night with a woman of flesh and blood.

In the doorway of one of the stables in the courtyard of rich Raphael Joseph's house, Barot'ali stood looking up at the new moon. His right hand rested on the sleek head of Leilia, the younger of the two goats that Sarah, Shabbatai's new bride, had given him as a present when she arrived in Cairo. Leilia was a much daintier creature than her older sister, whom Sarah had named Rosalinda. Rosalinda was merely patient under Barot'ali's caresses. But it was Leilia to whom the idiot's heart went out. Leilia, whose long-lashed, clear yellow eyes looked into his with something like his own gaze of longing. Now, with the new moon starting off across the sky in this strange city, where, though he never came to any harm, Barot'ali was often lonely, he was glad once more to have his goats near him. The tall Sarah with the long dark hair, who was taking up so much of Shabbatai's time, was a good woman, Barot'ali thought. She had kissed him and stroked him on the neck, and had sent him Leilia and Rosalinda.

It was a cool night, and Barot'ali had a fine new *burnous* — a gift from Shabbatai that very morning. It was a burnous made of camel's hair, with a long silk tassel which he dangled before Leilia's nose. She put out her slender tongue to lick it, but Barot'ali swung it away, then dangled it near her again. She leaned toward it, and again he snatched it away. The goat wearied of the game sooner than the man. She put her head down and butted him gently, then reared up on her hind legs as if she meant to climb into his arms. He squealed and sat cross-legged beside her so that she could lunge toward his armpit.

It was salty and warm there, and once she got her narrow head past the folds of his burnous and under his greasy shirt, Leilia began a happy snuffling. Barot'ali leaned against the stable wall and grinned. Undoing his sash, he pulled down his baggy trousers and slipped them off. He laughed toward the moon and stroked Leilia's head; then, taking her up, he moved her down over his spread legs and put her dainty forehooves on both his shoulders. The touch of her fine long hair against his stomach made him giggle. Occasionally, her hind hooves cut against his inner thighs, making a delicious pain. Leilia still struggled to reach the salt in his armpit. The idiot, clumsy in every other situation, had acquired considerable skill in dealing with his favorite. Ignoring her nuzzling, he held her steady while he stroked her udder.

It was a beautiful night, and he loved Leilia's springtime smells: hay and grass, mingled with the odor of urine and dung and freshly ploughed fields. Leilia's lunges in the direction of his armpit made her teats quiver over his erection. Inside the stable, Rosalinda, Leilia's older sister, bleated. She was larger and thicker-boned than Leilia, and endured Barot'ali with stolidity. When he had dealings with her, he always came to Rosalinda from behind, treating her like the goat she was. But to delicate Leilia, who was constantly in motion, who quivered when he so much as scratched her head, Barot'ali came in the way of a man with a woman.

Now, as her squirming all but overwhelmed him, he

reached behind her and spread her nether lips with his right hand. As her flesh received him, he clutched her flanks and pulled them firmly down. Leilia, invariably startled by the gesture, lunged and kicked and bleated. Barot'ali, surging toward the skies, called in answer to her cry of pain, *"Allah Akbar."* Then there was a rush of motion, and he fell away.

The new moon was but a little way advanced across the night.

Leaning on perfumed pillows, Shabbatai and his third wife, Sarah, sat a proper brother-and-sister distance apart, watching the myriad floating wicks drifting their soft yellow light back and forth across the pool of oil in the copper bowl at the foot of their bed. The shadows made by the tongues of flame created a restless mosaic on the blue-domed ceiling. It was a cool Cairo night, and Raphael Joseph, who had promoted their marriage, and whose guests they were, had seen to it that the bridal bed was furnished with silk bedclothes and prettily stitched coverlets, one of which, bunched together in his lap, Shabbatai was nervously stroking. Almost fifteen years had passed since he had been with a waiting bride on a wedding night.

Raphael Joseph was sixty years old, hawk-nosed, pious, and stern. He was called Raphael Joseph the *chelebi,* or lord, a title with which he was honored as head of the Jewish community of Cairo. To the Turkish Viceroy in Egypt, he was the *saraf bashi* — a very important man, the comptroller of the Egyptian treasury. Raphael Joseph, skillful in the Viceroy's business, and wise in presiding over the Jews, was, as pragmatists sometimes are, prey to unreasonable nighttime fears. It was his dreams that told him that he was in danger of being barred from heaven. Angels with malevolent faces showed up there and heaped scorn on him: "What are you, Raphael Joseph, besides rich and powerful and shrewd? What is that but to plough in the slime of wickedness? You have reaped iniquity; you have eaten the fruit of lies . . ." Raphael bowed his head, knowing that the angels were right. He had done all those things and had taken pleasure in them.

Knowing how tainted his soul was, the saraf bashi often thought of abandoning his responsibilities. He would, he told himself, walk away from the seats of power and the displays of pomp. Dressed in a loincloth and carrying a staff, he would go the long hot way to Jerusalem, where, in a cave on Mount Zion, he would immerse himself in the permanent calm of the Torah. The days and nights would slip away like the grains of sand in the hourglass. He would live, solitary and serene, until the most benign of the nighttime angels would appear at the foot of the straw mat on which he slept. It would be the angel of death beckoning him, and Raphael Joseph would rise and follow him into the cave of forgetfulness, at the other end of which there glowed the Throne.

It was pleasant to have such thoughts. They served his piety and his pragmatism. When he shook himself back to business, he would tell his sons that a man was his acts and not his dreams. The sons, who were unaware that their father had dreams at all, ignored the saying. Meanwhile, the chelebi, the saraf bashi, grew daily richer and more powerful; and devoted more and more of his money to Jewish charities. He founded *yeshivot,* he redeemed Jews who had been sold into slavery; he contributed to the welfare of the Jews of Jerusalem. In his Cairo household, Raphael Joseph entertained more than a score of hungry Talmudists and holy men.

His dinners were lavish affairs, with course upon course of roast, broiled, and boiled meats and fish, mountains of rice and almonds, and wine pouring endlessly into the cups of his guests, who almost never noticed that Raphael Joseph himself hardly touched the food or drink. Only Mikhael, his personal servant, knew that his master subsisted on a handful of roasted peas and a cup of water taken late at night.

Even Mikhael did not know that before Raphael Joseph went to his bed, he removed his stiff embroidered coat of office and his blue and silver robe of silk himself so that no one might see him retightening the bands of the hair shirt that gnawed ceaselessly at his pale, freckled skin.

It was inevitable that Raphael Joseph, lusting for holiness, should have sent for Shabbatai Zevi, the prodigy of illumination. Raphael Joseph had listened carefully to the widespread stories of Shabbatai's beatific wanderings, and for a long time now, it had seemed to him that he could discern in Shabbatai's life a certain thrilling pattern. Shabbatai's clear eyes, his deep learning, his entranced meditations, seemed more than marks of uniqueness. They were, Raphael Joseph had come to believe, possible signs of messianic power.

These were strange, portentous times. Out of the deserts of Arabia there had come the story of a multitude of warriors — Jewish warriors — who were said to be battalions of the lost tribes of Israel. The warriors, according to some reports, were already on the march, moving toward Baghdad, Damascus, and Tyre. Then they would make their way to Constantinople, where, it was prophesied, the Sultan would be toppled from his throne.

And what was one to make of the ship that had been seen off the western coast of Scotland — a ship with scarlet and gold and green sails that moved without wind but to the accompaniment of sweet music? At the ship's mast there flew a purple banner inscribed with the legend THE TWELVE TRIBES OF ISRAEL.

Such things were reported in distant places, but Shabbatai Zevi was before his very eyes. Shabbatai, who could turn the Friday evening blessing of the wine into a miraculous communion. Raphael Joseph had never heard anything like it. Shabbatai made the weekly courtesy to the Creator an occasion for enclosing the world in a web of

163

faith. From one pole of being to another, men, women, beasts, birds, stones, lightning, joined, *and became* the song that issued from his lips.

A man who could do that over a simple cup of wine might well be the Messiah, as some audacious rumors out of Salonika and Smyrna claimed. Raphael Joseph sighed. A hair shirt was not enough; fasts and penances were not enough; gifts for scholars and the Jewish poor were not enough to ensure that the gates of heaven would open to a man who had ploughed in the slime of wickedness. But —

To have been the Messiah's patron on his first coming into the world! Now *that* might be enough. Surely the man who walked with the Messiah as he led the multitude to the gates of heaven, surely Raphael Joseph, true comrade-in-arms of holiness, would be admitted through those gates after the Messiah bade them open. Then, ah, then, the malevolent angels of his dreams would have their mouths stopped once and for all.

Meanwhile, Raphael Joseph, nurturing in secret his suspicions of Shabbatai's true greatness, had had a piece of news. From the Jewish notables of Livorno there had come a series of letters describing the presence in their city of a young woman who claimed to be the destined bride of the Messiah.

Her name was Sarah, and Raphael Joseph, reading the letters, was struck by the note of muffled longing betrayed by the dry rabbinical accounts. Sentence after sentence *almost* described the woman's free behavior. Each time, the writer almost gave details, only to excuse himself from precision at the last moment.

Raphael Joseph, who had a keen memory of the excesses of his own youth in Livorno, smiled. He seemed to be reading an account of Susanna's bathing written by a committee of the spying elders. The prose was like a veil with ragged holes in it, delicately hiding or coarsely revealing the motions of the woman at her bath, even while it expressed horror at the sight of the water lapping at the curve of her breast or the folds of her belly.

She was, the letters said, as bold as she was beautiful. A woman who took her lovers where and when she liked. She had come to Livorno from Paris, but before that she had moved from Amsterdam to Geneva; from there to Brussels and Frankfurt. But everywhere she went, she told the same story: she was not subject to the usual constraints on women, because it was her destiny to be the Messiah's bride. Her loose behavior, she implied, was a preparation for that role.

And therein lay an authentic mystery. Scandals by themselves did not interest the chelebi. But that profligacy might be linked to holiness — that was an idea that gave him pause. For something like it had happened once when the Prophet Hosea had been commanded by God to marry a whore and to beget children of whoredom as preparation for prophesying to a whorish generation.

Raphael Joseph, thinking of the letters from Livorno, which had arrived while Shabbatai was a guest under his roof, could not believe that he was merely in the presence of coincidence. Luck was for ordinary people. It was their easy word for dealing with events too large for their understanding. The chelebi, whose dreams were instructed by angels of the Lord, and who was one of the great pragmatists of his time, discerned at once the outlines of a grand design. He sent for Sarah, who arrived in Cairo in such good time that the old saraf bashi was assured that the winds of heaven were in the sails of the ship that brought her.

Shabbatai, who had not been thinking of marriage, was disconcerted.

He was in mourning for his father and mother, who had died within a month of each other. Shabbatai acknowledged his father's death with the *kaddish*, the prayer for the dead. But his mother's death shook him into discontentment. He examined his face in the mirror and studied it for signs of advancing age, and found them. He was thirty-eight years old, and there were white hairs at his temples. His eyes, which his mother used to tell him were "her" eyes, showed a puffiness in their lower lids, and the feverish light he was accustomed to find in them looked a little less piercing than before. His lips still had their sculptured lines, but there was no question that he was beginning to develop a double chin.

His mother was dead, and he was not yet standing in the midst of glory! What had happened to the youth who had seen, in the mirror, his head surrounded by a nimbus of healing light? He had grown fat at the chelebi's table. Shabbatai, to whom the Patriarchs had spoken, saying, "Shabbatai, Shabbatai, take up your burden. Yours is the task," was in danger of drowning in a mire of baked meats and pastries and expensive wines.

No! He was still the same Shabbatai. Still attentive to the grief of the night birds and the watchman's cry, to the shriek of the Moslem heretic flayed in Baghdad, and the gasps of the children dying in the Ostropol pogrom. The *power* was still in him. He had only to put out his hand, and he could retrace the course of the mightiest river or fill the deepest chasms. If he wished, he could pluck down stars from the skies and put out volcanoes with his spittle.

Now, here was Sarah, the woman from Livorno, who was destined to be the bride of the Messiah.

His bride.

❦ ❦

Shabbatai watched Sarah covertly, wondering what there was to say. Even at the distance that they sat apart, he could feel the warmth that came from her. She was a tall, deep-bosomed, slender woman with thick, arched eyebrows. Her slender, graceful hands were folded in her lap. Shabbatai cleared his throat and searched for the sentence that a bridegroom who might also be the Messiah should speak to his bride. Sarah, who had been looking straight before her, turned slightly in his direction and moved her left hand toward him in the bed. "Hmmmmm," Shabbatai said.

Sarah was silent, but her hand continued its subtle drift toward him.

"My ring," he said, and cleared his throat again. "See."

"Yes," she said, glancing politely at the ring. "I see."

"It's *my* ring. Because the serpent . . . the serpent is my sign." He moved his hand toward her. Sarah looked more closely at the ring, then turned away her eyes. The ring was formed of a snake coiled upon itself, its mouth open, fangs exposed, forked tongue out.

"I hate snakes," she said. "They are evil."

"Yes. You would. You're a woman, and there is enmity between woman and the serpent, because the creature beguiled Eve in the Garden."

"No." Sarah shook her head. "I just hate snakes."

"But mine is the holy serpent. He represents me."

"They live in holes and darkness," she went on. "They are cold to touch. And they don't blink."

Shabbatai regarded Sarah with renewed interest. "The serpent doesn't blink," he said, "because he is beyond surprise."

"He is cold and evil," she insisted, and her warm hand crept closer to Shabbatai's.

"And yet he guards a great treasure. A great mystery."

"He slithers in dry leaves. He swallows mice and takes days to digest them. He spits poison. How can there be a mystery in a snake?"

"I mean God's mystery. And also mine. The serpent's name in Hebrew letters has the same numerical value as those that spell *messiah.*"

The talk was making Sarah uncomfortable. It seemed inappropriate. Yet Shabbatai had a rapt, an inward look, which seemed to reflect a mood that might be dangerous

167

to disturb. She moved her hand closer to his and sought for a dissembling word. Deceit, however, was never one of Sarah's talents, and she found herself saying stubbornly, "I don't care. I hate snakes."

He went on, as if he had not heard, "Of course the serpent is low and cold and evil. But it may be that the Messiah too will have to sink into great depths. The shards of the broken vessels of light have fallen into evil places. The Messiah, who has to gather them up, may have to immerse himself in the most repulsive slime, descending down, down, down into the Abyss, and there fall victim, level after level, to its great temptations. There may be a descent into the darkness in order to achieve the gathering of light."

He seemed to be crooning — no longer speaking to her. But the talk of immersing himself in slime had a whiff of insult in it. Enough, anyway, to make her say, more sharply than she had intended, "Shabbatai! Can you think of nothing better to entertain me with on our wedding night than this talk of abysses and snakes?"

As if she had slapped him, he leaped from the bed and stood with his back pressed against the wall tapestry, as if he wished to turn into one of the lions or acanthus leaves woven in its design. He breathed hard, struggling between bitterness and anger. She was, it now appeared, no more than a woman, despite her warmth and her beauty, despite the reports of her intelligence. He felt a deep weariness, a sense of repetition: bride after bride — Leah, Esther, and now Sarah.

The female. The female. The mist rising from the earth. The yearning of the female for the male. An exigent perfume that poisoned the night with desire. Shabbatai's back ached; his lips were parched. He pressed his hands against the tapestry.

Sarah's first impulse was to be scornful of the man who could leave a bed in which she lay. No one had ever treated her that way. On the other hand, Shabbatai was not just any man, as she had testified by marrying him. She was to confirm him, to define him as the Messiah.

Then Sarah, in her turn, was confused, remembering the hand that dropped from her mouth on the night of the trotting horses. The hand that had turned cold — so cold that the greedy sows had taken it as a signal that they might be as ravenous as they pleased. They had tossed and mouthed it, tearing at the newly stilled flesh. Flesh that had been . . . someone! A hand that had been pressed against her mouth with — what was it? Love? Or anger? A hand that should have caressed, that hurt. That suddenly let go, though she had done nothing to make . . . whom? . . . angry . . .

She shivered as if, here in midsummer Cairo, she were suffering from the cold. Shabbatai stood against the wall like a man caught in the flare of a torch. Sarah left the bed, and filling a cup with water, took it to Shabbatai.

For a wonder, he took it and drank thirstily. As he drank, he breathed in also Sarah's fragrant breath. When the cup was empty, Sarah took it from him and set it on the bedside tray. "Shabbatai," she said. "Shabbatai." She pressed her lips to his forehead and put her hand to his cheek, his chin. He felt her touch, as if rose petals had blown against his skin. Her hand was in the hair over his ear, on the side of his neck; then it pressed firmly, warmly on his shoulder. "Shabbatai. Ah, Shabbatai." Gently, she led him back to bed.

"Shabbatai," she said, and pressed him against the silken cushions. He sighed, and slowly his rigid body relaxed. Sarah, still stroking his face, put her left arm around him and brought him into her embrace, his head on her breast.

He was thirty-eight years old, and it was once again his wedding night. Looking into his eyes, she saw the glitter of what might be fever or fear or terrified desire. With one hand, she slipped her gown off her shoulder so that Shabbatai's cheek touched her naked breast. Then she sang.

169

"And what shall we eat when the Messiah comes?" she sang, her voice a clear tremolo. "The behemoth and the messiah-ox." The great creatures would turn on a spit, and all who were hungry would need only to put out their hands, and the roast flesh would leap to their fingers.

"And what shall we drink when the Messiah comes?" she crooned, rocking Shabbatai, as her song told him that there would be a river of wine flowing through the Kishinev market square, and for the children, a river of honey.

It would be a great day in Kishinev, when the Messiah came. The Jews of all the world would be there. There would be music played by angels; King David himself would lead their songs. There would be dancing and holy drunkenness. Endless rejoicing, embracing. There would be trees on which roasted almonds grew, and wells in which cherry brandy sparkled.

The song ended on a lullaby note:

> *Sleep, my child, and do not wake me,*
> *Sleep, my child, he'll soon be here.*
> *Close your eyes and the Messiah*
> *Will come to wipe away your tear.*

In Sarah's arms, Shabbatai, if not exactly asleep, was nevertheless supremely tranquil. She rocked him a while longer, and they both forgot it was their wedding night, lulled by the music and their warmth into a middle space of hushed affection. Then Shabbatai stirred and turned in Sarah's arms and touched his hand to her lips.

She shuddered, and it was her turn to grow rigid. She leaned away from him; her hand against his shoulder bit into it like a claw. Looking into her eyes, he was in time to see the light of intelligence fading from them. He sat up. "What's the matter?" he asked. "Whatever's wrong?" He had taken his hand from her lips, and now she caught it and pressed it to them again. When he tried to pull it away, she resisted, crying, "No, no!"

"There," he said. There's nothing to be afraid of."

Tears sprang to her eyes, and there came again her muffled "No, no."

He put his free arm around her shoulder. "There," he said, "I'm holding you. Whatever it is, it will soon go away. There . . ."

"I hear them," she whispered, hunching over in the bed, her long hair strewn across her shoulders and in her lap. "I hear them. The horses. Always, the horses."

"No," he replied. "No, no, Sarah. No." He patted her shoulder and repeated her name and wondered why her mysterious fear was starting a surge of love in him. She was Sarah. His Sarah. Not the profligate whom the letters from Livorno spoke of. Sarah. Frightened, pale, bowed. "Hush," he said. "Hush."

At last she sobbed against him. Between her tears and his caresses, he got from her the story of the horses and the men. The shouting and the shooting. The clinking of harness gear, the smell of the sows, and the hand pressed against her mouth . . .

"Sarah." His lips were at her ear. He caressed her hair. When she turned in his arms, he enfolded her like a child, cradling and cuddling her. Then, to make her close her eyes, he sang to her. The song of Meliselda bathing.

> As I rode down a winding way,
>   Down through a valley winding,
> I chanced on Meliselda there,
>   Her dark long hair unbinding . . .
>
> I combed her hair, I kissed her lips,
>   I whispered love and wonder,
> But when I bent to kiss her breasts,
>   The sky grew dark with thunder.

When he was done, Shabbatai sat, afraid to move. In an almost inaudible whisper, he said, "Now, Sarah. You sing."

She rubbed her face against his chest and sang again the lullaby of the Messiah in the market square of Kishinev.

171

The song of the rivers of wine and honey; then he sang of Meliselda's unbound hair. She sang of Jews dancing in their Sabbath clothes, and he sang of Meliselda bathing. Stanza by stanza, they sang toward each other, and Sarah's fingers found occasion between her singing to unloosen the cord of her robe. Then Shabbatai sang; then Sarah touched him; and there was no further singing.

Over the room there reigned a silence like a remembered fragrance. For the virgin Shabbatai, and for the endlessly experienced Sarah, the emergence of their ecstasy came stroke by stroke with the crescendo of approaching bells.

19

Gaza
1665

Rabbi Nathan Ashkenazi, also known as Nathan of Gaza, turned his gelding's head toward the desert. Nathan was twenty years old, and nearly ten years had passed since he had watched the scene at the bottom of the tower room, in which Shabbatai Zevi had been beaten by the officers of the Rabbinical Court. In those years, the image of Shabbatai had haunted his dreams and his waking imagination. If the world was indeed a place in which miracles were displayed to the discerning eye, surely Shabbatai's silent scourging had been miraculous. There was a poignant loveliness to the event. The frightened Shabbatai, crying that he could not bear stripes; then Shabbatai leaning against the whitewashed wall, uncannily silent as the cat-o'-nine-tails rose and fell. Shabbatai's naked shoulders receiving blow after blow and, at the thirty-ninth stroke, still clear and white and beautiful as ever. And always, the silence.

Now Shabbatai was coming to Gaza, and Nathan, who had been having disturbing dreams about the visit, was riding into the Negev, toward Jebel Yunis, eight miles away, where the annual Running of the Horses would take place in the midday heat.

The Running of the Horses was an event of the Bedouin Mansouri tribe. Each spring, the Mansouris gathered at the foot of Jebel Yunis, where the young men who felt themselves ready to take their place among the warriors were feasted by their sheikh, Ahmad ibn Mansour. After the great meal, they were sent up to the top of the mountain, from which, at a signal, they sent their horses racing down its craggy slopes. It was a fearful running that lasted less than twenty minutes. Before it was over, it cost the lives or health of animals and men; but the Mansouris held it to be necessary, because it contributed to the tribe's survival by sorting out, in one swift, cruel test, those which were the sure-footed horses and the skillful men.

The Running of the Horses was, properly speaking, not a race. There were no prizes at the foot of the mountain. There were no bets won or lost. All that was required was that man and horse, alive and body-whole, should reach ibn Mansour's camp within the time set for the running. But that required a full-tilt gallop down the trackless mountain. The unskilled, the ill-mounted, or those with otherwise unhappy destinies, died or were crippled. It was too bad. The dead were quickly buried, and the crippled learned to tend sheep and goats and to gather brushwood with the women and boys.

Nathan of Gaza, riding toward the Bedouin encampment, sat straight in his saddle, his heels well down in his stirrups, trying to achieve in his bearing that blend of arrogance, indifference, and equine style for which the Mansouris were famous.

Sheikh ibn Mansour had been incredulous when the young Jew had begged for the privilege of riding with the Mansouris from time to time. The idea of a Gaza Jew on horseback among his warriors had been at first simply amusing. Then, ibn Mansour had been touched by the fierce earnestness with which Nathan urged his request. Later, while the sheikh was still hesitating, the news reached him that Nathan had married the one-eyed daughter of Samuel Lissabona, one of Gaza's wealthiest merchants. In the light of that information, ibn Mansour had seen his way to combining his natural instincts for courtesy with his equally strong sense of cunning, because, while the Mansouris were indeed a warrior tribe, they grazed large flocks of sheep and goats and held scores of oases given over to date palm cultivation. It had never done the Bedouin any harm to have friendly contacts with the important merchants of Gaza. If Samuel Lissabona's son-in-law wanted to risk his neck riding with his warriors, then he should have the chance.

Nathan urged his horse to a trot. He was very frightened, but he was determined to be in the Running of the Horses today. It was his way of putting to God a question about Shabbatai.

Nathan's horse was a spirited animal — a three-year-old chestnut with a honey-colored mane, a gift from ibn Mansour, who understood the investment value of rich presents. Nathan had been riding with the Mansouris since October. On his own, he had run his horse over ever more demanding terrain, racing it across the dunes that stretched for miles south of the scraggly port of Gaza. At night, as a way of training himself and his horse, he had galloped through the jagged, boulder-strewn wadis to the north of the city, and as the horse's hooves sent sparks flying into the night, he had breathed the rushing wind and exulted in himself and his flying animal, whose strength was a gift from God. Nathan, cantering toward Jebel Yunis, prayed that his horse was like the one in the Book of Job, who "mocketh at fear, and is not affrighted . . . He saith among the trumpets, Ha, ha; and he smelleth the battle afar off, the thunder of the captains, and the shouting."

But Nathan was not riding down Jebel Yunis simply to test his courage. He was using the ride as a way to give God an opportunity to clarify a mystery for him. Ever since hearing that Shabbatai Zevi meant to stop in Gaza on his way from Cairo to Jerusalem, Nathan had been troubled by dreams in which Shabbatai seemed *about* to appear, *about* to be saying something of great importance; but always, at the final moment, the dream had collapsed into a mere swirling of golden mist, and Nathan woke with the sense of having missed a crucial message. Nathan, who had for years been receiving instruction in Kabbalah from his personal *maggid,* an angelic tutor, understood that his dreams were inchoate because there was something unclear in *him* that prevented him from reading God's message. Being a practical mystic as well as a passionate horseman, he had determined to ride in the Running of the Horses. His idea was to subject himself to an exhilaration so intense that it would shake his soul loose from its impediments of flesh and bone.

At the foot of Jebel Yunis, the preparations for the ride moved forward. The Mansouri tents were scattered along the flint-strewn flatland at the mountain's base. A score of feasting rugs had been laid end to end before Sheikh Ahmad ibn Mansour's tent, and there the young men, joined by their fathers and uncles, were being feasted. From the other tents, worried women — mothers or sisters or brides-to-be of the riders — brought copper platters of rice, boiled kid, and roast fowl. Nathan, who had been welcomed by ibn Mansour, sat at the place of least honor, at the very end of the long series of rugs. He did not mind. It was enough that the old sheikh had not driven him away; indeed, he had greeted Nathan courteously and had instructed the slaves to put before him a dish on which clean boiled rice, some hardboiled eggs, several flaps of bread, and an assortment of carrots, onions, and cucumbers had been placed — the only foods the Jew was permitted to eat with his Bedouin host.

Ibn Mansour, who had two sons of his own to worry about this morning, had little enthusiasm for speculations about Nathan's motives for being at the running. With a corner of his mind, he respected the Jew's decision. No doubt it was madness for a town Jew to set his life at hazard in a ritual that did not bind him; nevertheless, it was a madness that smacked more than a little of honor.

Nathan ate diffidently and watched the young Mansouris pretending indifference as well as appetite in these final moments before they risked their lives. The fathers, the uncles, the older brothers — the other kinsmen who had survived the Running of the Horses in other years — sat among the candidates and told stories of how *they* had made the ride, what obstacles they had overcome, what tricks of horsemanship had saved their lives. No one painted the running as anything but dreadful. In each tale, the rocks were jagged, the jumps deep and wide, the disasters that overtook the riders ghastly. Nathan, with no kinsman to tell him stories that would teach him what he might need to know, leaned forward to catch snatches of detail from the Bedouin, but it was hopeless. One kinsman urged sharp spurs; another, no spurs at all. Some praised long stirrups; others, Hebron beads tied to the headstall to keep away the evil eye. The secrets and the tricks flew back and forth. The candidates grew paler by the minute.

Sheikh ibn Mansour cleared his throat to give his guests notice that he meant to speak. When they were silent, he said, looking toward the sun, "In two more mouthfuls, it will be time for you to ride up Jebel Yunis. There is little to tell you but this: ride slowly to spare your horses. When you have reached the top of the mountain, you will find my brother Kemal there. With him is the Mullah Suleiman. The mullah will give you his blessing, after which you will take your places in a circle facing the descent. You will wait the time it takes to breathe ten breaths. When you hear the sound of my brother Kemal's musket, you will ride.

"May it be the will of Allah that I see you all again, alive and well and full of honor. Now, two more mouthfuls, and farewell." The old man put a ball of rice into his mouth, and his guests followed suit. After the second mouthful, there was a sudden milling about as the riders scattered to their horses.

Nathan, having no one to embrace, was among the first to be mounted, but he waited to be last among the file of riders. This was the Bedouin's ceremony. It would be wrong for him to be obtrusive. There was a shout, and twenty-two young men moved at a quick trot toward Jebel Yunis.

Jebel Yunis, as a mountain, was an anomaly. It was as if one of the lower peaks of the Sinai had been transplanted here to be the lone example of the Sinai's grimmest manner. It was not particularly high — no more than twenty-five hundred feet — but as a course for horses it was bad enough. The riders making their way to its summit wound in and out among great boulders, which had been, or were still being, cut by springs spurting from overhanging stone lips that looked as if they had been hacked out of the cliffs by frenzied axes. Sometimes the horses had to be ridden up gravel-strewn canyons, where their hooves started slides that could be heard pattering long after the first gravel was disturbed.

Nathan, trailing the Bedouin, had never seen anything so somber. Rocks as high as tall trees cast their shadows into chasms. Occasionally a horse whinnied and reared in protest against a snake winding its way across the track. As the men rode higher, a cool wind began to blow. What with the shadows and the wind, and the now-evident danger of the mountain, each man grew solemn. Voices died away, and in a little while there was nothing to be heard except the patient clicking of horses' hooves over rock. Nathan's heart failed when he considered that soon he, along with twenty-one honor-crazed Bedouin, must come rushing down these turns and twists of stone. He swallowed and leaned forward to make his horse's way a little easier.

After an hour and a half of steady upward winding, Mustapha, the older of Sheikh Ahmad ibn Mansour's sons, who was leading the column, passed under two pillar-shaped stones leaning into each other. There was a cry as the first of a flock of vultures took to the air. There were more than a dozen of the birds, their voices like the rattling of sticks against a wooden fence. They wheeled and uttered their cries of rage as if they meant to be avenged that minute for an affront against their rotten dignity. Nathan, passing his tongue across his teeth, discovered a scummy new taste of fear.

Then they were at the summit, standing in a wind-swept space that was as gently round as a bald man's head. There, as Sheikh ibn Mansour had promised, Kemal Mansour and the Mullah Suleiman waited. Mansour, on a quiet gray horse, sat with the hood of his burnous pulled well over his head. In his right hand, he held a musket with a silver-mounted stock. Mullah Suleiman, in a purple turban and a fine black robe, sat on a gaunt white mare.

When the riders were all in the open space, the mullah made a sweep of his arm to indicate that they should form a circle around him. There was a final noise of whinnying, the jangle of stirrups, and the ringing of bridle bells, then an intense silence. The mullah closed his eyes, then opened them. Spreading his arms and turning in a circle as he spoke, he called, "Listen. Listen, my brothers. Listen to this tale and know it is meant for you. The tale of Shaytan, the deceiver of mankind and of God.

"The story is told that the enemy of man, Shaytan, the dark accuser, who is permitted on this earth to seek the destruction of mankind, came one day before Allah, the Lord our God, where he sits among the myrtle trees in paradise with the Prophet Mohammed on His right hand, and on on His left, holy Adam and the Patriarchs.

" 'Allah il Allah,' said Shaytan. 'O Lord, Thou art God . . .'

" 'Shaytan,' the Lord replied. 'Why have you come?'

" 'To indict Your justice, Lord. To complain of my ill treatment.'

"Patiently, the Lord replied, 'How are you mistreated, Shaytan, say.'

" 'See. Ah, see,' the wicked Shaytan said. 'See how all of heaven sneers at me. On your right hand there stands the Prophet Mohammed; on your left is Adam. It is not justice, Lord. Adam stands where I should be.'

" 'Why?' inquired the Lord. 'Say why you should stand in Adam's place.'

" 'Because the substance of which you formed Adam is merely clay, but mine is fire. Fire must have precedence over clay. It is simple justice.'

" 'Fool,' the Lord replied. 'Ah, wicked, wicked fool. Have you learned so little during all these years? Know, Shaytan . . .' and the sound of the Lord's anger made all of heaven tremble, 'know that I, and I alone, determine who is made of fire and who of clay. Begone, fool. The judgment is mine.' There was the sound of thunder; Eden grew dark; and Shaytan, the accuser, went away, ashamed.

"There you have the tale, my brothers. A tale meant for you. Now turn your horses toward the descent. Allah . . . Allah, and not you, will determine which of you is made of fire and which of clay. May He be good to you."

The horses were turned. There was a wait. Overhead the vultures renewed their cries. Then a musket shot and a wild halloo.

Nathan drove in his spurs, his horse leaped, and there was the sound of hooves striking stone — and they were off, sliding, scrambling, racing. Nathan prayed and kept his heels down and his eyes fixed open, as in a trance. Sometimes he saw the passing world; sometimes he did not. Once he was aware that his horse had flung itself across a wide chasm. He opened his mouth to scream, but before he could utter a sound, he was on the other side, the wind in his ears. Sometimes, at his right or left, he heard the shriek of a horse or a man as hooves skidded on wet rock and something broke — a horse's neck . . . a rider's back. Nathan kept his reins a little above the pommel of his saddle and his heels down. Through the tears streaming from his eyes, he tried to find the least slippery, the least jagged way, but it did no good. Whichever way he turned his horse's head, there was a stream through which to plunge, a teetering boulder to leap over, a shale-filled wadi to scramble through. Once, a rock as large as a man's head, dislodged by another rider, came flying toward him. Nathan crouched and twisted and heard the rock clattering against a boulder on his left.

Fire or clay. Keep your heels down. Trust in God. Words that were not skittering gravel or spilled riders, their heads split open, lying between two rocks; or legs snapped, the white bones exposed, and faces, carved into tortured masks, to ride by. Fire and clay were not sweat and breathlessness, and flying stones that cut his temple, and the cramping muscles in his arms as he tried to hold the reins loosely enough to give the horse freedom of motion but tightly enough to guide it down its way. Clay or fire, and phlegm in his throat, and a permanently held breath, and his horse panting in the wind, and the clattering and the skidding and another leap, and the smell of hell as hooves struck fire out of the stones.

Nathan rode and turned and gasped. His horse plunged and slid and twisted. Once it stumbled and skidded. Nathan felt the animal's body suddenly disengaged from any contact with the earth as he and it were carried far into space, only to land, still running, on the slope beneath the low cliff over which they had slid.

Then it was warmer. The horse still raced among rocks, but now the ground was leveling off. Nathan sweated and groaned. Then he heard the sound of his horse's hooves striking, not rock, but hard-packed sand. Almost too frightened to believe he had come down alive from Jebel Yunis, Nathan ventured to look to the right. There was the mountain. To his left, a quarter of a mile away, were the tents of the Mansouris. Before him and behind, other riders as grateful as he were beginning, like himself, to take in their reins, to murmur lovingly to their horses, to slow down. Overhead, the vultures were already narrowing the circles of their wheeling — but not for him.

All the way back to Gaza, Nathan sat exhausted in his saddle, feeling a great numbness. After the first moments at the base of Jebel Yunis, when he had been included in the Mansouris' jubilation, there had come the slow return of his more usual reality. Murmuring a respectful phrase or two of thanks to Sheikh ibn Mansour, whose sons had also survived the running, Nathan pleaded pressing business in Gaza and left the camp. Once away from the Bedouin, Nathan felt his mind emptying of memory and sensation. He and his horse seemed to be riding on a gray, somber dish. Mile after mile he rode, aware that sometimes his flesh still quivered, but essentially unconscious of anything but the fact that he was alive. He had no memory of the mountain or of the ride down, beyond the recurrent echo, as from a great distance, of the rattling cry of the vultures.

Approaching the cultivated fields on the outskirts of Gaza, Nathan looked around him. Under a palm tree, near the road, three *fellahin* sat eating their flat bread while a fourth slept on a green hillock near his goats. Still nearer to Gaza, there were the first mud huts of the outlying villages rising from the soil, their walls smoothed by wind and rain. In a heavy spring storm, the huts could turn back into the mud from which they had been formed.

Nathan stirred weakly and tried to remember why he had gone to Jebel Yunis. A donkey, carrying two deep baskets filled with silver fish, trotted toward him, urged on by a boy from Gaza. Nathan, from his saddle, looked over a wall into a lush garden, where a wealthy Arab householder was taking his tea under a fire tree, whose branches made a lewd daub against the cloudless blue of the sky. The fire tree was red; the jacaranda beside it, purple; and the tray beside the merchant was gleaming brass. On the other side of the garden, two acacia trees sent cool whiffs of their golden blossoms into the air. Nathan turned giddy.

When next he was able to see, he was no longer on his horse, but sitting with his back against the garden wall. Above him, there was a blossom-laden branch of the acacia, and he could hear the hum of bees and flies. Before his eyes, though he was looking away from the sun, there was a swirling brightness that was, at first, only part of the vertigo that had assailed him.

Slowly, the swirling took the shape of a throne, whose substance was an unconsuming fire. As Nathan watched, the fire moved, but the throne retained its shape, except that where the headrest had been there now appeared, as if inscribed, fire upon fire, the indistinct letters of a Hebrew word. Nathan found himself panting as the smell of the acacia penetrated his lungs. The fire of the throne and the fire of the letters began to expand. The throne and the letters grew huge, and Nathan could see that the word spelled by the letters was S H A B B A T A I.

Nathan whispered the name and felt how it tasted of acacia. He whispered it again, and the flames that made up the throne moved and shifted, growing more intensely golden. More and more flame detached itself from the throne and played like a whirlpool of light, until it took the shape of Shabbatai himself, who smiled and, with great solemnity, took his place upon the throne, which, until that moment, had seemed impossibly too big for any man.

Shabbatai sat easily on the throne of fire, his name blazing above his burning head. Nathan heard a voice like the one that Moses must have heard beside the burning bush: "Nathan. Nathan, be not afraid. I am the God of thy father, the God of Abraham, the God of Isaac and of Jacob. I have seen the affliction of My people; I have heard their cries, and behold, I send for their salvation him whom My soul loveth, Shabbatai Zevi. Shabbatai Zevi, armed with My spirit, is he who shall slay the dragon; whose curse shall slay the wicked; whose blessing shall restore the good. He is the true Messiah, the Redeemer of Israel. Behold, Nathan. Behold Shabbatai Zevi, in whom I am well pleased."

Nathan watched the throne, the man, and the name. Shabbatai continued to smile, to nod, to raise his hands in benediction. The throne blazed on, but the fiery letters that spelled S H A B B A T A I began to change. In ripples of writhing fire, they merged into each other to form a new and more intensely brilliant word, S H A D D A I, another euphemistic spelling of God's name. Then Nathan heard the voice again: "Shabbatai Zevi is the hammer with which to shape the metal of salvation. Though he be reviled and scorned, yet shall he be greater than the angels."

And there he was, no longer indistinct, as in Nathan's recent dreams, but calmly present, and seated on the *merkabah*, the flaming throne of God, while God's fire played around him and God's voice announced him for what he was. As Nathan reached his hand out toward the vision, it faded.

Nathan got to his feet slowly. The acacia above him smelled as fresh and keen as before. His horse stood quietly grazing at the edge of the nearby ditch. When Nathan mounted, he felt a great sweetness in his mouth. He had ridden down Jebel Yunis as a way of enticing God to clarify his visions. Now they were clear.

He was alive — and Shabbatai Zevi, the Messiah of Israel, was on his way to Gaza. Nathan, approaching the city's gates, put his horse into a canter.

20

Cairo–Gaza–Jericho
1665

"Declare yourself," Sarah said. "The man I married is the Messiah. Declare yourself."

Shabbatai shook his head. Nothing was as it should be. After the wedding night, there came the marriage. After the singing and the perfumed caresses, there was Sarah, tall, unyielding, her fingers playing restlessly along her sides, as if feeling for the pattern in her green and gold silk robe.

Morosely, Shabbatai said, "There is nothing to declare."

"There is. I *married* you. I am your omen. *I* confirm you. Now, declare yourself."

It was so easy for her, thought Shabbatai. She lived in a world all of whose colors and shapes were clear, sharply outlined. Not as with him. Perhaps it was marriage, perhaps it was middle age that blurred experience and shaded horizons to their gray color. In her arms, on their wedding night, he had experienced a resurgence of his old sense of power and had believed that in the morning he would need only to step out on the balcony of their room in Raphael Joseph's house and announce to the multitudes that he, Shabbatai Zevi, the Redeemer of mankind, was in Cairo. After that, the shroud of gloom that dulled the

185

luster of the Creation would be lifted, and there would be joy in the world. But in the morning — and in the weeks since then — it had been quite otherwise. Sarah was swift, deft, reckless, and wanted him to act; he felt slow and vague.

Sarah was so vivid that Shabbatai, for the first time in his life, felt that he was no longer the brightest star in his firmament. It did not matter that he matched her robes, color for color, gold with gold. She moved in a fragrance like one whose garments "smell of myrrh, and aloes, and cassia, out of ivory palaces."

"Declare yourself," she insisted, and Shabbatai, thinking of the taste of her skin above her right shoulder, nerved himself to make the effort. He went and he returned and went again. Often, in the synagogue, remembering the ease with which, as a young man, he had spoken the Shem ha m'foresh, he formed the words with which to announce himself, but though his tongue moved, the declaration remained unspoken.

He asked the chelebi for advice, but Raphael Joseph, his heart under his hair shirt singing to the music of the Immanence that his house was nourishing, only echoed Sarah's words: "Declare yourself, Shabbatai. I have done all I could. You are the Messiah, and she is your bride. Declare yourself. The world is waiting." The saraf bashi's eyes shone.

Still, Shabbatai could not think how it should be done. His perplexity was intensified by the sudden disappearance of dreams from his sleep. Once, his nights had been as theatrical as the Patriarch Jacob's, and Shabbatai had counted on his dreams for portent and for counsel. Now, he slept the stunned sleep of a day laborer, but unlike the workman, he did not wake rested. Instead, he felt the squirming behind his eyes of undreamed dreams, of visions aching to be seen. The pain of undreaming was so intense that Shabbatai would have welcomed the reappearance in his sleep of the children of Na'amah, fluttering their bats' wings, mewing their filthy noises, pressing their women's breasts without nipples against his cheeks. But even his horrors failed him, and his nights stayed as unmemorable and as fitful as his days.

Then, one drizzly Cairo morning in early March, Shabbatai sat, exhausted and headachy, in the House of Study, trying to ignore a conversation between the sexton and the cantor, who seemed not to believe that Shabbatai might be engrossed in the pages of the Mishnah over which he was bent. The sexton was saying, "He is a learned man, this Nathan of Gaza, though still very young. Learned and rich. Oh, rich. He leads a blameless life."

"For a rich man, even that is possible," the skeptical cantor said.

"Before he married Lissabona's daughter, he spent years in the yeshivah, studying with the great Jacob Hagiz in Jerusalem."

"Now, that's more like it," the cantor said. "Hagiz was a scholar after my grandfather's heart."

"And they say," the sexton went on, "that young as Nathan is, he can move through the pages of Kabbalah like a fish through seaweed."

"How old is he?"

"Twenty."

"A Kabbalist at twenty? It's not permitted." It was the wisdom of the rabbis that no man should study Kabbalah until he was in middle life; otherwise, its mysterious twists and turns might drive the unripe scholar mad.

"No rabbi taught him. Nathan of Gaza, they say, is blessed with a *maggid,* an angel of the Lord who comes each day and leads him through the texts."

"No!" said the cantor.

"Yes, not no," the sexton replied.

"No!"

"Yes. Yes. And again yes. Not only that, but because of the maggid, Nathan has acquired a holy gift. Men and women whose souls are sick go to him for help. From

187

Jerusalem, from here in Cairo, from Constantinople. He has only to look into their eyes, and he knows at once which *tikkun,* which penitential gesture, to prescribe for their suffering. They say he gives hard penances."

"Of course. Being a rich man, he does not need to take bribes."

"Scoff if you like, Reb Uriel," the sexton said. "Men like you would drive the Messiah from their doors."

Shabbatai at the table turned over a page in his book.

꘎꘎꘎

Shabbatai left Sarah and Barot'ali in Cairo, in Raphael Joseph's house, and journeyed to Gaza, intending to see Nathan and get from him a tikkun for his soul.

It was early on a hot spring afternoon when he arrived in the dusty city. He found his way to Rabbi Nathan's synagogue, only to learn that the rabbi had ridden that morning into the desert to perform a penitential act. No one knew when he would be back. Shabbatai, whose name was known to the scholars in the House of Study, asked for permission to sit with them so that he might be refreshed with a bit of Torah while he waited. It was a request that could not be denied.

When, at evening time, Nathan still had not returned, Shabbatai, overcome by fatigue, asked the sexton to let him lie down in Nathan's study. His head no sooner touched the wooden bench than he was fast asleep.

He slept deeply, but he was conscious of the presence inside his head of rolling shadows that were not precisely dreams. There was motion and portent behind his eyes; he felt his body bound and unwound. Then he was floating and spinning in the dark, after which he floated to a high, high place, the black tip of a precipice, from which he was dropped . . .

To the sound of an ear-splitting yell that tore him out of his sleep. He staggered to his feet, gasping. Through the open window of the study there streamed the light of a crescent moon. Outside, in the courtyard, the branches of a carob tree waved, and Shabbatai could hear the rustling of its pods. Again there came the dreadful yell, like the sound of a soul tearing at the throat of a body it meant to leave. Shabbatai stumbled about in the half-light until he found the study door. He opened it and moved down the dark corridor that led, as he remembered, to the House of Study. He came to a door beneath which there gleamed a ribbon of light. Shabbatai put his hand on the cool iron handle, pressed down, and wrenched open the heavy door.

He stood, looking down a short flight of stairs that led to the House of Study, in which there now blazed scores of candles. Half a dozen men and a sprinkling of graybeards and youths were drawn up in a respectful half-circle around a lean, tall figure — a young man with a bony face who stood at the foot of the staircase, his arms outstretched, and who now opened his mouth and for the third time uttered a yell. The scholars drew nearer to each other. One of the older men begged softly, "Control yourself, Reb Nathan. You have a guest from Cairo. Reb Shabbatai. Reb Shabbatai Zevi."

Nathan's head jerked toward Shabbatai; then, as if his tongue had been stuffed inside his throat, he choked out his question: "Shabbatai?"

Shabbatai, still falling from the high place of his sleep, had to think before he replied, "I am Shabbatai."

Nathan trembled; his shadow in the candlelight flickered. "Shabbatai Zevi?"

"Yes," Shabbatai answered.

"Then. Then. Then. Oh, Lord God be praised for a true vision. Oh, Lord. Lord. Lord. Lord. Lord. Then . . . then . . . Shabbatai . . . . . THOU ART HE."

Shabbatai, looking into Nathan's entranced eyes, wanted to reach out, to touch the suffering man. He wanted to tell him why he, Shabbatai, had come to Gaza. He wanted to say, Nathan, Nathan. You, who have a maggid to guide you, guide *me*. I am a man deeply troubled. My soul is sick. Bless me, Nathan. Give me, I beg, a tikkun for my soul, for I thirst for peace.

Just then, Nathan leaped, as if the earth had flung him high into the air, as if the floor were a catapult. He fell with a crash among the benches. The frightened scholars huddled away from him, and he lay, his arms and legs flailing, among the volumes of Talmud, among the spilled prayer shawls and *t'filn*. Nathan's body writhed like a dying serpent. His head whipped from side to side; his legs and arms banged against whatever lay nearest. Then he was seized by a great rigidity and lay like a toppled statue while a voice greater than his own, but issuing from his mouth, reverberated through the House of Study: "SHABBATAI ZEVI. THOU ART HE. THOU ART HE. THE ANOINTED OF THE LORD. OF WHOM THE VISION SAID, 'I AM THE LORD THY GOD . . . I HAVE SURELY SEEN THE AFFLICTION OF MY PEOPLE: I HAVE HEARD THEIR CRIES, AND BEHOLD I SHALL SEND FOR THEIR SALVATION HIM WHOM MY SOUL LOVETH, SHABBATAI ZEVI.'

"AND THOU . . . AND THOU . . . AND THOU, SHABBATAI ZEVI, THOU ART HE. HIM WHOM THE SOUL OF THE LORD LOVETH." Nathan's nose was bleeding. His forehead was bruised, his eyes locked open as they had been throughout the Running of the Horses, and still the huge voice poured from him: "SHABBATAI ZEVI, THOU SHALT SLAY THE DRAGON. THOU SHALT PUNISH THE WICKED AND RESTORE THE GOOD. THOU ART HE, THE TRUE MESSIAH, THE REDEEMER OF IS-RAEL."

There was a long silence in the House of Study. Shabbatai stood at the top of the low staircase. From Nathan, there came the smells of sweat and horses; and from no-where at all, Sarah's fragrance — myrrh and aloes and cassia out of ivory palaces. The candlelight blazed up like torches, until the House of Study became a point of in-candescence, and Shabbatai held it in the palm of his radi-ant hand. Nathan lay below, his arm stretched out toward Shabbatai, and Shabbatai felt the power flow into him, filling him. He rocked with the motion of his lungs as they breathed light, and there was light playing in bands around his heart, light behind his eyes, under his fingernails, surging from his heels. He was Adam Kadmon, the creature of light. A fountain, an erupting volcano of illumination. Light everywhere, restless and turbulent. His nostrils, his eyes, were on fire; his hair, his lips, his member. He was alive with light, and it was truly time that he declare himself.

He flung his arms out in an all-embracing gesture. He opened his eyes inside the sphere of brilliance at whose center he stood. He opened his mouth and sang:

> *Lord, Lord, Lord, in Thy name and for Thy sake*
> *And the salvation of Thy people, Israel,*
> *I take up the burden, O Thou Lord of Light.*
>
> *Though my beginning was but small,*
> *Yet in Thy name and for Thy sake*
> *My latter end shall yet be mighty.*
>
> *I will ascend into the heavens,*
> *I will exalt my throne above the stars,*
> *Upon the mountain of the congregation.*
>
> *I will ascend above the clouds,*
> *I will lead the blind in paths they know not,*
> *I will make the darkness light, the crooked straight.*
>
> *Lord, Lord, Lord, in Thy name and for Thy sake*
> *And the salvation of Thy people, Israel,*
> *I take up the burden, O Thou Lord of Light.*

Shabbatai stood and felt himself expanding into the space that the Ein Sof, the Infinite, had once contracted from before there was Creation. There was no House of Study; there was no Gaza. Shabbatai was an infinitely radiating pulse of light, whose waves sought the Infinite in the abandoned space It had created. And Ein Sof, the Infinite, which had been yearning for Shabbatai, sent pulsations toward him in return. There was a moment, infinitely long, supernally radiant, when the waves of yearning met, and they were One — and SHABBATAI.

Nathan had been still while Shabbatai sang. Now, in the silence, he stood. Slowly, slowly, he walked toward the stairway. His clothes were soiled and bloodstained; his face, bruised and scratched. When he reached the foot of the stairs, he knelt before Shabbatai. His palms together, his head bowed, he waited, until, one by one, the Jews in the House of Study emerged from the cluster of fear they had made and joined him, kneeling, their eyes lifted, like his, toward Shabbatai. It was then that Nathan, in the calmer ecstasy of a fulfilled vision, raised his voice in prayer. "Blessed art Thou, O Lord our God, Who has sent us Shabbatai Zevi to redeem Thy people, Israel."

Shabbatai, still engrossed in being the light that streamed from his own eyes, did not hear how every voice in the House of Study spoke a hushed Amen.

❧ ❧

Shabbatai, Nathan, and their donkeys were resting. They were on a rocky shelf cut by wind and water on the slope of a red mountain overlooking the Salt Sea. The afternoon's great heat had begun to relent, and with it some of Shabbatai's irritability.

Nathan watched Shabbatai. For the last three weeks he had lived face to face with the Messiah as the two men made their way from Gaza to Hebron, from Hebron to Jerusalem, and from Jerusalem into the Judean Desert. It had been a grim journey on foot and donkeyback. Shabbatai was an uncomfortable walker, and he hated the smell of donkeys. For every distress of the road, he blamed Nathan. His armpits and loins chafed in the heat. He got specks of dust in his eyes. When they stopped at a roadside teahouse, the Arab waiters did not serve Shabbatai quickly enough. The heat, the dust, the poor food, and awkward service were Nathan's fault. As if, having proclaimed Shabbatai to be the Messiah, Nathan also bore the responsibility

192

to turn the physical world into a more convenient place.

Nathan was patient under the abuse. He had God's word that Shabbatai was the Savior. Surely the pain that Jews had endured over the centuries while they awaited his coming was measured in more dreadful units than those which Nathan suffered as his prophet. It was not written anywhere that the Messiah would be easy to live with. His faith in Shabbatai remained serene.

It was Shabbatai who had reverted to doubt. In Gaza, after the Recognition in the House of Study, he had been content to be adored by the Jews of the city; and as long as respectful worshippers filed by to kiss the hem of his garment or to beg a blessing from the Redeemer of Israel, Shabbatai had made gracious gestures. But when the multitudes were gone and he was left alone with Nathan, Shabbatai collapsed and begged Nathan to undo his prophecy.

Nathan, foreseeing scandal if a doubting Shabbatai stayed in Gaza, had proposed that they make a pilgrimage to the holy places in Hebron, Bethlehem, and Jerusalem. The journey, he argued, would give them both time to think, to confirm their visions. Shabbatai at first resisted the idea, but when Nathan added a retreat into the desert to their itinerary, he consented to go. Both men forbore to say aloud what was on their minds: that Christ had spent forty days in the wilderness, where Satan had offered Him temptations.

Shabbatai had proved a mercurial pilgrim. In Hebron, he had had a series of visions as he stood before the grille in front of the tomb of Abraham. Hebron's Jews would testify that they too, like the Jews of Gaza, had seen Shabbatai's face glowing like the morning sun. And yet, that very night, Nathan had been wakened by Shabbatai shaking him by the shoulders and crying, "Nathan . . . Nathan. If you love me, kill me. Spill me. I am unworthy. Nathan. Nathan. What have you done to me? I am unworthy. A fool. Oh, Nathan, kill me quickly. Kill me now." Nathan wiped the tears from Shabbatai's eyes and patted the older man's shoulders. "Nathan," Shabbatai complained, "I am a mere monster. A creature of Na'amah, formless and hideous. Oh, Nathan, I have swallowed a serpent and am with child by it." Eventually, his terror subsided, and he slept. In the morning, when they resumed their journey, he was as querulous as ever.

Now, resting in the shade of a red rock that was so finely balanced on the slope of the mountain that it looked as if it would tumble at any moment to the Salt Sea, they watched the rays of the setting sun elongate the mountain's shadow into the water. The tethered donkeys, their heads bowed, stood before the entrance to a shallow cave. The weak waves of the Salt Sea, unstirred by any wind, rippled toward the shore. To their left, in the distance toward Jericho, there stretched miles of scoured-out salt basins from which the sea had receded hundreds of years ago. Southward, the copper-colored cliffs marched along its blue metallic shore. Behind them, higher up the slope, the eye could catch occasional glimpses of green — no more than tinges of grass, where the winter rains had stirred up some life. As the sun dropped westward, the sky, which had been pale blue, acquired shades of purple, green, and gray. The heat faded from the desert, and, as evening approached, they could hear, with a new clarity, the sound of the bells on the Bedouin's goats and sheep.

There was a clattering noise. Shabbatai gave a startled shout. Nathan, who had been moving a thorn from one side of his mouth to the other, looked up and said, "It's nothing. Probably a goat." The noise of rattling pebbles had barely subsided when a Bedouin boy, his short stick in one hand, a reed flute and a basket of woven straw in the other, appeared on the path above them. He was followed, almost at once, by his goats in a straggly line. The boy watched the Jews closely, but as they made no hostile gestures, he was prepared to lead his animals past them in silence.

"*Salam alaykum,*" Nathan called. "What have you in the basket, *habibi?*"

The boy stopped. The Jews looked tired and were not armed. "Figs," he said. "My sister brought me figs. They were a present to my father from an uncle who visited Jerusalem two days ago. My father, who lies in a tent on the other side of the ridge, sent my sister with a share of figs for me. I mean to eat them by the pools at En Fashga, where my goats will drink." It was a long speech for him, and the boy stood, breathless.

"Sell me two handfuls of your figs," Nathan said.

"How much will you pay for two handfuls?" the boy asked indifferently, making no move. His goats had stopped and were eyeing the tethered donkeys.

"If the figs are ripe . . ." Nathan began.

"They are ripe."

"If they are whole . . ."

"They are whole."

"And if they are cool . . ."

"They are packed in leaves that have been frequently sprinkled," the boy assured him.

"And *if* your figs are sweet, I will give you two *pruth* for two handfuls."

"Two pruth!" The boy laughed scornfully. "Two pruth for figs my uncle carried two days' journey from Jerusalem? That my sister carried for two hours from my father's tent? That I myself have carried for this hour? Ah, Yahoudi, Yahoudi, my father's son is no man's idiot. Farewell."

"Then tell me, wise son of a wise father, how much two handfuls of your figs are worth."

"For you, because you are travelers and weary, I will sell two handfuls of my figs for six pruth."

"Buy them," Shabbatai urged softly. "Buy them."

"Six pruth?" Nathan was indignant. "For six pruth I can buy a basket of the coolest, ripest figs in Jerusalem."

"But not in the desert beside the Salt Sea," the boy said merrily and turned as if to go.

195

"That is well said," Nathan conceded. "I will give you four pruth, because you are so wise a youth."

It was the boy's turn to bend a little. "Give me six and you may milk a nanny over your figs into the bargain."

"Buy them. Buy them," came Shabbatai's whisper.

"Five, and it is done," Nathan said.

"Five it is." The boy laughed. He squatted before the Jews and opened his basket. Shabbatai reached both hands toward the figs. "No," the boy said sharply. "One handful for you. One for him."

Shabbatai grumbled. Nathan rose, went to his tethered donkey, and brought back two gourd bowls from the baggage on its back. He handed one to Shabbatai. "Which of your nannies shall we honor?"

"Your money first, my lord." the boy said.

"Ah, yes." Nathan counted five pruth into the boy's tough palm. Shabbatai scooped a handful of figs into his bowl; Nathan, less eagerly, followed suit. The boy closed his basket, turned and caught a black-headed nanny by the horns, and brought her to Nathan, who set Shabbatai's bowl under her and pulled at her teats. When the second bowl had been filled, the boy walked off, followed by his goats. At the turn of the path, he called back, "You are in a bad place to camp. Late at night, there will be hyenas. Very late, there is a lion. You will do better down below, beside the pools at En Fashga, where the smell of man is always strong." Then he was gone.

Shabbatai was already poking at the figs, which bobbed in his bowl, making green islands. "I love ripe figs," he said.

✷✷✷

The stars were out, and there would soon be a full moon edging its way over the mountains on the other side of the Salt Sea. Nathan and Shabbatai, taking the boy's advice, had moved their camp to a pool made by a series of freshwater rivulets that tumbled out of the mountainside to

196

wind among the rocks until they spilled themselves into the Salt Sea. Off to the south, a newly freshened breeze stirred the dense, high reeds in the nearby marsh. Northward, as the shore curved, they could see the lamplight flickering in the sparsely scattered huts on the hills near Jericho. The air was cool; the western sky still held fading streaks of the sun's fire. The Salt Sea, in which no life could live, shimmered as if it were not deadly.

Shabbatai, in a contented mood, was telling Nathan stories of his childhood and youth in Smyrna. Nathan listened, wondering at the change that had come over him. It was wonderful what a dish of figs could do. Shabbatai had cut at them with the edge of his spoon, then pressed them down, spilling their seed-laden syrup into the pungent goat's milk. When the figs were gone, he had tilted the bowl and taken slow, languorous sips of sweetened milk, swirling them about in his mouth. Now he leaned against a donkey's saddle, feeling relaxed and easy.

He was telling Nathan the story of his night walk up the mountain in Smyrna with Barot'ali. "It was the first time that I ever had a prophetic dream. I woke from it to find my mother and my grandmother beside my bed. Later I went back to sleep, and woke a second time. I left my bed and went outside to find whether the waking world was as dreadful as the one I had dreamed. The dream had been awful. Everything was wet and dark. Even the weather was in pain. The trees seemed to have no skins, and when the wind moved their branches, or a dragonfly walked across their trunks, they winced.

"When I got out into the street, I remembered that a serpent had stolen the rooster's voice and the world would stay dark unless I could find some remedy. It was up to me to save the sun. And Barot'ali, an idiot, taught me, though it first cost me my only sesame cake. 'Crow,' he said. 'Stand on your toes, open your mouth, flap your wings, and crow.' And I did as he told me. I crowed . . .

and the sun rose, and . . . and . . ." He stopped in confusion.

"Yes," Nathan said, and waited. The two men sat watching the full moon rise above the eastern shore of the Salt Sea. It made a glistening yellow streak across the water.

Shabbatai took Nathan's hand. "In Gaza," he said, "in your House of Study, I felt myself to be the center of a sphere of light. I was Adam Kadmon, with the fires of all the suns streaming from my eyes." Shabbatai's voice quivered. "Nathan! It isn't true, is it? None of it is true. Neither your vision nor mine. We are two madmen, mutually deluded."

From the slope of the mountain behind them, from the place where they had made their first camp, there came the cough and then the roar of a lion. A tentative, inquiring roar. A branch of thorn crackled in the fire and sent sparks flying out of the circle of its light. Nathan said, "You are Shabbatai Zevi, whom the Lord God has promised Israel as its Redeemer."

Shabbatai shook his head, rocking back and forth as if he were making a contentious prayer. "No. No. I am a clever Talmudist. An unhappy dreamer." On the mountainside, the lion roared. Nathan got to his feet and brought more thornwood to the fire. The hobbled donkeys shifted uneasily.

"You are the true Messiah, Shabbatai," he said.

"Nathan." Shabbatai groaned. "Ah, Nathan, even if it were true, who would believe it?"

"The world will believe it, as now they believe it in Gaza."

"I am nothing. I am no one. The Messiah, when he comes, will have authority."

Nathan stood. "You will have authority," he said, and left the circle of the firelight, only to return at once.

Shabbatai, his head bowed, spoke as to himself: "I am too soft, too vague, too weak. Where would I get authority?"

"From me," Nathan replied. "From me." Shabbatai lifted his eyes. Nathan stood above him at the edge of the fire, holding a rainbow-colored vial of glass. As Shabbatai made a movement of protest, Nathan tilted the vial. Shabbatai felt the sweat break out on his forehead, in his groin, under his arms. Then there was only the sensation of the fragrant oil creeping through his hair, down his temples, into his beard. As the oil trickled down the sides of his nose, into the corners of his mouth, there came, from high up on the mountain, the lion's final roar.

"Nathan!" Shabbatai wept. "In God's name, what have you done?"

"In the name of God, Shabbatai Zevi, I have anointed you King of the Jews."

※※※

Shabbatai woke frequently all the rest of that night.

Each time he woke warily, only to find, when he searched with his fingers, that the oil of anointment was still there. It had moved down his neck and inside his caftan and had made a sticky trail along his side. Each time he woke, the stars were still in the sky.

The King. He was the King of the Jews. Three paces away there slept Nathan the Prophet, curled into a tight ball, sleeping with the intensity of a child who has ministered to God.

The King. Shabbatai Zevi, the King of the Jews. The world was round and fragile; its waters sparkled; its deserts were dun; its winds howled. He was Shabbatai Zevi, who would lead a suffering people to stand before the throne of God.

The King. He was the King of the Jews.

※※※

In the morning, when Nathan woke, he took Shabbatai by the hand and led him to a grotto near the shore, where the trapped waters of a brook had made a pool. There, he removed Shabbatai's clothes and washed him in the cold, sweet water. Shabbatai submitted to Nathan's care in silence, but when he was dressed in clean clothes, he asked, "Is it true, Nathan? Is it true?"

"It's true," Nathan said brusquely. "It's true. Thou art he."

Shabbatai smiled, faced the east, and put out his arms to bless the day. There was a haze of dust, stirred by a stiff morning breeze, rising over the water. In the early light, the reeds in the nearby salt marsh gave off a silver glimmer. The cliffs behind them were red. The desert to the west and south was a cruel and scarred terrain, yet Shabbatai was pleased with it. There was a heretical idea abroad somewhere in the world that God Himself had been born in such a desert at the collision point of four great winds. It was a lovely notion.

Later that morning, when the sun's heat was on the desert, the world looked malevolent once more. The copper-colored cliffs glowered; the white, scoured basins along the shore of the Salt Sea seemed to leach light from the air. The water of the sea had the blue opacity of an old man's eyes.

It was a poisoned sea, which, though it swelled with motion, made no true waves. A nearly soundless sea, with a foam-scummed shore. The nearby hills and valleys looked bruised, not carved, out of a heat-cracked soil.

Looking down, Shabbatai was cheered by a fresh-water rivulet that flowed from him toward the Salt Sea. He followed it, engrossed by its brightness. It was living water, sweet and clear. It rippled over pebbles, turned and twisted among rocks. A good-humored rivulet, scurrying, hastening, teasing.

To the very last, it kept its healthful look, even as it spilled into the dead waters. To the last, the rivulet supported life — moss at its banks, water spiders hurrying across pools, tiny fish darting from rock to rock in alert, swift schools. Even when it entered the poisoned waters, the rivulet was a visible current for half a dozen yards more. The fish continued to play in it, until, at a mysterious distance from shore, they turned and hurried upstream for their lives.

Yet, to the eye, it was still the same rivulet that had come tumbling out of the rocks of the grotto. But the eye was a poor judge of purity, Shabbatai discovered, because when he bent to taste the water in the current, he started up, spitting and gagging.

As Shabbatai joined Nathan beside the packed, unhobbled donkeys, he felt impatient with himself. He was no longer young and should not have been surprised to learn what everybody knew: that the only way to tell the dead from the living water was to bend and drink.

21

❧

Smyrna
December, 1665

The Turkish fisherman displayed his catch — sturgeon, sea bass, and flounder — in three red tubs tilted on their sides so that the sun would catch the silver of the fish and make them dazzle. Itzhak ben Shimon, the hide dealer's son, who had just paid for a flounder and sent his servant home with it, was still arguing respectfully with Samuel Pena, the plump, rosy-cheeked merchant who could not make up his mind between sea bass and flounder. He walked from tub to tub, trying to choose at the same time as he attended to his quarrel. Samuel Pena was usually a good-humored man, but the very mention of Shabbatai Zevi soured his digestion. The quarrel with young Itzhak was more complicated still because Itzhak, heir to a prosperous business in hides, was a bachelor, who had lately taken what the attentive women in Pena's household had reported to be a decided interest in the older of Pena's two unmarried daughters.

Pena walked between the tubs, and Itzhak waited. There was the smell of salt water and sun-warmed wood in the air, mixed with the odor of fish frying in a shallow pan tended by a boy who sold a plateful of smelt with a round of bread for a copper. There were two old trawlers, their rigging bare, moored to the dock, and a galleass, its striped red and black sails now furled, bobbed in the water. Samuel Pena, unable to make up his mind, stopped midway between the sea bass and the flounder. "No, no. You'll never convince me. He's Mordekhai Zevi's son. A poultry dealer's boy . . ." Pena cleared his throat and smoothed his capacious belly so that he could speak with more authority. "The thing is a charade. Shabbatai Zevi the Messiah! A wide-eyed nothing of a boy who used to hide among the linen bales. A poultry dealer's son. Shabbatai of the strange acts, whom the rabbis sent packing for blasphemy. No. For the time being, it's only unreasonable. If he persists — if the Smyrna Jews persist in their folly — it will turn wicked."

"What *you* say borders on blasphemy," Itzhak said gently.

"Blasphemy? I? Never," Pena huffed.

"Yes. Because you limit God's power. Why may not the Messiah be the nearest beggar, if God wills?"

"Ah, yes," Pena conceded. "You are clever, but not as clever as the rabbis of Jerusalem, who have written letters warning us against Shabbatai." Pena turned impatiently to consider the sea bass and the flounder.

Itzhak ben Shimon was thirty years old. In the years that had passed since Shabbatai had kissed him at the conclusion of the whirling exercise on the beach, Itzhak had grown into a handsome man. Though only a little past ordinary height, he had a supple look to him. His hair was nearly inky black, tightly curled, and framed a lively face. His eyes were pale blue, his lips soft and full. When he remembered the way Shabbatai had kissed him long ago, Itzhak experienced again the surge of ecstasy that had overwhelmed him on that occasion. It had been a blessed moment, cold and intense, with the sea lapping at his neck and shoulders, and dizziness fading from his eyes. "You . . ." Itzhak had murmured. "You are the celestial lion. No one but you."

And Itzhak had been proved right after all. Shabbatai,

whom the rabbis had exiled and reviled, had returned to Smyrna in triumph. He was Shabbatai Zevi, the Anointed of the Lord, the Messiah, and the King of the Jews.

And he had remembered the kiss of his first disciple fifteen years ago! Itzhak closed his eyes, feeling again that joy. Shabbatai had come, and, overlooking the claims of richer, more powerful disciples, he had gone directly to Itzhak's house. He had given him the kiss of brotherhood and had accepted Itzhak's home to be the seat of his court while he stayed in Smyrna. More! He had designated Itzhak as one of his chief disciples and entrusted to him the management of his busy life. Itzhak saw to it that the Messiah and his bride and his idiot servant were properly cared for. Itzhak arranged the visits of important guests, and stored or sold the gifts they brought. Shabbatai, moved by Itzhak's indefatigable service, promised the younger man a kingdom on the day when he, Shabbatai, would divide the world among his favored disciples.

"A fool," Samuel Pena was growling, "a scoundrel, a charlatan, a blasphemer, and a madman . . . Oh . . . oh . . . I have seen him at work. He turns cities upside down. The Jews in Aleppo gave away their gold. The Jews of Gaza have turned into praying machines. God help Smyrna, now that this rush-light Shabbatai is here."

"He has come in the Lord's good time," Itzhak murmured. His tone caught the distracted Pena's attention. Leaning forward, he looked into the young man's intensely blue eyes. "Itzhak ben Shimon? You . . . you . . . are one of the . . . madmen?"

"May all the world be affected by my madness." Itzhak smiled. Slowly, Samuel Pena understood that his older daughter's marriage prospects were fading away before him. He turned and signaled to the Turkish fisherman. His mind was made up; he would buy the largest of the sea bass. The Turk smiled and sprinkled fresh water on his dazzling fish.

✤✤

They sat around a table under the boxed lemon trees on Itzhak's terrace overlooking the Aegean. Shabbatai nibbled from a bowl of nougats; Sarah sipped from her cup of tea. Itzhak, still thrilled by his good fortune, and unsure whether he had a right to be any closer, sat at a measured distance from the Messiah. Barot'ali, the idiot, slept under a stone bench shaded by a laurel bush near the garden wall, and snorted at the attentions of a hovering fly.

"He writes me reasons," Shabbatai complained. "He must write his letters from Gaza. He is busy announcing me to the world."

Sarah, her voice level, said, "He will always be too busy."

"That's a lie," Shabbatai snapped. "What do you know of Nathan? He promised to come. And he will. Write to him, Itzhak. Say that . . . I *need* him."

"I have written. He writes me what he writes you: he is busy with his letters to the world."

"I need him . . ." Shabbatai protested.

"No," Sarah said. "He is nothing to you. He never was."

"He recognized me. He proclaimed me . . ."

"I recognized you . . ."

"If it comes to that," Itzhak ventured, "I recognized you, Shabbatai. Long ago."

"Yes! Yes! And between you, I remained an unknown, dreaming, wandering rabbi. The crazy Smyrna rabbi, the pious fool. I know what I was . . . and what Nathan made me."

Sarah put down her cup impatiently, then looked away. Itzhak studied her through veiled eyes. She amazed him. She was so dark-haired, so quick. When she moved, she pushed the glossy strands of her hair from her eyes as if she were throwing them away. Her eyes searched people's faces swiftly, intently. And when her eyes failed to understand something, she touched or smelled or tasted it. Itzhak had seen her put her tongue to a sword blade so that she could, by means of its taste, understand its function.

She was sensual, richly colored, swift. And difficult to

205

know. He had seen her in Joseph Zevi's house one afternoon, sitting among the women — sewing, weaving, drumming her fingers on the table. Joseph, Shabbatai's younger brother, had a wife, Rachel, who had taken a fever when her son was three months old. Rachel recovered from her illness, but found that her milk had dried out. She was, that day, complaining of her problem to the women.

Sarah, ignoring Joseph's presence, rose from her seat and took the baby in her arms. "Poor thing," she whispered. "Poor baby. Let's see what I can do." Tearing open her bodice, she pressed the child's mouth to her breast. The baby nuzzled toward her nipple and found it, held it, and sucked intently while over Sarah's face there passed an expression of contentment. She stood, her eyes closed, rocking and crooning, as if she and the child were the only two creatures in the world. Then the child, pulling at a dry teat, squirmed and gasped and howled, its head twisting back and forth. But Sarah would not be cheated of her happiness and tried to keep the protesting mouth around her nipple by main force. The infant shrieked and squawled, kicked and howled, until Sarah, waking from her daze, looked down and saw what she was doing. She shuddered and contritely released the child to its mother, saying, "Take him. I am as dry as you. I thought . . ." Then, seeing Itzhak, she said, "I thought . . . the wife of the Messiah . . . I don't know what I thought." A moment later, she had entirely recovered her poise.

Sarah puzzled Itzhak, but more than that, she frightened him. If he stood too near her, he conceived intolerable images of her body under her clothes. His mouth turned dry, his throat ached, and he felt himself yielding to an impulse to bend over her and, in some way he could not imagine, drink her fragrance or her breath.

Shabbatai had left the table and stood at the edge of the terrace, looking out to sea. "Do something, Itzhak. Get Nathan here. I don't care what you tell him. Make him come."

"Is it Nathan whom the crowds follow?" Sarah asked scornfully. "Or is it you? In Aleppo, when the Jews tore your clothing for relics, was it Nathan they called for? In Damascus, when the women spoke in tongues, the name they cried was 'Shabbatai! Shabbatai!' Not 'Nathan!' The triumph is your own. You are the Messiah. Why do you need Nathan, who sits in Gaza spilling ink?"

"Because," Shabbatai began, "because . . ."

He was interrupted by Aryeh, Itzhak's servant, who hurried out to whisper something in his master's ear. Itzhak excused himself and went into the house, from which, a moment later, he returned, leading a palsied old man. "Shabbatai," Itzhak began. He looked pale. "Here is Rabbi Gamaliel, whom you remember . . . ?"

"Rabbi Gamaliel!" Shabbatai said warmly, resuming his public manner. "How could I forget Rabbi Gamaliel, the sniffing rabbi." He smiled and took the old man's left hand, tactfully avoiding the right, which quivered too hard to be held.

"He brings important news, Shabbatai," Itzhak said, as he seated the rabbi. "Frightening news."

"Itzhak," Shabbatai chided. "What is there to fear when the Lord's Anointed is in your house?"

"Shabbatai . . ." panted Rabbi Gamaliel. "Ah, these are wicked times. Bad. Bad. And worst of all in Smyrna. And yet" — the tears came to his eyes — "and yet, I remember . . ." He looked about him, trying to focus the faces he saw, but they stayed misty. Then he remembered what it was that had started the tears, and that Shabbatai was before him. "Yes . . . yes . . . there were other days in Smyrna, once. You remember, Shabbatai? It was in the *mikveh*, in the ritual bath. And you were young, and I was . . . younger than I am. They said . . . this boy's father, may he rest in peace, swore you were a wizard. But I stood beside you, Shabbatai, and I smelled you . . . And you smelled good. I stood there. I did, and there were no evil thoughts, as I was told there would be. You smelled good. As if" — and the old man wept — "as if fresh flowers were passing by . . . Oh, Shabbatai. And now the rabbis . . . the rabbis . . ."

"What about the rabbis?" Shabbatai demanded.

"There were . . . Last night . . . certain rich men and the rabbis met. Ah, Shabbatai, when I remember that smell . . . And you stood there, so young and clean, and did not scorn me for my foolish duty . . ."

Coldly, Sarah interposed, "What happened last night?"

Rabbi Gamaliel shivered. "I said that you were blessed, and you replied that I might be blessed as well. Do you remember, Shabbatai? So you see. I had to come . . . I couldn't let them do it. I had to warn you."

"About what?" Shabbatai asked, restraining his impatience.

The palsied right hand shook still harder, and Gamaliel clasped it with his left but was unable to still its motion. "They say . . . It's because they're afraid. They say . . . they say . . . they want quiet . . . the rabbis want quiet in the synagogues; the merchants, quiet in the bazaars. And so . . ." With his palsied hand he failed to wipe the tears from his eyes.

"And so?" Itzhak encouraged.

Sarah stood and faced the wondering men. "It's clear enough," she said. "They've hired an assassin."

Old Gamaliel stopped sobbing and looked at her, as if he were peering through the mists in his own eyes. "How did you know?" he wondered. Turning to Shabbatai, he asked, "How did she know?"

Barot'ali, under his stone bench, sneezed and woke and called out, "Shabbatai?"

Shabbatai, his face gone ashen, nevertheless bent to scratch the idiot's pate. "I am here," he said. "Now, hush."

22

Peter Harleigh, in Smyrna,
to Nicholas Tyrell, in London
December, 1665

. . . impossible to believe that one has learned from his mistakes. It is only that with the passage of the years, the sense of surprise with which we used to meet our errors is blunted, creating the illusion of less pain.

It did no earthly good, Tyrell, my flight from Shabbatai. My five-year absence is as if it had not been, though I had you and all of England to console and to beguile me.

For a quiet space, I lived away from the tumultuous empire of the Turks. Away from their *pilaffs* and perfumes, their moustaches, their turbans, and their endless conniving. Away from the busy swarming of the Jews. Away from Shabbatai.

Then why, Nick, did I leave England, where there is honest beef and mutton, to come back to this sun-broiled stink-hole of the universe, where lamb is old goat served small, and friendship is a wily arrangement between dishonourable men?

Again, Shabbatai.

I wish you had spared me the news of my father's death — and yet . . . it was your duty. I thank you for your brevity and for your words of consolation. I take it, from your silence, that my father sent no words of counsel or farewell to his only son.

It matters not. I am a very genius at molesting memories. Ah, yes. Shabbatai.

He has fearfully prospered in the years that I was gone. He is a new Shabbatai, always in the public eye. He commands, he sings, he prays and fasts and bathes surrounded by adoring multitudes. The soft, frequently uncertain man of theatrical temper I left behind has hardened into a new mould. Gone are his questioning looks to see if he has played well his bit of staging. He strides where he once walked. When he speaks, it is with the voice of one used to thundering out of whirlwinds. All of Smyrna, nay, all of Jewry, is in turmoil because of him.

Yet all is not well with him, Tyrell. He is ablaze indeed, yet were I his physician, I should be troubled for his health, but whether of the body or the soul I should be hard put to say. There is in his eyes the light of some barbarous fever, a demonic infection, which, I think, he has confused with the motion in his soul of grace.

This new Shabbatai is wholly the creation of an obscure young Israelite named Nathan Ashkenazi, or, as he signs himself, Nathan of Gaza, from the Egyptian town in which he lives. This Nathan, this stripling — for he is but twenty years old to Shabbatai's thirty-nine (and my forty-five) — seems to have sprung up out of that madman's breeding ground we call the Holy Land. Young as he is, he has set himself up to be the John the Baptist to my Shabbatai's Jesus Christ.

Now how does a dazed African provincial rouse a Jewish world to the coming of its Messiah? Why, Tyrell, he writes. Endlessly, indefatigably. His letters proclaiming Shabbatai's mission flow from Gaza in a torrent. There is hardly a city in Asia or Europe in which Jews live where his letters have not been received. Surely this Mephisto of the inkpot neither eats nor sleeps, but sits chained to a stool and a high desk, on which unroll, mile upon mile, the foolscap on which he writes . . . and writes . . . and writes.

To my English ear, what he says is but sad and paltry stuff, resounding with promises of joy and power, music and feasting, and an end to grief — all in the name of Shabbatai, whom he has designated as the Messiah of the House of David. This is to say that Shabbatai is descended from King David, from whose line, so goes the ancient Jewish prophecy, the true Messiah will emerge. And that Redeemer (whatever we Christians may think) is our Shabbatai, who brings the new Law and the new dispensation. In the belief in Shabbatai no act may be sinful; outside it, there can be no salvation.

Thus, Nathan of Gaza on high matters, but his pen runs as swiftly on the low. To the Jews in the empire of the Turks, Nathan promises that Shabbatai, very soon, will take the Emperor's crown from him. Shabbatai, then, will lead the uncrowned Mehmet the Fourth around on a leash. After a certain time (so prophesies Nathan), Mehmet (like the Anti-Christ in Revelation) will revolt against his bondage, and, with the help of evil spirits, will turn loose wars and bloodshed, death and devastation. There will be a time of weeping and wailing, until Shabbatai, riding a lion, will return from a journey to the River Sambatyon, holding in his hand a seven-headed serpent for a bridle.

Shabbatai's coming will inaugurate the longed-for End of Days, in the course of which he will reunite the ten lost tribes of Israel with their brethren. The new Jewish nation will follow its Messiah to Jerusalem, where the holy Temple, refurbished and shining with crystal and rubies, diamonds and gold, will descend from heaven and take its former place again on Mount Moriah.

Joy, of course, will reign supreme.

Thus, Nathan of Gaza — and so speaks my Shabbatai. If you think such language is all moon-madness, you forget that it is spoken by Jews, to Jews. Who else but Jews could nourish themselves in the desert for forty years on vermin and hoarfrost, then swear the stuff was sent by God and tasted of coriander and honey?

Moon-madness or Jewish madness, I confess myself caressed by the notion of the End of Days. In the sound of those words, the world's real danger seems to be enclosed in a compelling loveliness. It is a thrilling notion — as thrilling as life may be in a cabin at the edge of a cliff, from which, each morning, over-powered by the beauty of the sunrise, one is beset by the temptation to leap. The "End of Days" makes a fine, sweet music. Surely it is the burden of the sirens' song. For who would not wish the present moment to end? Who does not long for chaos to crack the circle of the horizon and reclaim its own? Finality has its temptations: darkness, silence, and an end to the pain of love.

But I have drifted away from my theme, which is Shabbatai. It is all very well for Nathan in Gaza among the date palms and the camel dung to invent a messiah who will snatch the Emperor's crown. It is quite another matter for Shabbatai to repeat such stuff in the bright daylight of Smyrna, under the watchful eyes of the Kaimakam Pasha. The Kaimakam Pasha is a fat official, who has, to his credit, a keen eye for well-made Greek boys. But he is, for a Turkish provincial, reasonably ambitious. He wishes to become as rich as possible; and he hopes to be remarked by the Emperor in Constantinople as an effective provincial governor. For the moment, the Kaimakam's money hunger has kept Shabbatai safe from the too-scrupulous attention of the police spies of Smyrna. But this state of affairs cannot last long. A report of Shabbatai's childish threat to take the Emperor's crown from him will soon reach Constantinople.

There is another matter, too. Shabbatai, a prisoner of his own innocence, seems never to have heard of the word *sedition*. He moves through Smyrna's streets creating civil turmoil, as his besotted adherents, many of them men of substance, sell their goods or give them away. Business, which in Turkey is chiefly in the hands of the Jews, threatens to break down. Add such confusion to the "Emperor's crown" story, and the prediction is easy that the Kaimakam Pasha will take steps soon.

In the mean while, our Messiah walks like a man who has discovered that there is no dividing line between his dreams and the waking world. There is nothing he can want that is not instantly his. His robes of state are the finest blue or scarlet or purple wool. The feasts over which he presides are sumptuous. The crowds that stream after him are agog with adulation. And always, the Kaimakam's spies are there and taking note.

Shabbatai offends the Turks, but he outrages the still-powerful Council of Smyrna Rabbis more by flouting the old laws and fixed traditions of the Jews.

Every afternoon, when the day's heat has subsided, Shabbatai and his wife create new rituals.

His wife! Yes, he is married to a Polish woman named Sarah. A woman in all ways marvellous, not least in her flashing beauty. She is a tall, raven-haired woman, with a complexion dark enough to seem Levantine, but glowing with the vitality of the more vibrant North. She has the high cheekbones of a Tartar, and the commanding motions of a fretful queen. Had Kit Marlowe had the making of her, he would have framed a female Tamburlaine. Her forehead is open and smooth, her eyebrows arched as with the very pencil of a Leonardo, and her nose — for she is a Jewess, after all — is so delicately carved that it hints of the aquiline. She has the finest shape, the loveliest neck, and the most beautiful arms in the world. She is compelling and gracious, although if one looks deeply into her eyes, one may glimpse the motions of a heart-breaking wistfulness. You have guessed, Tyrell, that, did my tastes run that way, I could be smitten with the woman.

See how I wander.

Let me return to the rituals. See them, then, my glorious pair, Shabbatai and Sarah, on a platform erected in the square before the Central Synagogue of Smyrna. He is robed in scarlet and gold, and stands at one end of the platform, his hands folded, his head bowed as if in meditation. She, at the other end, garbed in black and gold, faces him. Her hands are at her sides; her head is held high; her lips are parted. In the square, the adoring multitude waits.

From Shabbatai's end of the platform, a sustained drumroll is heard; from Sarah's end, the thin, solitary keening of an *hautbois*. The music is a signal for the appearance in the square of five white-clad youths and five black-robed women. Each of the youths holds aloft a silver brazier, from which the smoke of burning charcoal drifts. The young men form an arc on the platform facing Shabbatai. The young women, each of whom is carrying a plain black earthenware bowl, form a similar arc facing Sarah. The drum begins a measured beat while the young men tilt their braziers first towards Shabbatai, then towards the crowd so that all may see the glowing charcoal. At the sound of the *hautbois,* the women tilt their vessels towards Sarah, then towards the crowd, revealing glistening lambs' kidneys still embedded in their fat.

It is the sight of the kidney-fat that sets the crowd murmuring, for there is not a Jew, from high to low, in all that crowd that does not know how forbidden it is to eat.

The music quickens. One by one, the young women kneel before Sarah, who makes V's of her palms in a priestly gesture and says:

"With the coming of the Messiah, there is an abrogation of the Laws.

"With the coming of the Messiah, the curse of Eve is lifted.

"With the coming of the Messiah, Woman, the *Shekhina,* the Indwelling Presence of God, is freed from her bondage."

The young women rise, turn, and walk to the other side of the platform, towards Shabbatai, while the youths carry their braziers and kneel before Sarah. Again, she makes a blessing:

"With the coming of the Messiah, there is no shame in the body.

"With the coming of the Messiah, there are no unclean members.

"With the coming of the Messiah, there is no shameful love.

"With the coming of the Messiah, the loins and the light are one."

The youths now join the women before Shabbatai, who goes from couple to couple, where, with surprising deftness, he cuts bits of the fat-dotted kidney and throws them onto the coals. There are splutters of roasting fat, spumes of smoke, and a smell that sets one's spittle flowing.

"Khelev," somebody says with a sigh. "Forbidden *khelev."*

Shabbatai, as if replying to the unhappy voice, raises his eyes to heaven and offers a sonorous prayer: "Blessed art Thou, O Lord our God, King of the universe, Who permits what is forbidden." Then, when he judges the moment to be right, he completes the outrage: he spears a bit of the roasted fat and puts it in his mouth. The watching crowd is hushed, as much with fear as with wonder. "This," says Shabbatai, "is the communion of the redeemed. Thus do we celebrate the new mysteries. In the name of the Lord, Who permits what is forbidden. Blessed is Y H V H. Blessed is the Lord of Hosts Who has sent Israel its Messiah. Blessed is he who sets out the table of salvation and bids all that are hungry for eternal life to come and eat. Come ye, then, who are famished to be saved; come now, in the name of the Lord Who permits what is forbidden. Come, and eat."

Sarah joins Shabbatai at the center of the platform, where the acolytes have placed the glowing braziers. One by one, like sleepers putting their trust in the last dream they will ever have on earth, they come: pious grandfathers, mothers with infants at the breast; schoolchildren, their

215

slates clutched in their arms; bridegrooms clinging to their brides. They come, and there is a great hush over the square as they bow and eat the roasted, forbidden fat, which, before the New Dispensation, they would have chosen martyrdom to spurn.

I dreamed, Tyrell, that the Thames was on fire, and that my father stood on its banks and blessed the flames when he saw me, in a pitch-lined boat, drifting like the infant Moses, downstream towards the fire.

☙

Does not the truth stare at you? Nathan of Gaza — and Shabbatai!

I can see it all. There, in Gaza, in those hot desert sands, the serpent Nathan coiled around my Shabbatai. They were lovers! The two of them on mountains, prancing and leaping, naked and yowling like cats. I know it. I swear it. They defiled each other with the sweetest copulations. Kisses amongst thorns; moist embraces at the edge of marshes.

While I — corrupt and godless Christian that I am — I kept my distance from His Holiness. Oh . . . Oh . . . I could have had him. Who shall tell me no? Whether by fraud or money; whether by rape or witchcraft. I could have had him.

And I did not! I shall run mad. *I* could not bring myself to offer insult to his holy flesh, fearing to break some gland of purity in him, without whose essence he might fail to be a saint.

I am a mockery unto myself.

Messiah. Messiah. Messiah.

They were lovers — in the flesh. There you have the meaning of the new Shabbatai. That squint-eyed stripling, Nathan, took Shabbatai's true virginity. While he whispered "Messiah!" in Shabbatai's ear, you may be certain his hand had slipped inside Shabbatai's robe to toy with what is surely the loveliest member ever made.

216

23

Lvov to Odessa
October, 1665

It was fifty miles of slowly leveling Carpathian foothills to Galichova, the first village on the Dniester, where Nehemiah could hope to find a raft or boat that would take him downstream to Odessa. Nehemiah chose to be on the road in the late afternoon, when the peasants, driving their cattle in from the fields to the villages, were too tired and too hungry to be curious about a Jew moving south. Not that he was often mistreated. He was still as thick-bodied and powerful as ever, despite his sixty-five years, and the axe hanging loosely at his side warned meddlers that it could be used for more than chopping wood. No. Nehemiah moved late in the day, because in his later years he had learned to love the waning light, when human voices hushed, and the night noises of the world started up. The dark, when it came, kept the roads empty, cool, and still.

After Danielov, the road wound through a not very dense forest of beech trees, whose silver trunks shimmered in the early starlight. A warm wind moving through their branches made a soughing like a distant lament. Sometimes there came the hunting call of an owl, or the rustle of the undergrowth when a weasel or a hedgehog moved.

Nehemiah walked on, breathing the odor of rain-soaked leaves.

Anyone watching him might suppose him to be a traveler going somewhere with a will. In fact, though he walked purposefully toward Galichova, he was far from knowing whether he indeed meant to go as far as Odessa, or, from there, to Constantinople. He argued the matter with himself, but without slowing his pace. That is itself something, he conceded. My feet seem to know the way; on the other hand, there is my head, which is not interested in Odessa and much less interested in Constantinople. Well, I'll follow my feet as far as Galichova, and pay attention to my head on the way. Who knows, we may arrive at an accommodation.

The beech forest gave way to open country, with farmhouses scattered among fields of rye.

Shabbatai! That Smyrna fellow, who, more than a decade ago, had been merely a nervous rumor out of Turkey, had been turned, by a young rabbi of Gaza, into a ubiquitous paper presence throughout Europe, where Nathan's letters were creating mischief — or hope. Letters like this one:

To the Children of Israel, peace!

Praise, praise unto the Lord.

Know that you have been found worthy in your generation. The fulfillment of God's words pronounced by the Prophets and our ancestors is at hand.

Praise! Praise unto the Lord! Shabbatai Zevi, the Messiah, is come to transform your bitterness into joy, your fast days into festivals.

Lo, the celestial lion descends from the heavens, and the Messiah will mount him soon, holding in his right hand the seven-headed serpent for a bridle. Then, he will lead all Israel toward Jerusalem, where God will cause the Temple of Solomon to descend from the sky . . . The holy Temple, new-built with gold and emer-

218

alds, amethyst and chrysoprase; with opals, topaz, and jade, will float down from the sky to rest on Mount Moriah.

After these wonders will come the resurrection of the dead and an end to mourning.

I send you these words that you may know: Shabbatai Zevi, the Redeemer, is come.

Make yourself worthy of his redemption.

Nathan of Gaza

Shabbatai Zevi. Shabbatai. How the rumors about the man had persisted. His name, like other iridescent bubbles, should have vanished. It had not. And now, this Nathan, reputed a learned man, had transformed himself into a speaking trumpet for Shabbatai. And serious men and women everywhere wanted Nehemiah's judgment about the prodigy that had risen in the East.

Was it madness born of grief? Or was it a sign of hope? Madness and hope! What was Jewish history if not a single rope braided of those two strands?

Nehemiah shook his head and admired his feet, which, having no part in the debate, kept walking toward Galichova.

Suppose God *had* roused Himself after all? Suppose He had determined to ease the pain of His Creation? But would God's Messiah write a letter such as the one Nehemiah had lately received, brought to him in Lvov by a messenger who had carried it all the way from Turkey? This letter?

To the Rabbi Nehemiah Ha-Kohen in Lvov, peace!

I write at the command of Shabbatai Zevi, the Anointed of the Lord, the true Messiah and King of the Jews.

Know that three weeks before the Feast of Tamusz, there appeared in the Messiah's court two rabbis of Lvov, pious men, come on a pilgrimage to my lord Shabbatai Zevi. They saw with their own eyes his sancti-

219

fied majesty; they heard with their own ears his exalted speech.

Having communed with these rabbis, Shabbatai had discourse with them; and the rabbis were much refreshed in body and soul and believed that Shabbatai Zevi was the Messiah of the Lord and the Redeemer and King of the Jews.

Then my lord Shabbatai inquired after the welfare of the Jews of Poland, and comforted the rabbis over the Polish disasters, and promised revenge on the oppressors. After which, he inquired of them who among the rabbis of Poland was most worthy to be brought to Turkey to be a witness to his mission so that, being illuminated and transfigured, such a man might be a light of truth concerning Shabbatai to the Jews of Poland?

The rabbis of Lvov, with one voice, replied that there was such an one. That his name was Nehemiah Ha-Kohen — a *khakham* and doer of pious deeds.

Wherefore, I write at the command of Shabbatai Zevi, the Anointed of God, the celestial lion, the Redeemer of souls, the Messiah and King of Israel, to bid Nehemiah Ha-Kohen come forthwith to the blessed city of Smyrna, in the land of the Turks, so that our lord may meet you and greet you and cause his light to shine upon you.

> *Itzhak ben Shimon*
> Scribe to Shabbatai
> Given this day, the 27th of Ab

Below the scribe's signature was written:

Nehemiah Ha-Kohen,
Come!

> *Shabbatai-Messiah* in *olam hazeh*
> (The Present World),
> The Lord God in *olam haboh*
> (The World to Come)

Nehemiah's feet — as if *they* had read the letter — were on their way. He shook his head. Who but a madman, dazzled by the Turkish heat, would sign himself "The Lord God in *olam haboh*"? On the other hand, how did one say no to a direct command from God?

Crossing the wooden bridge across the Dniester, four miles above Galichova, Nehemiah heard the quick patter of hooves in the road behind him. With surprising quickness for a man of his bulk, Nehemiah was across the bridge and crouching in a hazel grove on the other side, his unslung axe across his knees. His flight was a wise precaution, because a moment later a small troop of Tartar irregulars, wearing wolfskin hats and creaking leather armor, trotted by. The Tartars were not especially cruel as captors, but it was the better part of prudence not to put oneself in their way. It was more prudent still to sit quietly in the hazel grove, lest this group of horsemen prove to be outriders of a larger troop yet to come.

From the starlit pools along the Dniester's banks there came the croaking of hundreds of frogs. Nehemiah smiled. If only he were Solomon, who understood the voices of the Creation, he might know what sort of advice the frogs were giving him.

Half an hour later, when no more Tartars appeared, Nehemiah strode on toward Galichova, his feet still in command. He looked up at the stars; he inhaled the fragrant night air; then he had a vision of how the Messiah should look: a broadly built man, an outdoorsman, gruff and brisk; a man who had lived among outcasts and the poor, who had broken bread with bandits and beggars. A strong, dark, striding man with dirt under his fingernails, with teeth strong enough to crack a marrow bone. A brawny fellow whom the winds had seared and death had frequently touched.

Nehemiah, within sight of Galichova, laughed out loud at the glimpse he had of the axe swinging freely at the Messiah's radiant thigh.

24

Peter Harleigh, en route, Smyrna to Constantinople,
to Nicholas Tyrell in London
January 2–February 8, 1666

You have developed in middle life an unexpected flare
for satire. Your tales of high-bred horses and ill-bred
whores do honour to your pen. As for Bennet, Sandwich,
and Buckingham, how well you have hit the mark: they
have found their *métier* and make a most excellent committee of pimps to serve King Charles's diviner lust.

You write well, Nick. But be cautious. The satirist who
begins by hating mankind not infrequently ends disgusted
with himself in his mirror.

Tyrell, you know the wind that blows across the south
downs of Sussex in January? A plaguey wind that enters
the pores and continues its whining in the muscles and
the bones. A wet and steady wind that breathes behind
the eyes and ears; and makes a clammy whirlpool of the
brain. There's such a wind now in the rigging of our ship.

It is four days since we left Smyrna. We are: myself and
Shabbatai, Sarah and the young merchant Itzhak, and
Barot'ali with his two goats. There is, too, a rabble of
pilgrims, followers of Shabbatai, who have sold all they

owned to follow him to Constantinople, where, they believe, Shabbatai will take the Emperor's crown from him.

Why, since I do not have the Jewish Messiah-madness, am I in this crowd of exalted lunatics? What can I say? Love may be one excuse; perhaps another is curiosity to see how this tangled children's mystery play will end. What is certain is that here in the Aegean Sea I hear the soughing of that death-song Sussex wind.

January 4

The wind has died down, but there is a swelling of the sea that has turned Shabbatai green. The Turkish sailors snicker as they pass the Messiah holding to the rail, his teeth clamped to keep his breakfast down. Less than an hour later, the swells give way to a tempest that leaps at the ship as if it means to tear it and ourselves to bits. The wind howls and tosses us about like a chip on a millpond, driving us to the peaks of obsidian cliffs, or dropping us into troughs that seem to be the very bottom of the sea.

Shabbatai is thoroughly sick. I am much afraid that his gut forgets it was meant to minister to the King of the Jews.

Waves crash across the deck; the ship trembles like a frightened horse. The sailors, learning there is a leak in the hold, race about in a panic, until one cries, "The Jew Messiah. A Jonah. Over the side with him." The shout is taken up, and, despite thunder, lightning, lashing rain, and breaking waves that threaten to drown them *and* Shabbatai, they plead with their captain to let them throw the infidel Messiah overboard. "A Jonah!" they cry. "A Jew! A Jonah!" The captain, a clean-shaven fellow, except for a pair of wicked moustaches that stick out from the sides of his face like daggers, is nothing loth, and there follows a lugging and a pulling intended to send Shabbatai into the belly of a whale. But when an over-zealous third mate swings a cat-o'-nine-tales at him, Shabbatai wrenches it away, and, swelling like a Hercules, flings sailors aside like ninepins and, roaring commands, moves through the tempest towards the ship's bow.

The men, who would fain follow him, perforce scatter to save their lives as a twelve-pound gun amidships breaks loose and races the ship's length to the stern, where, breaking through the rail, it plunges into the sea. The wind, in the mean while, has lashed itself into a killing rage. Spars fly; canvas is ripped; seas wash across the deck.

Shabbatai, as if he fed on gales, is mounting to the crow's-nest, where, with a ship's wisdom no Smyrna Jew ever acquired, he lashes himself with a rope. The ship plunges and shudders, the thunder rolls, and Shabbatai, his arms raised to the skies, commands, "Enough, O troubled sea." Then, "Wind! O wind, what is thy grief? Why dost thou wail?"

"The man is mad!" a sailor cries, and the heavens, as if of his mind, hurl a lightning stroke that seems to shatter over the ship, transforming the storm-racked night into a pale, yet sunless, version of dawn. In that brightness, we all see each other as if painted on a canvas: the captain at the wheel, Itzhak and Sarah at my side, the sailors huddling with the passengers who have braved the storm to be on deck. Shabbatai, on his perch, calm and cajoling, is heard: "Enough, thou frightened sea; all's well again; be still, O troubled wind; sink into sleep."

As swiftly as the lightning-forged dawn came, it yields to the night again, and our ship, which moments before had been close to foundering, sails smoothly northward.

January 16
The men say it was the devil who stopped the storm, they walk cautiously past Shabbatai, making signs against the evil eye.

Shabbatai is restless with exaltation. "Did you see me,

Englishman?" he says. "Was there ever anything like it?
Jacob, struggling with the angel beside the ford at Jabbok,
was not more mighty." He leaps to his feet; he strides
about the deck, muttering; or he stands at the ship's bow
as if it were he, indeed, who was sending us scudding to
the Hellespont.

January 17

It is twenty hours since we have been becalmed. Shabbatai refuses to notice.

Sarah, who, since the sea grew calm, has been much
preoccupied, sits beside him. "Shabbatai," she says, "I
have been thinking. We are going to Constantinople. Have
you . . . have you thought of the . . . dangers?"

Shabbatai sees neither her nor the motionless sea. He
says, "You have seen my power. It is written that I shall
take the Emperor's crown."

Sarah shakes him and tries without success to make him
look at her. "Listen, Shabbatai. You are the Messiah, but
the Messiah may face danger, like an ordinary man . . ."

"I am not ordinary," he says, and closes his eyes.

Sarah turns to me. "Englishman, you tell him. He is
still flesh and blood."

I want to say: Enough, both of you. I am sick of you
and your Jewish delusions.

But I am unmanned by love and by a conviction that
truth is a trivial thing, compared with what Shabbatai sees
behind his eyes. Still, I say lamely, "Shabbatai, Constantinople is not Roman Jerusalem, but . . . what if the Turk
be no wiser than Pilate?"

Shabbatai's smile is not of this world. "What happened
to the Other has nothing to do with me."

I look away. Just then we are interrupted by Itzhak and
a Smyrna matron, who keeps shoving away Itzhak's mollify-
ing hand. "Lord, lord!" she cries to Shabbatai.

"Yes?"

"Lord, surely *some* things are forbidden . . ."

"Speak," Shabbatai says, as relieved as Sarah and I are by the distraction. "What troubles you?"

"Your servant, Shabbatai. Your witless one . . ."

"Barot'ali? Yes?"

"Filth!" the woman rages. "Abomination! He is there, in the hold. With those . . . with Leilia, with Rosalinda . . . Goats. Female goats. He treats them . . . Oh, unspeakable . . . They are his concubines!"

Shabbatai studies the woman. The Smyrna dowager looks angrily at the rest of us and waits. At last, Shabbatai gives his judgment. Kindly, he inquires, "Yehudit bat Mattityahu?" She nods, proud to be remembered. "Before my coming, there were Filth and Abomination and Unspeakable Acts. But Yehudit, I am here. All things are clean unto you as long as you have me."

Uncertainly, she bows and backs away. As she moves towards the afterdeck, her silk scarves barely stir.

January 18

Still becalmed.

Can it be that our ill luck on this voyage is repayment for a piece of wickedness that took place in Smyrna?

You know what triumphant days Shabbatai spent there. He preached the salvation of all mankind, an end to the subjection of women. He abolished every constraint the Jews had ever made on love. Men and women danced in the streets. Shabbatai's repeated prayer, "Blessed is the name of the Lord Who permits what is forbidden," was heard by the multitude as a call to licence. There was no behaviour so wild, so lecherous, so free, that the prayer did not seem to countenance. Men whored after their neighbours' wives, or their own daughters. Mothers lay with their sons, their fathers, or with each other. The very children, repeating "Blessed is the name of the Lord Who permits what is forbidden," imitated the sins of their elders.

In the midst of so much stink and sweetness, there were Jews in the city who did not accept Shabbatai's New Dispensation. Samuel Pena, one of these *kapharim*, unbelievers, had (so Shabbatai was made to believe) hired an assassin to murder him.

That very afternoon (it was late on a Friday) Shabbatai, without wasting an instant, put himself at the head of a mob, which stormed Pena's gate. With Shabbatai calling for vengeance, the multitude smashed in the gates and over-ran the old man's house, seeking for Pena and his two daughters. Pena, at first, was nowhere to be seen. But the daughters were found at the top of the house, whirling like tops from whose centers came cries of "Shabbatai . . . *Amirah*, our lord and king, may his majesty be exalted." The crowd understood by this that another miracle had happened. The former *kapharim* were become *ma'aminim*, believers. The daughters spun, piping like birds, "Shabbatai. Shabbatai. *Amirah!*" A little later, old Samuel Pena crawled out from behind an arras and joined his twirling daughters, to make a final miracle.

In the event, there was no real harm done, although I think it was an ill thing, so to frighten the old man and his daughters.

This long, long calm feels like an omen.

January 19
The inevitable has happened. Blue-eyed Itzhak and Sarah have discovered each other. Well, they have been tow and tinder all this while. The wonder is only that it took them so long. They wander the ship like Tristan and Isolde, their fingers and eyes straying towards each other.

January 20

Shabbatai and I are at the after-rail, watching the immobile sea. There is a cry. We turn to find Itzhak thrashing on the deck. "Forbid it," he begs. "Shabbatai, forbid it. I love you. I don't want to betray you."

A dozen paces behind Itzhak, Sarah stands, her cheeks glowing.

"Forbid it," Itzhak pleads. "She is a succubus. I cannot help myself."

Shabbatai casts a look at the motionless sea, then says, "There is no betrayal, Itzhak. Go to her. She is a woman with the need of woman. Go. It will be a *tikkun* for her soul."

"What about my soul?" Itzhak asks.

"For yours, too. Go."

The young man gets to his feet. Torn between guilt and greed, he hesitates, then yields to greed and hurries towards Sarah, who is already moving towards her cabin.

We have been at sea for twenty-two days.

January 20

There is a spanking breeze from the south. We should make Abydos by night-fall.

January 20 (*late afternoon*)

Our captain, who has been watching signals from a *galleass* on our port bow, comes to tell us that it is the Emperor's coastal guard. We are to make towards shore at once, unless we wish to be fired upon.

Abydos, January 21

Shabbatai is in prison, although not charged with any crime.

What a hell-hole. Broken bodies, vermin, darkness.

Shabbatai is calm, as if he had not been dragged from the ship and made to ride on horseback seven full hours, only to be flung into the den in which he lies.

I have poured out money, and, although his prison is vile, he is well fed and decently clothed. He has access to visits from me and certain wealthy believers, with whom, tonight, I am to meet to plan what can be done. With their gold and mine, much may be accomplished in this land of *bakshish*.

No one, thank God, has yet spoken the word "sedition."

Sarah, Itzhak, Barot'ali, and his goats, lodge with me at my inn.

Our group of monied well-wishers has met. Tomorrow, we will call on Köprülü Pasha, who, it is said, caused Shabbatai's arrest. Köprülü is a young man reputed to have a civilized mind. Like all Turks, he can be swayed by gold.

One of the merchants at our meeting, seeing how I gnawed my lip over Shabbatai's plight, leant over to say, "Lord Harleigh, our sages tell us that when the egg is no more, and the chick is not yet, it is wise to sit very still."

25

Abydos
May, 1666

After months of bad weather and bad food, Nehemiah
Ha-Kohen had reached Smyrna, only to learn that Shabbatai Zevi was in prison in Abydos. There followed a final
eight days of gusty sailing, and now, here Nehemiah was,
leaning into the wind as he stepped from the caïque that
had brought him from Smyrna. Behind him on the Bospho-
rus, there was a constant sea traffic, bringing and carrying
away Jewish pilgrims to the Imperial Prison on Abydos,
where Shabbatai was held. The dock was thronged with
Jews and with Turkish boatmen made suddenly prosperous
by the new source of income the holy prisoner had brought
them. The wind, blowing from the Aegean, turned the
normally blue sea a choppy gray, but neither the passengers nor the boatmen let the weather discourage them
from their haggling. Nehemiah asked some questions of
passersby, then adjusted the axe at his side, and strode
through the crowds on the docks toward the prison, a
quarter of a mile away.

Shabbatai's worshippers called the old fortress in which
he was kept "the Tower of Strength." The great hillside
below the prison teemed with Jews living in tents, in shacks,
in mud hovels. They clustered around food stalls and

bought bits of skewered meat roasted over charcoal, or fried sardines, or fresh split cucumbers dipped in salt, or rose-flavored sweets, sesame cakes, boiled horse beans. The air was heavy with the smell of cooking fires, garbage, horse dung, and the reek of human feces. Children ran about underfoot; parents scolded, horses whinnied, donkeys brayed. Wealthy Jews, preceded by their uniformed *kavaslar*, who bawled, "Way, way for the honorable Yeheskiel of Damascus. Way, way . . ." carried their bellies through the crowd. The yelling kavaslar did little good, since their gold-braided uniforms and their carved sticks attracted more people than their cries dispersed. From time to time, a squad of Janissaries, sinisterly mustached, rode through the turmoil, their long-sleeved caps jiggling over their shoulders, and snapped their whips, to remind the Jews that Pasha Sami ibn Sami, the governor of the District of Abydos, was keeping order.

Nehemiah made his way through magicians, flame-drinkers, storytellers, knife-swallowers. Almost against his will, he stopped at the edge of a throng watching a young Anatolian Gypsy with dirty blond hair making her way across a tightrope strung eight feet above the ground on two poles set fifteen yards apart. The young Gypsy was in no special danger, but as she moved across the rope, great tears welled from her eyes and coursed down her dirty cheeks. Once she brushed them with her sleeve; the movement made her lurch, and to recapture her balance, she ran forward, then back a couple of paces, after which she was calm again and resumed her progress across the rope, the tears still streaming down her face. Nehemiah, watching her, tried to shake the Gypsy's resemblance both to his limping Hanna and to the fragile — and broken — Feigele. It was an old trick his eyes sometimes played on him. Soon it would pass. Nehemiah flung a coin into a greasy cap that was shoved at him by a toothless woman with a wen on her cheek, and went on toward the walled fortress where Shabbatai Zevi waited.

Before the prison gates, long lines of poor folk waited at each of several tables, where Turkish officials collected a flat fee of one silver coin, which admitted these lowly pilgrims to the prison. There, if they were fortunate, they might see Shabbatai taking his morning or afternoon walk through the prison courtyard. At other tables, in shorter queues, stood more prosperous men and women: cobblers, weavers, smiths, milliners, innkeepers, and their wives and children. From these people, various Jewish officials collected two silver coins, a fee that permitted them to walk about in the courtyard in the near presence of Shabbatai himself. Still more prosperous citizens who were willing to pay ten silver coins — physicians, notaries, tax-farmers, rabbis — received bright blue passes that entitled them to join Shabbatai's train as he made his progress through the courtyard. Finally, in the shortest line of all, there stood the richest of the would-be visitors: merchants and money-lenders, government officials, jewelers, lawyers, and their wives or widows. At this table, presided over by Itzhak ben Shimon, Shabbatai's blue-eyed young private secretary, these wealthy folk paid enormous sums of money for the right to sit with Shabbatai and his disciples at the midday and evening meals, or when he preached or held court. The rich pilgrims fingered their long silk robes and looked about them disdainfully or kept their eyes on the chests their servants carried, in which there waited the gold or the jewels that would buy them places of honor at the right hand of redemption.

Nehemiah, watching the financial transactions, was not pleased. Nowhere in the course of his journey from Lvov to Abydos had it occurred to him that to reach the Messiah one might have to pay cash. Wrapping his heavy Polish coat around him like a prayer shawl, he muttered to himself, then took his place in line with the wealthiest Jews. At first, the rich men or their wives sent him icy looks, but Nehemiah growled like a bear and opened his coat to let the breeze blow a whiff of his many travel odors toward them. A plump goldsmith, second in the line, signaled to his *kavas* and said something in his ear. The kavas, his staff of office gripped in both hands like a tourney-stick, slouched toward Nehemiah, to whom he said, "My master, the honorable Shlomo of Salonika, sends you greetings. Also, he wishes me to tell you to take yourself elsewhere. He cannot abide your stink."

Nehemiah looked up at the loose-limbed kavas and hitched his axe farther forward on his belt. "So. So." He nodded. "Does he, now? Does he? Cannot abide, is it? Cannot! Well . . ." Catching the servant's elbow in a woodsman's grip, Nehemiah said, "Come on, then, let's pay our respects to your honorable master." He rushed the man forward in a lame trot, until, almost on the goldsmith, he tripped the kavas. There was a liquid thump as the servant collided with his master's belly; then man and master rolled in a heap. Nehemiah adjusted his axe, turned, and resumed his place in line.

The shouts of the goldsmith and the groans of his kavas brought an angry Itzhak ben Shimon running to confront Nehemiah. "Just who . . . just who . . . do you think you are? You . . . you . . ."

Nehemiah, indifferent to the bleats that came from the overturned goldsmith, said, "I know who I am. Nehemiah Ha-Kohen of Lvov."

Itzhak paled. "Reb Nehemiah . . . of Lvov? The axeman saint? Reb Nehem——"

"You." Nehemiah wiped the sweat from the back of his neck. "You have a name?"

"Itzhak . . . Itzhak ben Shimon. Shabbatai's scribe. It was I, Reb Nehemiah, who wrote to you. And now this! You must forgive us . . . you must forgive me. There is so much to look after. We had hoped to greet you. To heap honors . . . to . . . to . . . There's been a dreadful mistake . . ."

"Perhaps," Nehemiah said ambiguously, but he allowed the young man to lead him past the Turkish guards and

233

into the cool stone labyrinth of the prison, where Itzhak, remembering something, cried, "Wait! Wait here for one moment, Reb Nehemiah. I'll be only a minute." He darted away, and Nehemiah watched him return to the unattended table. There, he made brushing gestures at the goldsmith's cloak; then he ran about until he found a man to take his place dealing with the wealthy Jews. There was a final set of apologetic gestures over the goldsmith, after which Itzhak returned to an increasingly irritated Nehemiah. "How good of you," Itzhak said, panting. "How good of you to wait."

Like a deer startled by nettles, Itzhak plunged down the long corridor. Nehemiah followed him slowly, trying to absorb a host of new sensations. He looked down at his heavy hobnailed Polish boots, and attended to the sound they made striking the Levantine stone.

"This way," Itzhak called. "This way, Reb Nehemiah." And Nehemiah went, feeling the distance between the sun-struck hillside, swarming with God-hungry Jews, and the calm of the stone corridor down which he walked. At intervals, he passed turbaned prison guards standing in pairs before arches to other corridors. The soldiers stood at ease, their long pikes held loosely, indifferent to the movement of these privileged Jews.

Itzhak tried to slow his pace so that Nehemiah could walk with him.

"Where are we going?" Nehemiah inquired.

"To Shabbatai's Court of Audience."

"A Court of Audience? In a prison?"

Itzhak laughed. "Shabbatai is no ordinary prisoner."

"Tell me," Nehemiah asked, "is it true, as I have heard, that the Emperor of the Turks brings Shabbatai water in a silver bowl so that Shabbatai can wash his hands before saying his morning prayers?"

"Ah, Jewish exaggeration." Itzhak shrugged. "The Emperor is in Constantinople. And yet, Shabbatai does reign in splendor here."

"They tell me," Nehemiah pursued, "that Shabbatai is very beautiful. That light pours from him like the sun. Is that true?"

The level curiosity in the older man's voice made Itzhak squirm. "Shabbatai, when the blessed mood is on him, is certainly — radiant."

"Is he a holy man?" Nehemiah rasped.

Itzhak looked up toward the vaulted stone ceiling. "He is the Messiah. The Anointed of the Lord. He has spoken the *Shem ha m'foresh*. He commands the lightning, and he stills the seas."

"And yet, he is a prisoner of the Turks."

They were approaching a corridor that turned to the right. At their left, a line of eight Turkish prisoners waited their turn before a smith, who was applying leg irons to their ankles. "He is a prisoner," Itzhak agreed. "But not like those men. He is more like . . . Daniel cast into the lions' den — 'And a stone was brought, and laid upon the mouth of the den' — And Shabbatai, like Daniel, has shut the mouths of the lions and turned the Emperor's tower of punishment into a Tower of Strength . . . into which the righteous may run and be safe . . ."

"Yes," Nehemiah said dryly. "But where is it written that Jews must pay admission to be safe in the Messiah's tower?"

Itzhak stopped and looked at the weather-worn rabbi from Poland. "I know," he said. "It must seem strange to you . . . the money. But, as long as we are still in olam hazeh, in this world, money is needed, both for the Messiah *and* for those who believe in him. Soon, when Shabbatai leads us to olam haboh, the world to come, there will be an end to money. There, we shall all sit at God's right hand and . . ."

"No doubt. No doubt," Nehemiah said. "Well, never mind. Let's get on with it."

Itzhak, watching the rabbi's blunt fingers moving along the sharp blade of the axe at his side, made his voice gentle

235

as he said, "Reb Nehemiah. You've been on a very long journey. You are tired. It might be better for you to rest for a day or so before meeting Shabbatai. You ought not to face our Redeemer in a troubled mood."

"Never mind my mood," snapped Nehemiah. "If I am to be redeemed, the Messiah will redeem me, fatigue and mood and all. Now! Take me to your Shabbatai."

"Of course," Itzhak said. He nodded to a couple of guards, who leaned their weight against the huge brass-studded doors before which they stood. The doors swung inward. Nehemiah and Itzhak passed through.

Nehemiah's first thought, after the gloom of the stone corridors, was that the world had changed to gold and red and green. He found himself standing at one end of a rectangular open court, on every side of which there ran a roofed, wooden gallery, thronging with men and women whose clothing shimmered with color. In the court-yard itself, there was a luxuriant, if slightly dusty, garden, arranged to display lawns, orange trees, date palms, box hedges, and bamboo-shaded rock gardens. Six fountains, at regular intervals, sent water sparkling toward the sun.

"This," an awed Nehemiah said, "is a prison?"

"These are the Pasha Sami ibn Sami's private quarters. Turned over to Shabbatai's uses," Itzhak said.

"Out of the Pasha's kindness of heart?"

Itzhak refused to be goaded. "He was paid, of course. There are devoted bankers in Constantinople . . . believers . . . who have made . . . who make . . . generous contributions."

"Generous," echoed Nehemiah.

"Come," Itzhak said, growing weary of Nehemiah's disapproval. "Let me take you to Shabbatai." The scruffy woodchopper was corrosive as lime. Later, under Shabbatai's scrutiny, Nehemiah would learn that even a man with a reputation for holiness could study the uses of humility.

"Yes," Nehemiah said, shaking his head like a bull getting ready to charge. "Where is he?"

236

Itzhak pushed through the crowd, past the coming and going of petitioners, of servants swinging trays of tea and cakes and lighted *narghil;* past pilgrims, still dusty or sea-stained, pressing toward the far end of the courtyard, where, as Nehemiah suddenly saw, the Messiah, robed in scarlet, sat on a raised golden throne.

Itzhak made one final effort to deter mischief. He put a hand on Nehemiah's shoulder and said, "Speak softly to him, Reb Nehemiah. It may be he will give you a tikkun for your soul." Nehemiah, gazing at Shabbatai, murmured, *"Nu, nu."* Itzhak shrugged and, making a trumpet of his hands, he shouted, "Way! Way! Way, for Rabbi Nehemiah Ha-Kohen of Lvov."

The man is plump, Nehemiah thought, absorbed in Shabbatai; he is plump and soft and *clean.* He remembered his half-whimsical hope that the Messiah would be an out-doorsman, with a face roughened and tanned by wind and sun. A dark, striding fellow, with dirt under his fingernails. A carpenter, a sailor. Perhaps even a logger, with an axe slapping against his thigh. He shrugged and walked through the crowd, which parted at his approach to the throne of redemption.

Shabbatai was on his feet. "Blessed is the womb that bore you. Your name for righteousness has preceded you." Even as Shabbatai spoke, he was hiding some confusion. The rabbi's name and reputation were familiar, but why was he here? He turned to Sarah, who sat on a throne to his left, surprised to find her intently studying the rabbi.

Nehemiah, still engrossed in the mood and melody of Shabbatai's voice, was thinking, He is tall and graceful — and clean; his hands are clean and his eyes. His lips are moist. Neither his brow nor his cheeks nor his throat are wrinkled. Bah! The Messiah of God could not be such a piece of honeycake.

Then he saw Sarah. It was nearly nine years since he had faced her in Zamosc, but she was still the intense woman into whose dark eyes he had looked. She was the woman, found in a cemetery, who was suspected of being possessed by a *dybbuk.* "Where have you been?" he had asked her, but she had refused to remember. She had frightened the Zamosc rabbis with her talk of marrying the Messiah. Now, here she was.

He felt the weight of incredulity pressing on his shoulders. Was it God or Satan who had put these two on thrones in this prison in Turkey? The melody of Shabbatai's voice still rang in his ears; the honeyed beauty of the man glowed before his eyes. And beside him? A pliant, radiant Eve? Or the temptress Lilith? The bride of Adam Kadmon, or the consort of hell? He tried unsuccessfully to avert his gaze from her.

He wrenched his head toward Shabbatai and asked, "Why am I here?"

Shabbatai, unable to remember, turned to Sarah, who was now on her feet beside him. "Welcome to the Tower of Strength, Reb Nehemiah," she said. "I trust you are well."

Nehemiah remembered suddenly how dusty he was; his hands touched the worn spots in his coat; for the first time, he was ashamed of the thick usefulness of his Polish hobnailed boots. His hand went toward his crotch, but he arrested the movement and seized the handle of his axe. "Why," he asked again, "am I here?"

"It was I who urged it, Reb Nehemiah. When my lord Shabbatai was still in Smyrna, there were Polish visitors there who spoke of your piety and of your *mitsvot,* your holy deeds. And I . . . I remembered you . . ."

Shabbatai brightened as he recalled the conversation. "Yes. Yes. She told me to send for you. She said you had shared the anguish of my people in Europe; and would welcome a tikkun for your soul. Then, seeing the truth of the redemption I bring, you would carry back to Poland a persuasive witnessing . . ."

Sarah winced at Shabbatai's disingenuous confession, but Nehemiah found himself touched by it. Whatever the ruse that had brought him, he was glad to be here. He felt himself seized by a rush of power — the scholar's power, or the woodsman's — in the near presence of the mystery that surrounded Shabbatai.

Sarah was another matter. What was it he had said about her to the fearful rabbis of Zamosc? "What is in her, God's will . . . will manifest." It had been a face-saving phrase to hide his helplessness. Now here she was, a madwoman turned prophetess, who had gone out into the world and found a messiah to marry. Was this not God's will manifesting itself? Sarah and Shabbatai, as bright and glorious as a couple of morning stars. Did they not make a pattern in a world where — so Nehemiah had taught himself — there was no design?

He trembled. What if there was design? He closed his eyes and tried to pray, but in the voluntary dark behind his eyelids he saw instead the money-takers at the prison gate, the splendors of the courtyard, the multicolored garments of the pilgrims. He saw Shabbatai's plump, well-washed body and his scarlet robe, and Sarah, beside him, like an unwavering flame.

Was it God's will? Or Satan's.

Unslinging his axe, he set it before him with the haft to the ground. The spittle in his mouth tasted like steel. There was a sound like a wind blowing from distant caverns, and he heard himself saying, "Are you truly the Messiah ben David?"

"I am he. The Anointed of the Lord."

"Anointed by whom?"

It was the gage unmistakably thrown down. There was a nervous movement among the disciples around the throne, but Shabbatai replied serenely, "Anointed by Nathan of Gaza, prophet of the Lord. In the desert of Judea, by the Salt Sea."

From behind Shabbatai's throne, there came the slap, slap of sandals, as Barot'ali moved into the space between Shabbatai and Nehemiah. The idiot sniffed the air, trying

239

to localize the scent of menace that drifted toward the throne. Barot'ali weaved from side to side like a Golem, one of those clay monsters twitched into life by rabbinical piety. The idiot waved his hands before him like the weapons they were. Itzhak reached out and tugged at his sleeve, but Barot'ali looked from Nehemiah to Shabbatai, from Shabbatai to Nehemiah, and mewed until Shabbatai said, "Hush." Barot'ali sank down cross-legged before the dais, his huge hands in his lap.

Nehemiah rocked back and forth over his axe like a man reciting the "for-the-sins-I-have-committed-against-Thee" prayer in the synagogue on the Day of Atonement. But what he prayed for was humility, judgment, strength so that he might not betray the weeping Gypsy on her tightrope, nor Lame Hannah's unfinished alphabet, nor Feigele, with the child in her womb, who had slipped so easily into the grave beside the wheatfield.

There was a voice, Shabbatai's, expounding the meaning of a gold medallion he wore around his neck. "See, Reb Nehemiah. It is the image of the serpent biting the womb of a doe struggling to give birth. You understand its meaning?"

Nehemiah did not reply. Shabbatai resumed his explanation: "The whole scene represents the coming of the Messiah; but note, Reb Nehemiah, that the serpent represents the Serpent of the Right, the Lord's serpent, enlarging the womb of *tsvi*, the deer, to permit the Shekhina, the Indwelling Presence of God, to enter into the world, thereby preparing the way for the Messiah. See" — Shabbatai held out his hand — "I also wear the serpent's ring."

"Why?"

"Because the Serpent of the Right is my creature. He has prepared my way."

"Hmmm. I see. Hmmm."

"*Nakhash, Meshiakh . . . Meshiakh, Nakhash,*" Shabbatai explained, setting the Hebrew words for serpent and messiah side by side for Nehemiah to appreciate the mystery:

the two words had the same numerical value, and therefore represented each other.

"Yes, yes . . ." Nehemiah tapped the stone of the court-yard with the haft of his axe.

There was a rustle of approval from the crowd around the throne. The ragged old man from Poland was being taught what the adepts already knew. Nehemiah tapped the stone again and said, "Beware, Shabbatai Zevi. Beware lest you rejoice too soon. Is it not written that Palestina shall not rejoice for out of the serpent's root shall come forth a cockatrice, and his fruit shall be a fiery serpent?"

Sarah put her hand out to restrain Shabbatai. "My lord," she said, "the Polish rabbi is weary. Perhaps tomorrow . . ."

"No, Sarah. No. Reb Nehemiah asks in love, and lovingly I reply . . ."

Sarah withdrew her hand. She felt the blood rush from her head to her heart. This . . . this Nehemiah chirping his questions around Shabbatai was a dry cicada. A man in pain, and wedded to his pain. A man without hope who could mangle hope. Whose madness had brought him here? Then she remembered and bowed her head.

Shabbatai, unable to hear the rasping wings of the dark cicada, spoke sweetly. "Lovingly, then, I reply, It is certainly written, as you say, Reb Nehemiah. But it is not written for me."

A hushed murmur of approval rippled through the audience. A Salonika banker in a green silk robe sighed and said, "They that be wise shall shine like the brightness of the firmament."

Nehemiah looked soberly from the banker's face to Shabbatai's and then to Sarah's. It was time to make an end. Hefting his axe with both hands, he said, "Where, if you are the Messiah, Shabbatai Zevi," he demanded, "where, if you are the Messiah of the House of David — *where then is the Messiah of Joseph's house?*"

Silence fell on the courtyard like a stone. The left side of Shabbatai's face twitched as if he had been bitten by an insect. His lips, as he licked them, moved in silent repetition: *Where then is the Messiah of Joseph's house?* Shabbatai saw, rather than heard, the question: it had the form of the night sky dotted with cold stars, and a rooster stood on cruel, blue-plated feet, its beak parted, getting ready to crow up the sun. It lifted itself on tiptoe; it stretched its neck and strained and flapped its wings until it uttered, instead of a rooster's crow, a silent serpent with malevolent yellow eyes that wound itself through the sky looking for a victim. Calmly, it writhed its head to the north, to the south, to the east and west. The serpent flowed and searched and swam through the heavens, searching and searching until it found — him.

"Rabbi . . . Nehem—— Nehemiah," Shabbatai began, but his throat was filled with the dust of the Judean Desert, and his tongue tasted of the dead Salt Sea.

26

Abydos
March, 1666

Seen from the perspective of the morning star shining
down upon the scene eighteen hours later, the courtyard
was a tableau of weariness. Nehemiah Ha-Kohen stood
leaning on his axe. Shabbatai, too, was standing, but he
had the look of a scarlet-clad scarecrow, as he clung to
the pillars of his throne. Both men were hoarse. All afternoon and all night, the argument had gone round and
round while Shabbatai and Nehemiah gnawed at the question of the Messiah of the House of Joseph. All afternoon
and all night there had been a scurrying of disciples bringing books and manuscripts, which lay now in a disorderly
pile on a hastily constructed table before the dais.

As the afternoon wore on and neither man prevailed
or retreated, disciples and pilgrims — and servants —
found places for themselves in the grass and settled down
to watch the endless struggle. Every four hours, the muezzin called the Moslem faithful to prayer with his cry:

> *Ashadu an la ilah illa 'llah,*
> *Ashadu an la ilah illa 'llah.*

And every four hours, shortly after the muezzin's call,
the clanking of arms was heard as the Turkish guard in

the courtyard was changed. But the debate wore on.

The Messiah ben Joseph, according to messianic tradition, was the anonymous messiah who was destined to come into the world before the Messiah ben David. The earlier messiah would be a humble man, low and despised, fit only to be a precursor, a servant of the greater, the *true* Messiah ben David. The prophecies held that the lesser messiah, though he would take vengeance on the enemies of Israel, would nevertheless die a martyr's death. That sacrifice was necessary before the world would be deemed worthy to be saved by the Messiah of the House of David. And the core of the debate was whether Shabbatai, who claimed to be the Messiah of the House of David, could prove that the Messiah ben Joseph had already fulfilled his destiny.

An hour after the battle of the citations began, Sarah tried a second time to bring it to a stop, but by then Shabbatai, fully in command of his rhetoric and pleased with the cunning and subtlety of his scholarship, waved her away.

Now, the two exhausted men panted and stared at each other. At last, Nehemiah, like an all but defeated wrestler picking himself off the ground, gasped, "A name . . . Shabbatai. If . . he has come . . . and died . . . his name!"

A sweat-drenched Shabbatai took a deep breath and said, "Rabbi Abraham Zalman, may his name be blessed."

Nehemiah's head drooped between his shoulders. It was a time to roar, but he could hardly whisper. Still, a reply was needed. "Rabbi Abraham Zalman? How . . . how, Shabbatai, do you dare?"

"Rabbi Abraham Zalman, the messiah of the House of Joseph. The martyr who died in the massacres at Nemirov, cut down by the Cossacks, one of whom he slew."

The tears streamed down Nehemiah's cheeks. Tears of fatigue and outrage. He spat three times, then cried, "Oh, sinner, sinner! There were six thousand Jewish dead at Nemirov. *Six thousand!* Men and women and children. And scores of Cossacks dead. How, in that Polish mound of agony, would *you,* among your silks and nougats here, know which of those corpses was the Messiah ben Joseph? Pfoo! You shame the dead."

Shabbatai, shaken by the reply, looked about wanly, and then yielded to a shabby impulse. Slyly, he said, "Reb Nehemiah, many times since your name and your learning and your *mitsvot* — and your sorrows — became known to me, I have thought that you yourself might be the Messiah ben Joseph."

Nehemiah lifted his axe and brought it down with such force that it split the flagstone. "Oh, thou son of Belial. *I?* No . . . no . . . no . . . Now you shame the living. There is no such merit in me . . . I ask no better destiny than the covenant of Jacob."

"That covenant," Shabbatai said, drawing himself up, "I have come to fulfill."

"Not you," Nehemiah chided. "Not you. That covenant is steeped in pain, of which you know nothing. Look at you, as plump and coddled as a girl's pet lamb."

"I have known pain," Shabbatai insisted. "I am a man of sorrows and acquainted with grief. I have been driven from city to city. The rabbis of Jerusalem punished me with stripes."

"Ah, Shabbatai. You are one of those who makes the world glisten with words. But they won't do here. The dead are dead; the living live. The hungry ache; the full digest. And whom the whip touches, it marks. Show me, O man of sorrow, *show me the marks of the whip.*"

Nehemiah spoke the sentence caught up in the flow of his bitterness, but the chance words stunned his opponent. He paled.

"I will show you nothing, old man." Shabbatai stood and felt the nausea rise in him as he recalled the bound tax evader in Smyrna, and the rod-master's apprentice wielding his cutting knives on the strips of the victim's flesh. He remembered the dreamlike sequence with the men from the rabbinical court in Jerusalem . . . the cat-

o'-nine-tails rising and falling. "I will show you nothing.
I have had enough of you."

"But I, Shabbatai Zevi, have not yet had enough of you.
I will name you for what you are."

"I am Shabbatai Zevi, the Anointed of the Lord . . ."

"Shabbatai Zevi, who is filled with a lust for glory." Nehemiah spat. "But the cup of the Lord's right hand shall
be turned unto thee, and a shameful spewing shall be on
thy glory." Around the throne, the disciples stirred. In
the gray light of dawn, all faces looked as if they were
made of freshly dug clay.

Just then, Shabbatai, who felt the tug of the abyss over
whose edge Nehemiah was driving him, was assailed by
a strange longing. He thought how lovely it would be to
be like Nehemiah: so rude and yet so subtle. To be a woodsman, a forest dweller; to live with wind and storm, with
the axe and the alphabet for one's only wealth. Ah, if only
God had chosen to merge him, Shabbatai, with this angry
block of a man. What a messiah, together, they might have
made!

Nehemiah, too, felt himself softening. Shabbatai was so
young, so woebegone. Like a miserable child caught in a
lie before witnesses. A child. Learned and brilliant, but
with only charm and a patina of childhood with which to
defend himself. And he, Nehemiah, had rubbed that patina
away.

Sweat-stained and worn, he felt a great longing that the
last eighteen hours could be undone, a longing to take
Shabbatai by the hand and lead him down from his throne,
to take him somewhere to a dark cool room, where, surrounded by old books, they might sit, like father and son,
and refresh themselves in the study of ancient certainties.

So real was Nehemiah's reverie that he did in fact reach
a hand toward Shabbatai, but it was the hand that held
the axe. A startled Shabbatai stepped back. "Don't you
dare to touch me." Then, to reassert his authority, he used
his exquisite voice:

I am the Anointed of the Lord!
I will ascend into the heavens,
I will exalt my throne above the stars,
Upon the mountain of the congregation . . .

Nehemiah trembled at the appalling import of the words. Because what Shabbatai sang was but part of the dreadful imprecation spoken by Isaiah against Lucifer. There was no need to feel compassion for this Shabbatai, no need to embrace him. No doubt God had chosen Shabbatai's delusion for him, but it *was* a delusion. Above the sound of Shabbatai's singing, Nehemiah called the rest of Isaiah's words:

Thy pomp is brought down to the grave . . .
The worm is spread under thee,
And the worms cover thee.
How art thou fallen from heaven, O Lucifer,
Son of the morning!
How art thou cut down to the ground,
Which didst weaken the nations!

Shabbatai stared. Nehemiah took a step forward. Shabbatai cried, "Help!"

Barot'ali was on his feet, his huge hands swaying. Sarah, too, started up. The disciples around the throne scrambled out of the way. Above Barot'ali's head, Shabbatai called toward his adversary, "I am the Anointed of the Lord."

Nehemiah, stepping back warily from the advancing Barot'ali, replied firmly, "Thou art not he."

"I am the Messiah. I am the King of the Jews."

Barot'ali was already flexing his enormous hands. Nehemiah made fending motions with his axe.

"No, Shabbatai. Thou art not he."

"I am the celestial lion!"

"A blasphemer!"

"I am the King of the Jews."

Barot'ali advanced, smiling, a gleam of spittle moving

down his jaw. Nehemiah retreated, but cried, "Thou art a fool for glory!"

A despairing Shabbatai yelled, "Barot'ali! If you love me, kill him."

It was a command the idiot understood. He lumbered foward. Sarah, crying "Shabbatai, no," started from the dais, but Itzhak ben Shimon caught and held her in place.

Nehemiah continued to back away, waving his axe in wider and wider arcs. Barot'ali came on, driving him back toward the doors. There, before the portals, turbaned guards stood, their lances at the ready, pleased to see the fight moving their way.

Nehemiah was calm, but he felt empty — and tired. Tired of his journey, of the hours of debate without food or water. Tired of his life. What had it all been but a long fatigue: the axe, the alphabet, the cool green woods? He had had, and lost, more love than is given many men in one lifetime. What was the point any longer of carrying his bulk through the world? And yet, it came to him that he did not want to die. He wondered, as Barot'ali came on, why not.

The idiot, his hands out before him like a blind man, advanced. Nehemiah, weaving with his axe, stepped backward, and stumbled on the lower of the two steps before the doors. Barot'ali charged. Nehemiah, unable to wield the axe, went down, with Barot'ali's hands at his throat.

There began, for Nehemiah, a slow darkness in which he tried to breathe. He clawed at the idiot's robe and tore it, but the fingers round his throat squeezed harder, and the darkness deepened. His chest felt heavy; the blood vessels in his eyes throbbed; and what had been darkness became a red and swirling mist . . . in Zlitin. In a brothel roofed with thatch, where he, Nehemiah, sat drinking with a one-legged Turk. Abdul Hamid. His friend. His brother. The two of them drinking until they were dizzy with fumes and philosophy.

Barot'ali's fingers squeezed. The mist behind Nehemiah's eyes turned a deeper red. Man into meat. The meat looking into the mirror, hoping to find God.

The image quivered. The fingers around his throat still squeezed and he felt the lines of pain in his eyeballs like the crazed glass in a window of the brothel in which there sounded the cry *Allah Akbar*. It was a pain like the tearing of a seam, revealing a sudden Nothing where his memory had always been. An ugly emptiness, an insulting pain, through which there sounded the voice of his good friend Abdul Hamid, crying, "See. We are no longer cousins. Having put on the turban of Allah, you are my Moslem brother. See." The red pain, in a little while, would bring an end to breathing. After the red pain, there would be the gray, and after that, there would be no color at all. Only the pain itself.

Then Nehemiah felt himself growing still, as, in his eyes, there exploded a brightness in which he uprooted the hitching post and swung it against the Cossack's skull.

He heard a long-drawn cry and opened his eyes to discover that he was on his feet, the axe in his hand, while Barot'ali, blood oozing from a gash in his thigh, stood before him, howling. Nehemiah lifted the axe, and Barot'ali lunged, his hands set for throttling.

Nehemiah's courage left him. He could not sink into that red mist again. Not again. Out of the corner of his eye, he caught a glimpse of the guards making room to let the idiot kill the Jew.

Nehemiah, remembering everything, leaped toward the nearest guard and toppled him. Crying *"Allah il Allah Akbar,"* he snatched the greasy turban from the guard's head and clapped it on his own. The startled guard was on his feet again, his lance at the ready.

There followed a long silence as the guards here and at the other sides of the courtyard stood open-mouthed, absorbing what had happened. In solemn pairs, they left their posts, their lances leveled, and came to the portals before which Nehemiah stood. He was only a squat Jew in an ill-fitting turban, but as devout Moslems they understood their duty to this sudden convert. Slowly, piously, they formed a cordon around Nehemiah, who, his eyes closed, continued to call *"Allah il Allah Akbar,"* followed by the only other two Turkish words he knew, "Köprülü Pasha. Köprülü Pasha."

The guards nodded. Their lances erect, they waited while two of their number opened the brass-studded doors; then they marched the new Moslem into the darker corridors of the Emperor's prison at Abydos.

In the courtyard, Shabbatai knelt beside a whimpering Barot'ali. Unmindful of the staring Jews around them, Shabbatai, with a clean, white kerchief he had moistened in a fountain, was wiping away the blood oozing from the idiot's thigh. "There," he said. "There, there."

27

Adrianople
September, 1666

For Shabbatai, the days and nights that followed his confrontation with Nehemiah were equally unrelenting. He was hustled from the Tower of Strength by impassive guards and shoved into an enclosed cart; from there to a barge; and then to a stuffy, hot cubicle in a ship. Then back to a cart, until, bone-weary, he was delivered to a filthy, bare, stone room with only a single small grate built high up in the wall, through which he could see a tiny patch of daytime blue or nighttime starlit sky.

He was, perhaps for the first time in his life, absolutely alone. To the Turks who had the handling of him, he was an inconvenient object that had to be gotten to Adrianople as quickly as possible. If any of them did know his name, it served only to make them laugh. Shabbatai, the King of the Jews, in chains, on the way to Adrianople to take the Emperor's crown.

As for friends! There were no crowds of believers crying, "Shabbatai! *Amirah!* Messiah!" No wealthy delegations of Jews from Milan, from Munich, from Persepolis. Nathan? Well, Nathan had been lost to him for a long time. As if the anointing in the desert had been his climactic event. After which he seemed to tire of the real Shabbatai, and sent him off to complete the redemption of the Jews while Nathan retired to Gaza, where, day in and day out, he invented theology that he sent to the four corners of the earth. Now, Sarah was gone. And Itzhak ben Shimon. Harleigh, the rich Englishman. And Barot'ali, loyal Barot'ali, was taken from him, too.

His new solitude was not at all like the loneliness of an exalted spirit looking down on an admiring — or even a hostile — multitude. It was a loneliness that left him feeling vulnerable to the most trivial annoyances, as if, naked, he stood at the center of a nettle field, afraid to move.

Afraid! Not with the sorts of self-doubting fears he had had in Smyrna when he first became conscious of his powers, or later in Cairo, or on the shores of the Salt Sea. Those were, in a sense, the natural anxieties of an illuminated man testing his limits. No. He was afraid of the splinters in the carts that had hauled him, of the vermin in the ships that had brought him to Adrianople. He was afraid of the dark, of chains clanking in the night. And he loathed himself for being afraid. He detested the taste of fear, like vomit, on his tongue, and its texture, like scabs, against his skin. Fear had the sound . . . of his own name.

"Shabbatai!" The name spoken curtly, but without anger. "Shabbatai."

He was not in a prison cell now, and the man speaking was Ahmed Köprülü, the Grand Vizier. Ahmed Köprülü, known also as Fazil Ahmed, or Ahmed the Virtuous, sat back and stroked his black curly beard. "Understand me, Shabbatai," he said. "There is about you a certain remnant innocence that I find charming. I should not like to see you die." Köprülü looked about to see whether his attendants were alert. This was an almost private interview with Shabbatai, the holy Smyrna Jew charged with sedition. It was, therefore, a state matter, and Köprülü preferred that his servants take an interest in what happened. The Selam Agasi, the Master of Ceremonies, at his right had his head properly up and his hands folded over his paunch. His neat olive cloak with its scarlet lining hung down in generous folds over his crimson pantaloons, but the young Camasir Agasi, who looked after the ministerial underclothing, had twice been careless about stifling a yawn.

Köprülü fingered the ermine collar of his blue cloak and turned his attention again to Shabbatai. "I should not like to see you die. In that, I am like my father." The Grand Vizier, not yet thirty years old, sighed with the gravity of a much older man. "My father, let me tell you, detested justice. He was past forty when I was born. Forty-four, to be precise. Older than you. He did not become the Grand Vizier until he was seventy. It was a long time to wait for so much power. *He* had the sense of innocence that I admire in you, but he did not let it distract him from his duties . . . Let me tell you about him. Yes. Yes. Every Thursday morning, he took me with him to the fowlers' market, where he bought five cages full of larks only for the pleasure it gave him to set the birds free.

"You see what I mean? A lifetime spent liberating larks. Then he was made Grand Vizier, and learned that justice was expected from him. Are you following my story?"

"I do not understand it."

"No? Let me be clearer. In the five years that he was in office, my father signed the death warrants of thirty-six thousand miscreants, whom he caused to be executed for the good of the state. Yet he always hated blood. As I do. Now you understand my little fable?"

The friendliness in the Grand Vizier's face unsettled Shabbatai. "You mean to kill me?" he asked.

"Only if you make it necessary. Neither the Emperor nor I wants your blood. But you are charged with sedition. And by a Moslem. Never mind that the complaining Moslem is but a day old in the faith, that not so long ago he was merely another disputatious Jew. A miracle is a miracle."

Shabbatai tried to think who could best talk to this boyish

Grand Vizier: the Shabbatai who was the son of a monied Smyrna merchant, or the man who cowered at night as he listened to the quarreling vermin in his cell, or Shabbatai-Messiah, Amirah, the Anointed of the Lord? He said, "What do you want of me?"

"Let me ask you something. In your time at Abydos? Were you well treated?"

"Yes."

Köprülü consulted a memorandum. "And your eight thousand Jews — your visitors or pilgrims — were they well treated?"

"Yes," Shabbatai said, a hint of impatience in his voice.

"Ah, yes," Köprülü said quickly. "You are of course right. Rich disciples paid the Emperor's treasury many silver coins for that good treatment. But that was *before* you were charged with sedition." He shook his head. "I must say, you managed things badly there in Abydos. Well, what's done is done. But my task, today, is to keep you from managing as badly again. The punishment for sedition," he added icily, "is death. Now, what are you going to say to the Emperor tomorrow?"

Shabbatai tilted his head, evidently listening to or seeing something. *From the slope of the mountain behind them, from the place where they had made their first camp and eaten the figs, there came first the cough and then the roar of a lion . . . A branch of thorn crackled in the fire and sent sparks flying out of the circle of light. Nathan took his hand from Shabbatai's cheek and said, "You are Shabbatai Zevi, whom the Lord God has promised Israel as its Redeemer."*

Lifting his head, he looked into Köprülü's face and said, "I will tell him who I am and why I have come. *I* am Shabbatai Zevi, the Anointed of the Lord, the Redeemer of mankind, sent to take the Emperor's crown from him . . ."

For a long time, Köprülü considered what he had heard; then, shaking his head, he said, "That was well spoken. 'The Redeemer of mankind.' I am impressed. I, Köprülü, the Grand Vizier, the Burden Bearer. I am my master's horse, Shabbatai; his ox, his camel. Say what you will to me, and I will bear it patiently.

"But we are talking here about life and death. Your death, Shabbatai. The Emperor is a much different kind of man from myself. To tell you what is no secret, he is somewhat given over to drink, which makes him . . . impatient. Very impatient. I urge you, when you stand before him, to muffle a little the thunder of your voice. Because" — his voice dropped — "in this world, he, not you, hurls the lightning."

Despite the slow and repulsive pressure of fear in his gorge, Shabbatai forced himself to say "No. There are two kinds of power: the one, a lower kind, is the sort the Emperor wields over cities, towns, dominions; the other, such as is given me from on high, rules the eternal kingdom. In a struggle between the Emperor and me, *I* shall triumph." God, he remembered, had spoken the Creation. He, Shabbatai, would speak the redemption of the world. If only he did not totter.

Köprülü gnawed at a fingernail. "Shabbatai, if you are mad, then we are both wasting our time. I prefer to think that you have been . . . trapped by events. A trap from which, because it is good business and good statecraft, I prefer to rescue you. Listen now," he said reasonably. "I want us to compose a letter, you and I. The letter will say that the charge of sedition made against Shabbatai Zevi was made by a maligning Jew. Shabbatai makes no claims to be the Messiah; he denies that he has ever called himself the King of the Jews, or that it was ever his intention, as has been rumored, to come to Adrianople for the purpose of taking the Emperor's crown. Shabbatai Zevi claims no more for himself than that he is a humble rabbi and a pious man. If he is released from custody, Shabbatai Zevi will leave Adrianople immediately for Jerusalem, where he will spend the rest of his days in study and in meditation. He asks pardon of the Emperor for having caused confusion among the Jews, and he prays that the blessing of God may fall upon the empire and the Emperor forever and ever, and so on and so on, amen. Signed, Shabbatai Zevi . . .

"There," Köprülü said, rubbing his hands together. "That should do it. I will dictate the letter, you will sign it, and off you go to Jerusalem. A little rumpled, but alive."

"No," said Shabbatai. "I will not." His hands, compressed into fists at his side, looked like cold, carved marble.

"You *will* not?"

"No." Then, because Köprülü had moved him, a trembling Shabbatai, who felt unseen shadows gnawing at the light, said kindly, "Ahmed Köprülü, when I come to sit on my throne, I will keep in mind that you were one among the Gentiles who wished me well."

The condescension was too much for the Grand Vizier. "Guards!" he roared. "Guards!" The guards in their yellow tunics and their red and white turbans came running. "Get him . . . get him *out* of here." But when they rushed Shabbatai toward the door, he called, "Softly, softly. This particular meadowlark must be delivered to the Emperor unbruised."

When they were gone, Köprülü studied the upward curl of his green shoes. Turning to the Master of Ceremonies, he said, "You have some French, Ortughlu. What was it the Frankish ambassador said to the Emperor last night?"

The old man adjusted his scarlet-lined olive cloak and worked his mouth to get the required amount of spit for the strange accent. His hands folded over his fine stomach, he said, *"Rien n'avance les choses comme les exécutions."*

"Ah," said the Grand Vizier, "if only it were true."

❧ ❧

When he was sober, Mehmet the Fourth, the Emperor of the Turks, was inclined — with Ahmed Köprülü's help — to be reasonable, though in matters of importance he

256

was given to consulting three ancient and learned, but blind, astrologers, who, with a score of assistants, plotted charts for him in their observatory at Brusa. Mehmet, a florid and portly twenty-five-year-old, explained his confidence in the blind men. "It is a commonplace that when nature deprives a creature of one of its senses, it enhances the others in compensation. A blind astrologer, unable to see the heavens, has developed a superior sense of them. Living in darkness, his being is alert to the subtlest variations in the stars. *His* star map is no mere sheet of paper with lines and dots on it. Rather, he feels in the sympathetic tremors of his nerves the smallest changes in the patterns of the stars. My blind astrologers touch the skies they study with the fingers of memory and desire." Mehmet cocked his head and looked at his listener with keen, suspicious eyes. He was the Padishah, the Emperor of the Turks, and did not really expect an argument.

Now, as Mehmet sat on his purple dais with its green and gold tassels and faced Shabbatai Zevi, he recalled that his astrologers had marked this day as one "requiring an audacious act to avert an evil omen." How was one to deal audaciously with one more prophetling, another holy man — one of dozens in the empire who buzzed with the pride of gnats, making great men shake their heads.

Shabbatai, at least, had none of the scabby features of the desert madmen who were usually brought before him, claiming to have met God. Why, after their encounter, God should leave his worshippers looking like scalded scarecrows no mullah had ever explained. This fellow, anyhow, had no touch of poverty about him. His blue robe looked so much like the one worn by his Cavusbasi, his Minister of Justice, who stood beside Köprülü on Mehmet's left, that the sour-faced minister gnawed at his lower lip. The Celladbasi, the Chief Executioner, and his assistant, the Cellad, or Lesser Executioner, eyed Shabbatai's clothing with the proprietary air of men who get to share an executed prisoner's clothing. The Celladbasi would have the fur-trimmed blue cloak; the Cellad could look forward to Shabbatai's embroidered shirt and golden pantaloons.

"They tell me, Shabbatai Zevi," Mehmet began, "that you have come to take my crown from me."

Shabbatai, like a man reading a line from a play he has not studied, said, "Yes. It is written that I am to wear your crown . . ."

"So, it is written?" Mehmet's instinct was to dispose of Shabbatai with a judicious swing of his curved sword, but Köprülü had counseled against it. A mere beheading was hardly the audacious act advised by the blind astrologers.

"It is written, you say. And here" — he unrolled a few inches of a scroll — "here is written a long list of charges against you. Wherever you go, there is turmoil in the streets of the empire. There have been riots and brawling. Good Jewish merchants have abandoned their shops and are off to get a sniff of the salvation you promise. And there is the charge of sedition — which you confirm before my very eyes.

"On the one hand, the matter is very simple: you have earned your death. Against that, I have to consider the matter of one hundred thousand silver coins paid each month into my treasury by certain of your friends. Money I need, especially since my war with Crete. So you see, I have a problem."

"When I have taken your crown, and ushered in the redemption of mankind, you will no longer have that dilemma."

"Brilliant!" Mehmet turned to Köprülü. "What a clearheaded redeemer he is. But, Shabbatai. What shall I do in the meanwhile? It is always the meanwhile that grinds."

"I am no man for the meanwhile," Shabbatai said. Then, drawing a long, deep, and strangely weary breath, he said, "Now, Mehmet, Emperor of the Turkish Nation, give me your crown so that what is written may be accomplished." Shabbatai looked vaguely about him. He had said the words, and now, surely, there must appear a man's hand writing on the wall, over against the candlestick, the confirming message: *Me'ne, Me'ne, Te'kel, l'Shabbatai* — *God hath numbered thy kingdom and finished it; thou art weighed in the balances and art found wanting. Thy kingdom is taken from you and delivered to Shabbatai.*

Shabbatai waited, but there was no hand, no writing on a wall. The Emperor seemed to be considering. Then, "You want my crown," he said, "and you tell me that it is God's will that you should have it. Well, I am quite willing that you have it."

Despite his trance, Shabbatai heard the menace in the words. He stood as if rooted in stone.

"However," Mehmet continued, enjoying his game, "I must know whether it is *God's* will, and not Shaytan's. For, as we say, 'Shaytan has many lovely faces.' How am I to know that yours is not one of them?"

"My word is enough," Shabbatai said. "I am the Anointed of the Lord."

"For that matter, so am I." Mehmet laughed. "However, since I have the throne, the scepter, and the crown, the burden of proof is on you."

"It is written that men shall believe in me without signs or wonders."

"A convenient writing that leaves me uninformed. I need to know whether God or Shaytan moves in you. And so I shall." He made a sign to his Grand Vizier. "Come, Köprülü, show this Shabbatai what tricks my bowmen can perform."

The Grand Vizier clapped his hands. At one side of the archway facing the throne a lattice was thrown open, exposing a view into the Emperor's garden, where, in the shade of a heavily laden pomegranate tree, three Janissaries stood. They wore yellow parade uniforms; the sleeve tips of their long white bonnets hung carelessly over their left shoulders.

"What are you going to do?" a pale Shabbatai asked.

"You'll know soon enough. But first," Mehmet said, "let me tell you about these men. Like you, they have a destiny. Theirs includes bad rations, late pay, foul weather, and the miseries of love and war. They are steady men, and, though they grumble, they put up with what comes to them. Unlike you, they believe that they serve destiny; it does not serve them. With their help, I propose to consult God."

"How?" Shabbatai's voice was hardly a whisper.

"Target practice," Mehmet replied. "Watch." He nodded to Köprülü, who clapped his hands. In the garden, there was a whirr of wings as a freed dove mounted the air. Shabbatai saw the blurred motion of an archer's hand, and a transfixed dove died in the grass. The mustached bowman whose arrow it was stood, his free hand dangling lazily at his side.

"It may be," the Emperor said, "that his was a lucky shot. Let's give the second fellow a chance. The one with the belly who keeps scratching at his crotch. Köprülü!" Köprülü clapped his hands. Again there was a flurry of sound and motion as a bird beat the air and found its death. Again, the indifference of the bowman.

"They are lazy, my fellows," Mehmet said affectionately, "but they are skillful, too. Shall we see what the little fellow can do?"

Shabbatai, his lips working, said, "No. There is no need to kill another bird."

"You are generous, Shabbatai. A fine characteristic in an emperor. I wish it were my gift, but I am too impatient. Besides, I drink too much, which gives me a vile temper. Not a bad thing on the battlefield, but otherwise ugly to be around. I am not likable, Shabbatai . . . I have been known to . . ." Mehmet shrugged. "You see, Ahmed Köprülü, how your Shabbatai makes me run on. He has such a kindly face, he tempts me into confidences."

"What," said Shabbatai, "what are you going to do to me?"

"It is my archers and God and you who will do it all. You see that myrtle bush off there in the distance? You will stand before it, facing my archers. Each time Köprülü signals, an arrow will fly. If, as you believe, you are the Anointed of the Lord, you will have no trouble turning away one, two, or three of the arrows. They are fallible men. See, the little one looks sleepy, the fat one is stunned with drink, and the tall one is exhausted with fornications. Given their weaknesses and your God-given power, they may miss their target. If they do, my crown is yours."

Shabbatai heard it all, and was struck by how much there was still left in the world to wonder at. The ingenuity with which these men played with death, and his own detached calm. He felt a cold breeze blowing over the mountain peak on which he stood. It was the highest place in the world. Just above him, within reach of his hand, was the lowest place in heaven, and he, Shabbatai, had reached it.

It had been so easy to leave them all behind. Itzhak and Sarah and Nathan. Harleigh the Englishman, and Barot'ali. Köprülü Pasha, Mehmet, Rabbi Escapa, and Mordekhai, his wheezing father.

But even as he lifted himself onto the rim of heaven, by calling on the celestial lion, he remembered where he had seen it. In Cairo, hauled about by a ragged boy from the Atlas Mountains. An old, nearly toothless, weary beast whose scummy eyes and muzzle were besieged by flies. When the Arab boy poked its side with a stick, the beast did what it could to roar, making a sound like a shard scraping against a wall.

Shabbatai cleared his throat. "Will there be . . . one shaft from each bowman, or all three at once?"

"One from each bowman. In sequence."

"And if I am killed?"

Mehmet shrugged, "What promises can one make to the dead?"

"And . . . if I am hurt?"

"If no arrow touches you, you will be the Emperor. If so much as a thread of your robe is touched by an arrow, you are a dead man."

"There is no other choice?"

Mehmet's laughter shook the audience hall. "Shabbatai, do you want it written that you temporized before a test of God's will? Come now. Are you a peddler messiah? We are not setting the price of a bolt of cloth or a scullery maid's necklace. The game is greatness. Yours or mine."

Köprülü leaned over and whispered into the Padishah's ear. Mehmet listened, nodded, smiled.

"Well, Shabbatai, you continue fortunate in your friends. Köprülü thinks I am being harsh with you. He suggests that God's affection for you may show itself in other ways than in the random flight of arrows. You are a devout and learned man, steeped, until now, in the erroneous teachings of the Jews. But there are miracles and miracles. What if, under the guidance of your friends — Köprülü and myself — you should discover and acknowledge your errors, and learn the one truth: that Allah is Allah, and Mohammed is His messenger? Would not that be a miracle that served God and my treasury and the peace of the realm all at once?

"It's a happy thought, Shabbatai. If you take the turban, you will ensure your place in paradise without the inconvenience of arrows flying toward the myrtle bush. Moreover, to speak of lesser matters, as a distinguished convert you would be entitled to various honors of the Sublime Porte."

Shabbatai, his eyes open but unfocused, was praying, "O Lord, why hast Thou delivered me to the ungodly and turned me over into the hands of the wicked? I was at ease, but he hath broken me asunder: he hath taken me by the neck and shaken me to pieces and set me up for his mark. His archers compass me round about, he cleaveth my reins asunder and doth not spare me . . . O God, why hast Thou delivered me to the ungodly?"

His lips moved, but the words of the prayer seemed

leaden, inert. Finally, Shabbatai said, "Apostasy?"

"Why," Köprülü interposed almost merrily, "why use such an ugly word? Why not call it a miraculous conversion that leaves you still the darling of ten thousand eyes, with silks and jewels and satins, and rivers of gold flowing toward you?"

"Otherwise?"

Mehmet frowned. "Still merchandising, Shabbatai? Otherwise, the bowmen, and an end to the matter."

There was no rim of heaven and no mountain peak. Shabbatai Zevi, a prisoner in the Emperor's court in Adrianople, made a low bow and said, "It is a weighty matter, my lord. May I have a day to think it over?"

"Don't be a fool. I give you an hour in which to discover whether you are a miraculous Moslem, a holy Jew, or a corpse."

Shabbatai bowed and was led away.

Mehmet, seeing the droop of his shoulders, thought what a pity it was to reveal a man to himself. This Shabbatai, for instance — how presentable he was as a saint or an angel or a messiah. Then Mehmet had rubbed his face in the slime of his mortality.

It had been deviously done. But Köprülü Pasha was no doubt right: slyness was a form of audacity. The blind astrologers in Bursa would be pleased that he had averted the evil omen.

Then, into Mehmet's head, there obtruded a thought that made his eyes grow wide. What if Shabbatai chose to stand before the myrtle bush? And what if the bowmen missed?

The Jew would be back in an hour.

The rest was in God's hands. *Masa Allah!*

28

*Adrianople
September 15, 1666*

He has an earthquake in his soul, Sarah thought, as Shabbatai paced the library in the seraglio, where he had been
brought under guard to take counsel with his friends. It
was a handsome, quiet room that smelled of old vellum
and calf-bound folios. Peter Harleigh stood at the window
and looked out into the garden through the diamond-
shaped panes. Itzhak sat at a heavy dark table, at either
end of which there stood illuminated copies of the Koran
on mother-of-pearl-inlaid scrollwork stands. He was uncomfortable so near the heathen volumes and started up
constantly to follow Shabbatai in his wanderings past the
screened bookshelves, only to scurry back each time that
Shabbatai waved him impatiently away.

"He wants me *dead,*" Shabbatai said for the tenth time.
"You don't any of you understand that. He wants me to
die." Barot'ali, who could not sit cross-legged because of
the stiffness of his still-bandaged thigh, leaned against a
whitewashed wall and wondered at the room's clean brightness and at Shabbatai's distracted prowling. These days,
nothing was as it used to be with Shabbatai. He no longer
glowed, and though there was still sweetness in him, it
was like honey into which flies had fallen.

"I have an hour," Shabbatai complained. "An hour in which to decide whether to live or die, and you stare at me. What good are you? Why are any of you here? Why don't you *do* something?"

Sarah felt her heart contract. Shabbatai looked as if he were made of yellow wax. His eyes were sunk in his face, his hands trembled, and tears lurked at the edge of his voice. What, she wondered, can I say to a man with an earthquake in his soul?

She blamed herself because it had been her suggestion, in Smyrna, to send for Nehemiah, the axeman saint. It had seemed a reasonable idea. Shabbatai had been suffering seizures of impatience and uncertainty, because, though the Jewish Levant was swept up in his movement, the Jews of Europe were slow in giving him their faith. When the rabbis of Lvov spoke of Nehemiah, she had recalled him from their encounter in Zamosc. She had imagined his meeting with Shabbatai as a healing event: the dark anguished man of despair meeting the apostle of hope. Nehemiah might find comfort for his soul, and Shabbatai an important convert, who would return to Europe, where his witnessing would engulf the Jews of Europe in the tide of redemption.

She shivered. God, she had been told, writes straight with crooked lines. Well, Nehemiah *had* come. And now Shabbatai, who had been a confident flame, stood flickering before them, demanding, "Why don't you *do* something?"

The Englishman, Peter Harleigh, leaned against the window frame and looked out on the seraglio's central walk, where half a dozen aproned cooks were urging on a battle between a mute and a couple of dwarfs. The mute, a muscular giant with a thick waist that was tightly clasped by a broad, jewel-encrusted girdle, waved his arms to fend off the dwarfs. At intervals, he made eloquent gestures that pleaded with the little men to let him alone. Harleigh could hear the faint bleating sounds that came from the tongueless mouth.

The quarrel had begun innocently. The dwarfs had come at the mute like frolicsome puppies, meaning no more than a momentary wrestle with their friend. The preoccupied mute had thoughtlessly brushed one of them away so hard that he fell. The mute's bad luck was that the crowd of cooks had seen the incident, and all at once the dwarfs' honor was at stake, and what had started out as a game turned grimly serious. Urged on by the cooks, the little men swarmed over the mute, yapping and cursing like so many raging lap dogs. Despite the daggers the dwarfs carried, the mute was in no great danger. He plucked the dwarfs from him, one after the other, and set them down on the grass, from which, however, they returned constantly to the attack. Harleigh sensed the mute's mounting despair, because the dwarfs, as the mute well knew, were the Emperor's favorite toys. If any harm came to them, the mute would pay with his life. It was an impasse from which, had the giant been able to talk, he might have saved himself with cajoleries or bribes; but, wordless, he could only wave his arms and, like Hercules dealing with the Hydra's proliferating heads, pull at the chattering dwarfs one by one as they came on.

Harleigh wrenched his attention from the scene in the courtyard and turned to Shabbatai. The Englishman, too, looked exhausted. Not even his great wealth had been able to buy Shabbatai out of his present danger, but that was a truth he could not bring himself to report to Shabbatai. So, to comfort him, he offered with conviction what was at best only a halfhearted hope. "You're in no danger of dying. Mehmet and Köprülü are playing a schoolboy trick. You're worth a great deal more to them alive than dead."

"Tell me, Englishman," Shabbatai said, "what if I believe you, and I stand before the bowmen — and they shoot?"

Itzhak flung himself at Shabbatai's feet, crying, "No, no. They won't, Shabbatai. Their hands will be palsied; their eyes will go blind. You are the King of Love . . ."

Shabbatai spurned him with his foot. "Look at him, Harleigh. He has the stink of Sarah's loins about him still, and yet he speaks of love."

Itzhak burst into tears. Still clinging to Shabbatai's foot, he wailed, "You sent me to her, Shabbatai. You sent me to her. You sent me." His cheek against the stone floor, he sobbed, "Where . . . where is it written, Shabbatai, that the celestial lion will be a Moslem? Tell me, and I shall believe."

Sarah looked away in distaste. Catching Harleigh's eyes on her, she said, "Well, Englishman. Frightened Jews make an unpleasant sight, don't they?"

Harleigh glanced out the window in time to see the exasperated mute flinging a dwarf from him. The little man struck the ground hard and lay senseless, and the giant, his torso glittering with sweat, waited for a physician and for the inevitable guards who would come to arrest him.

"Not only Jews," Harleigh replied. Then, to Shabbatai, "Stop torturing your friends. And stop this talk of dying. It's only a Turkish game. If Mehmet can frighten you into a hasty apostasy, he'll have a pet Moslem to show off — and money, too."

Shabbatai stared in unbelief. "Peter Harleigh? You want me to stand before the bowmen, too!" He stepped closer to Harleigh. "Tell me, Englishman. Surely *you* don't take me for the Messiah?"

Harleigh waved both hands feebly, as if trying to brush away the image of the frightened mute, and said, "Shabbatai, you press too hard. The Messiah? How do I know? It seems to me that if I had known Jesus and loved Him, as I do you, I may still have doubted He was the Son of God. Doubt is the marrow in my bones. But, yes . . I believe that you are . . . something . . . I believe . . ." He shook his head, rejecting the next words that rose to his tongue.

"Yes?" Shabbatai asked, listening intently. "You believe . . ."

"That you are a . . . a force. An idea . . . a necessity

. . . a possibility of something . . . better . . . splendid
. . . But if you go back into the hall of the Divan and
beg the Emperor for a turban, you will have chosen to
be . . . nothing. Nothing at all."

"I see. I see," Shabbatai said bitterly. "And you, Sarah,
my best beloved. How do you counsel me?"

Sarah, her hand on Barot'ali's shoulder, was seeing
Shabbatai as well as a scene she had lived through countless
times as a child in the convent. The bells woke her before
dawn, and there was the patter of bare feet on the stone
floors as the women hurried to the chapel in time for mat-
ins. Forty women, their breath steaming with the winter
cold, lifted their eyes to Christ hanging on the timbered
cross above the chapel altar. He was one of those eastern
Christs, with a face that seemed twisted by an angry wind.
His eyes torn by suffering; His mouth, His bitten mouth,
open in a cry . . . the man-god, the god-man, each part
betraying the other, both meeting where the nails penetrated the flesh. And every day, to the slow tolling of iron
bells, forty brides looked into their bridegroom's face,
where was wrought the full price of the Word made flesh.

And Shabbatai, who was to reverse that process — who
was to be the flesh made word? How did Sarah, the bride
of Shabbatai, who had rubbed her cheek against his chest
and sung him a Yiddish lullaby of the Messiah in the market
square at Kishinev . . . and had heard him sing:

> As I rode down a winding way,
>   Down through a valley winding,
> I chanced on Meliselda there,
>   Her long dark hair unbinding . . .
>
> I combed her hair, I kissed her lips,
>   I whispered love and wonder,
> But when I bent to kiss her breasts,
>   The sky grew dark with thunder.

How was she to say to this messiah that dying as well as
song might be required of him?

"Shabbatai," she said softly, "I haven't been asked to make your choice. I can't tell you what to do."

"Why can't you? You were never shy of telling me before. 'Declare yourself,'" he mimicked. "'The man I married is the Messiah . . . Declare yourself.' Well, I declared myself. Now look at me."

"I do. I see you. You are Shabbatai Zevi, who spoke the Shem ha m'foresh; who is Amirah, the Anointed of the Lord . . ."

"And the arrows?"

"That is for you to say. You are the King of the Jews. And must do . . . what is needed . . ."

"That means die, doesn't it? Ah, what an ugly little scheme it is. That way, you and Itzhak are left to slaver over each other to your hearts' content. Look at them, Peter Harleigh! The pigs. The lecherous swine. You can see it in their eyes: they want me dead."

"No!" Sarah cried, trying to shut out the image of the grimacing Christ. "I want you to be . . . who you are."

"O Lord God in heaven!" Shabbatai shook his fists at them all. "Why hast Thou compassed me round with fools who darken counsel with words? Listen, Lord, how they love me: The arrows flying against me will make me live; the turban that will save my life will kill me. Sarah loves me and tells me I must die; Itzhak loves me and tells me I must die. The sodomite Englishman loves me and tells me I must die. Is there no one who loves me who wants me to live?"

He looked wildly around the library. "You — Barot'ali. *You* love me. What do you say?"

Barot'ali rubbed at the pain in his thigh. He had been listening intently without understanding much of what was said, though it was clear that Shabbatai was unhappy. When Shabbatai asked again, "Well, Barot'ali, shall I live or die?" the idiot got heavily to his feet. He was forty-eight years old, tall and shambling, with thick, unwieldy hands. His bushy gray eyebrows made fierce arches over his deep-set eyes. He wore a stained brown robe, from which there came the not unpleasant smell of the goats that were his nighttime companions.

"Mmmmm," he said. 'Mmmmmmm," and began an aimless shuffling around the room as he considered Shabbatai's question. Harleigh watched the twitching of Barot'ali's face as the idiot struggled to understand the half-formed notions rising in his head. Unable to grasp them, Barot'ali took refuge in motion and stumbled around the library like a puzzled ox, going from Sarah to Itzhak, from Itzhak to Harleigh, and from him to Shabbatai, pausing to sniff the air before each of them, as if hoping to find in the smells of their bodies something that would help him answer Shabbatai's question. When he came back a second time to Shabbatai, he stood before him for a long while, his huge shoulders drooping, shaking his head like a bear waving off flies. Shabbatai put a hand to the idiot's filthy head and scratched him behind the ear.

"Well, Barot'ali. You also love me. Tell me. What shall I do?"

Barot'ali raised his head. Into his vagarious eyes there came a fitful look of clarity. Thinking hurt, Barot'ali knew. It was a slow demon scratching pitilessly inside his head. But now Shabbatai wanted him to think . . . If he could find what it was, the demon might stop scratching that much sooner and leave him with something to tell Shabbatai. It had been like that once before.

Barot'ali *had* done it, once. Long ago. Very long ago. Before there was Sarah, or the man they called Peter Harleigh, or Itzhak. Before Leilia and Rosalinda.

It was when Shabbatai was a child. There had been a night when he asked Barot'ali a hard question. What was that question? Remembering was as hard as thinking. Loving was easiest. He had only to look into Shabbatai's face, and warmth flowed with a sweetness that had in it the taste of sesame-cake crumbs melting in his mouth — Shabbatai's gift.

It had been an important question. Put to him on an occasion just like this one, when something . . . *big* was at stake. Shabbatai had stood looking up at him, his beautiful face twisted with fear, his lovely voice harsh with it. As he was standing now, his face drawn, his eyes dark and worried, and the thin smell of fear coming from him. There had been the same fear, and it was a starlit night, and sesame cake and . . . and . . . and Shabbatai pleading for help to save the sun. That was it.

Could that be what Shabbatai wanted now? People used so many words. Everywhere the idiot looked, men and women were fountains of speech. They were always saying something or asking each other what it was that they had said. Words. Words. Words. Words — and none of them was ever as clear as the way things felt or smelled or tasted. People were always hissing or gabbling, and their speech amounted to nothing. Except for those times when Shabbatai told stories, but even then it was his voice that was beautiful, and not the stories that he told. What a lot of nonsense words were. And yet they could make people angry or sad or happy — if one only knew which ones to say. Once, long ago, Barot'ali had said something right in answer to Shabbatai's question, and Shabbatai had been happy. Was that the sort of speech Shabbatai wanted now? Something sweet? As sweet as the sesame cake that had melted on his tongue?

Barot'ali suddenly remembered what that question had been. Shabbatai had said, "Help me, Barot'ali. Help me. How shall I save the sun?" And Barot'ali had replied with good words. A reply that felt like the spurt of love he had when he embraced Leilia.

Barot'ali looked into Shabbatai's eyes. In their dark depths, he saw the stirrings of the sweetness he was trying to recall. Slowly, the old mood returned, and for the second time in his life he had an illumination. He let his mouth drop open as he savored the happiness he was about to give his friend. When Shabbatai shook him impatiently

271

and asked, "What shall I do, Barot'ali?" Barot'ali was ready.

"Crow, Shabbatai," he said, his face wreathed in smiles. "You must crow. Flap your wings. Open your mouth. Stand on your toes and crow. That's what you must do. Flap your wings and crow."

As if a lash had cut him, Shabbatai groaned, then leaped at the idiot, tearing at his face with his fingers. Barot'ali, bigger, stronger, older than Shabbatai, made no move to protect himself. In the first onset of the attack, he stood, feeling the fingernails raking his flesh like streaks of fire. Then, not to see the hatred in Shabbatai's face, he put his head between his hands and chose to fall to the stone floor, where he lay still as Shabbatai kicked and howled and screamed, "Bastard. Lump. Idiot. Son of a Moslem whore. Ah, you foul vermin. Own brother to a camel's turd. You morsel of scum. You stinking carrion. Ah . . . ah . . . you filthy abortion. You sickly dung beetle. Scurvy rat. You dead man's spittle. Oh . . . oh . . . you jackal. You toad . . ." Barot'ali lay curled at Shabbatai's feet, and covered his eyes with his hands while Shabbatai kicked and screamed, "Mock me, will you? Monster. Maggot." Shabbatai kicked Barot'ali's head, his shoulder, the unhealed wound in his thigh. "My life." Shabbatai gasped. "It is *my* life that you mock. My prophet. My friend. Me. Me . . . you mock. Who saved the sun; who swallowed a serpent. Who stilled the waves. Me. Shabbatai Zevi . . . to stand before the arrows to be mocked. Me. Oh, thief. Mock me, will you. There . . . there . . . You . . . You . . . Nathan . . . Satan . . . idiot . . . To mock me . . . as you have . . . always . . . mocked me." His feet struck Barot'ali's ears, his nose, his teeth. Barot'ali curled his great bulk like a child trying to sleep through a bad dream, consoling himself with the memory that once it had been beautiful.

Then, long ago, Shabbatai had stood on the summit

of Kadifekale, watching the sun come up, and there had
been the cry of the muezzin:

Allah, o Akbar,
Allah, o Akbar.

Ashadu an la ilah illa 'llah,
Ashadu an la ilah illa 'llah.

Shabbatai's foot smashed against his mouth, then against
the wound in his thigh. Instead of the taste of sesame-
seed cake, there was now the bitterness of blood, and where
Shabbatai had soothed the wound in his thigh with a clean
handkerchief dipped in the water of a fountain, there was
now fresh pain and oozing blood.

In the dark above him, Barot'ali heard voices meddling
with Shabbatai and wished that they would leave his unhappy friend alone. The Englishman was shouting at Shabbatai, and Sarah was bent over him, Barot'ali, trying to
shield him from Shabbatai's kicks. Itzhak sobbed as he
tugged at Sarah's shoulders, but all that Barot'ali saw was
the Prince of Light standing in his special space. His fingers
and toes and nostrils were blazing; his hair and his lips
were alive with fire. Light splattered and gushed from him;
there was an overflow of light that spilled into the vessels
below with such force that the vessels broke; and there
were shards and light subsiding into darkness. There were
broken vessels, and the question was whether they could
ever be mended, and the answer was that Shabbatai, and
not a scullery maid, would come and he would mend them.

Still, the unwearying kicks and blows and gouges, despite
the shield of Sarah's body. Barot'ali did not mind the pain,
and in his life, blood was nothing new. But there was something missing in the way he remembered the morning on
the summit of Kadifekale. Barot'ali prayed his Moslem
prayer, and when he was done, he waited for the boy to
stand away, to remember that he was a Jew, as he looked
out over the mountain toward the sun he had miraculously

saved. Barot'ali waited for Shabbatai to answer his Moslem prayer with his Jewish:

Kadosh, kadosh, kadosh
Adonai, ts'vaot . .

The boy was still there, cursing, screaming, tearing at his flesh, but though Barot'ali waited and waited and waited — the prayer in praise of glory did not come.

Epilogue

From Peter Harleigh, in Corfu,
to Nicholas Tyrell, in London
January, 1667

. . . and elsewhere as well, there is the wreckage of his love. In Salonika, those who once believed in Shabbatai throw stones at each other, crying, "Traitor! Seducer!" In Poland, the drunken rabbi, Nehemiah Ha-Kohen, who betrayed Shabbatai to the Turks, wanders bareheaded from city to city, crying that he killed God. From Gaza, Nathan writes endlessly, telling the world that it was a satanic spectre and not Shabbatai who took the turban in Adrianople. Itzhak, unable to bear Shabbatai's apostasy, died a suicide, leaping from a boat within sight of the Tower of Strength at Abydos. As for Sarah, beautiful, ambiguous Sarah has disappeared into the Troad, pregnant with what some disciples prophesy will be Shabbatai's son.

In Europe and the Near East, there is confusion. In Livorno, Frankfurt, Salonika, Jerusalem, heartsick believers continue to gather in synagogues, asking for news of miracles in Shabbatai's name. Devout Jews take the turban in Smyrna, in Damascus, in Aleppo, for his sake. Others sink back into the old tradition of devotion as into a gulf of failure.

We live in a dark time, Tyrell; but for the Jews who had — and lost — their Shabbatai, these are the darkest times of all.

My God, Tyrell, They've made him a doorkeeper of the seraglio. Shabbatai. Our Shabbatai is a paid servant in that labyrinth of exhausted flesh and faded intelligence. Shabbatai, whose name accords with Shaddai, the name of God, stands bowing and scraping for thirty talents a month before the black eunuchs and the white as they come and go. Thirty talents a month and silk scarves and all the greasy mutton he can eat.

I think, sometimes, that Shabbatai was too old when he had his encounter with the Sultan. A youthful Shabbatai meeting the arrogant young Emperor would have seized the occasion for a grand gesture. But Shabbatai was forty, and the only high gesticulation he could understand was that which *he* controlled. Forty is the age of prudence, which is a skill useful to merchants and survivors, but one that is fatal to heroes and saints. Prudence, as young men do not know, is a secret harbinger of death. Shabbatai, at forty, chose prudence — and middle age.

Or so I think when I hate him.

How . . . how could he leave us?

If he had been a madman, I could not feel a grief this strong. The madman goes to a place in his own mind where none of us wants to follow. His going makes us lonely, but it does not entice us after him. The saint, on the other hand, bidding us farewell, steals the life of our affections and creates the richest desolation by suggesting that it was *our* emptiness that made him go. The madman's departure ends with the closing of a door. The saint's bequeathes us the fable of our failure as he goes .

He escapes me . . . he escapes me . . .

Sometimes, I think his only genius was that he could sing. That his voice, being beautiful, made a glow around his banalities. Once within the tent of his music, music was all the belief we needed, or could bear. Then I remember the thousands who never came within sound of his voice, and I ask myself what it was that made *them* stand looking up at the sky waiting for the cloud to come that would carry them, in Shabbatai's name, to the newly descended Temple in Jerusalem.

In my darkest moments, I charge Shabbatai with having been an empty space filled by the longing of those who loved, and thereby invented, him. Then I remember his eyes, the touch of his hand, his smell, and the radiance of his smile, and I am baffled once more.

But my unhappiness is as nothing compared with Barot'ali's.

He lives with me here, on Corfu, he and his goats; and he cannot understand why Shabbatai spurned and beat him. He, even more than I, is pining away. The physician whom I sent for tells me that it is not uncommon for these idiots, when they have sustained a grief, to will themselves to die. I do not know whether Barot'ali has chosen such an end, but he looks ashen and soft. He wanders about the island looking for something — under shrubs, in caves, and by the sea. I provide him with everything he needs, regarding him as all that is left to me of Shabbatai, but I have no way to comfort him. He, more than any of us, had seen a great light and had it taken from him.

He is forty-nine years old, grey and stooped, but when I come upon him whispering the story of Adam Kadmon into the ear of one of his goats, he has on his face the radiant look of a saint.

Every morning, before dawn, he rises from his place in the straw and mounts to the ruined tower on the hill behind my house. There he stands, on the only battlement that is still complete, and faces the east. Then, at precisely the right moment, he stretches his arms out, flaps his wings and calls, *"Co co ri co."* Then *"Co co ri co."* And finally,

277

giving the full-throated call of the cockerel, *"Co co ricoricori-coricoricoricorico,"* he crows up the sun.

But when I meet him on the downward path, there are tears coursing down his dirty face. Every day, as I hold him to my heart, he tells me that no matter how hard he flaps his wings or crows, what rises is always the wrong sun.